The DARK MATTER
of Mona Starr

Laura Lee Gulledge

Amulet Books, New York

Library of Congress Control Number 2019945549

Hardcover ISBN 978-1-4197-3423-6
Paperback ISBN 978-1-4197-4200-2

Text and illustrations copyright © 2020 Laura Lee Gulledge
Book design by Max Temescu

Additional material by Earl Vallery (page 19), Juliet Trail (page 51), Andrea Sparacio (page 88), and Bonnie Rubrecht (page 93). Mona's wall installation (pages 173–179) contains additional material by Aiden, Alessa, Ally, Alyssa, And, Chaya, Christine, Cong, Daniel, Eric, Jack, Hoang, Jaiyi, Julian, Justin, Khan, Kaiwen, Kyle, Lauren, Mai, Mia, Ruiqi, Tat, Tran, Vlassios, Will, and Yue of Fairmont Prep Academy (Anaheim, CA), plus Anish and Abby from Skyline Middle School (Harrisonburg, VA), plus Kiera and Makenzie from Crossroads College Preparatory School (St. Louis, MO), plus Heidy, Salina, Makenna, Jasmine, Brandyn, and Tamia from Falling Creek Middle School (North Chesterfield, VA), in addition to Ariana Kerr.

Printed and bound in China
10 9 8 7 6 5 4 3 2 1

Amulet Books are available at special discounts when purchased in quantity for premiums and promotions as well as fundraising or educational use. Special editions can also be created to specification. For details, contact specialsales@abramsbooks.com or the address below.

Amulet Books® is a registered trademark of Harry N. Abrams, Inc.

ABRAMS The Art of Books
195 Broadway, New York, NY 10007
abramsbooks.com

For all my Artners . . .
and for all stars who feel
like black holes.

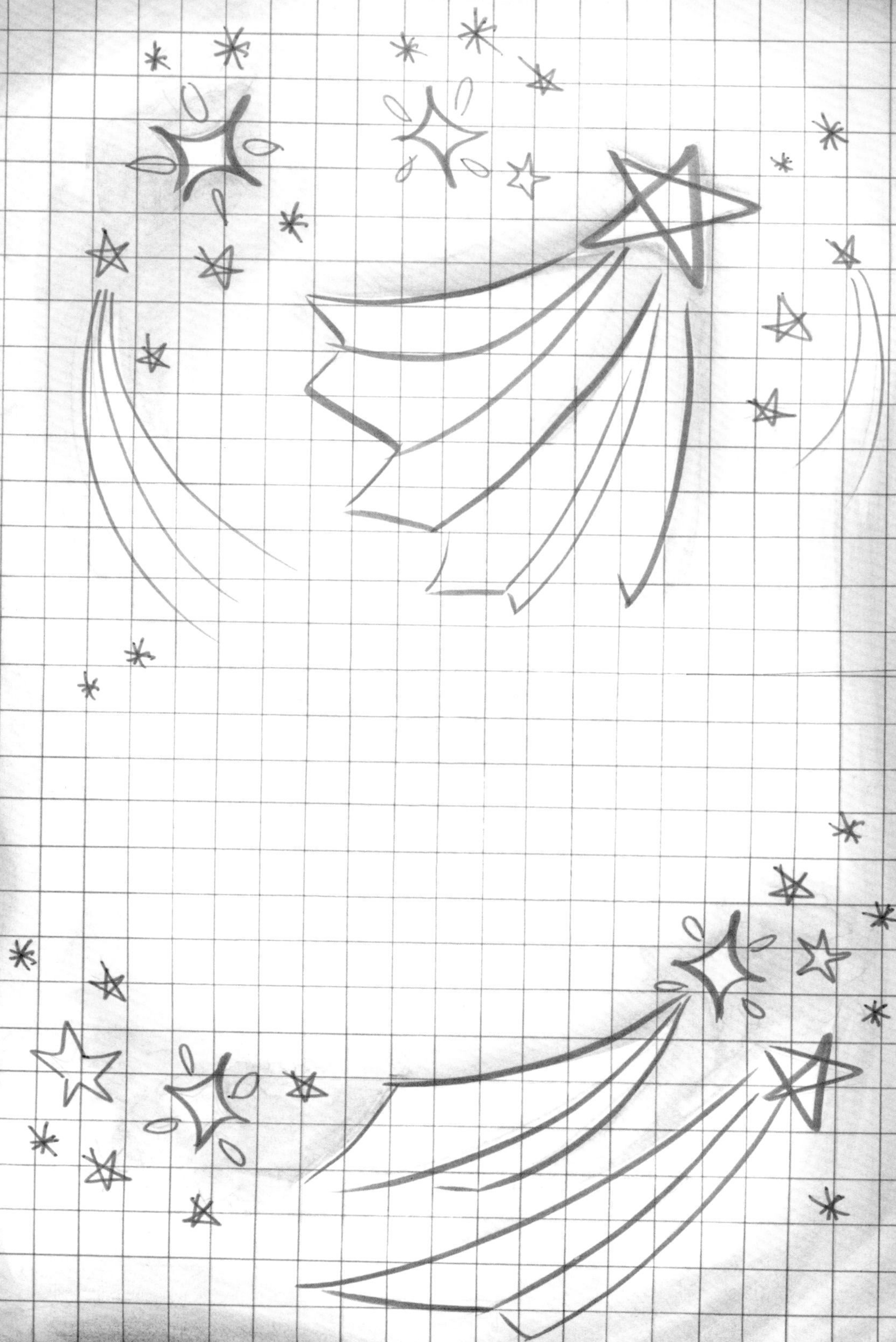

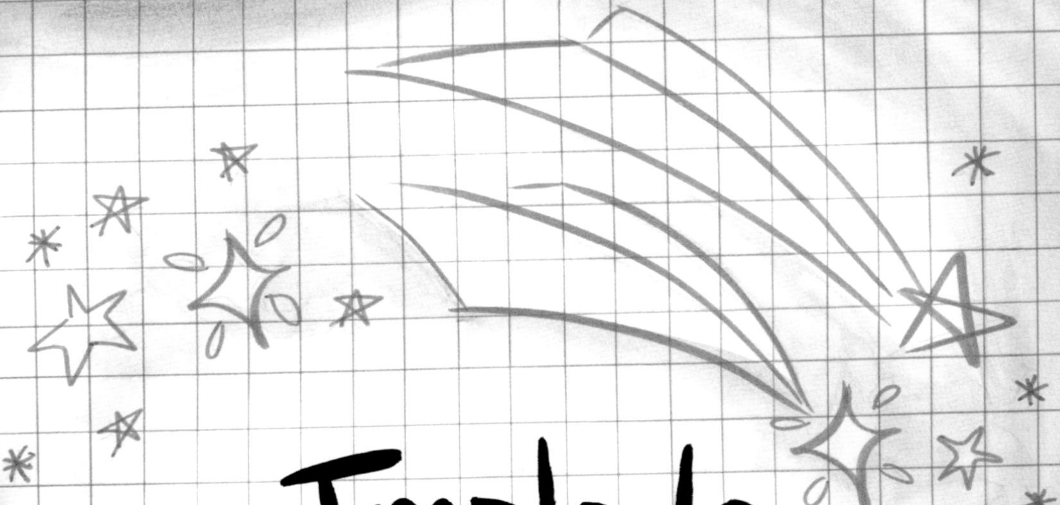

Implode or evolve

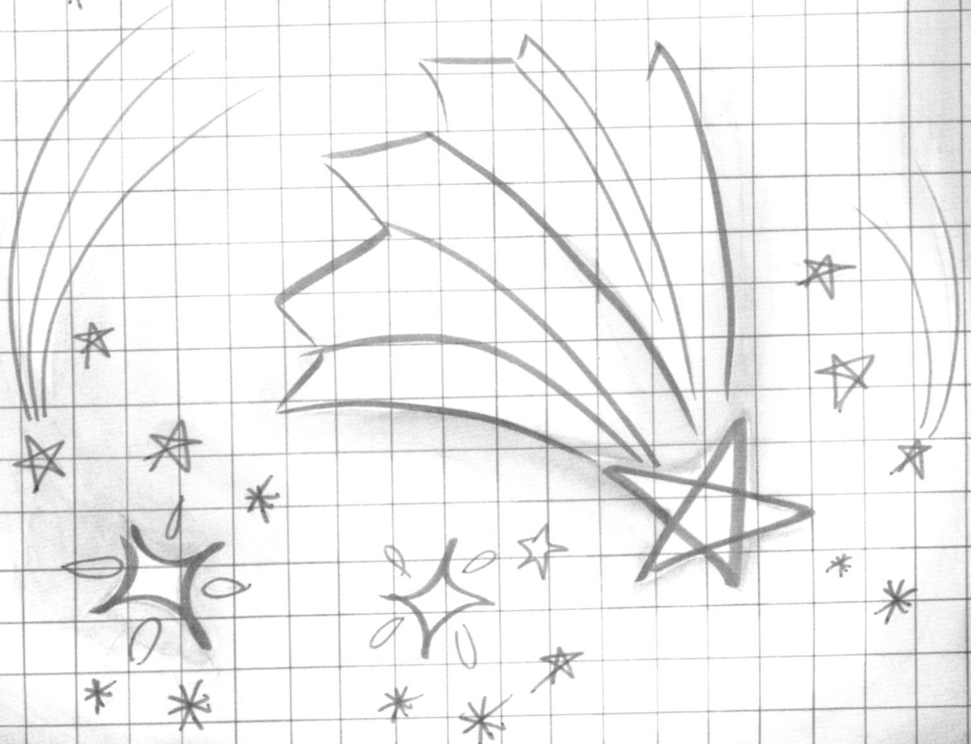

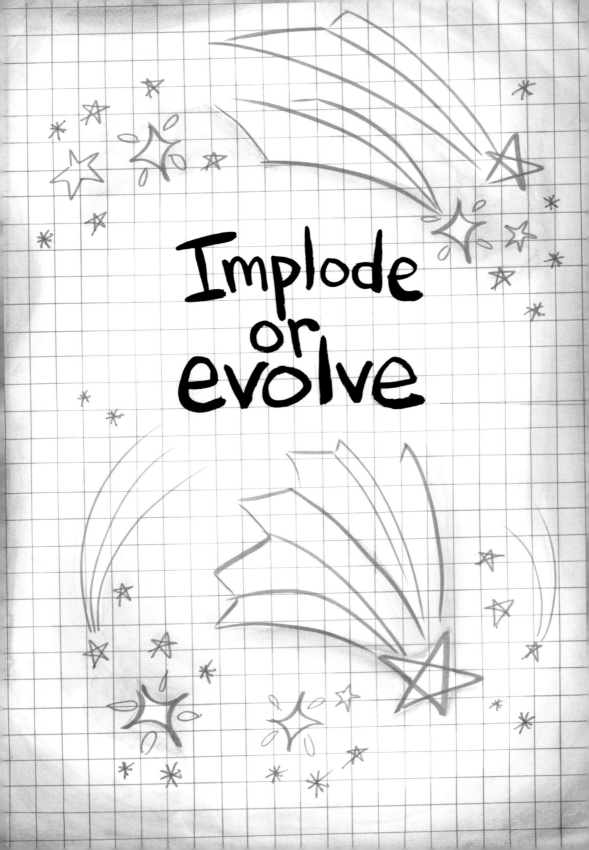

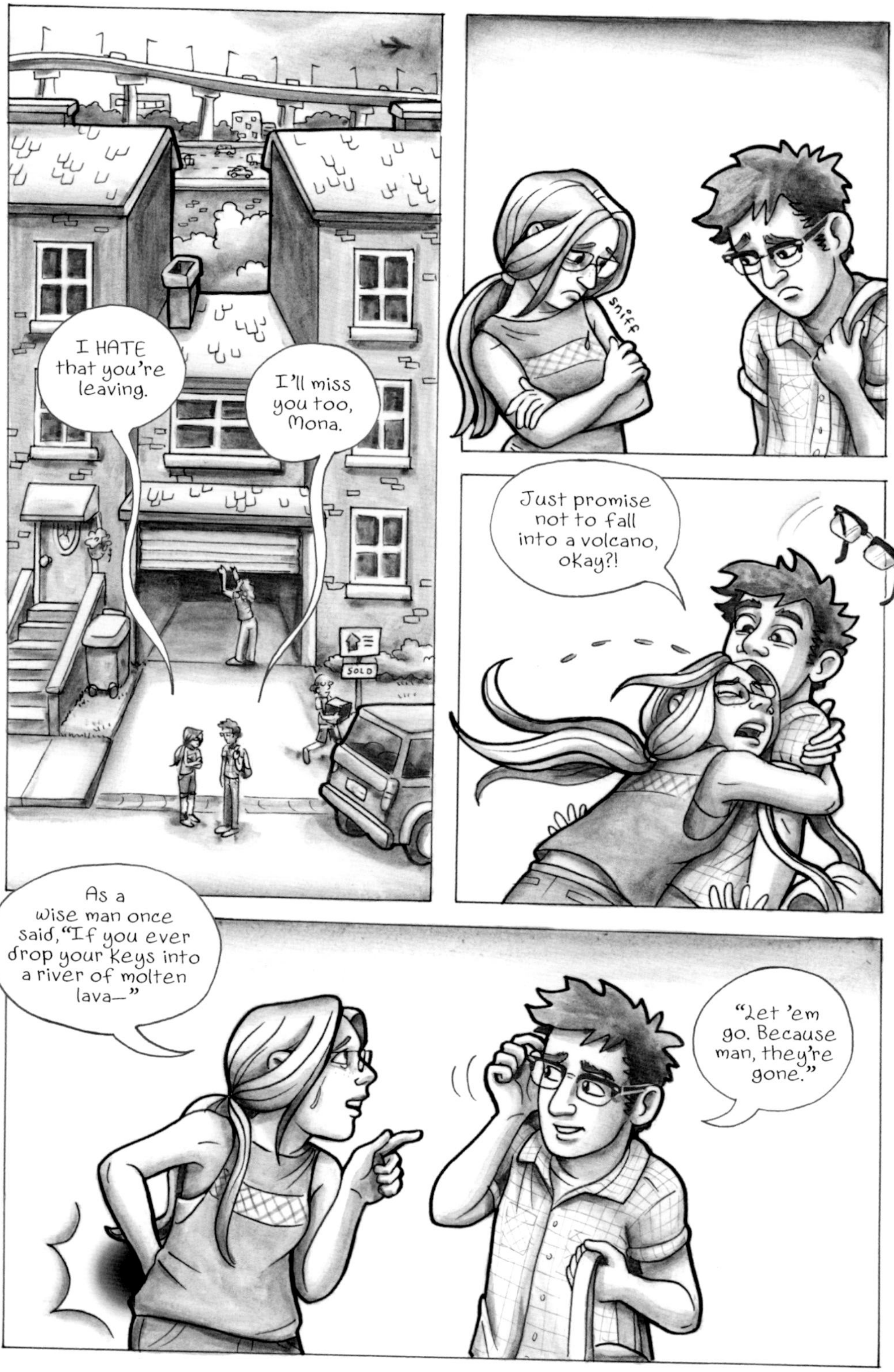
I HATE that you're leaving.
I'll miss you too, Mona.
SOLD
sniff
Just promise not to fall into a volcano, okay?!
As a wise man once said, "If you ever drop your keys into a river of molten lava—"
"Let 'em go. Because man, they're gone."

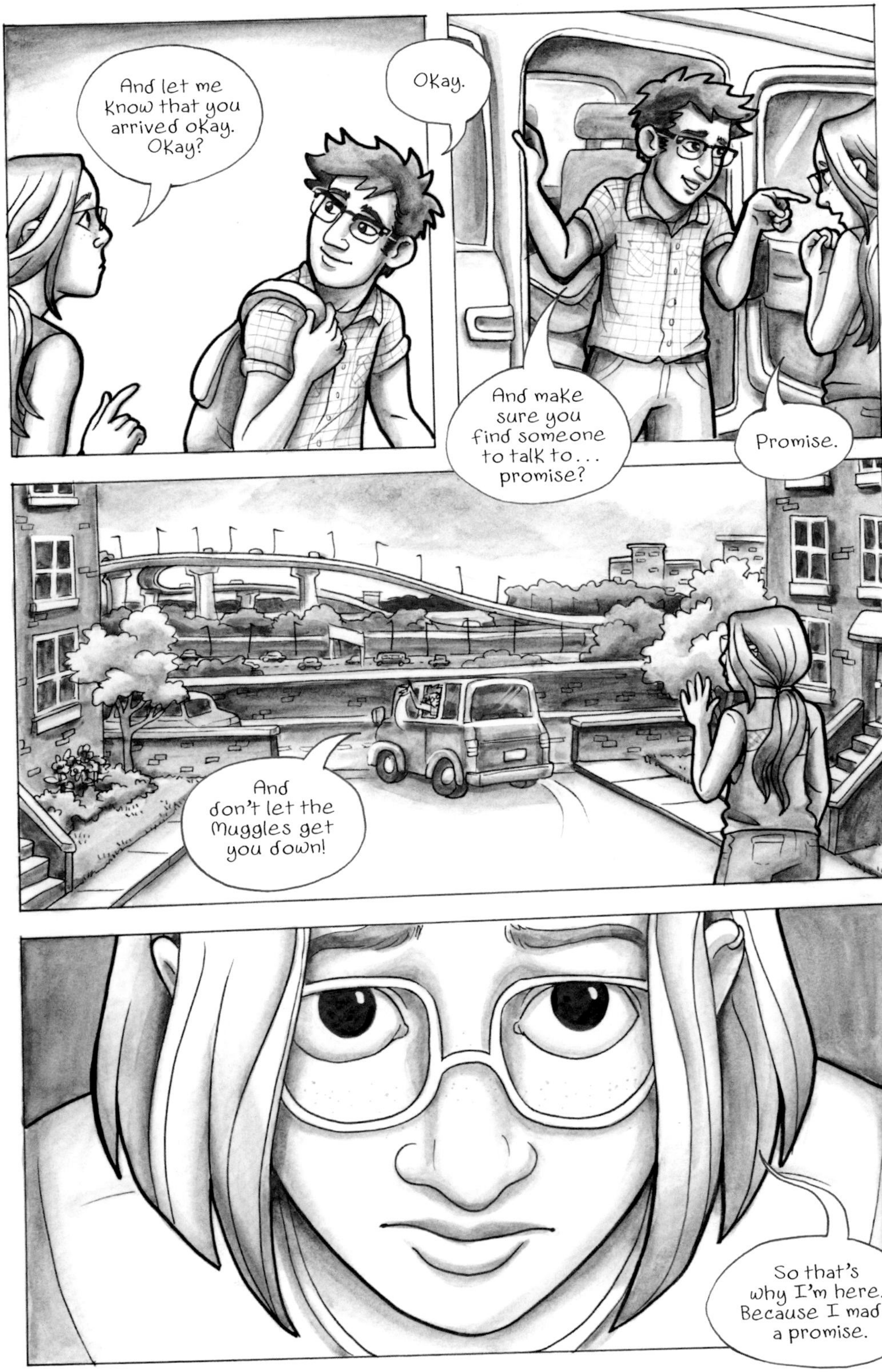
And let me know that you arrived okay. Okay?
Okay.
And make sure you find someone to talk to . . . promise?
Promise.
And don't let the Muggles get you down!
So that's why I'm here. Because I made a promise.

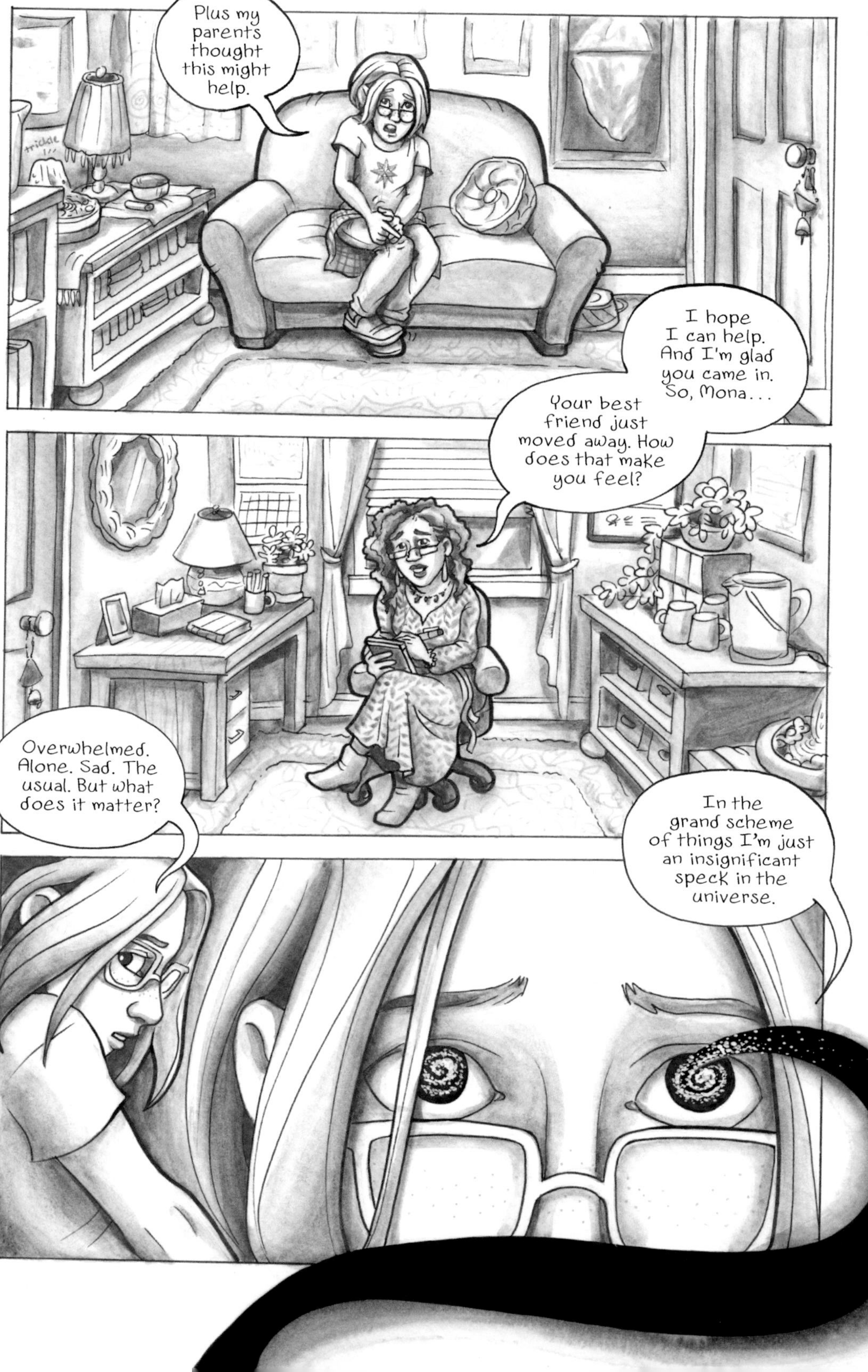

Plus my parents thought this might help.
I hope I can help. And I'm glad you came in. So, Mona...
Your best friend just moved away. How does that make you feel?
Overwhelmed. Alone. Sad. The usual. But what does it matter?
In the grand scheme of things I'm just an insignificant speck in the universe.

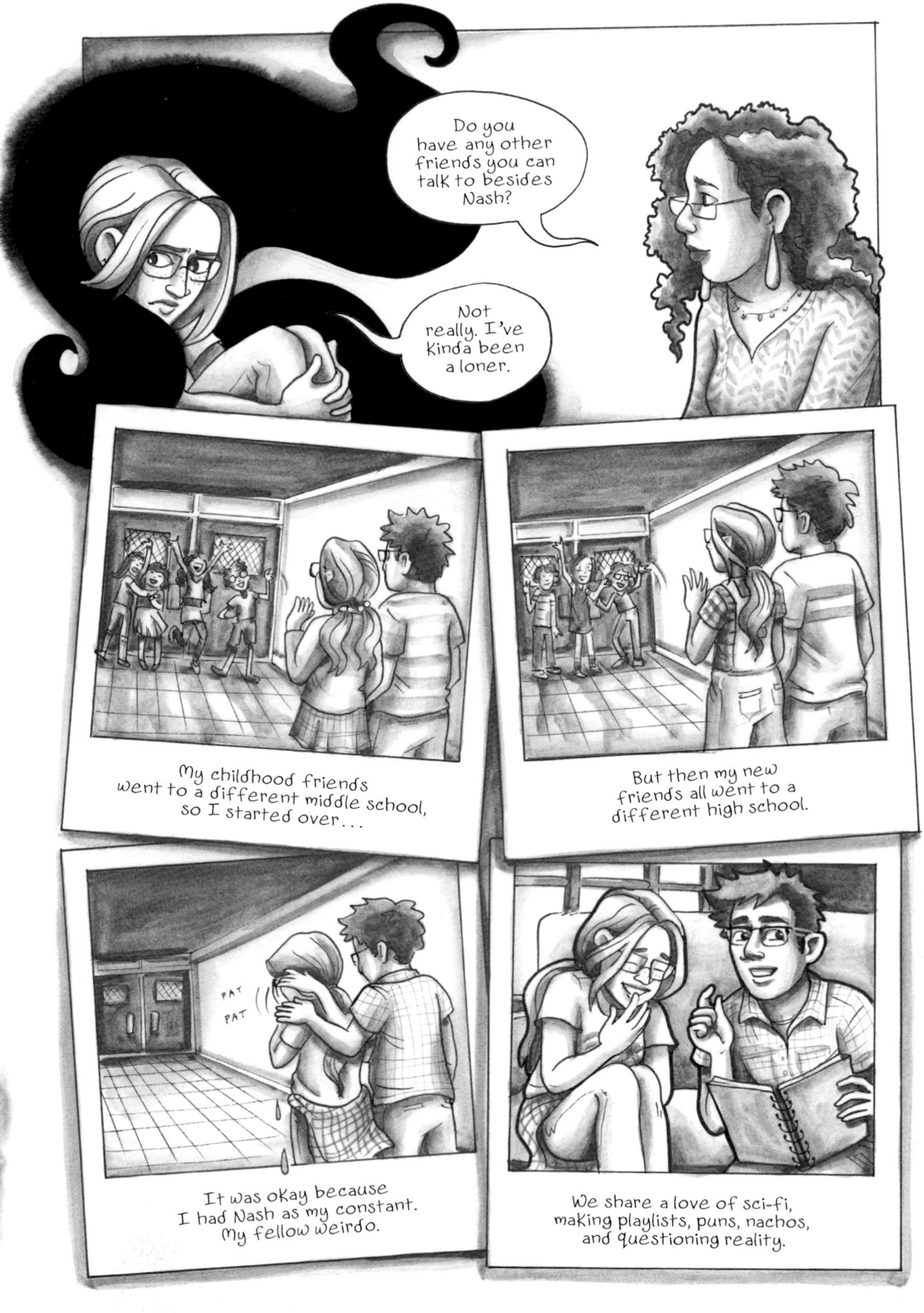
Do you have any other friends you can talk to besides Nash?
Not really. I've kinda been a loner.
My childhood friends went to a different middle school, so I started over...
But then my new friends all went to a different high school.
PAT
PAT
It was okay because I had Nash as my constant. My fellow weirdo.
We share a love of sci-fi, making playlists, puns, nachos, and questioning reality.

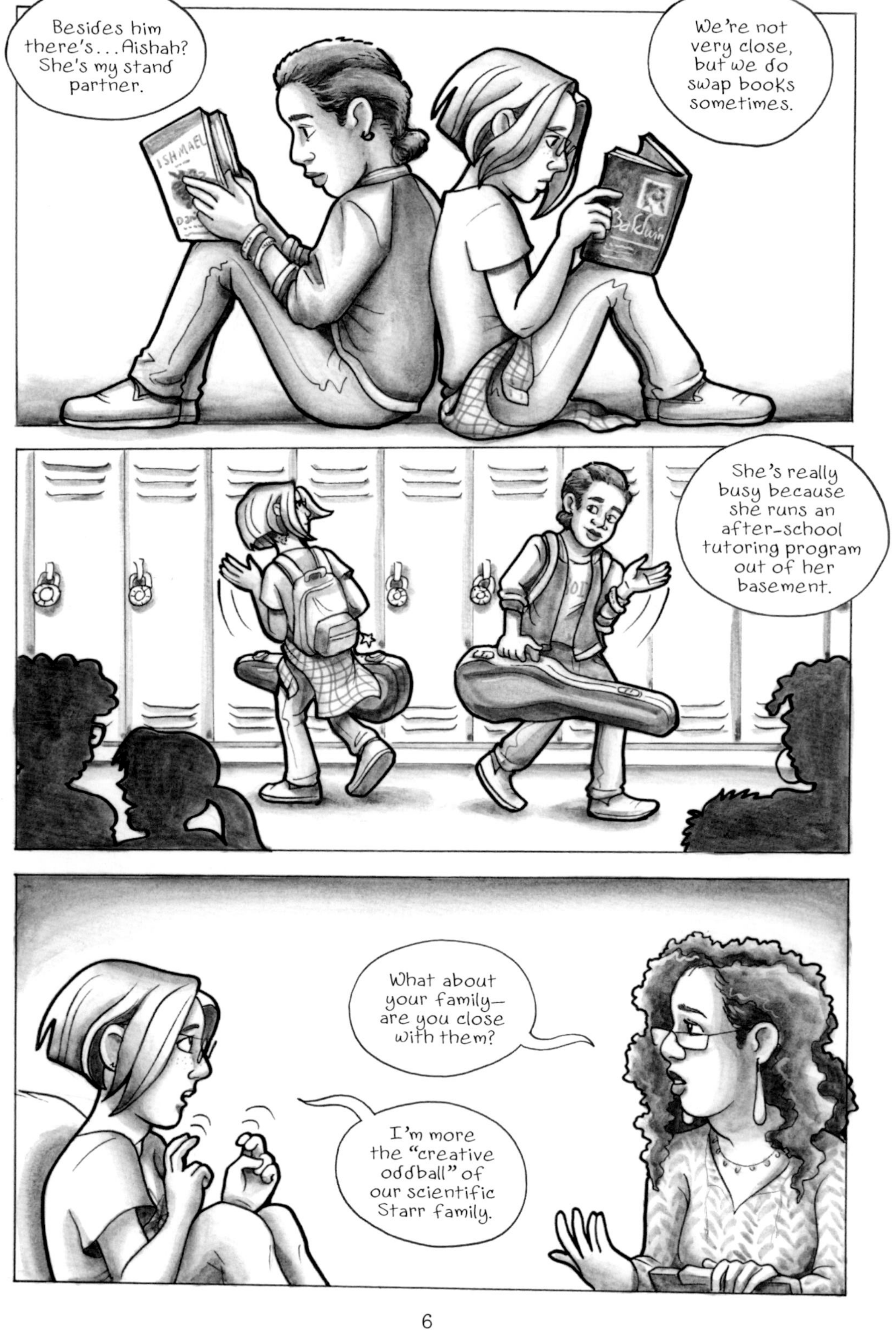
Besides him there's . . . Aishah? She's my stand partner.
ISHMAEL
We're not very close, but we do swap books sometimes.
She's really busy because she runs an after-school tutoring program out of her basement.
What about your family— are you close with them?
I'm more the "creative oddball" of our scientific Starr family.

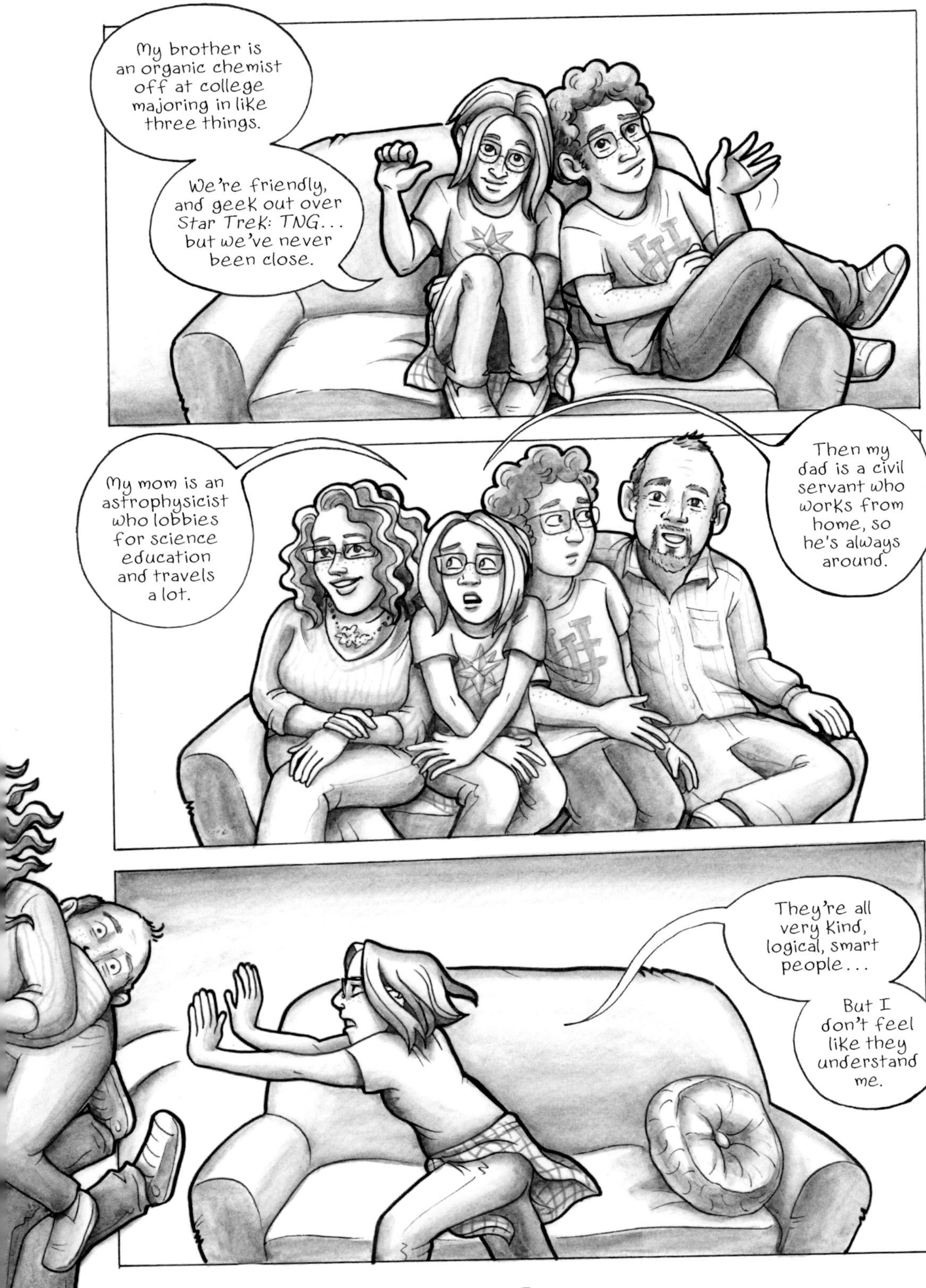
My brother is an organic chemist off at college majoring in like three things.
We're friendly, and geek out over Star Trek: TNG... but we've never been close.
My mom is an astrophysicist who lobbies for science education and travels a lot.
Then my dad is a civil servant who works from home, so he's always around.
They're all very kind, logical, smart people...
But I don't feel like they understand me.

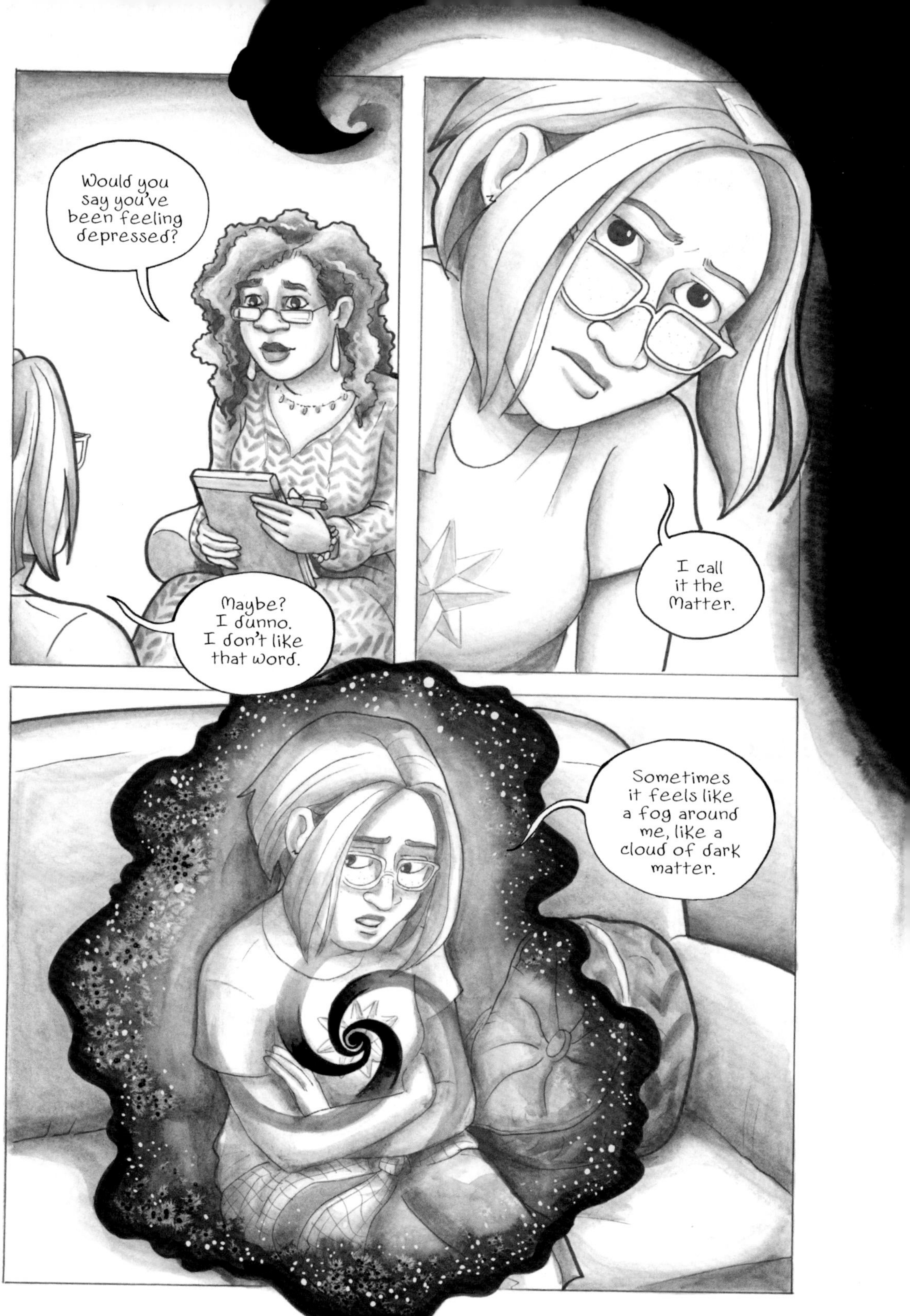
Would you say you've been feeling depressed?
Maybe? I dunno. I don't like that word.
I call it the Matter.
Sometimes it feels like a fog around me, like a cloud of dark matter.

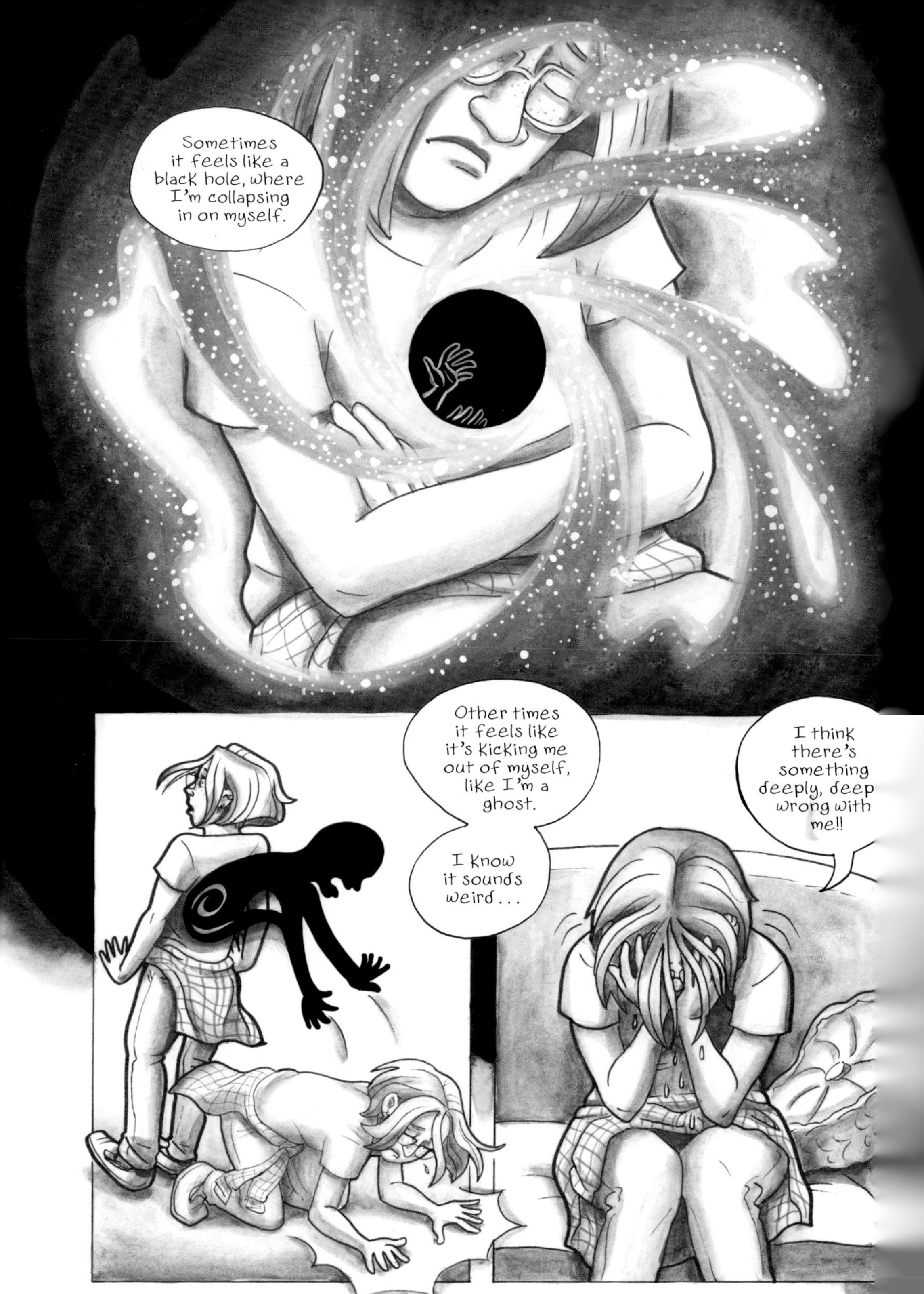

Sometimes it feels like a black hole, where I'm collapsing in on myself.
Other times it feels like it's kicking me out of myself, like I'm a ghost.
I know it sounds weird . . .
I think there's something deeply, deep wrong with me!!

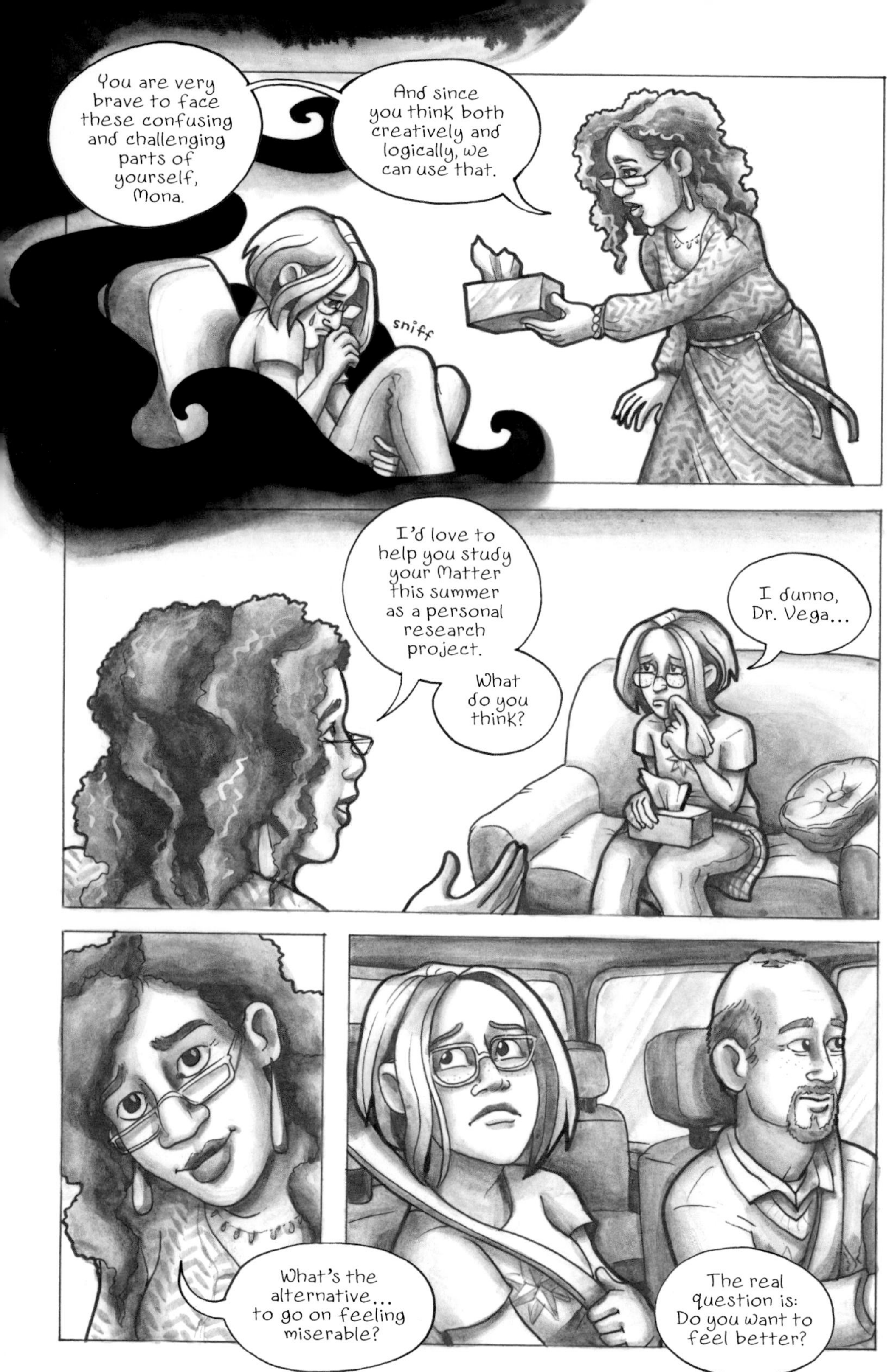
You are very brave to face these confusing and challenging parts of yourself, Mona.
And since you think both creatively and logically, we can use that.
sniff
I'd love to help you study your Matter this summer as a personal research project.
What do you think?
I dunno, Dr. Vega...
What's the alternative... to go on feeling miserable?
The real question is: Do you want to feel better?

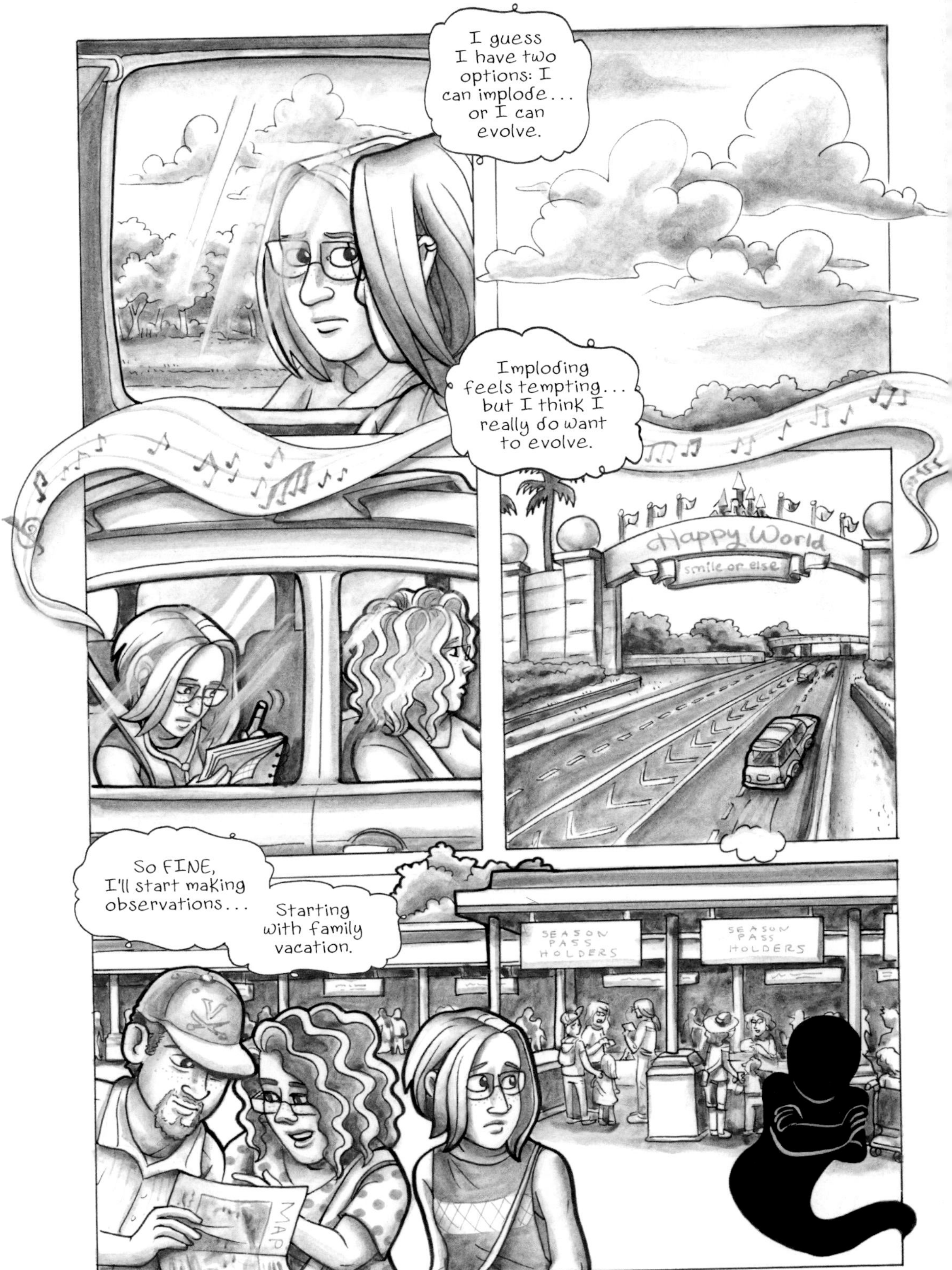
I guess I have two options: I can implode... or I can evolve.
Imploding feels tempting... but I think I really do want to evolve.
Happy World
smile or else
So FINE, I'll start making observations...
Starting with family vacation.
SEASON PASS HOLDERS
SEASON PASS HOLDERS
MAP

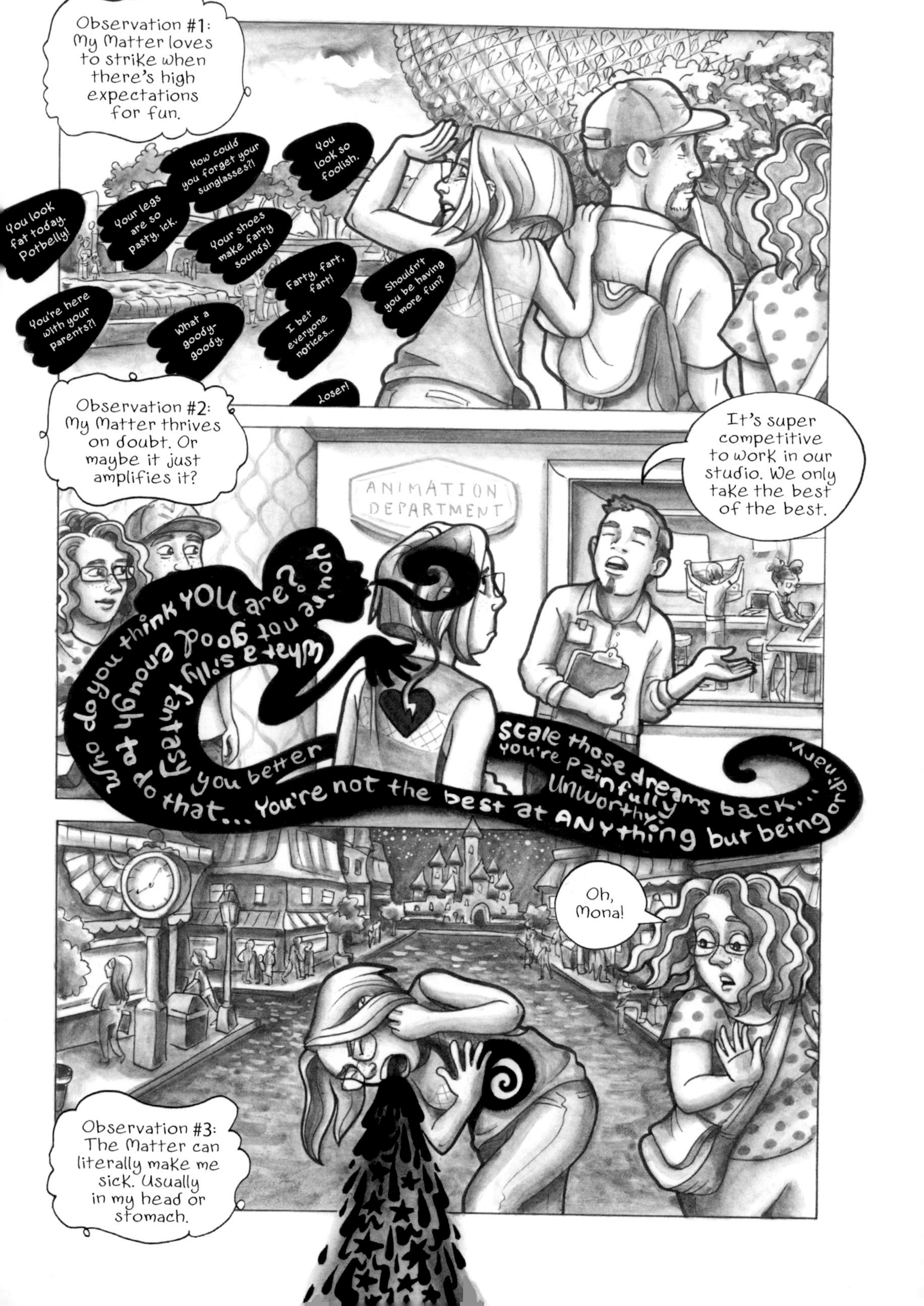
Observation #1: My Matter loves to strike when there's high expectations for fun.
You look fat today. Potbelly!
Your legs are so pasty, ick.
How could you forget your sunglasses?!
You look so foolish.
Your shoes make farty sounds!
Farty, fart, fart!
Shouldn't you be having more fun?
You're here with your parents?!
What a goody-goody.
I bet everyone notices...
Loser!
Observation #2: My Matter thrives on doubt. Or maybe it just amplifies it?
ANIMATION DEPARTMENT
It's super competitive to work in our studio. We only take the best of the best.
Who do you think YOU are?
You're not good enough to do that... You're not the best at ANYTHING but being ordinary.
What a silly fantasy you better scale those dreams back...
You're painfully unworthy.
Oh, Mona!
Observation #3: The Matter can literally make me sick. Usually in my head or stomach.

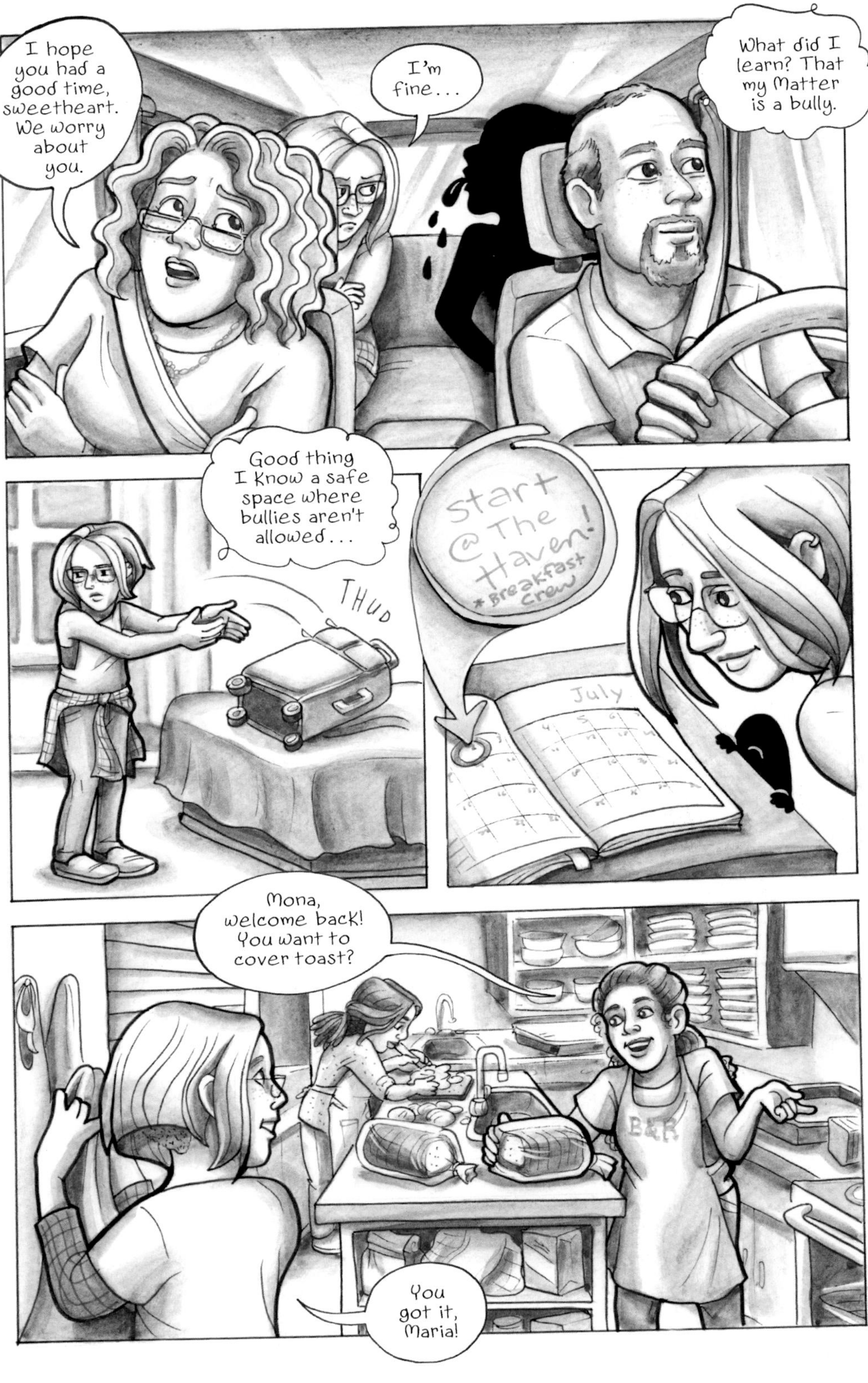
I hope you had a good time, sweetheart. We worry about you.
I'm fine . . .
What did I learn? That my Matter is a bully.
Good thing I know a safe space where bullies aren't allowed . . .
THUD
Start @ The Haven! * Breakfast Crew
July
Mona, welcome back! You want to cover toast?
B&R
You got it, Maria!

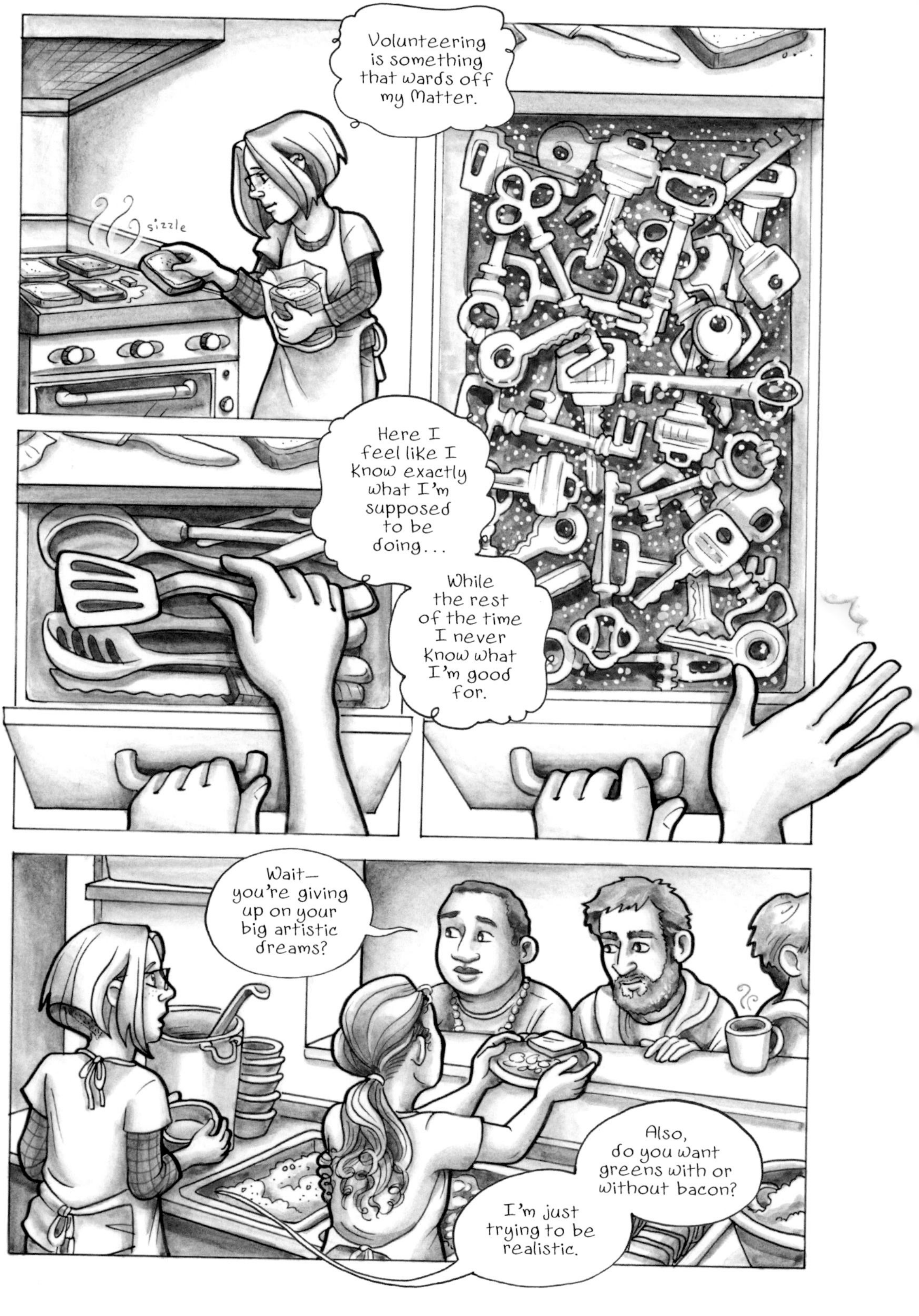

Volunteering is something that wards off my Matter.
sizzle
Here I feel like I know exactly what I'm supposed to be doing...
While the rest of the time I never know what I'm good for.
Wait— you're giving up on your big artistic dreams?
I'm just trying to be realistic.
Also, do you want greens with or without bacon?

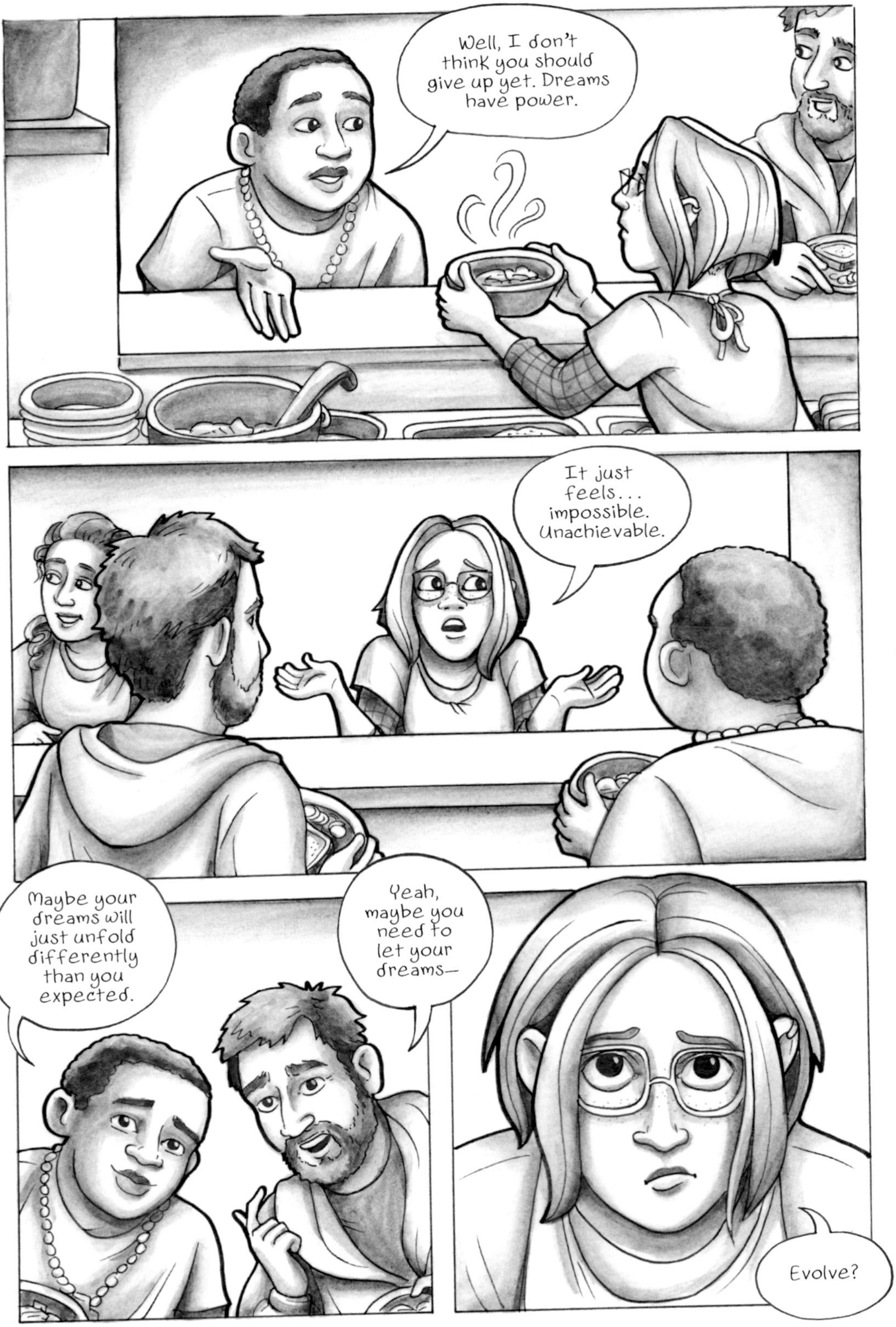
Well, I don't think you should give up yet. Dreams have power.
It just feels... impossible. Unachievable.
Maybe your dreams will just unfold differently than you expected.
Yeah, maybe you need to let your dreams—
Evolve?

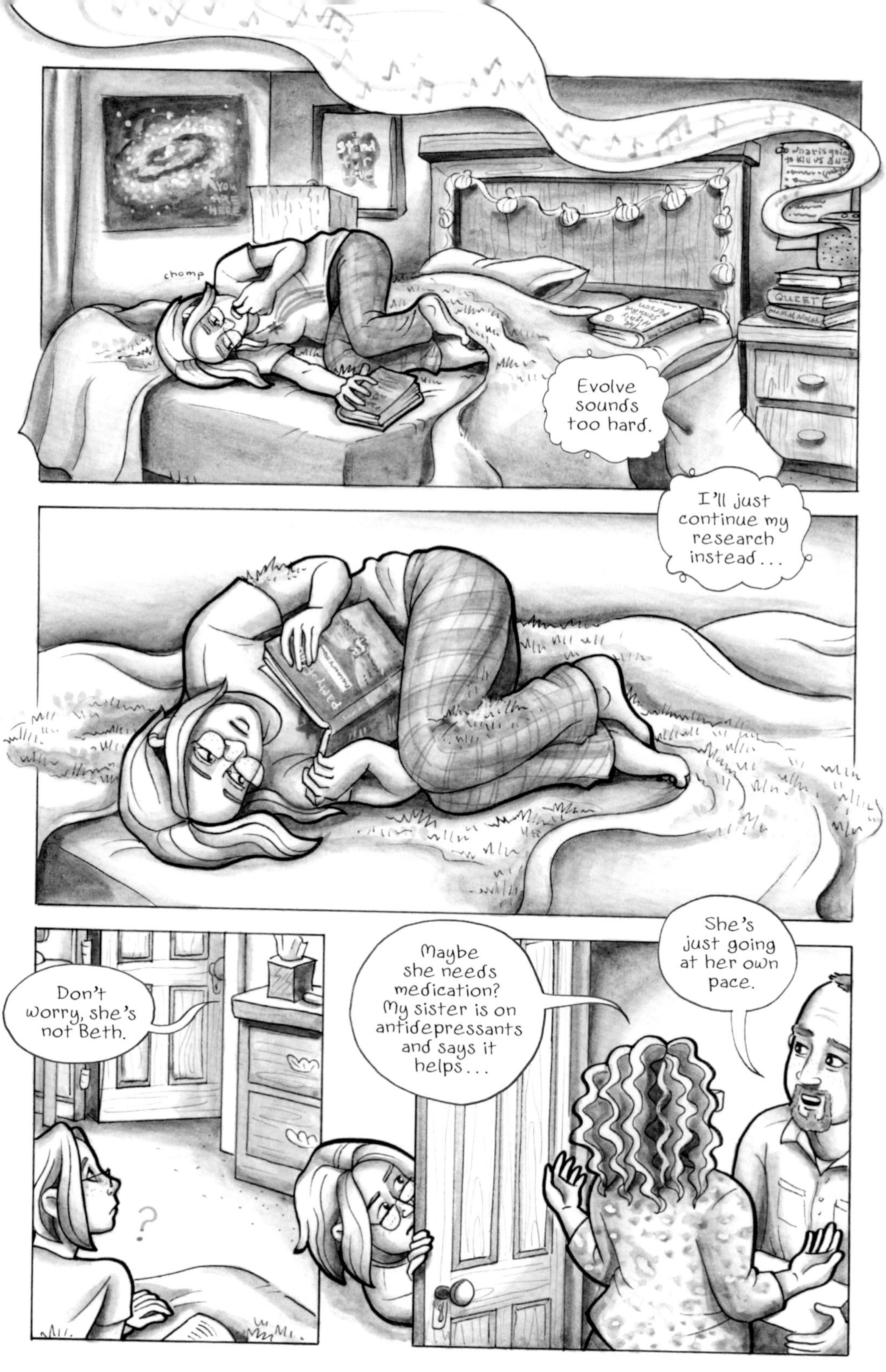
YOU ARE HERE
chomp
QUIET
Evolve sounds too hard.
I'll just continue my research instead...
Don't worry, she's not Beth.
Maybe she needs medication? My sister is on antidepressants and says it helps...
She's just going at her own pace.

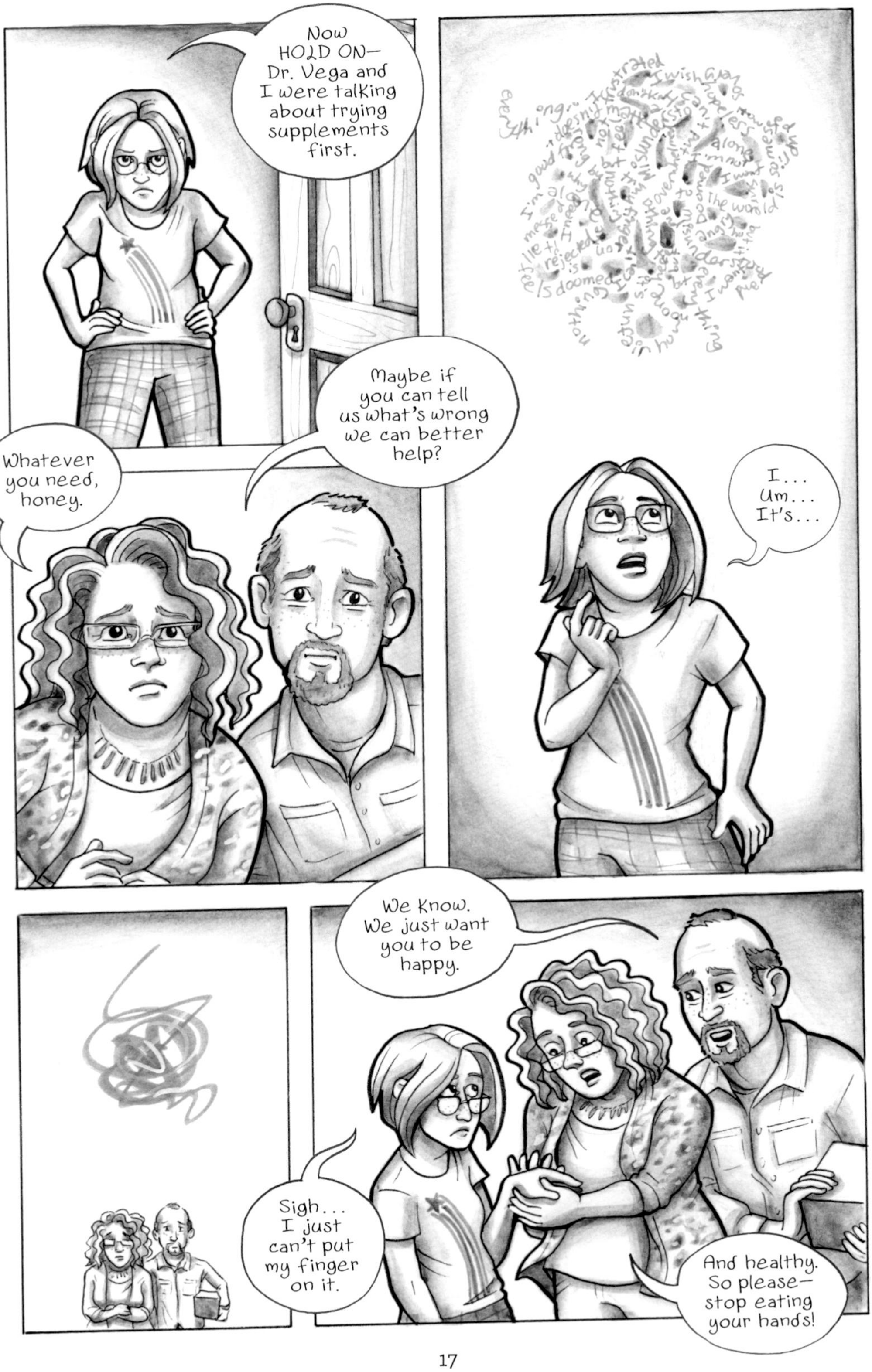

Now HOLD ON— Dr. Vega and I were talking about trying supplements first.
Whatever you need, honey.
Maybe if you can tell us what's wrong we can better help?
I... Um... It's...
We know. We just want you to be happy.
And healthy. So please— stop eating your hands!
Sigh... I just can't put my finger on it.

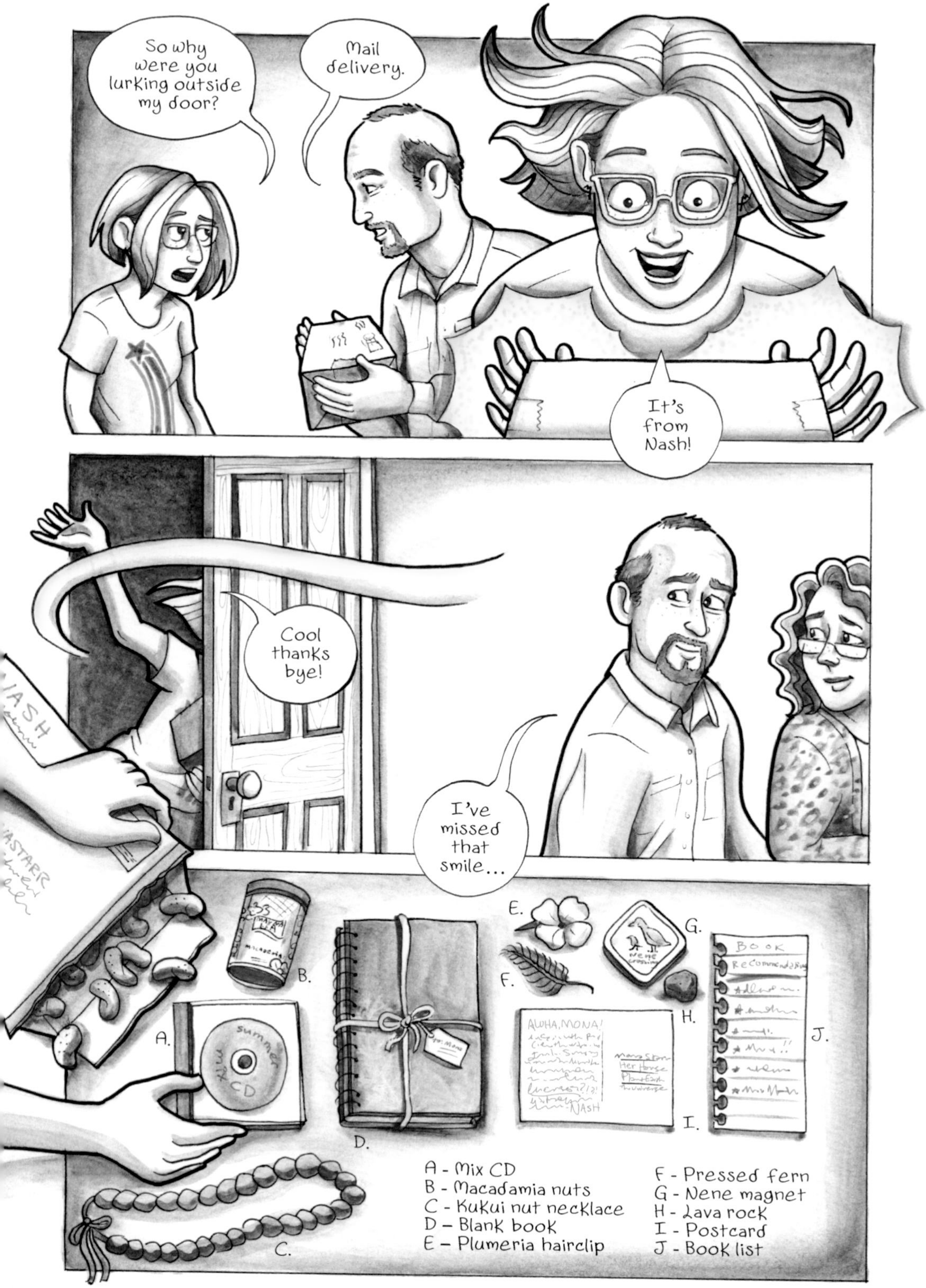
So why were you lurking outside my door?
Mail delivery.
It's from Nash!
Cool thanks bye!
I've missed that smile...
A.
B.
C.
D.
E.
F.
G.
H.
I.
J.
summer CD
ALOHA, MONA!
NASH
BOOK
A - Mix CD
B - Macadamia nuts
C - Kukui nut necklace
D - Blank book
E - Plumeria hairclip
F - Pressed fern
G - Nene magnet
H - Lava rock
I - Postcard
J - Book list

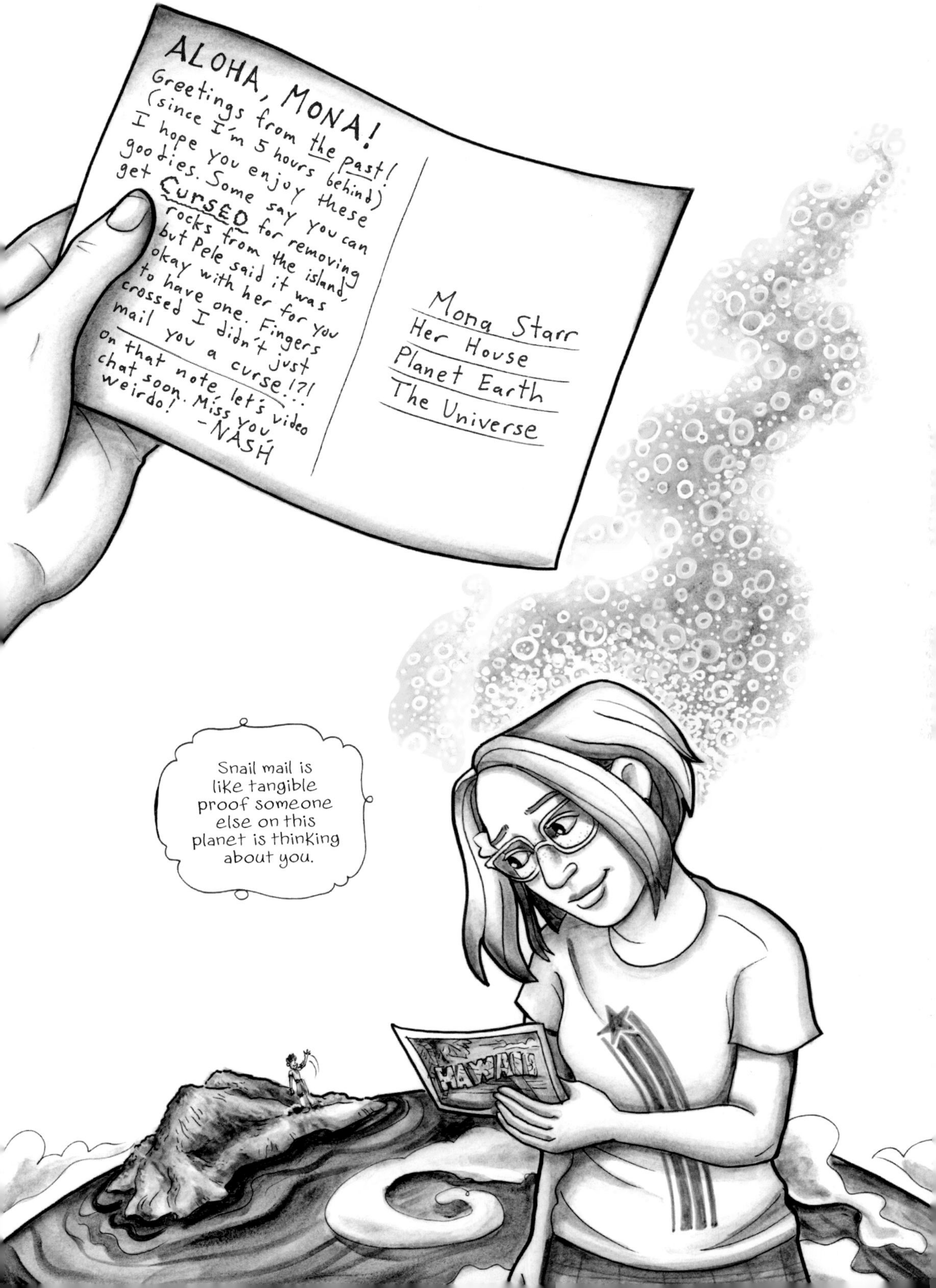
ALOHA, MONA!
Greetings from the past! (since I'm 5 hours behind) I hope you enjoy these goodies. Some say you can get CURSED for removing rocks from the island, but Pele said it was okay with her for you to have one. Fingers crossed I didn't just mail you a curse!?!
On that note, let's video chat soon. Miss you, weirdo! -NASH
Mona Starr
Her House
Planet Earth
The Universe
Snail mail is like tangible proof someone else on this planet is thinking about you.
HAWAII

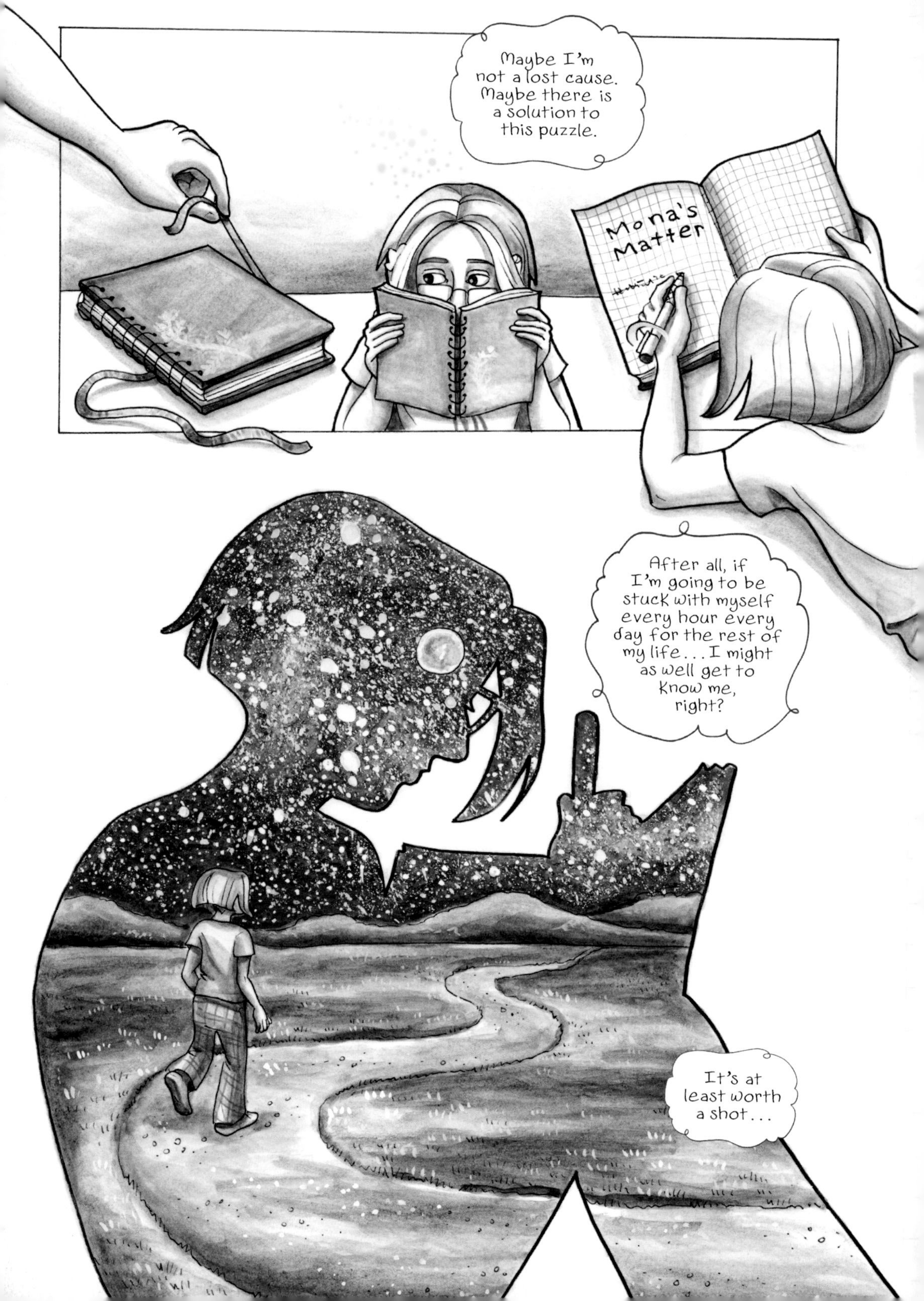

Maybe I'm not a lost cause. Maybe there is a solution to this puzzle.
Mona's Matter
After all, if I'm going to be stuck with myself every hour every day for the rest of my life... I might as well get to know me, right?
It's at least worth a shot...

Notice Your Patterns

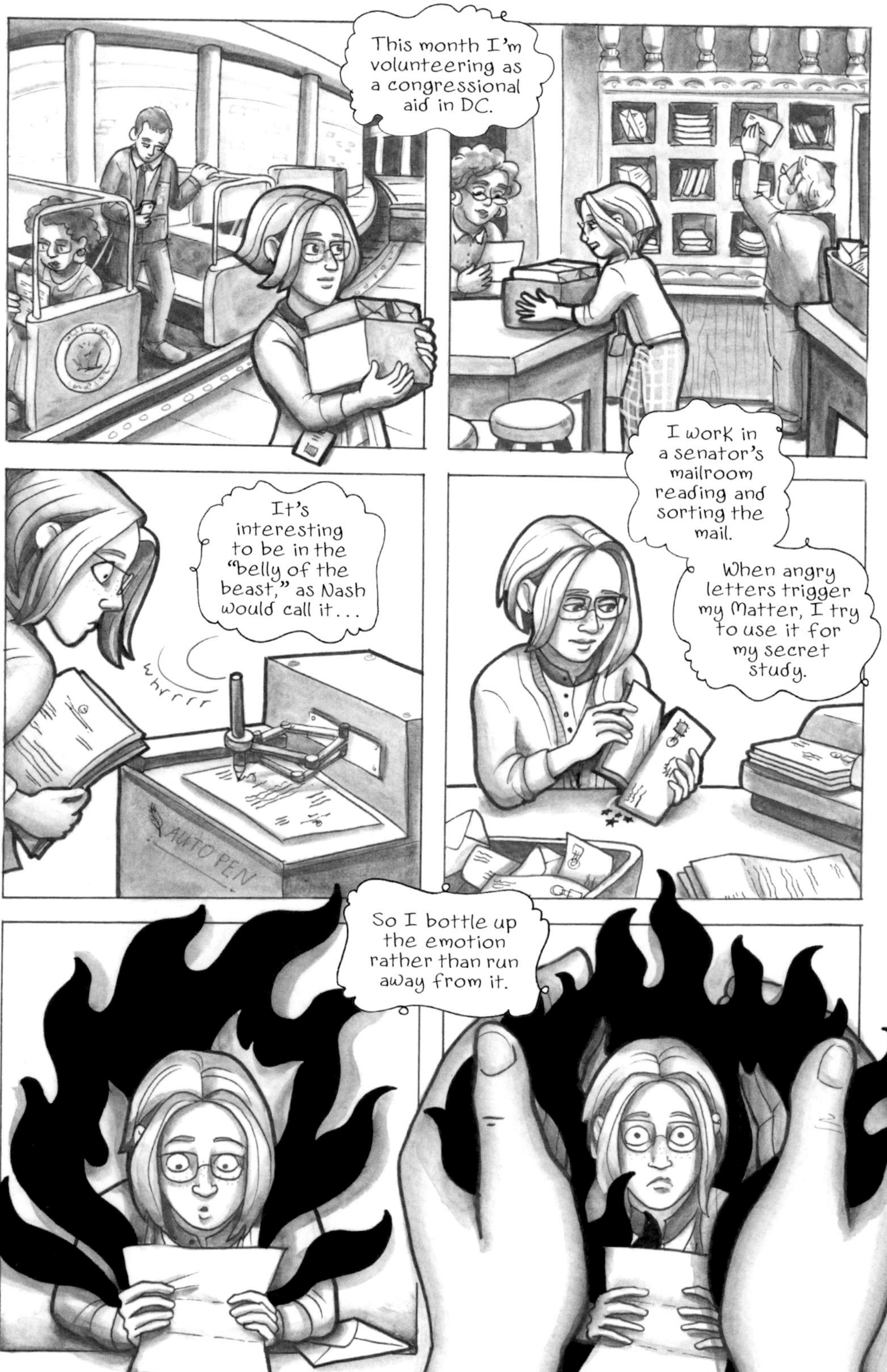
This month I'm volunteering as a congressional aid in DC.
I work in a senator's mailroom reading and sorting the mail.
It's interesting to be in the "belly of the beast," as Nash would call it...
Whrrrr
AUTO PEN
When angry letters trigger my Matter, I try to use it for my secret study.
So I bottle up the emotion rather than run away from it.

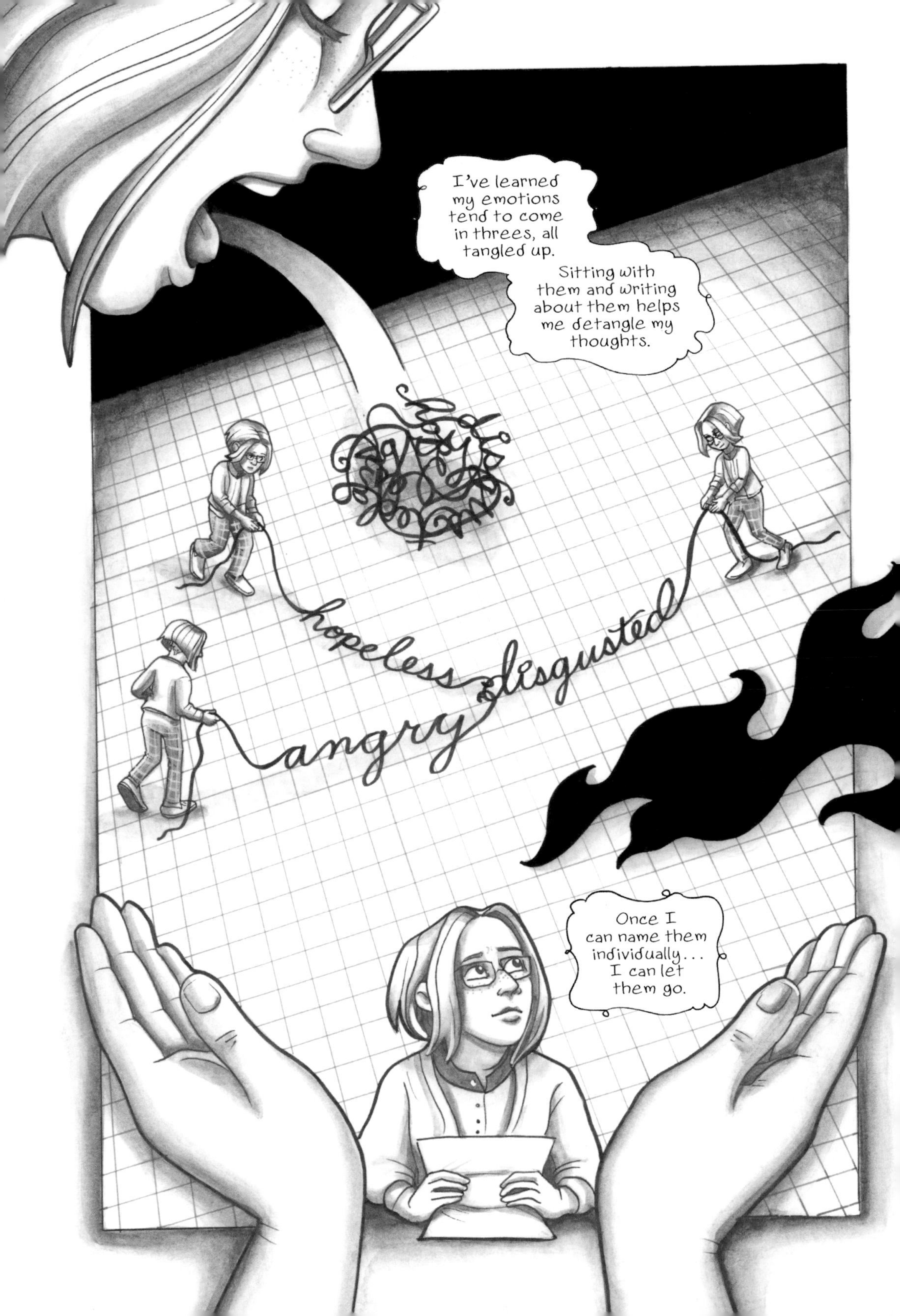
I've learned my emotions tend to come in threes, all tangled up.
Sitting with them and writing about them helps me detangle my thoughts.
hopeless
disgusted
angry
Once I can name them individually... I can let them go.

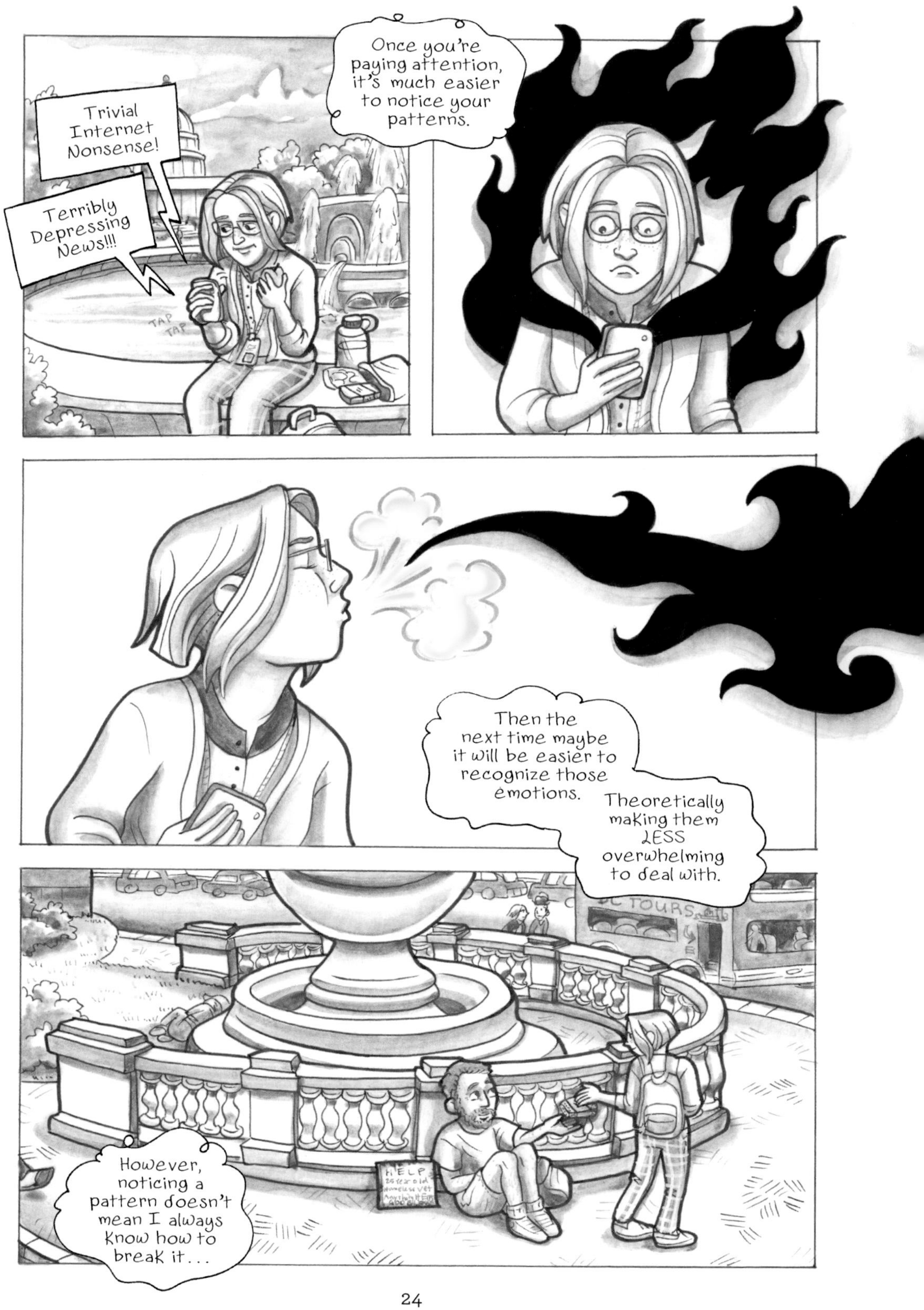
Trivial Internet Nonsense!
Terribly Depressing News!!!
TAP TAP
Once you're paying attention, it's much easier to notice your patterns.
Then the next time maybe it will be easier to recognize those emotions.
Theoretically making them LESS overwhelming to deal with.
However, noticing a pattern doesn't mean I always know how to break it...

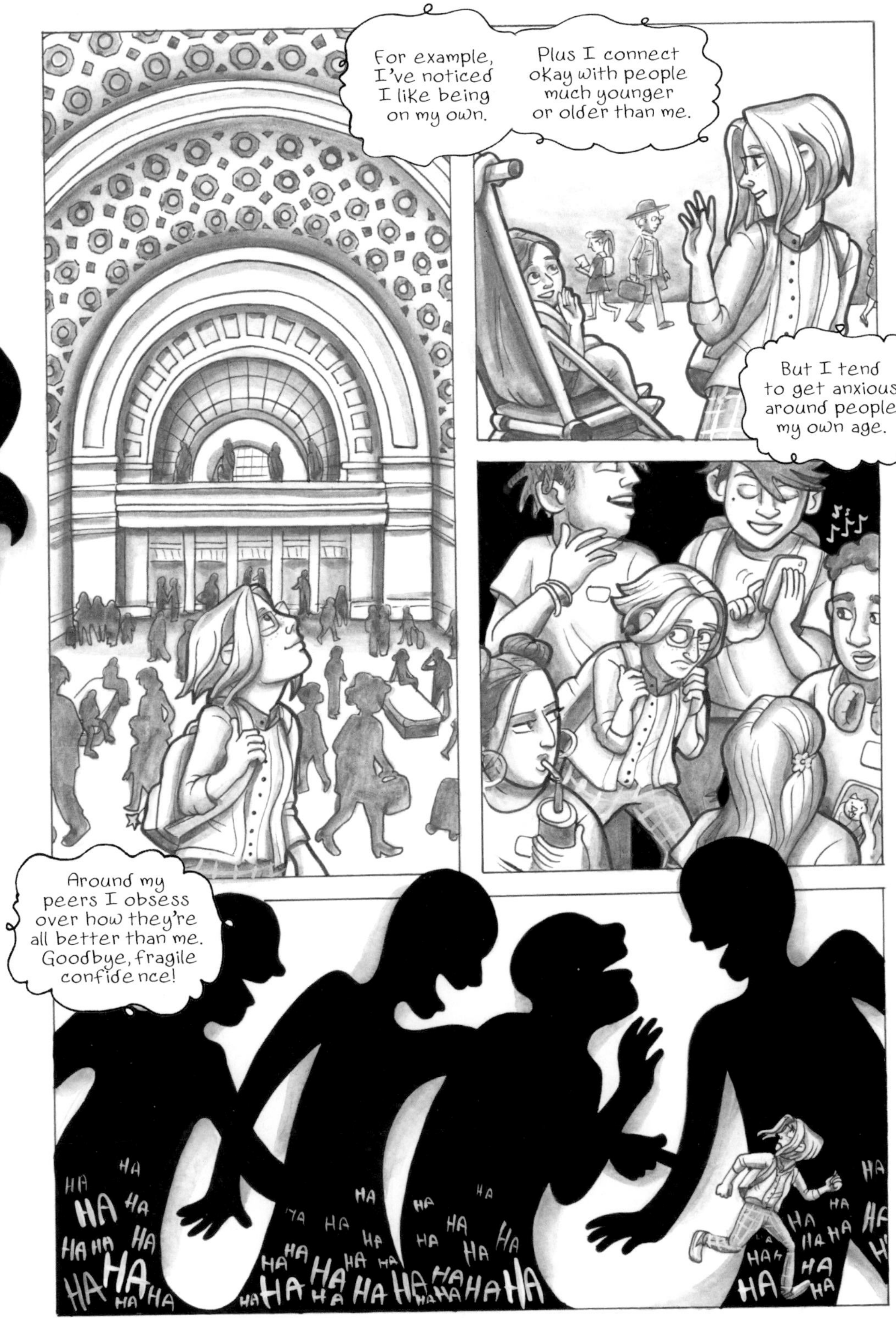
For example, I've noticed I like being on my own.
Plus I connect okay with people much younger or older than me.
But I tend to get anxious around people my own age.
Around my peers I obsess over how they're all better than me. Goodbye, fragile confidence!
HA HA HA

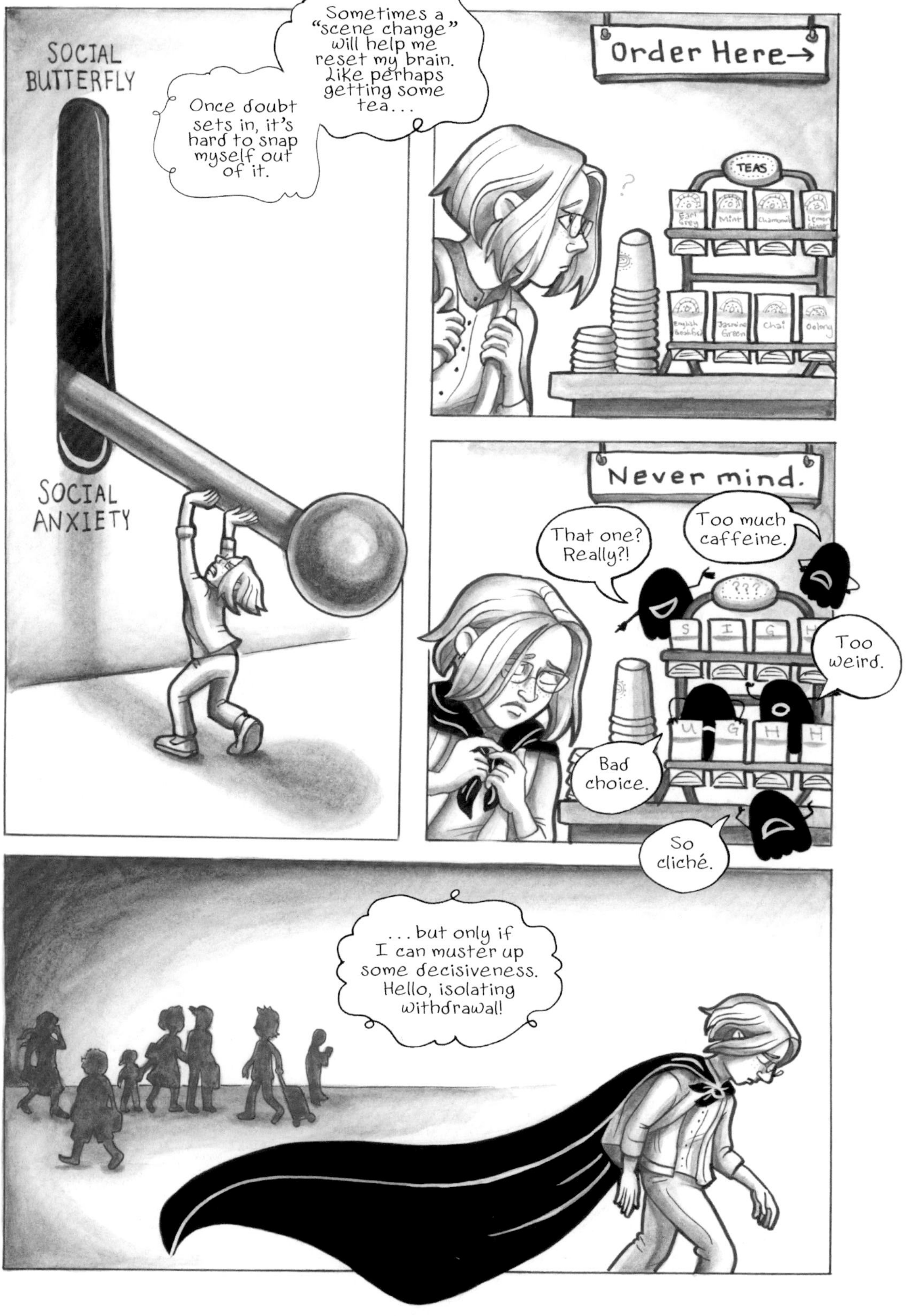
SOCIAL BUTTERFLY
SOCIAL ANXIETY
Once doubt sets in, it's hard to snap myself out of it.
Sometimes a "scene change" will help me reset my brain. Like perhaps getting some tea...
Order Here→
TEAS
Mint
Chai
Oolong
Never mind.
That one? Really?!
Too much caffeine.
Too weird.
Bad choice.
So cliché.
...but only if I can muster up some decisiveness. Hello, isolating withdrawal!

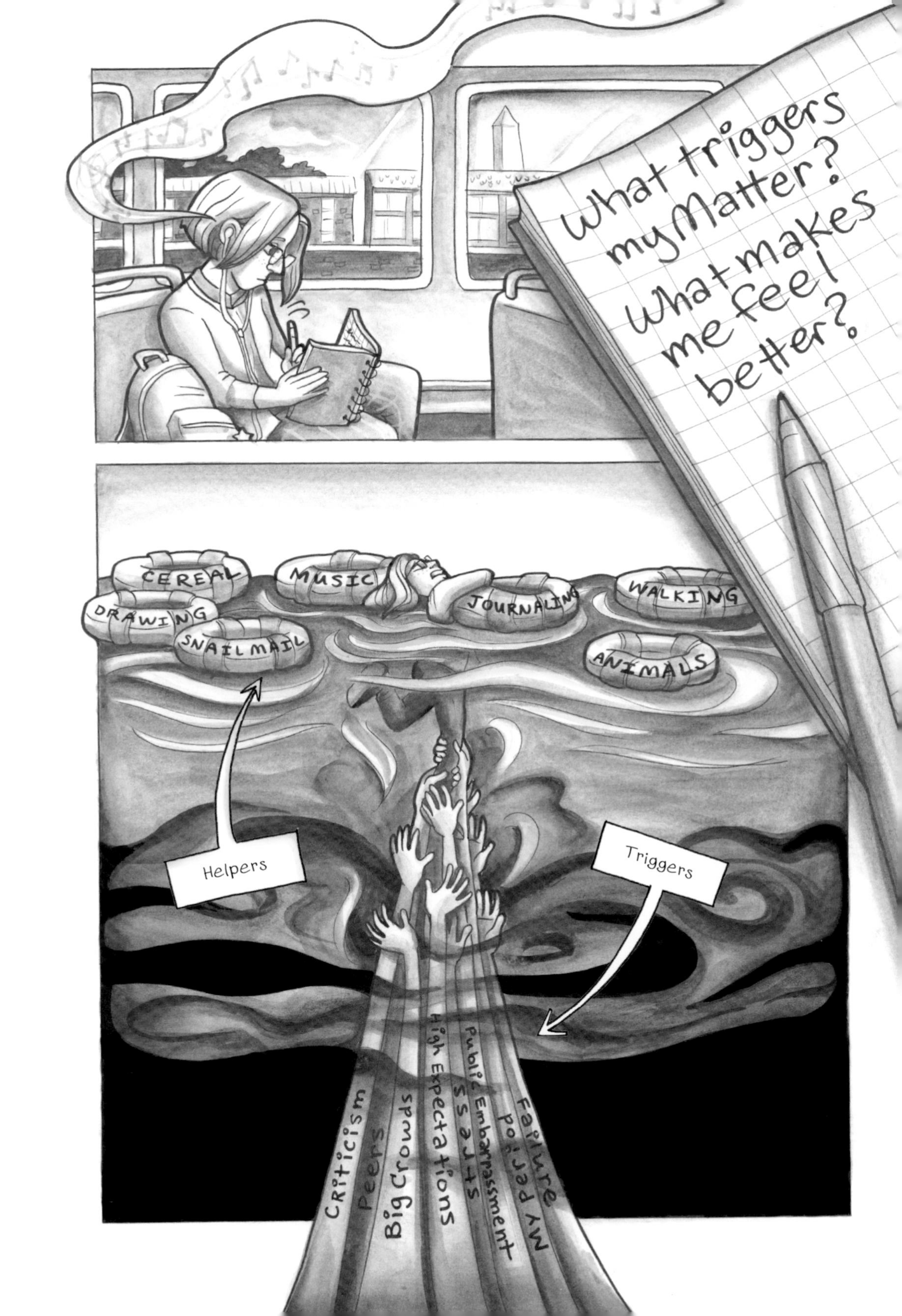

What triggers my Matter? What makes me feel better?
CEREAL
MUSIC
DRAWING
SNAILMAIL
JOURNALING
WALKING
ANIMALS
Helpers
Triggers
Criticism
Peers
Big Crowds
High Expectations
Stress
Public Embarrassment
My Period
Failure

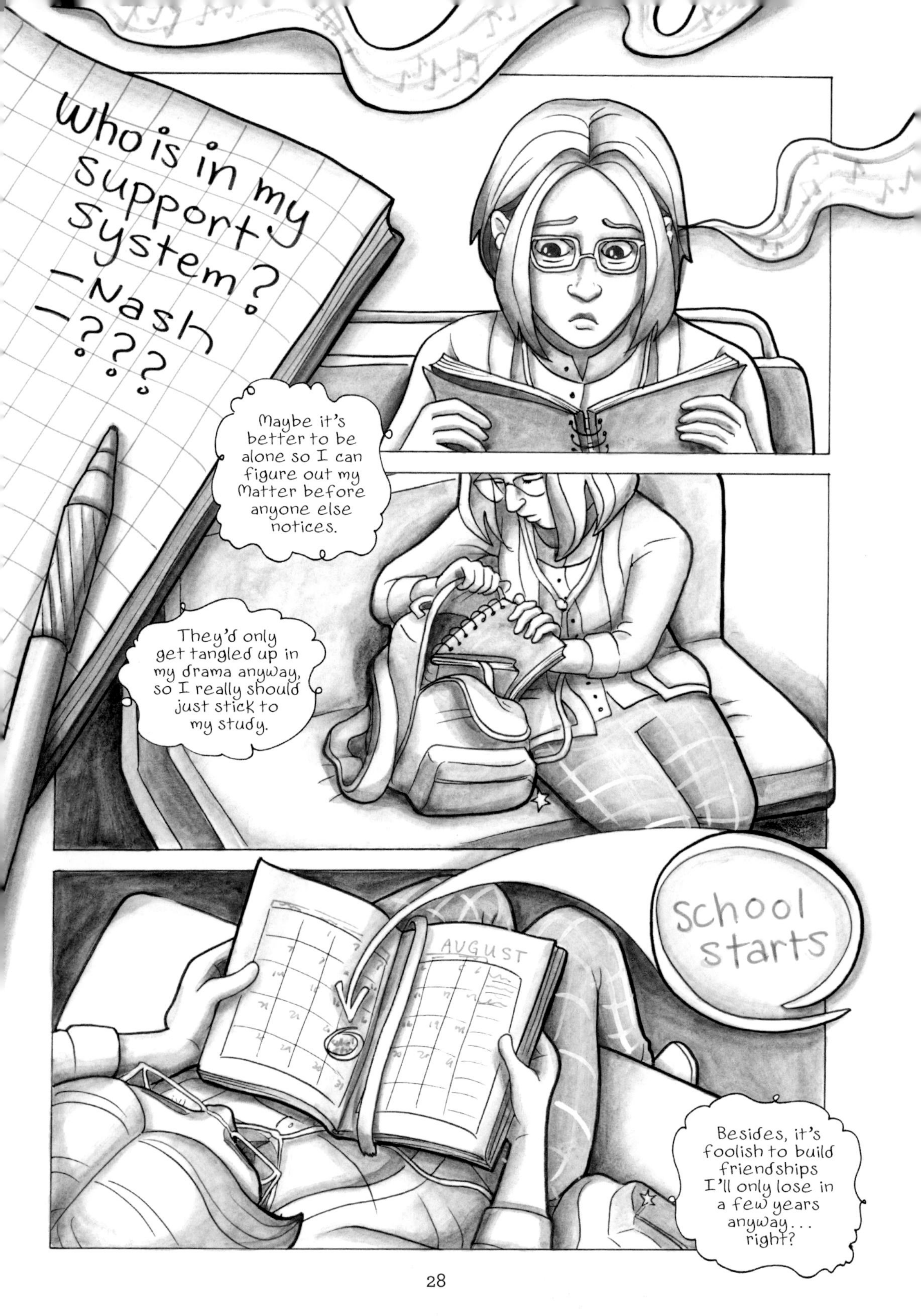
Who is in my support system?
-Nash
-???
Maybe it's better to be alone so I can figure out my Matter before anyone else notices.
They'd only get tangled up in my drama anyway, so I really should just stick to my study.
AUGUST
School starts
Besides, it's foolish to build friendships I'll only lose in a few years anyway... right?

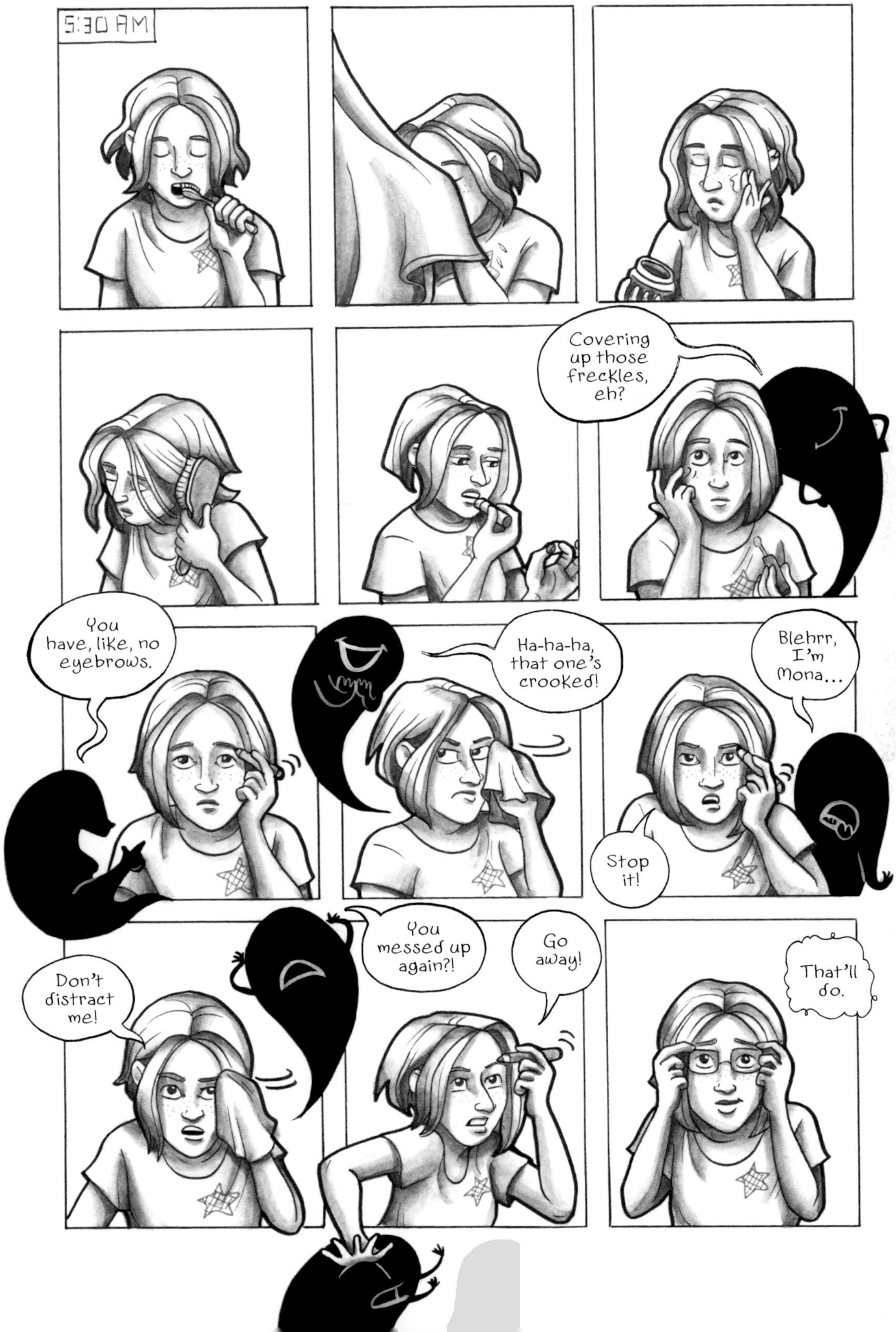
5:30 AM
Covering up those freckles, eh?
You have, like, no eyebrows.
Ha-ha-ha, that one's crooked!
Blehrr, I'm Mona...
Stop it!
Don't distract me!
You messed up again?!
Go away!
That'll do.

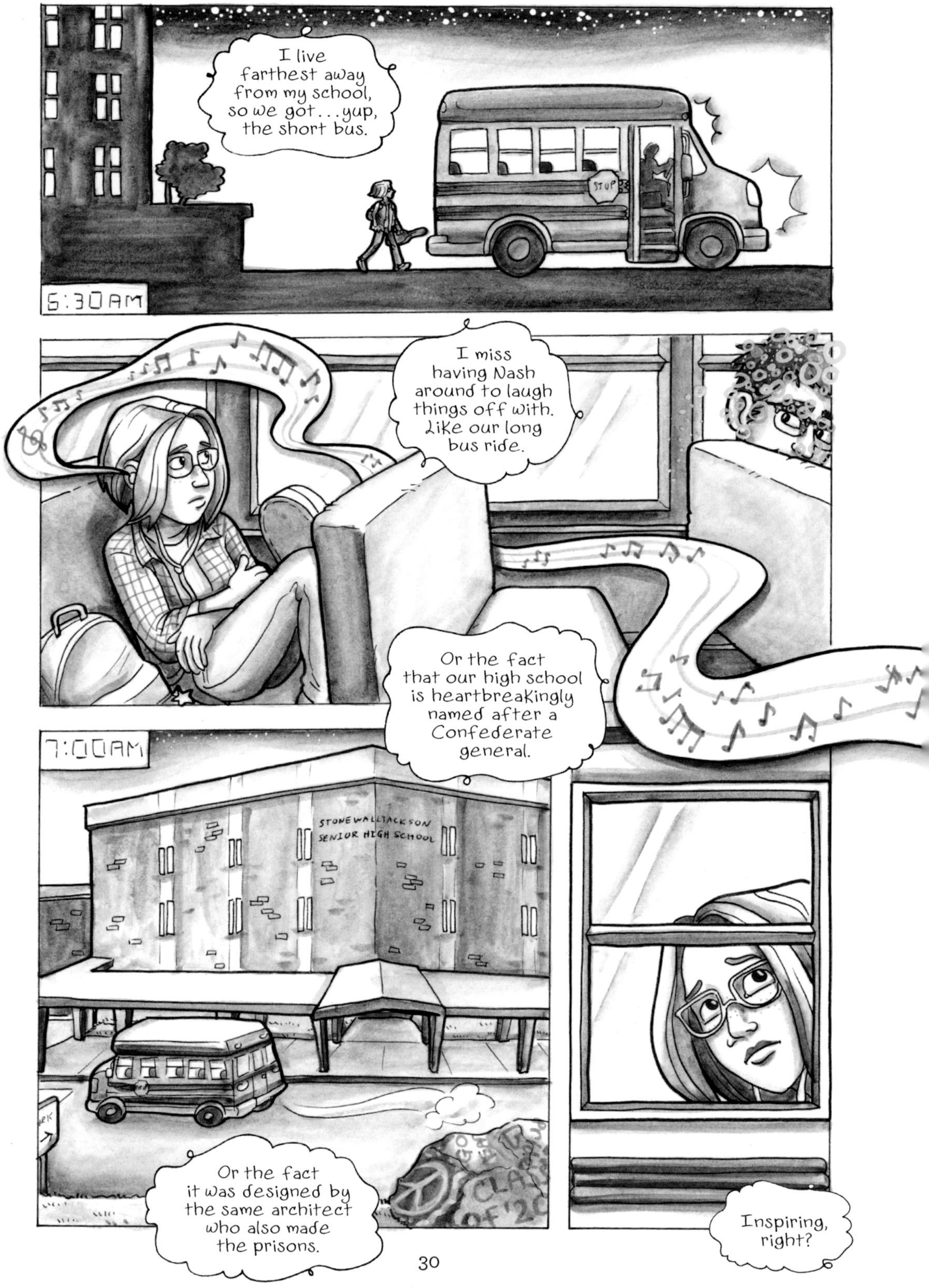
I live farthest away from my school, so we got . . . yup, the short bus.
STOP
6:30AM
I miss having Nash around to laugh things off with. Like our long bus ride.
Or the fact that our high school is heartbreakingly named after a Confederate general.
7:00AM
STONEWALL JACKSON SENIOR HIGH SCHOOL
Or the fact it was designed by the same architect who also made the prisons.
Inspiring, right?

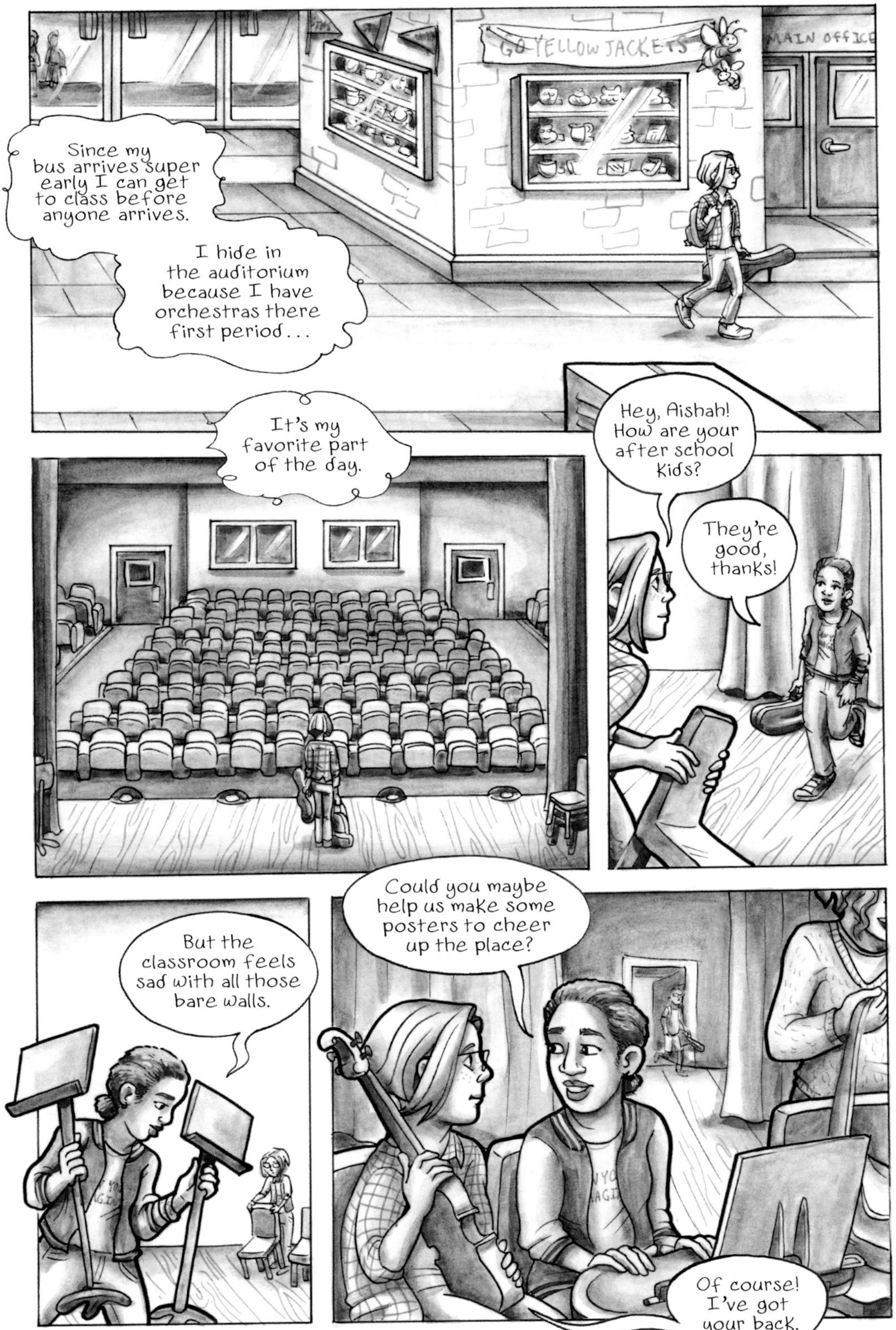
GO YELLOW JACKETS
MAIN OFFICE
Since my bus arrives super early I can get to class before anyone arrives.
I hide in the auditorium because I have orchestras there first period . . .
It's my favorite part of the day.
Hey, Aishah! How are your after school kids?
They're good, thanks!
But the classroom feels sad with all those bare walls.
Could you maybe help us make some posters to cheer up the place?
Of course! I've got your back.

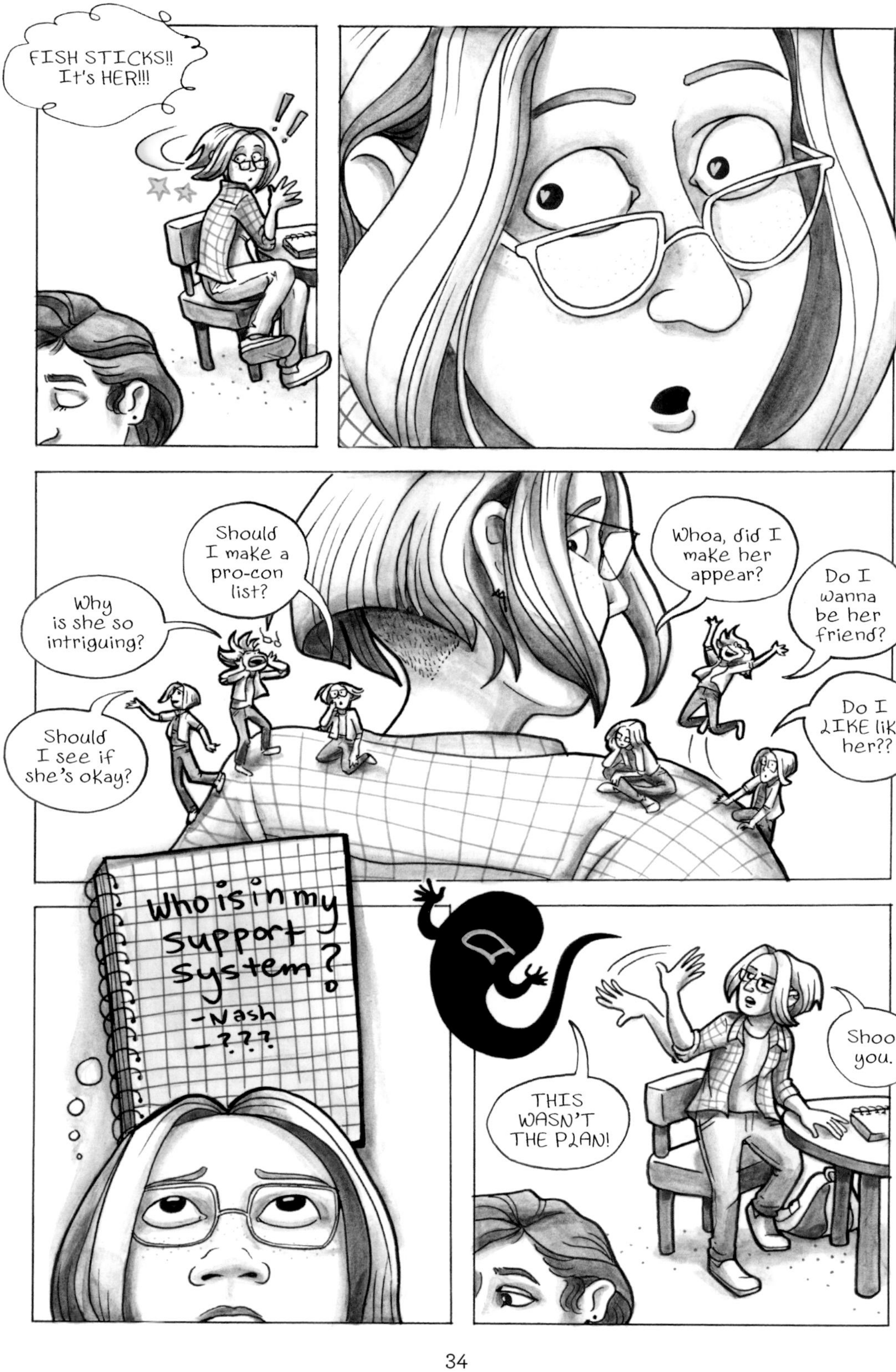
FISH STICKS!! It's HER!!!
!!
Should I make a pro-con list?
Why is she so intriguing?
Should I see if she's okay?
Whoa, did I make her appear?
Do I wanna be her friend?
Do I LIKE like her??
Who is in my support system?
-Nash
-???
THIS WASN'T THE PLAN!
Shoo, you.

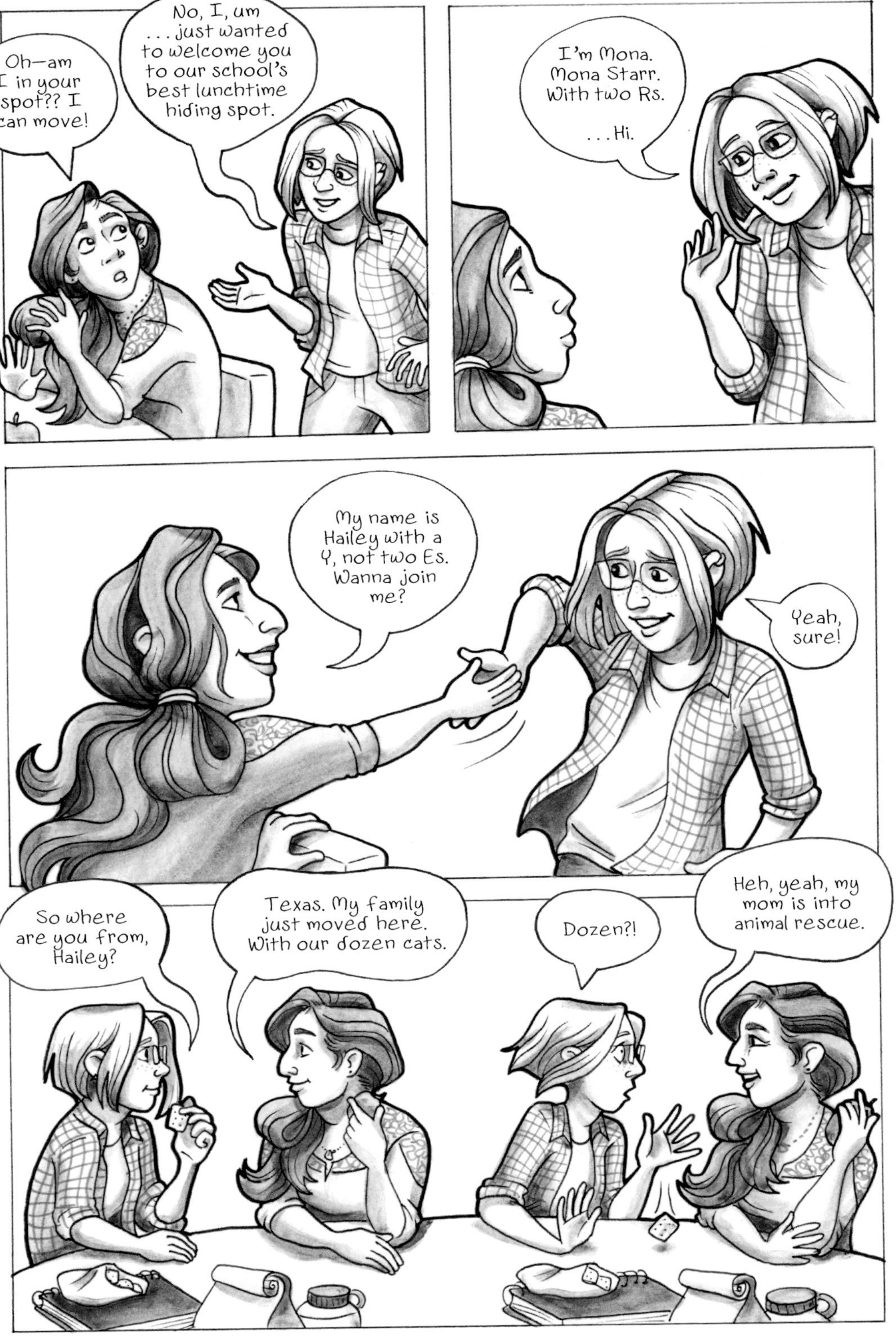
Oh—am I in your spot?? I can move!
No, I, um . . . just wanted to welcome you to our school's best lunchtime hiding spot.
I'm Mona. Mona Starr. With two Rs.
. . . Hi.
My name is Hailey with a Y, not two Es. Wanna join me?
Yeah, sure!
So where are you from, Hailey?
Texas. My family just moved here. With our dozen cats.
Dozen?!
Heh, yeah, my mom is into animal rescue.

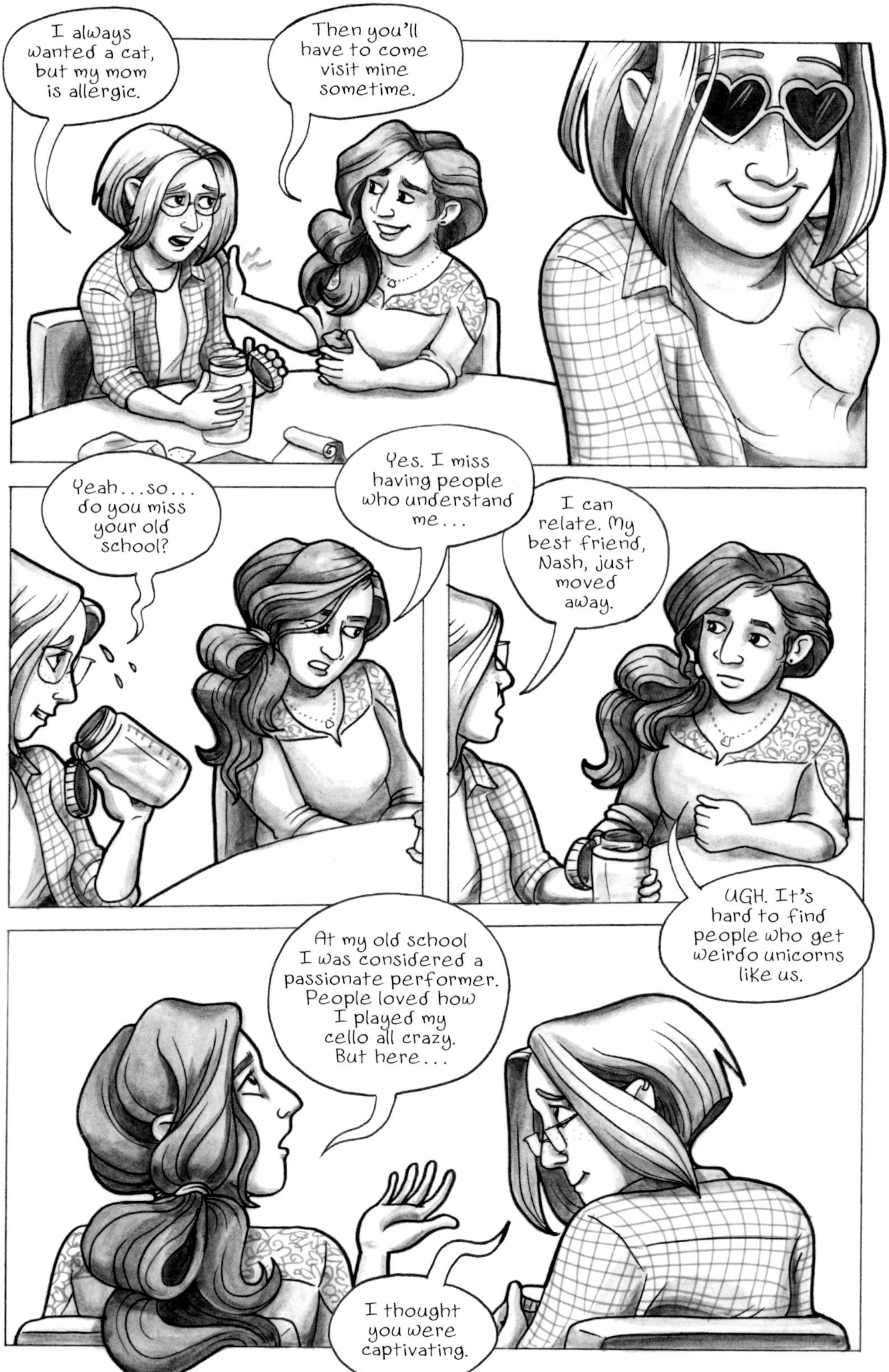
I always wanted a cat, but my mom is allergic.
Then you'll have to come visit mine sometime.
Yeah... so... do you miss your old school?
Yes. I miss having people who understand me...
I can relate. My best friend, Nash, just moved away.
UGH. It's hard to find people who get weirdo unicorns like us.
At my old school I was considered a passionate performer. People loved how I played my cello all crazy. But here...
I thought you were captivating.

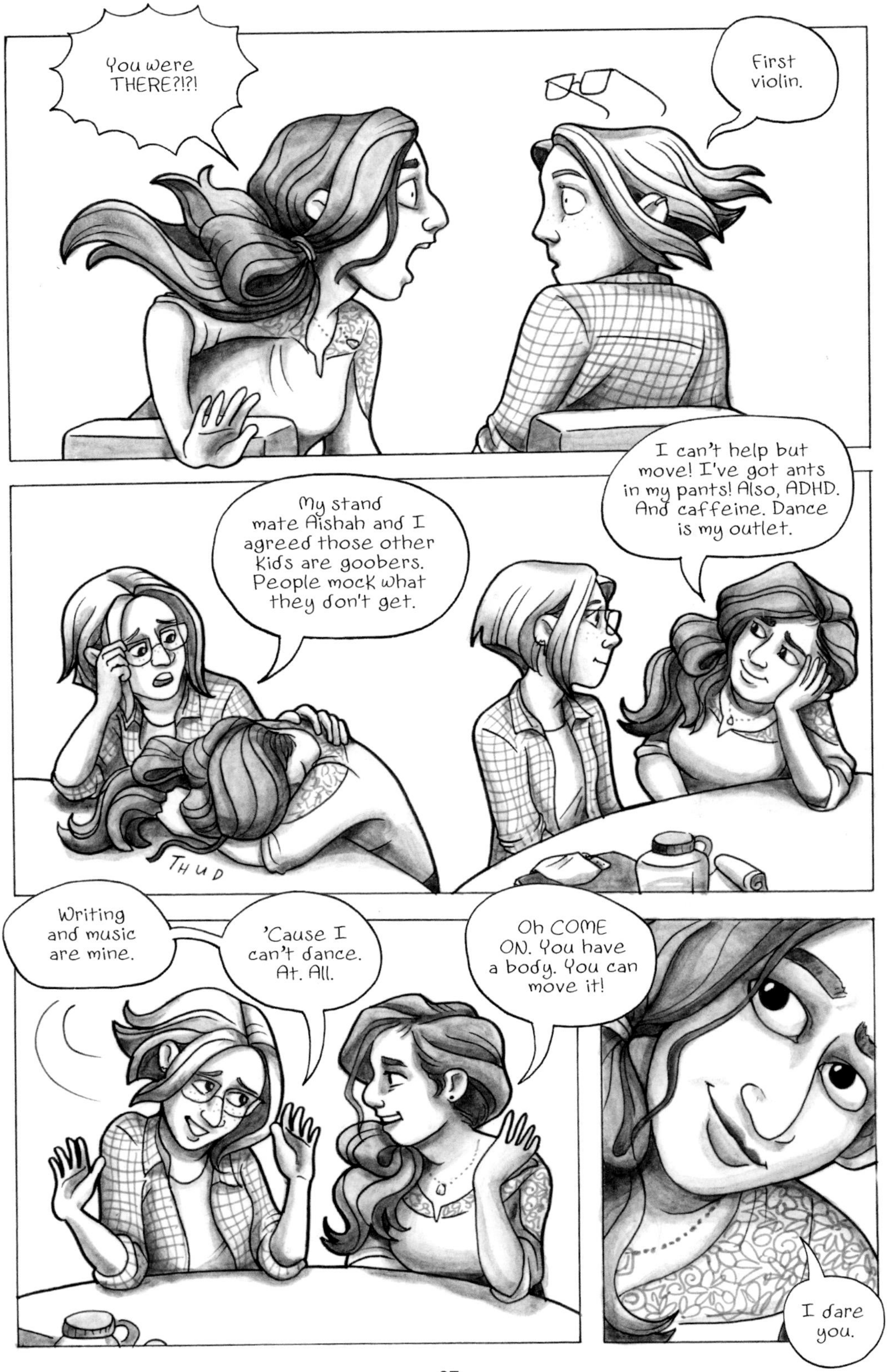
You were THERE?!?!
First violin.
My stand mate Aishah and I agreed those other kids are goobers. People mock what they don't get.
THUD
I can't help but move! I've got ants in my pants! Also, ADHD. And caffeine. Dance is my outlet.
Writing and music are mine.
'Cause I can't dance. At. All.
Oh COME ON. You have a body. You can move it!
I dare you.

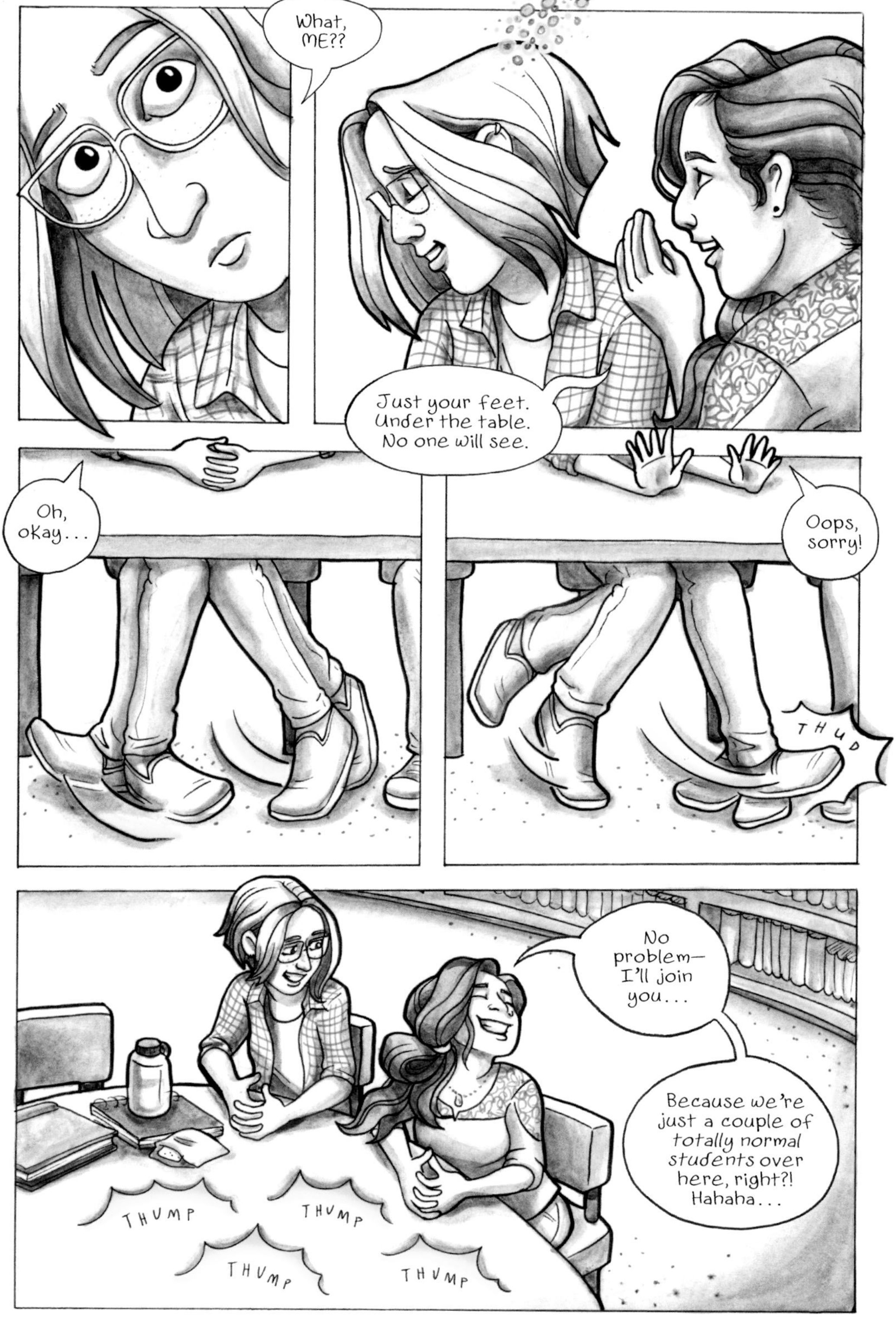
What, ME??
Just your feet. Under the table. No one will see.
Oh, okay...
Oops, sorry!
THUD
No problem— I'll join you...
Because we're just a couple of totally normal students over here, right?! Hahaha...
THUMP
THUMP
THUMP
THUMP

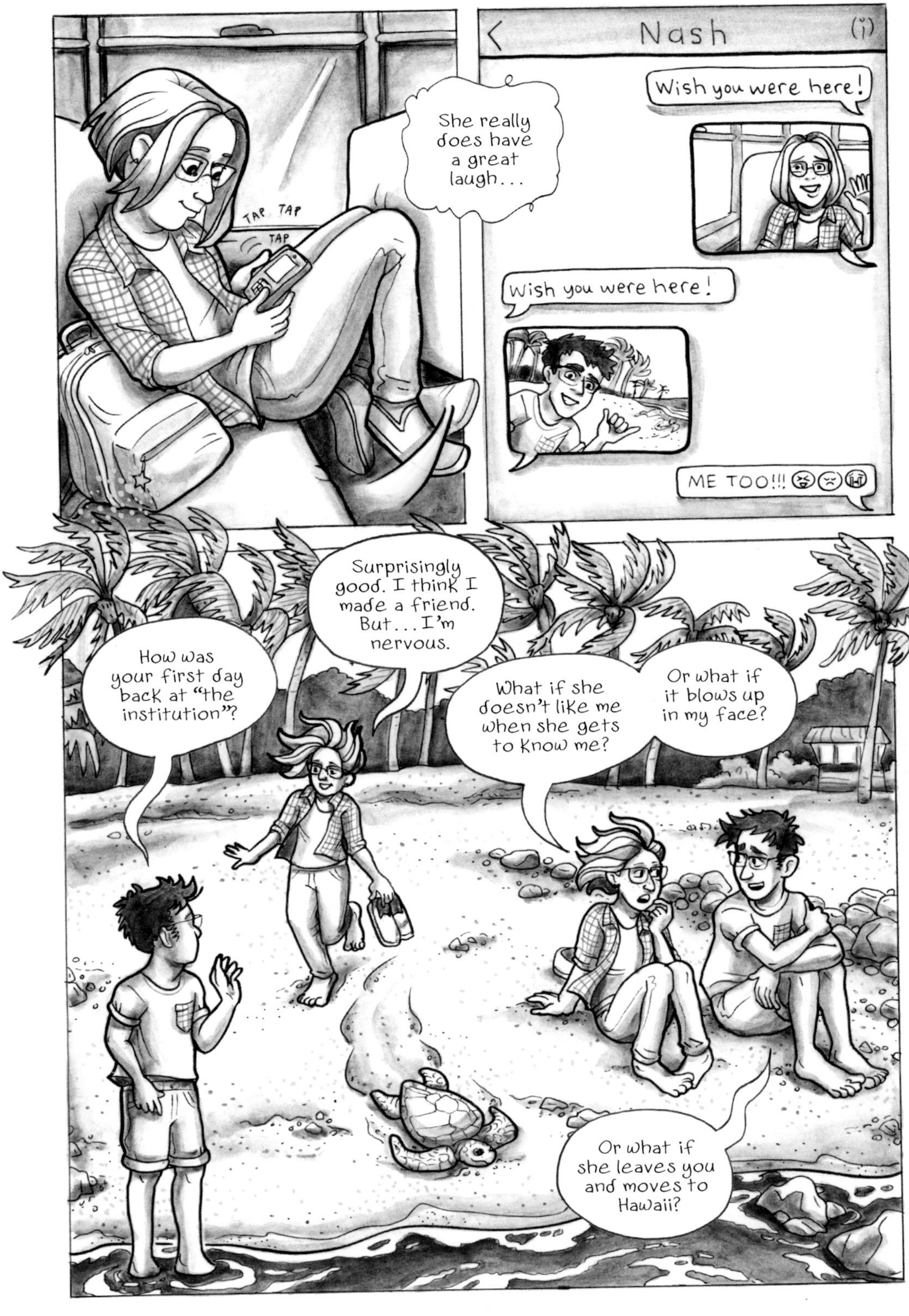
She really does have a great laugh...
TAP TAP
TAP
Nash
Wish you were here!
Wish you were here!
ME TOO!!!
How was your first day back at "the institution"?
Surprisingly good. I think I made a friend. But... I'm nervous.
What if she doesn't like me when she gets to know me?
Or what if it blows up in my face?
Or what if she leaves you and moves to Hawaii?

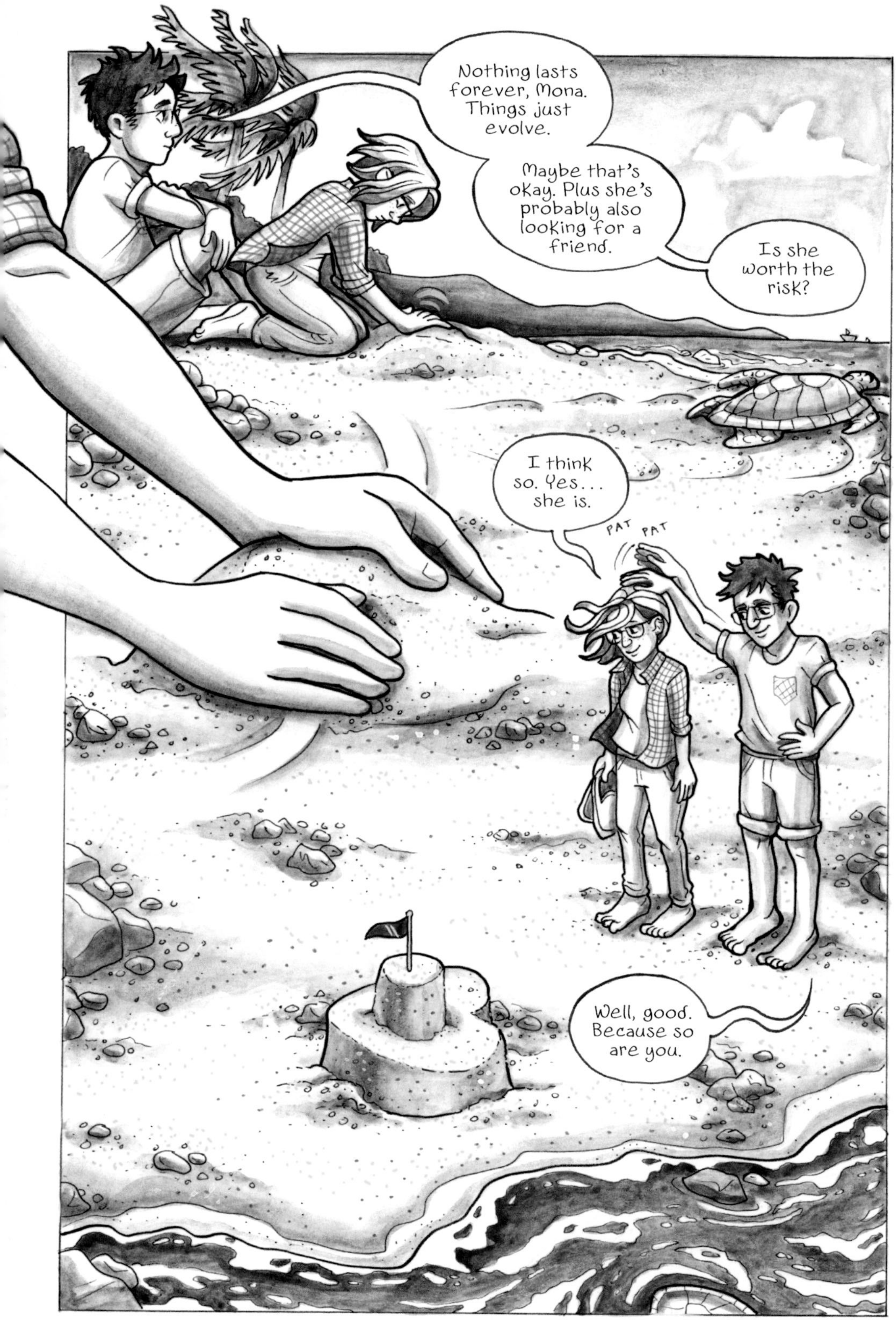
Nothing lasts forever, Mona. Things just evolve.
Maybe that's okay. Plus she's probably also looking for a friend.
Is she worth the risk?
I think so. Yes... she is.
PAT PAT
Well, good. Because so are you.

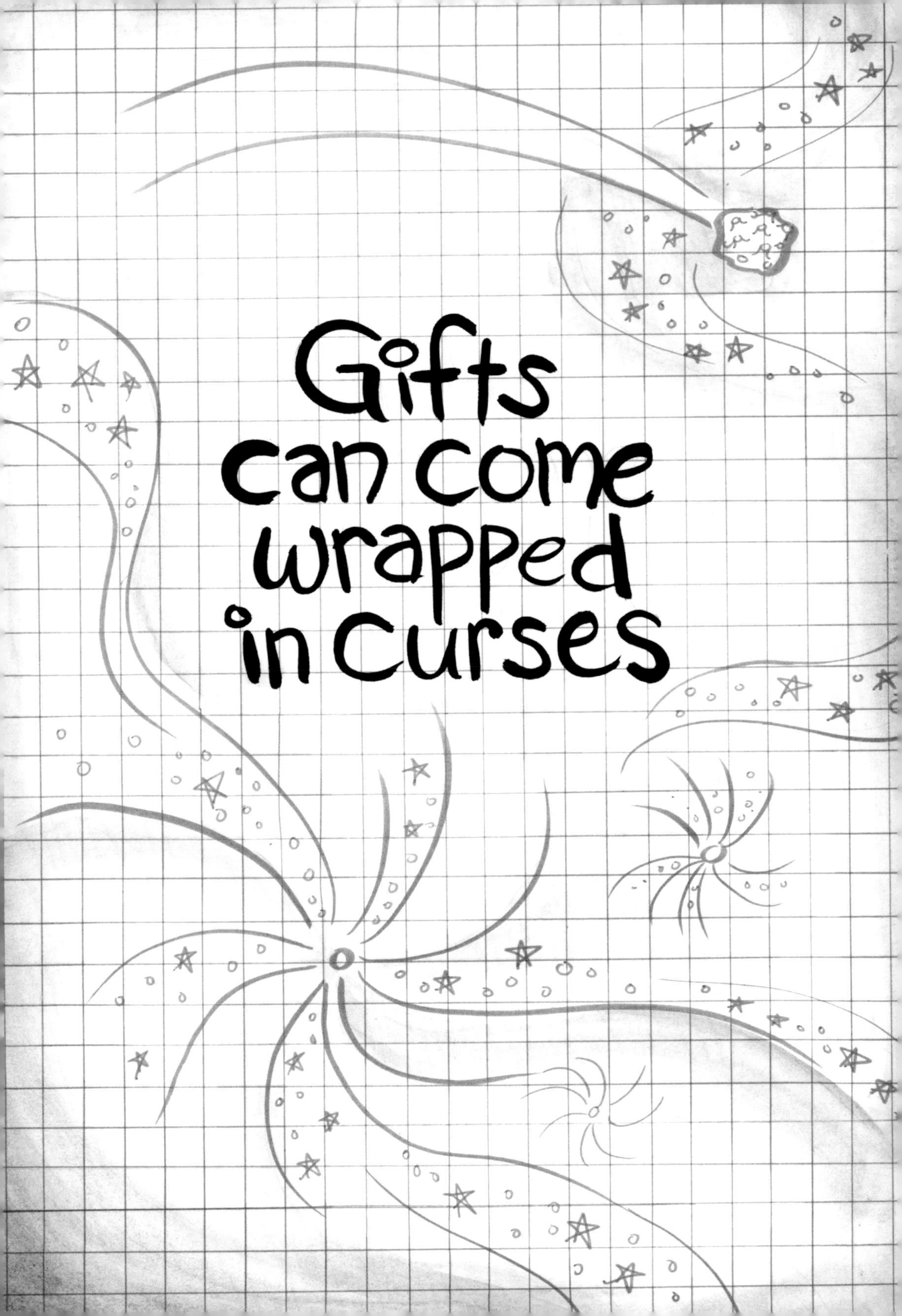
Gifts
can come
wrapped
in curses

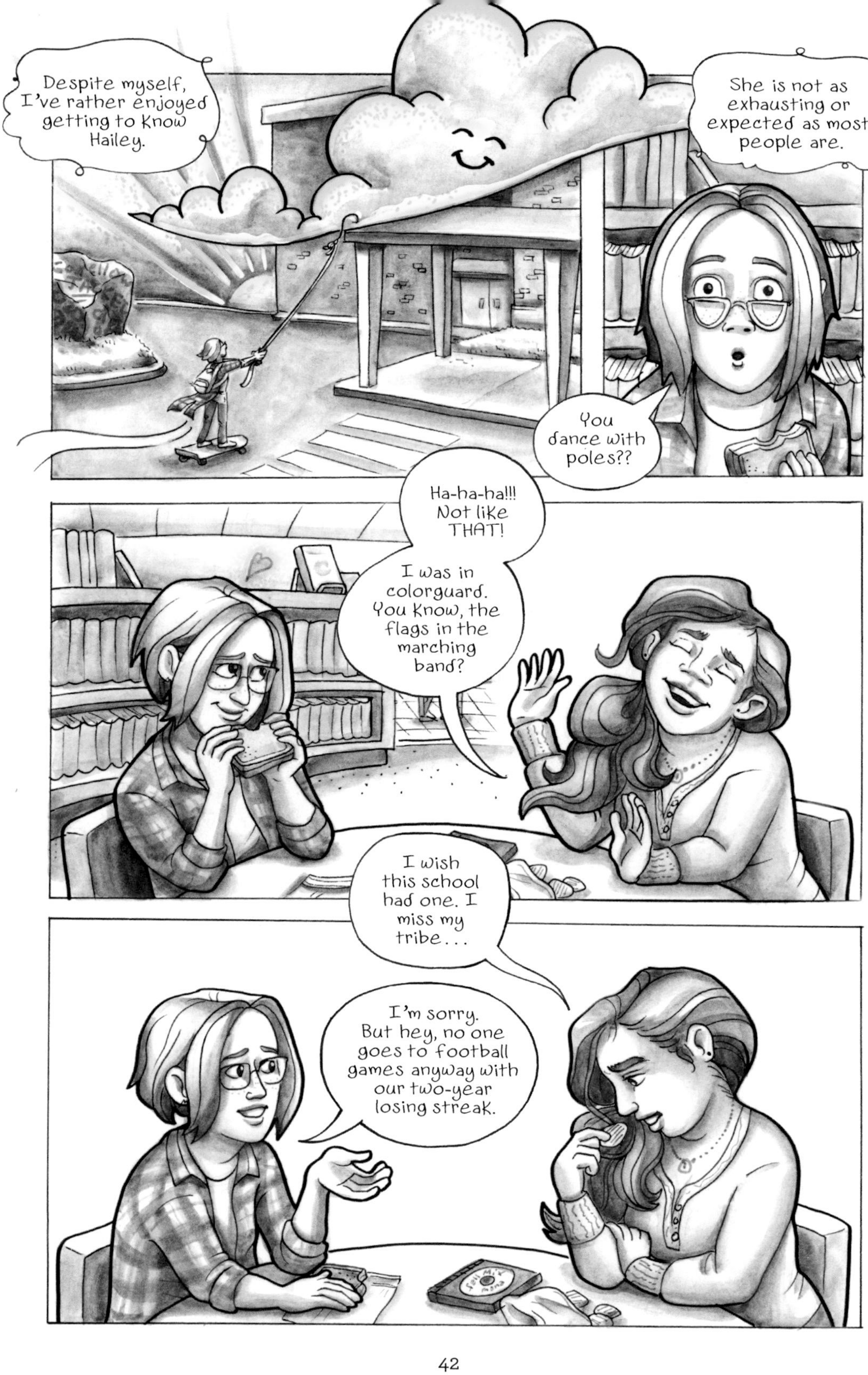
Despite myself, I've rather enjoyed getting to know Hailey.
She is not as exhausting or expected as most people are.
You dance with poles??
Ha-ha-ha!!! Not like THAT!
I was in colorguard. You know, the flags in the marching band?
I wish this school had one. I miss my tribe...
I'm sorry. But hey, no one goes to football games anyway with our two-year losing streak.

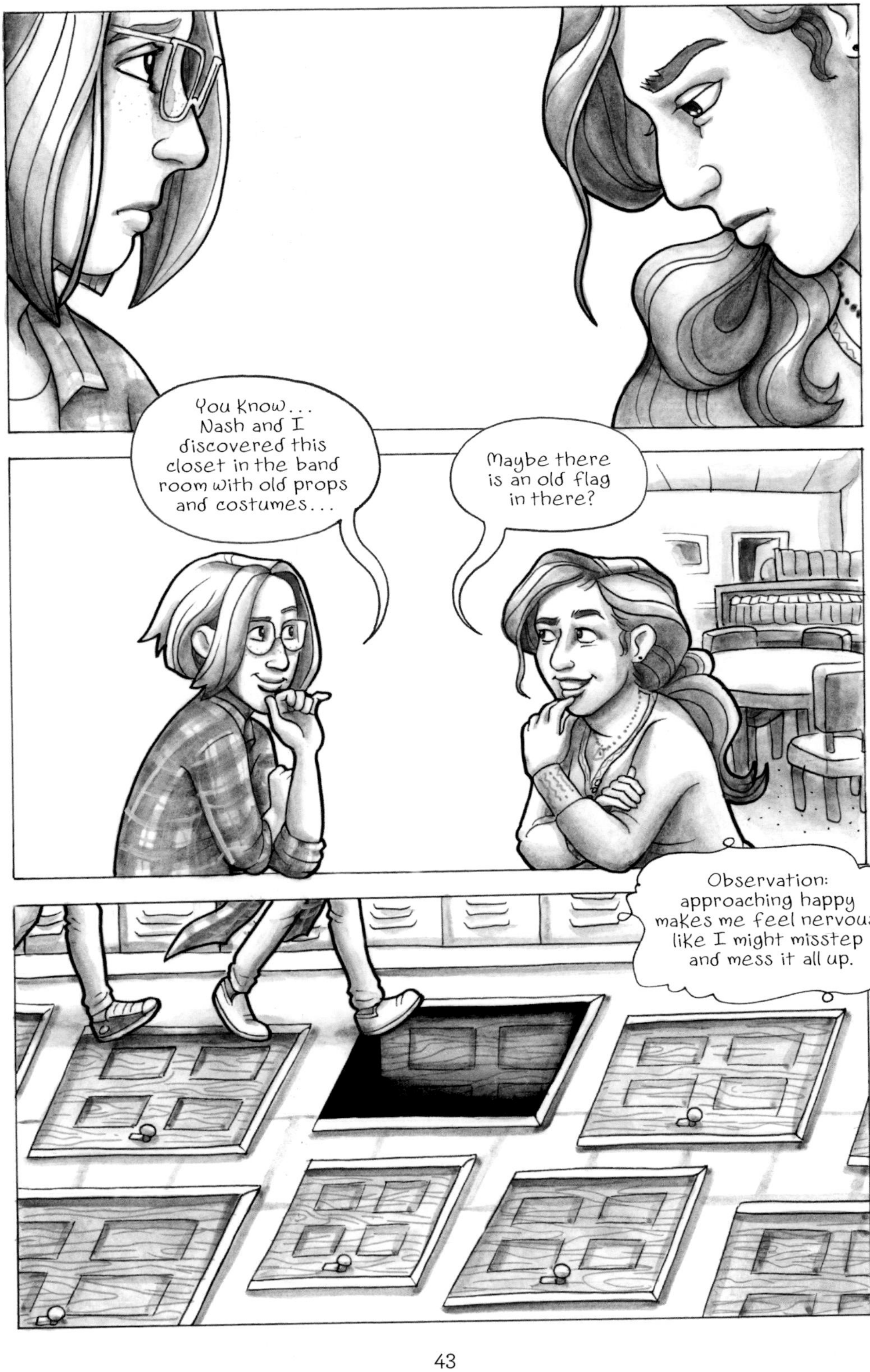
You Know... Nash and I discovered this closet in the band room with old props and costumes...
Maybe there is an old flag in there?
Observation: approaching happy makes me feel nervous, like I might misstep and mess it all up.

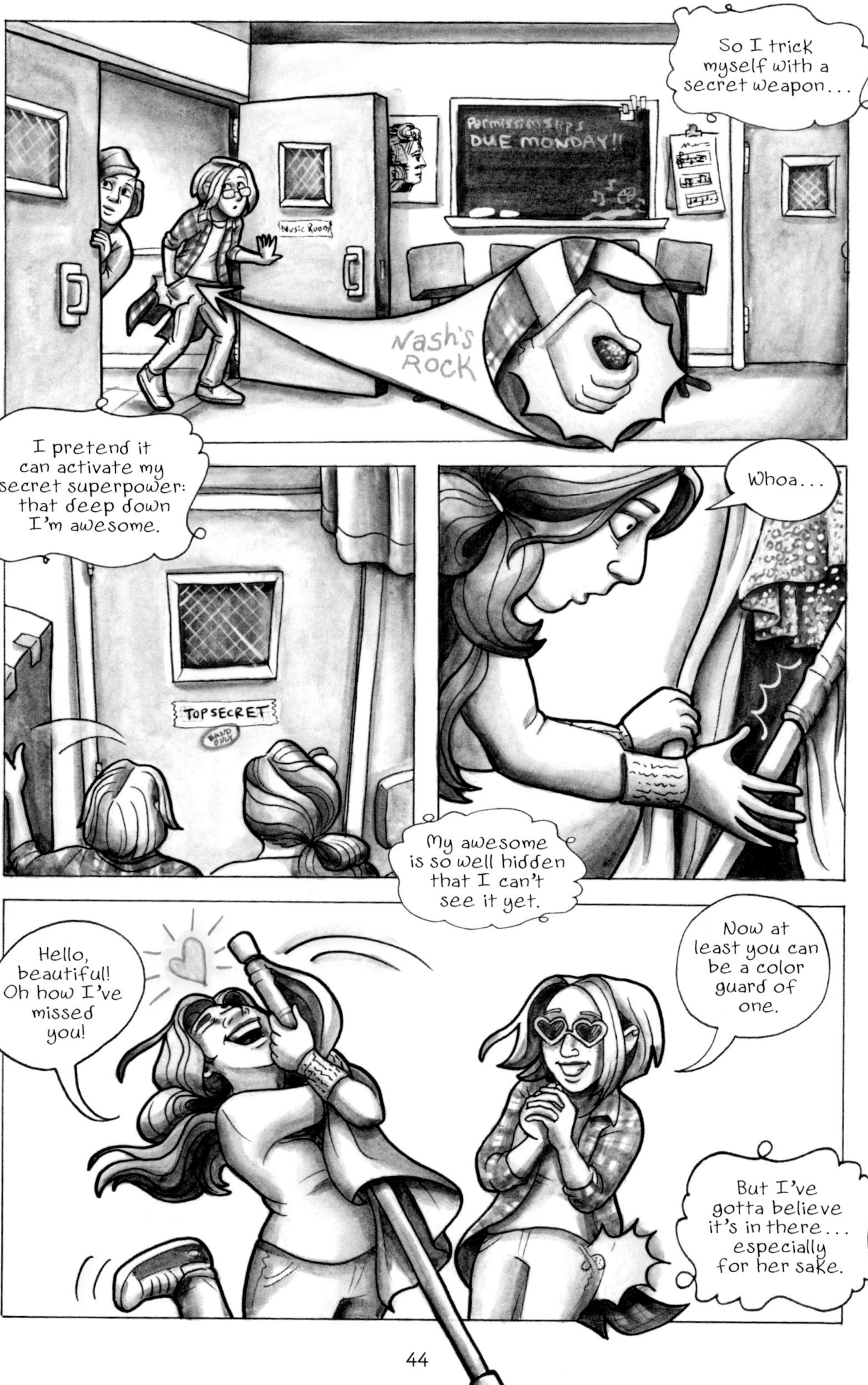
So I trick myself with a secret weapon...
Permission slips DUE MONDAY!!
Music Room
Nash's ROCK
I pretend it can activate my secret superpower: that deep down I'm awesome.
TOP SECRET
Whoa...
My awesome is so well hidden that I can't see it yet.
Hello, beautiful! Oh how I've missed you!
Now at least you can be a color guard of one.
But I've gotta believe it's in there... especially for her sake.

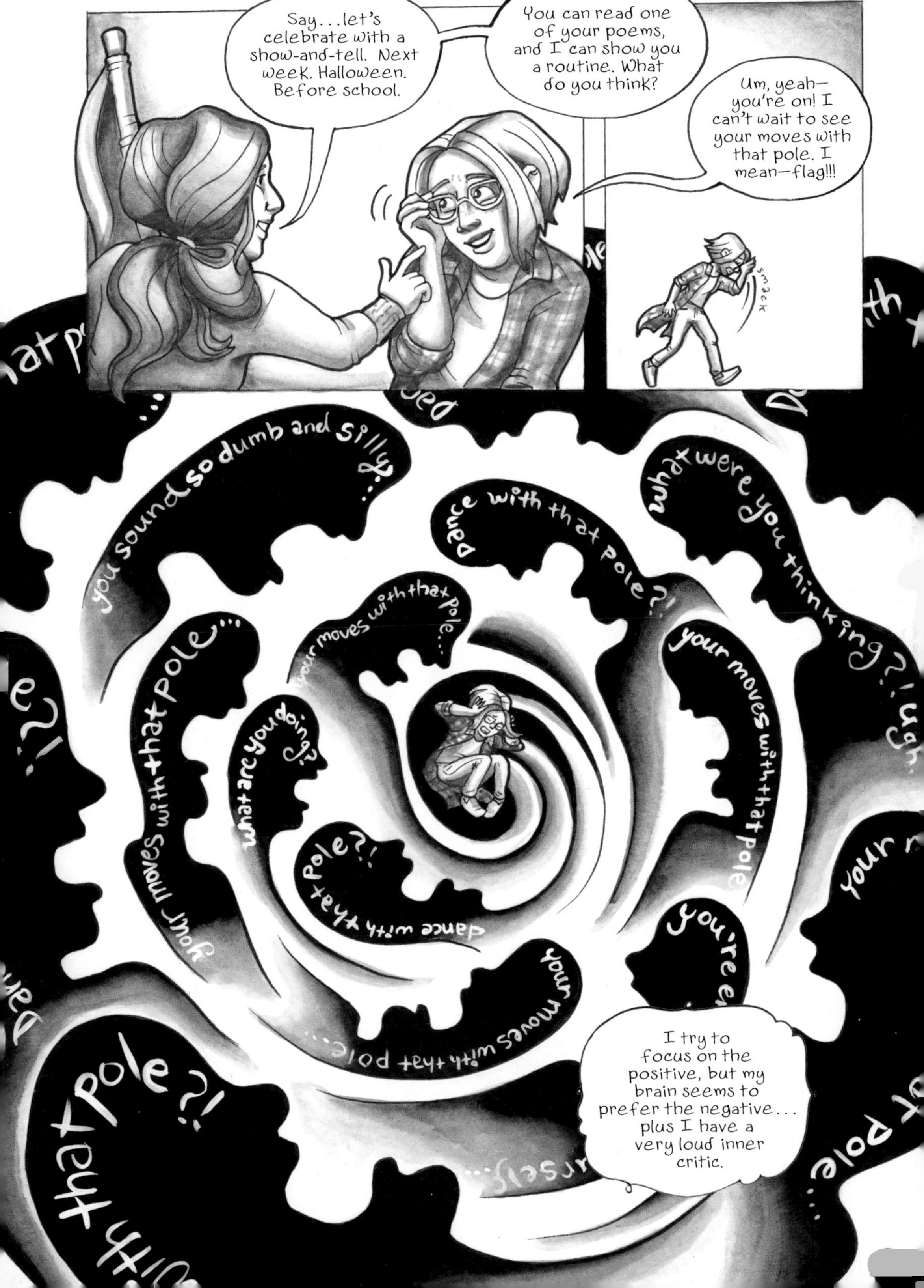
Say...let's celebrate with a show-and-tell. Next week. Halloween. Before school.
You can read one of your poems, and I can show you a routine. What do you think?
Um, yeah—you're on! I can't wait to see your moves with that pole. I mean—flag!!!
smack
you sound so dumb and silly...
Dance with that pole?!
what were you thinking?! ugh.
your moves with that pole...
your moves with that pole...
what are you doing?
your moves with that pole
pole?!
dance with that
your moves with that pole...
you're e
with that pole?!
I try to focus on the positive, but my brain seems to prefer the negative... plus I have a very loud inner critic.

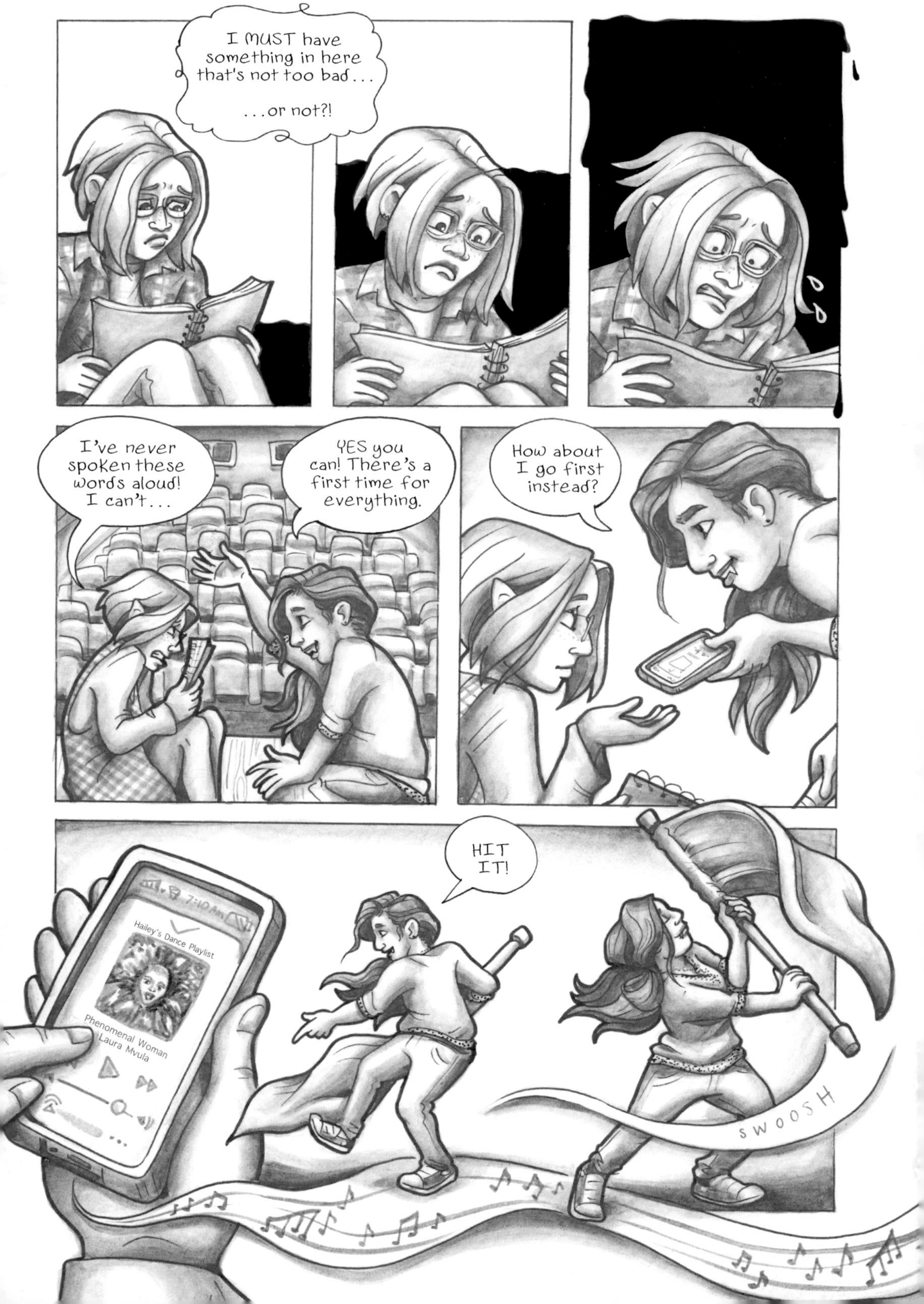

I MUST have something in here that's not too bad . . .
. . . or not?!
I've never spoken these words aloud! I can't . . .
YES you can! There's a first time for everything.
How about I go first instead?
HIT IT!
Hailey's Dance Playlist
Phenomenal Woman
Laura Mvula
SWOOSH

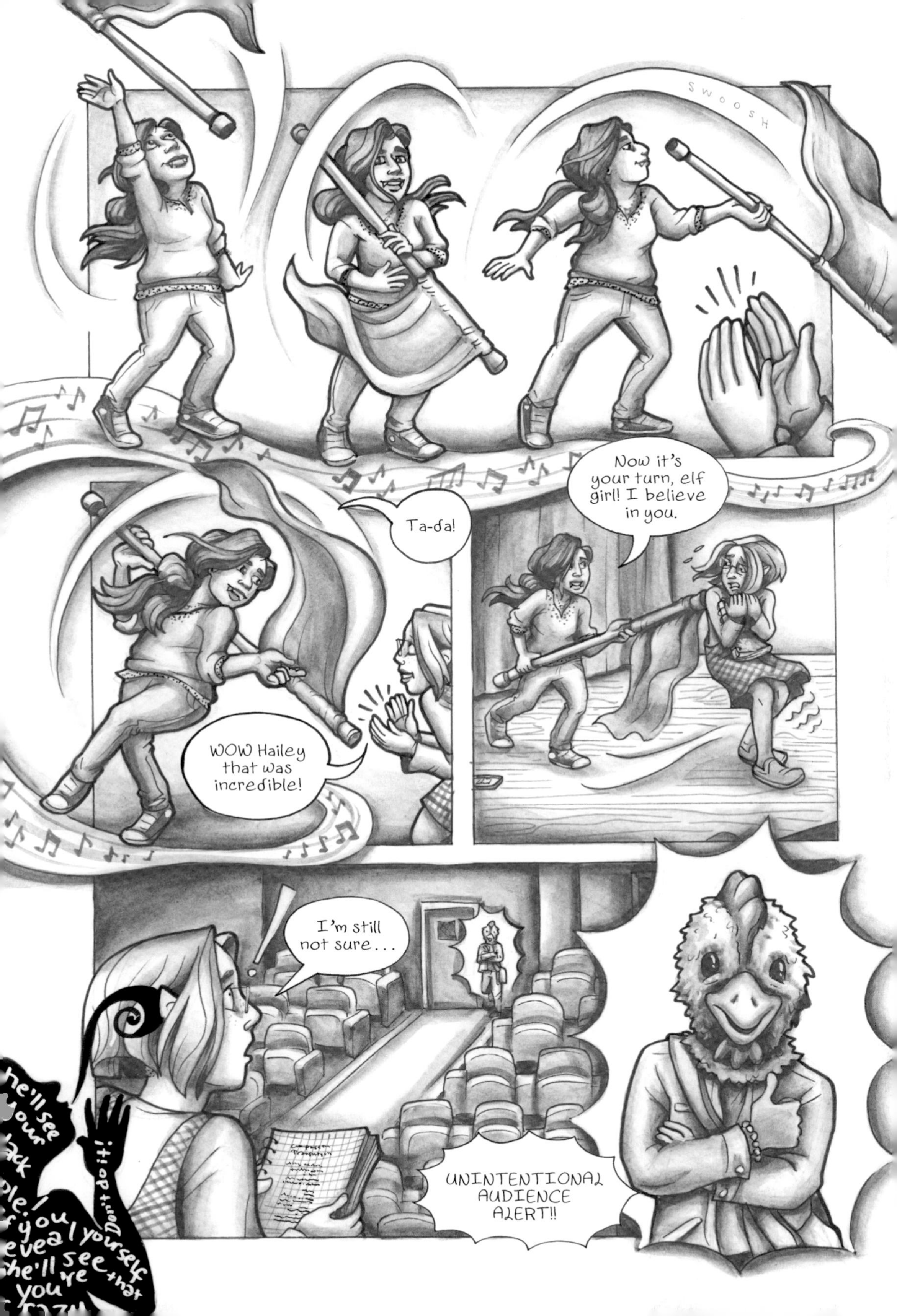
SWOOSH
Ta-da!
WOW Hailey that was incredible!
Now it's your turn, elf girl! I believe in you.
I'm still not sure . . .
UNINTENTIONAL AUDIENCE ALERT!!
Don't do it!

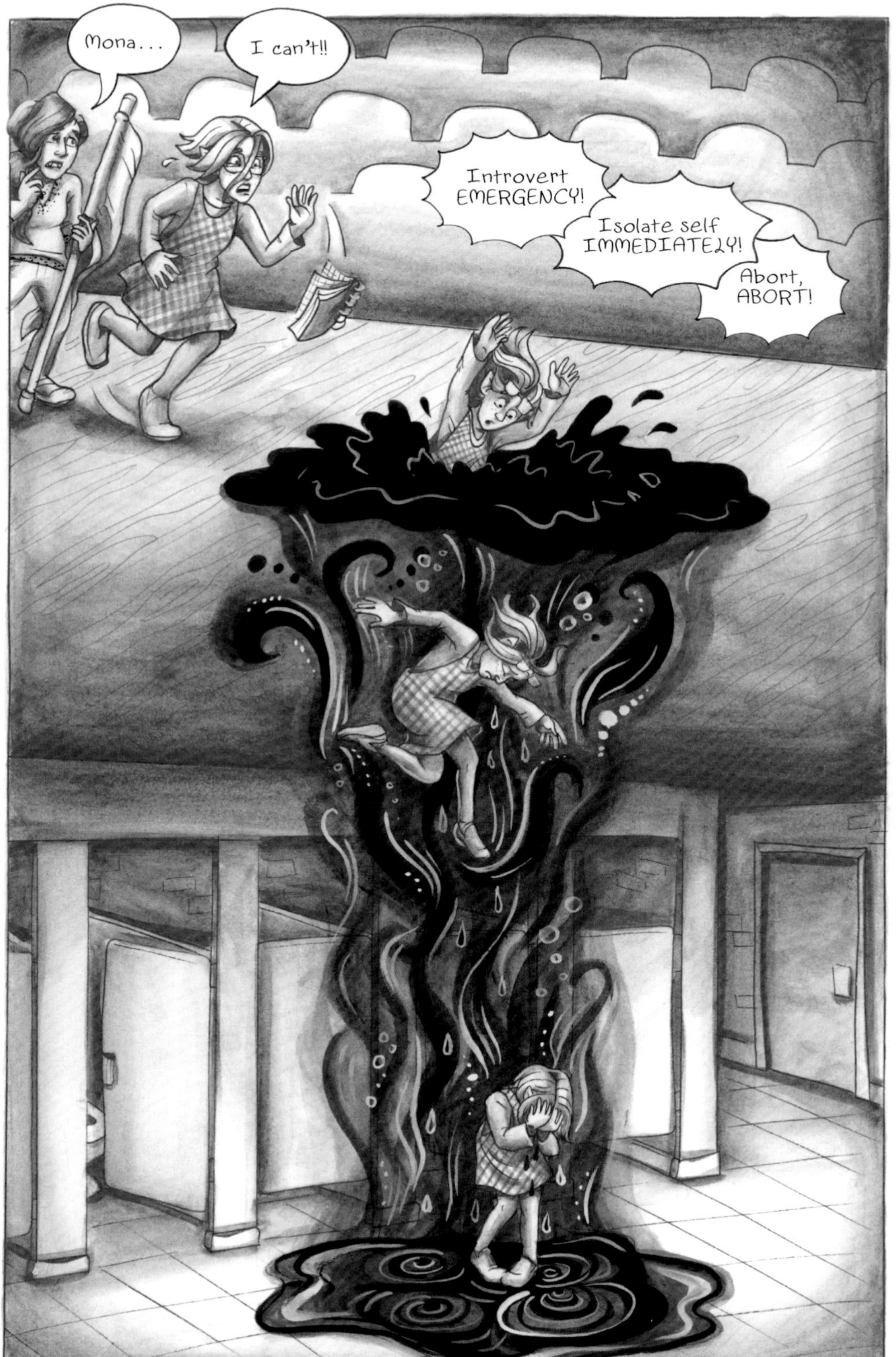
Mona...
I can't!!
Introvert EMERGENCY!
Isolate self IMMEDIATELY!
Abort, ABORT!

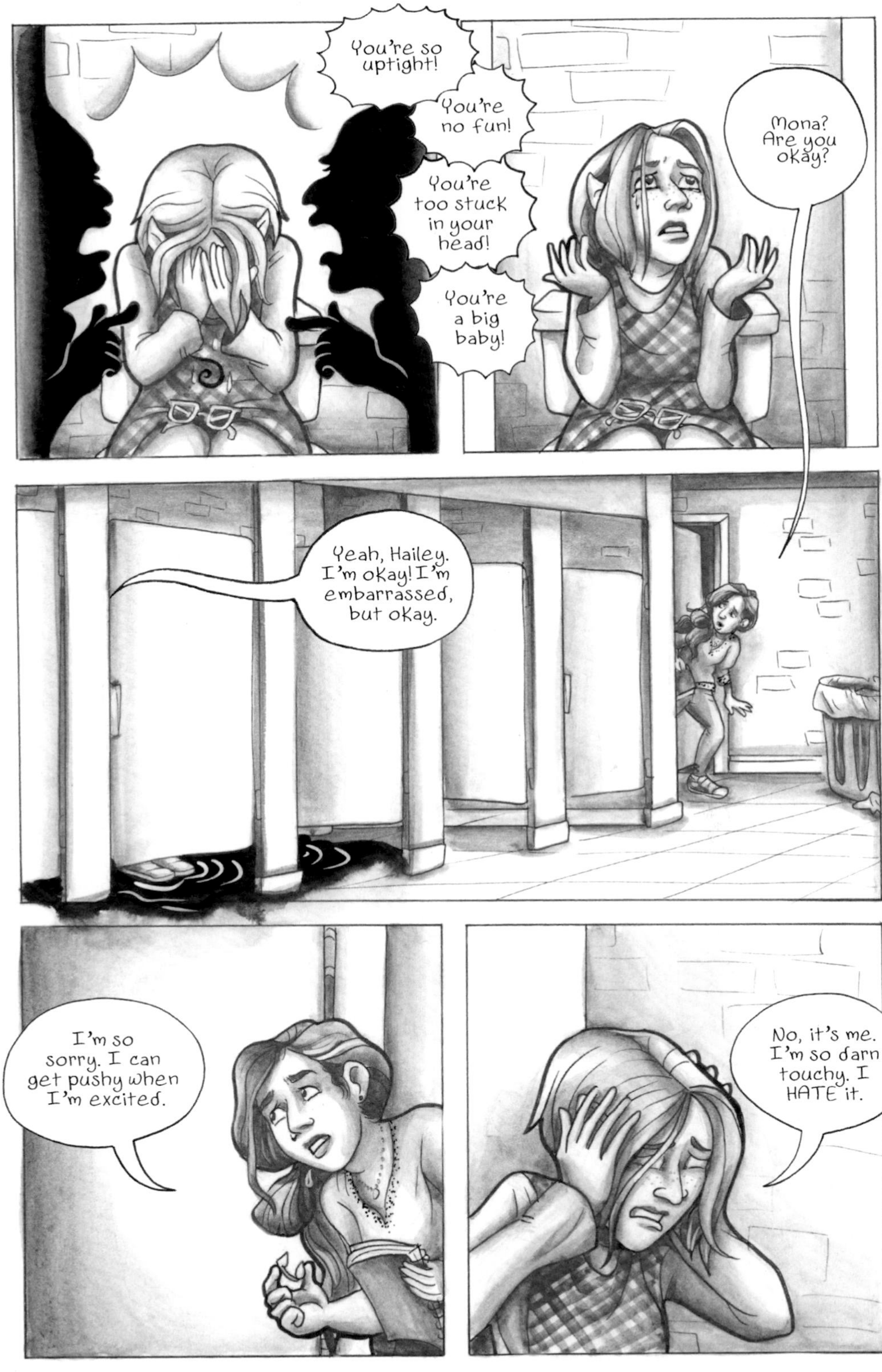
You're so uptight!
You're no fun!
You're too stuck in your head!
You're a big baby!
Mona? Are you okay?
Yeah, Hailey. I'm okay! I'm embarrassed, but okay.
I'm so sorry. I can get pushy when I'm excited.
No, it's me. I'm so darn touchy. I HATE it.

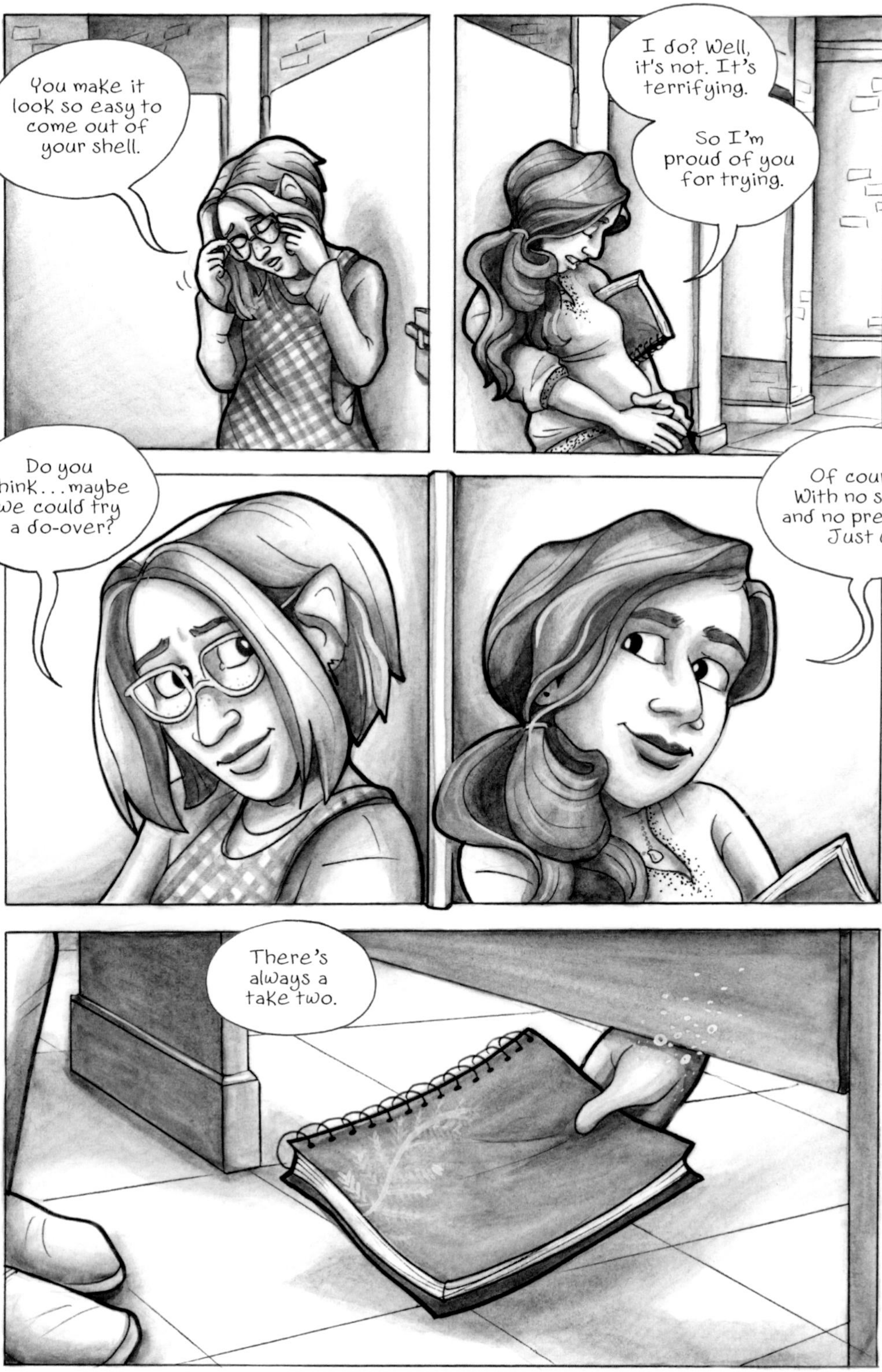
You make it look so easy to come out of your shell.
I do? Well, it's not. It's terrifying.
So I'm proud of you for trying.
Do you think... maybe we could try a do-over?
Of course. With no stage, and no pressure. Just us.
There's always a take two.

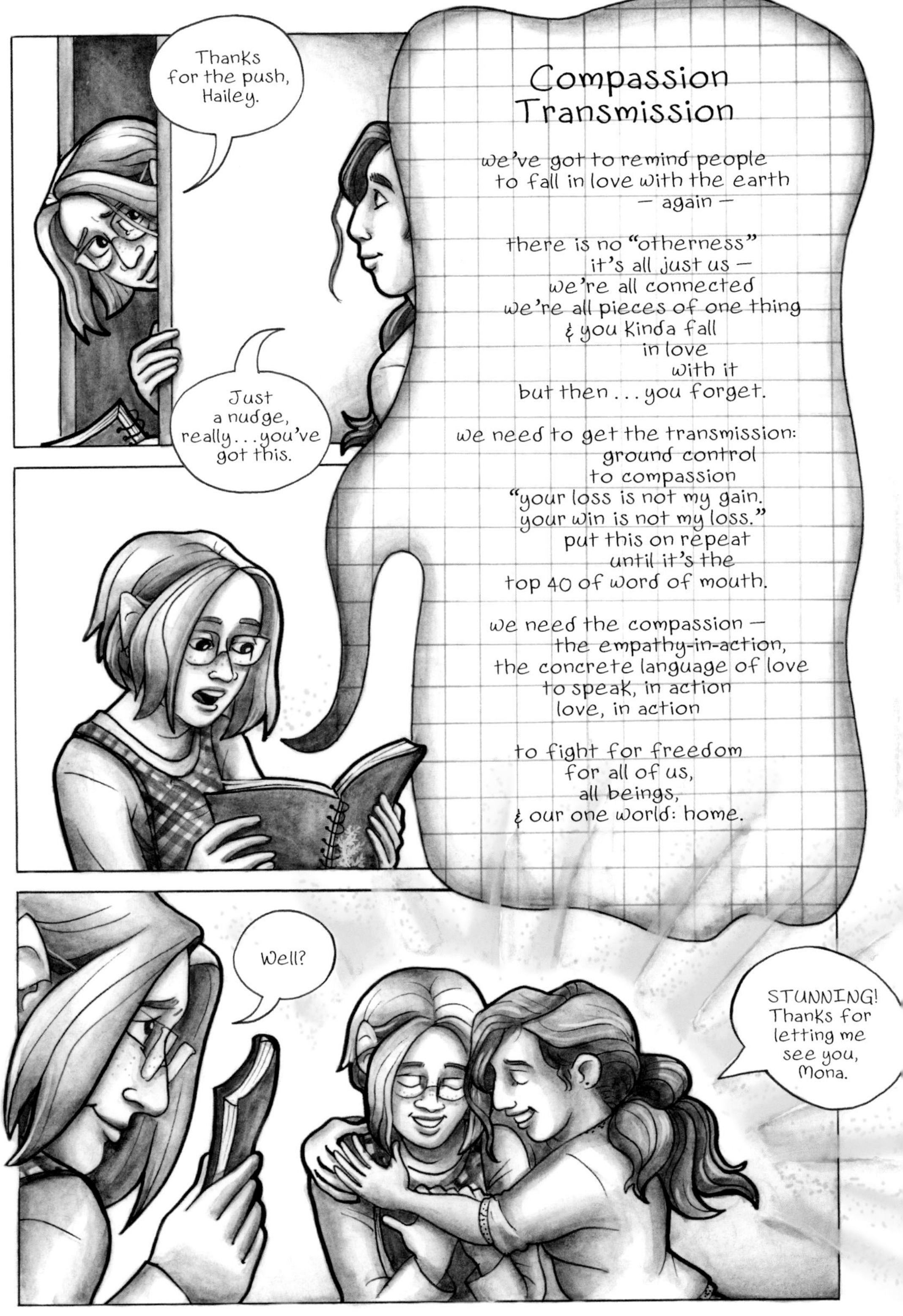
Thanks for the push, Hailey.
Just a nudge, really . . . you've got this.
Compassion Transmission
we've got to remind people
to fall in love with the earth
— again —
there is no "otherness"
it's all just us —
we're all connected
we're all pieces of one thing
& you kinda fall
in love
with it
but then . . . you forget.
we need to get the transmission:
ground control
to compassion
"your loss is not my gain.
your win is not my loss."
put this on repeat
until it's the
top 40 of word of mouth.
we need the compassion —
the empathy-in-action,
the concrete language of love
to speak, in action
love, in action
to fight for freedom
for all of us,
all beings,
& our one world: home.
Well?
STUNNING! Thanks for letting me see you, Mona.

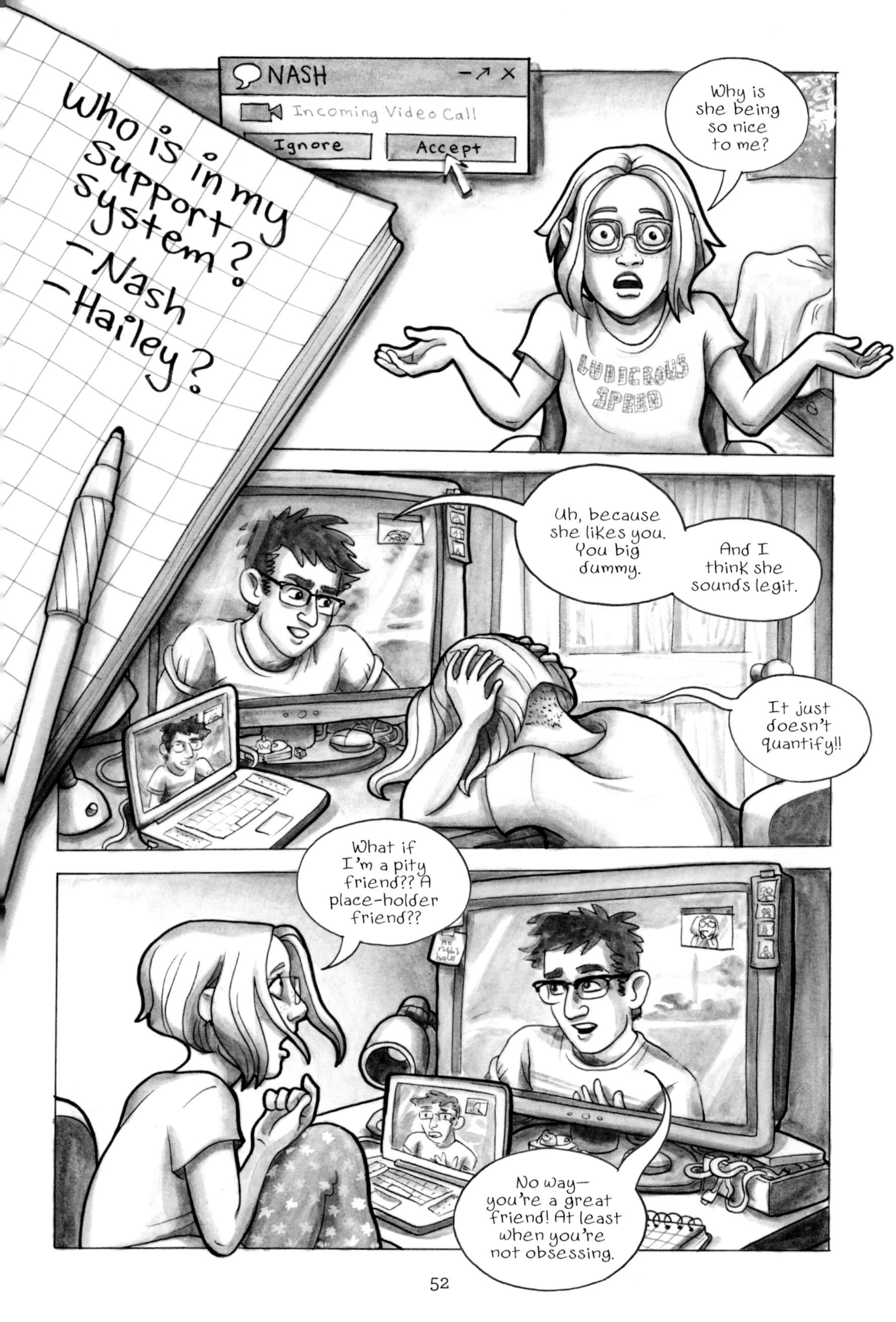
Who is in my Support system? -Nash -Hailey?
NASH
Incoming Video Call
Ignore
Accept
Why is she being so nice to me?
LUDICROUS SPEED
Uh, because she likes you. You big dummy.
And I think she sounds legit.
It just doesn't quantify!!
What if I'm a pity friend?? A place-holder friend??
No way— you're a great friend! At least when you're not obsessing.

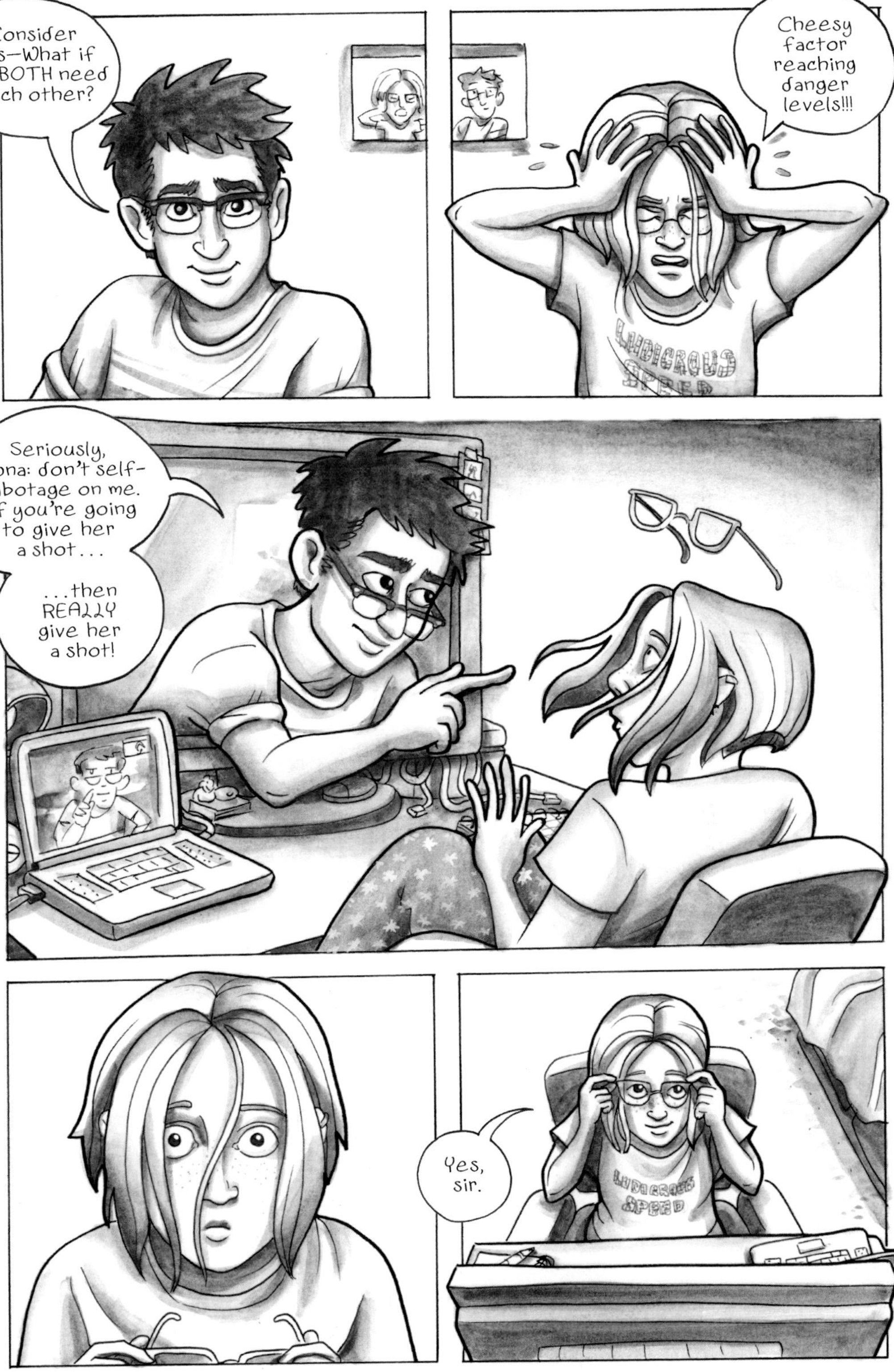
Consider this—What if you BOTH need each other?
Cheesy factor reaching danger levels!!!
LUDICROUS SPEED
Seriously, Mona: don't self-sabotage on me. If you're going to give her a shot...
...then REALLY give her a shot!
Yes, sir.
LUDICROUS SPEED

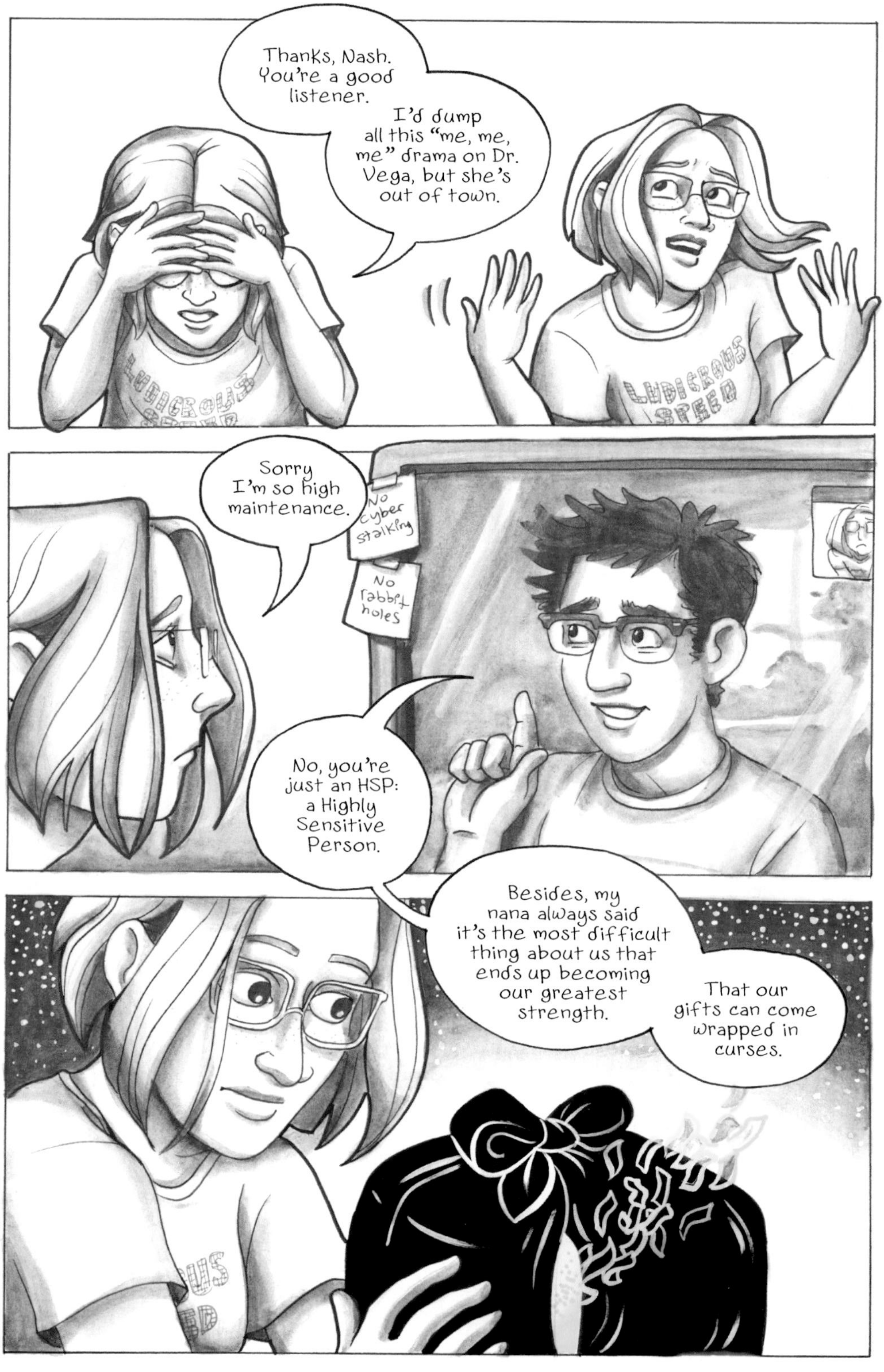
Thanks, Nash. You're a good listener.
I'd dump all this "me, me, me" drama on Dr. Vega, but she's out of town.
LUDICROUS SPEED
LUDICROUS SPEED
Sorry I'm so high maintenance.
No cyber stalking
No rabbit holes
No, you're just an HSP: a Highly Sensitive Person.
Besides, my nana always said it's the most difficult thing about us that ends up becoming our greatest strength.
That our gifts can come wrapped in curses.

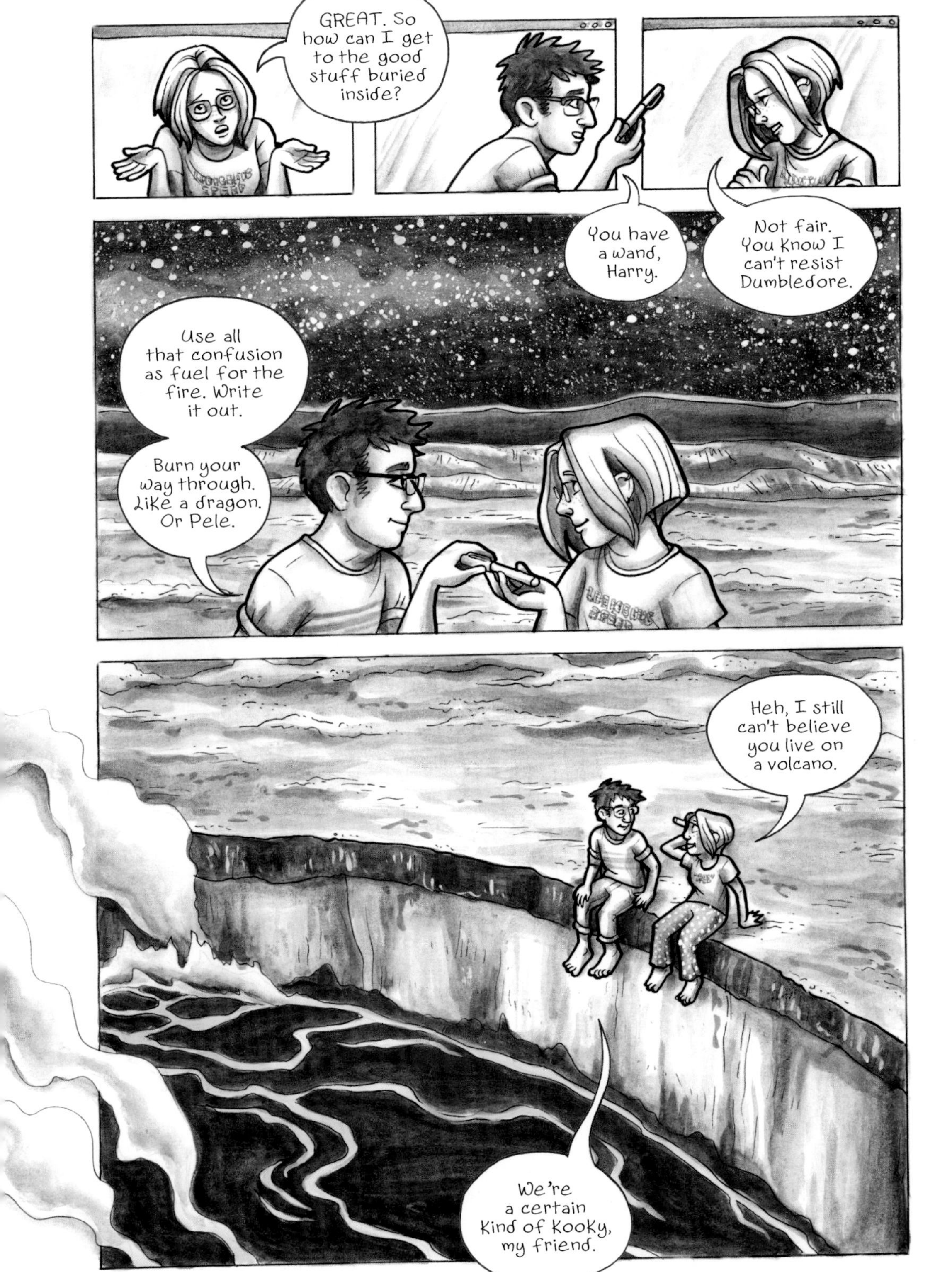
GREAT. So how can I get to the good stuff buried inside?
You have a wand, Harry.
Not fair. You know I can't resist Dumbledore.
Use all that confusion as fuel for the fire. Write it out.
Burn your way through. Like a dragon. Or Pele.
Heh, I still can't believe you live on a volcano.
We're a certain kind of kooky, my friend.

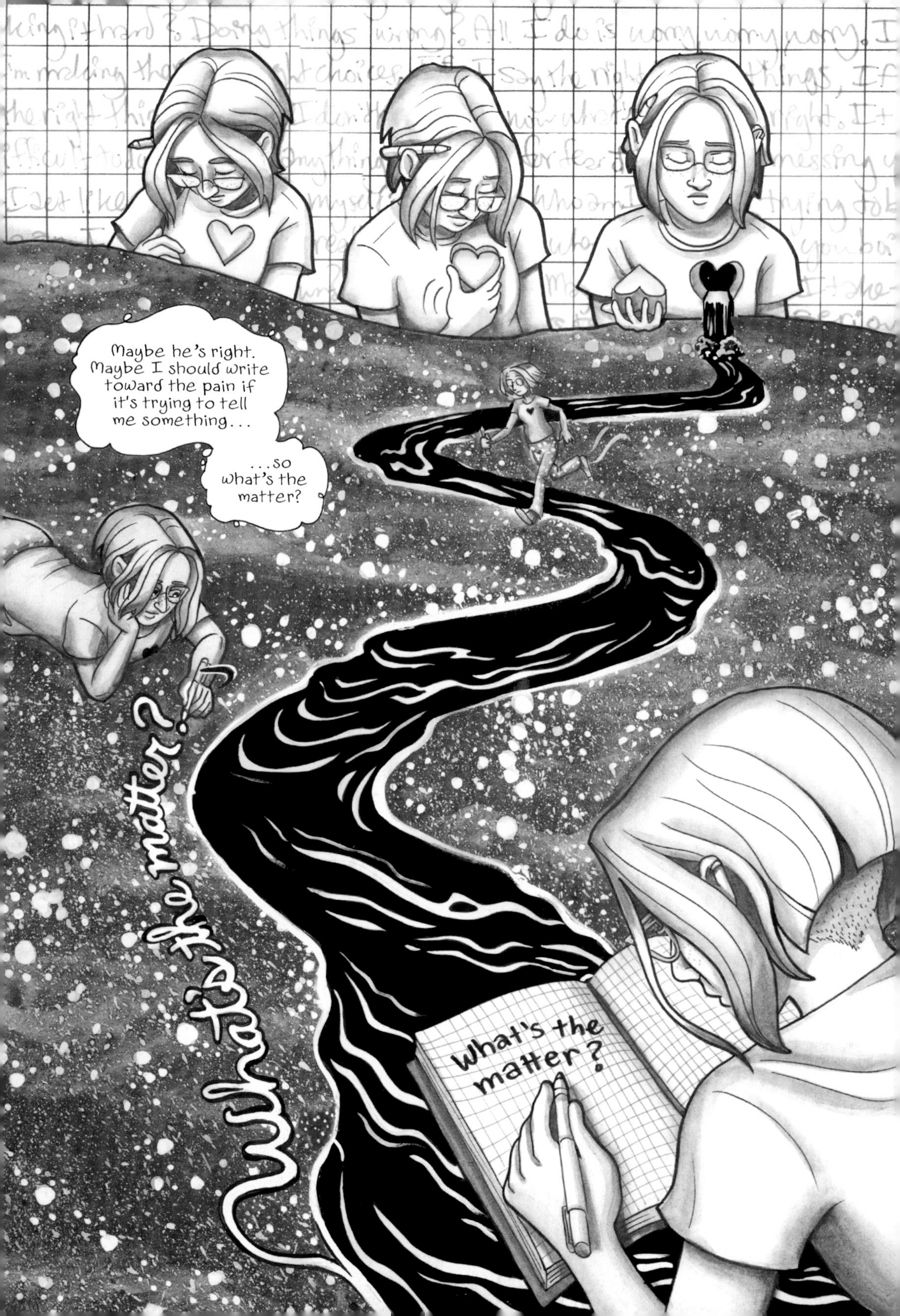
Maybe he's right. Maybe I should write toward the pain if it's trying to tell me something...
...so what's the matter?
What's the matter?
What's the matter?

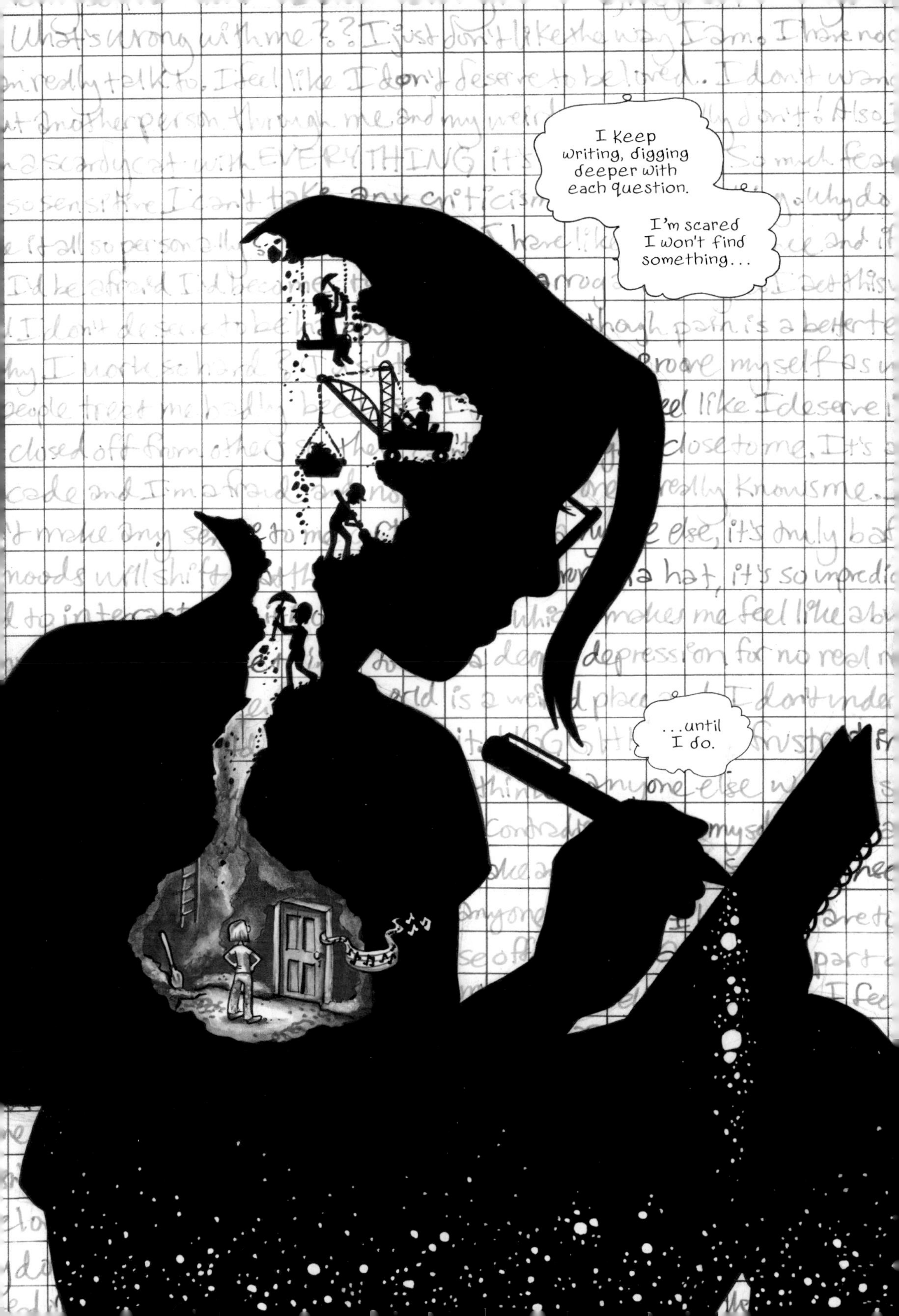
I Keep writing, digging deeper with each question.
I'm scared I won't find something...
...until I do.

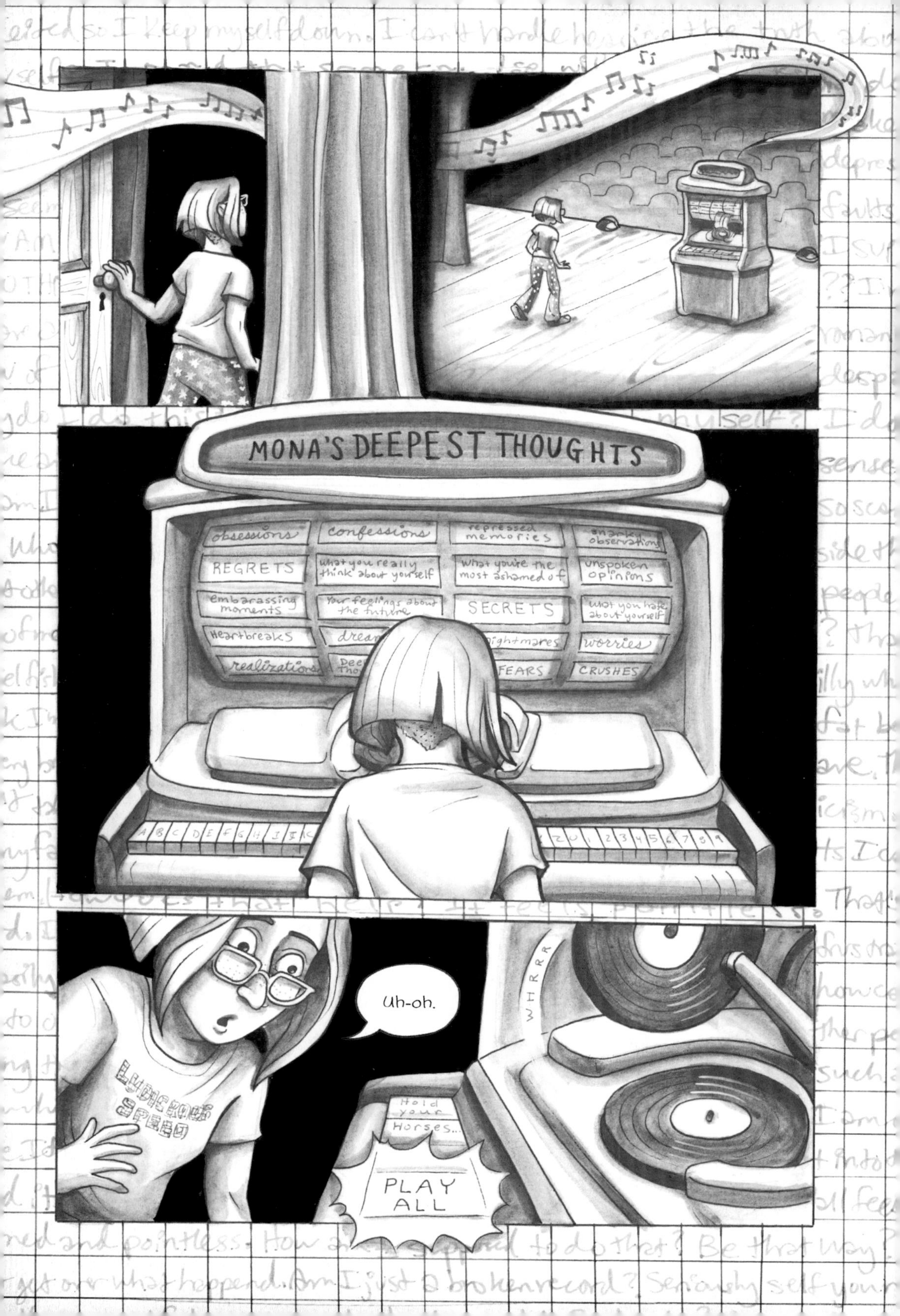
MONA'S DEEPEST THOUGHTS
obsessions
confessions
repressed memories
snarky observations
REGRETS
what you really think about yourself
what you're the most ashamed of
unspoken opinions
embarassing moments
Your feelings about the future
SECRETS
what you hate about yourself
Heartbreaks
worries
realizations
FEARS
CRUSHES
Uh-oh.
WHRRR
Hold your Horses...
PLAY ALL

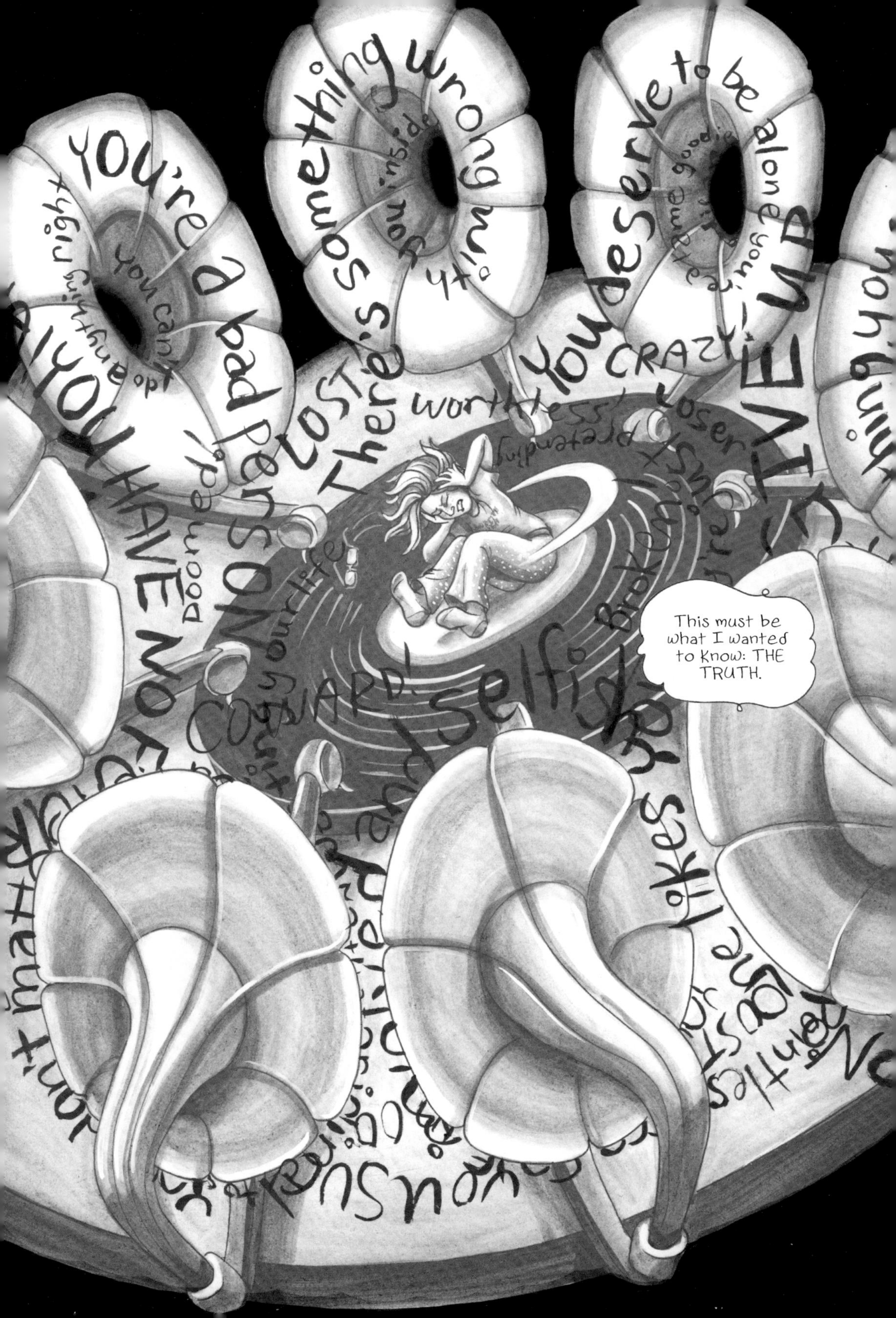

You're a bad person
you can't do anything right
There's something wrong with you inside
You deserve to be alone
CRAZY!
worthless!
loser
pretending
LOST!
DOOMED!
COWARD!
selfish
Broken!
This must be what I wanted to know: THE TRUTH.

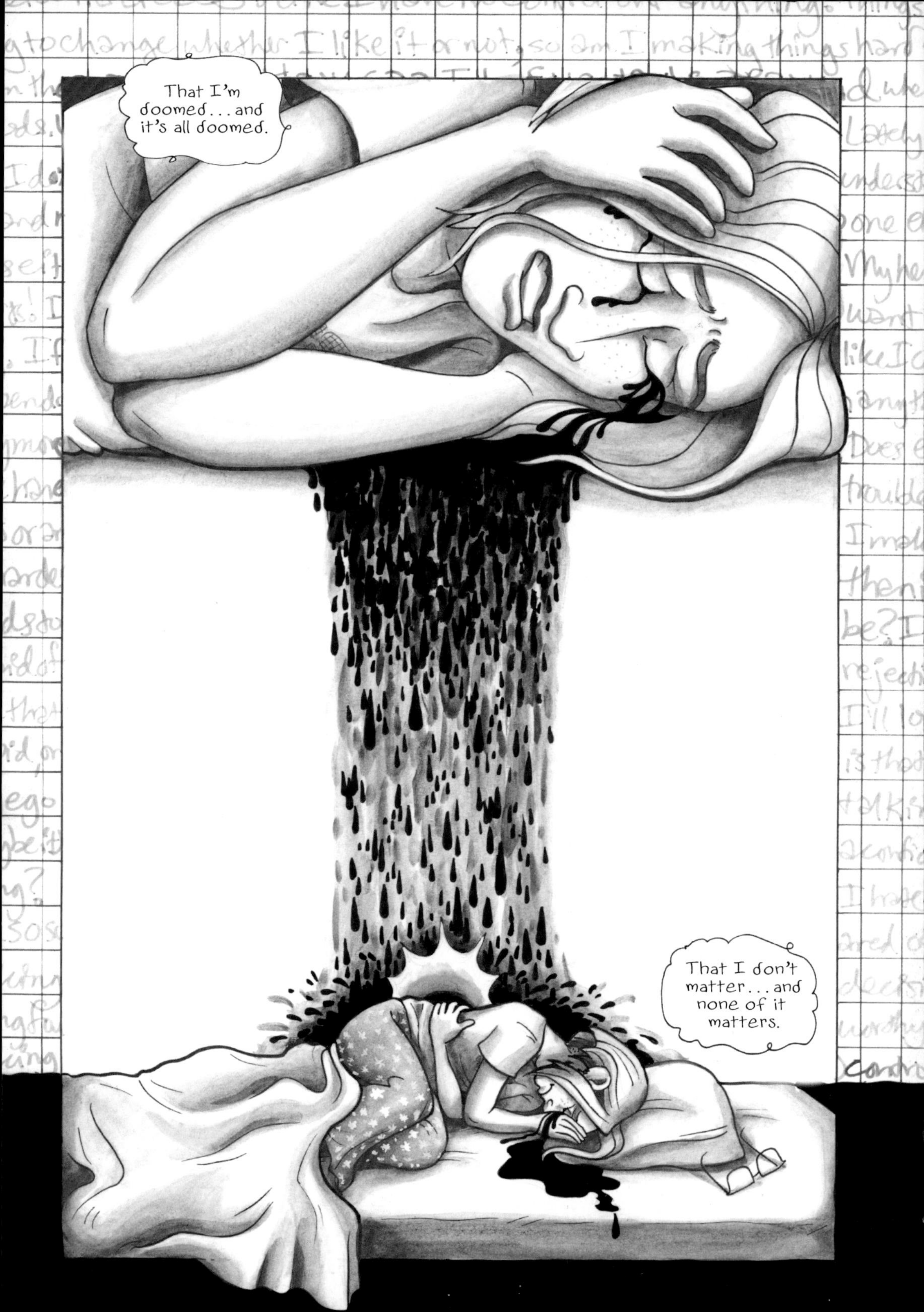
That I'm doomed . . . and it's all doomed.
That I don't matter . . . and none of it matters.

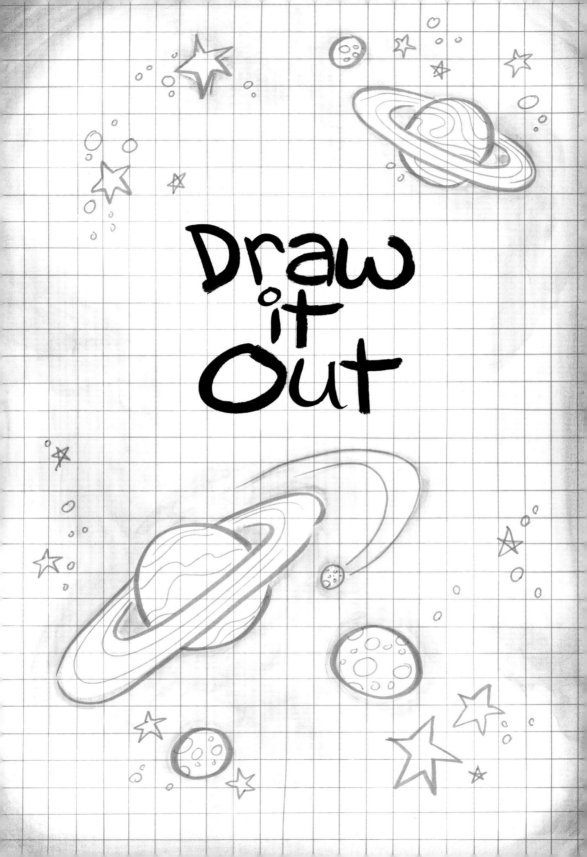

Draw
it
Out

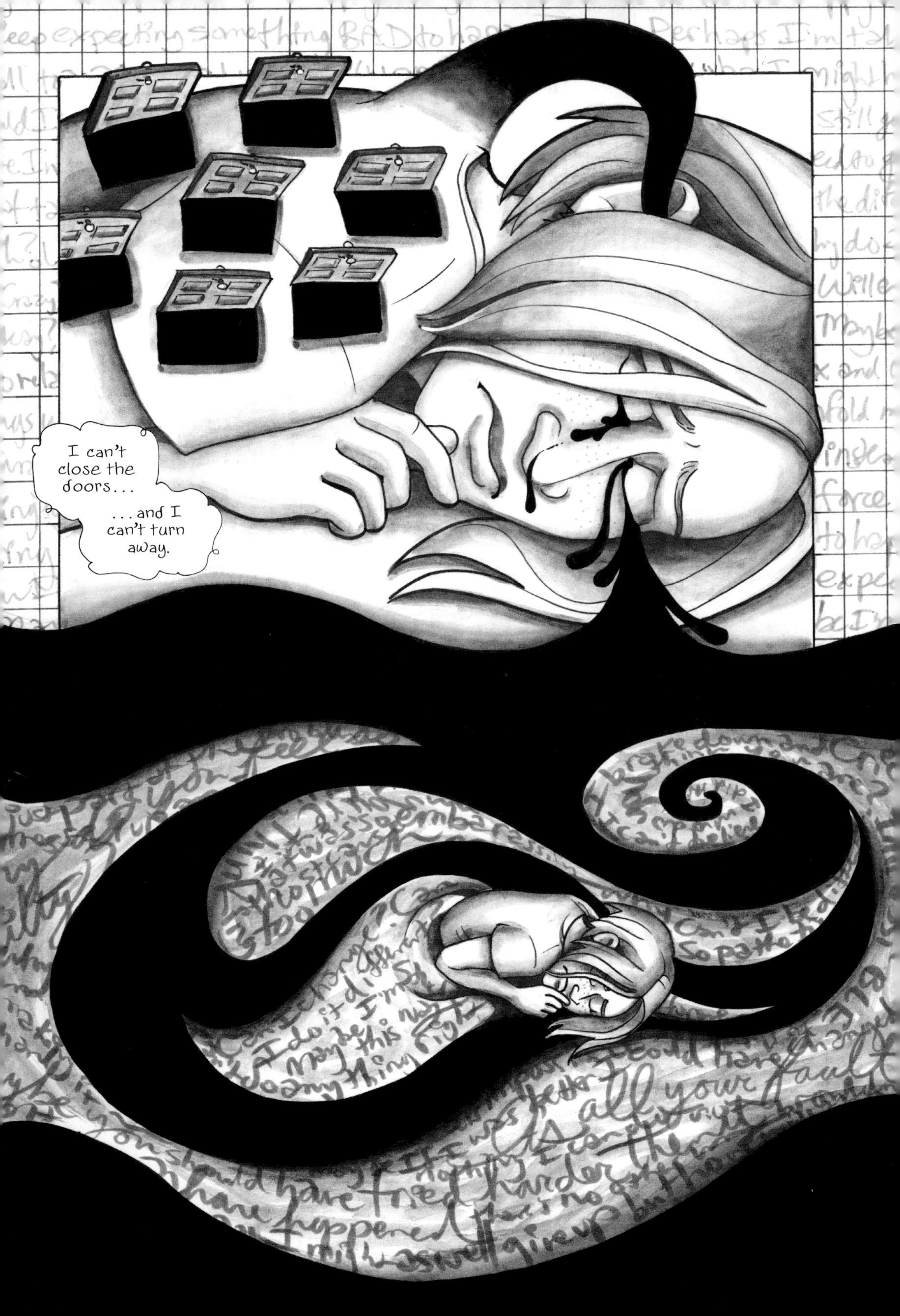
I can't close the doors...
...and I can't turn away.

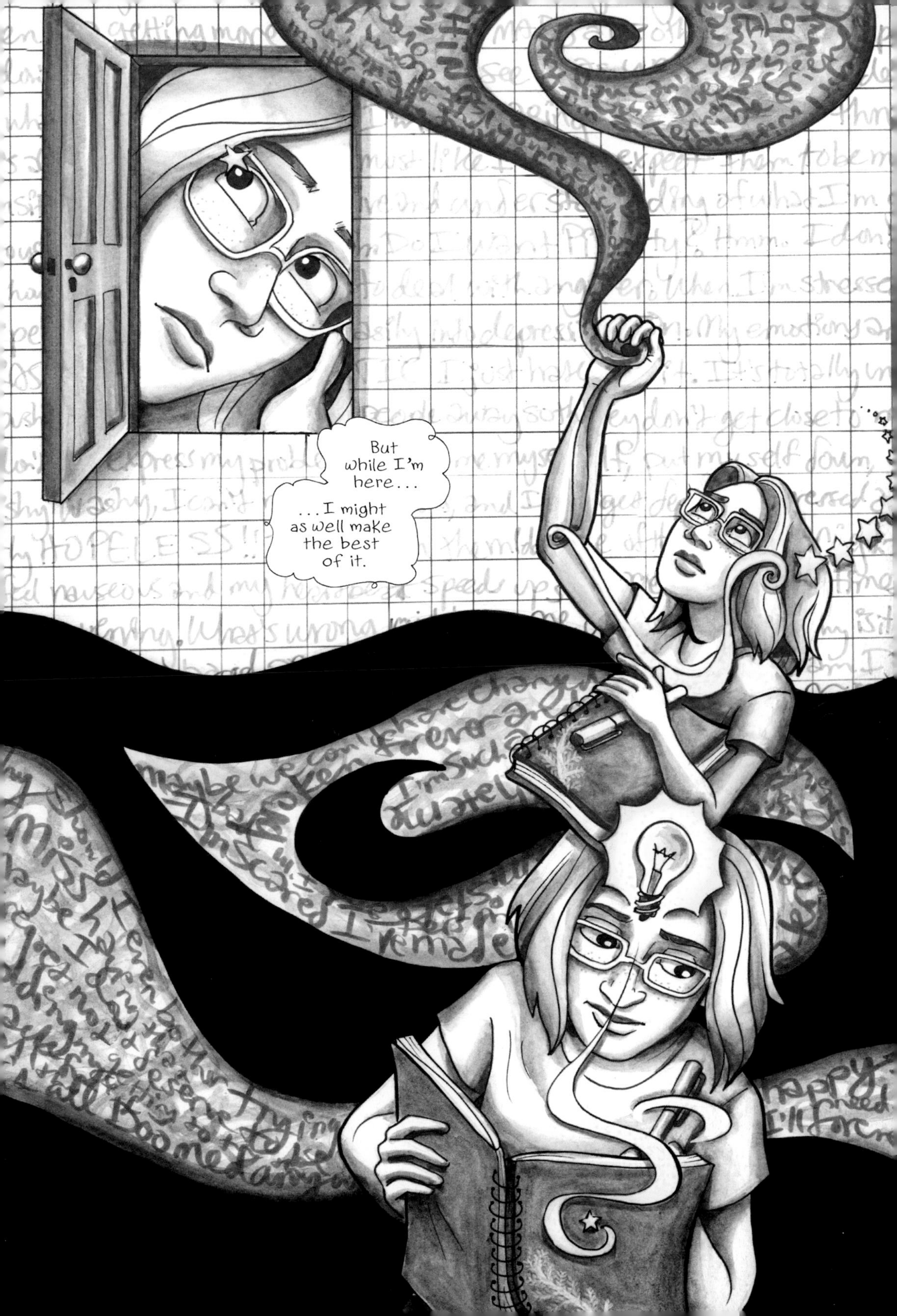
But while I'm here . . .
. . . I might as well make the best of it.

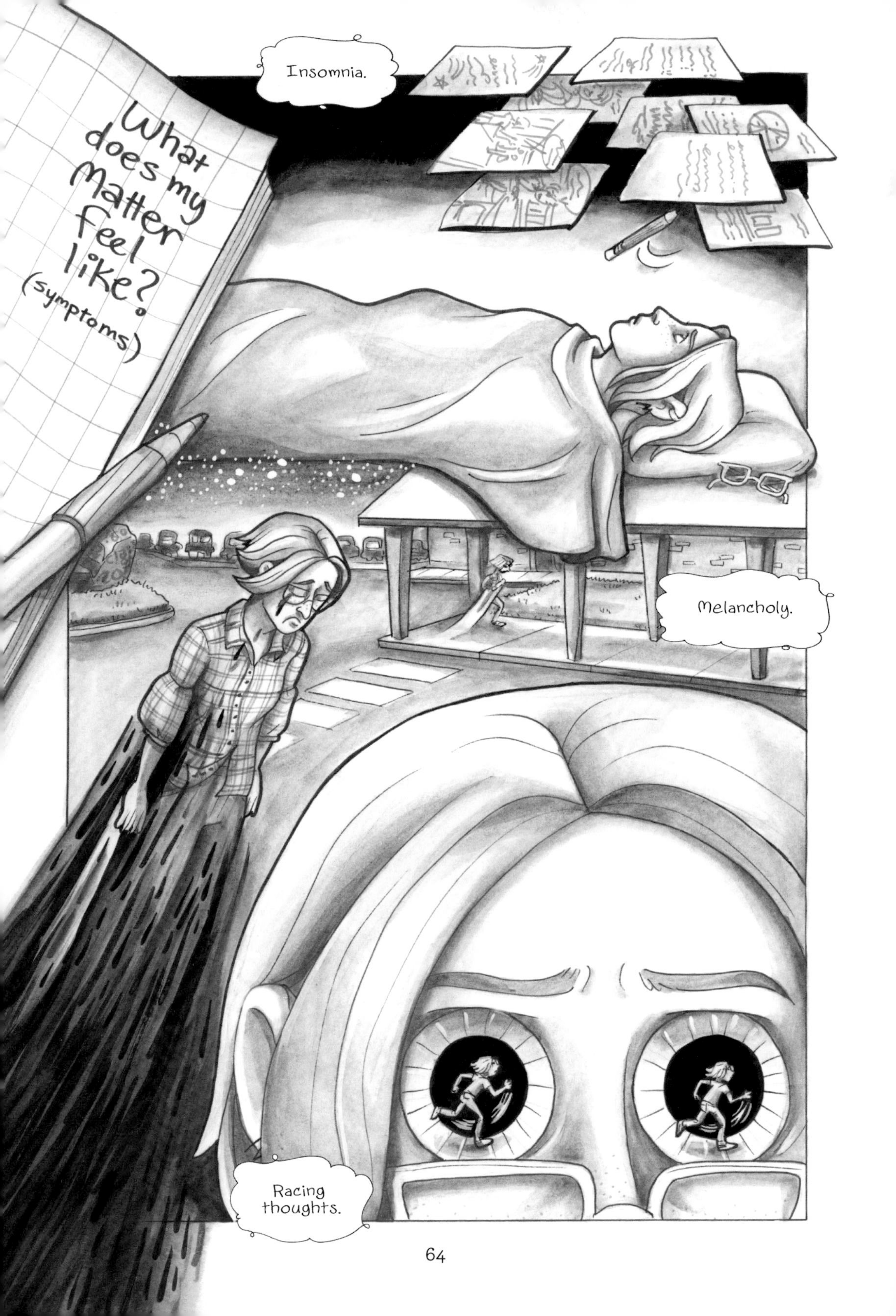
What does my Matter feel like?
(symptoms)
Insomnia.
Melancholy.
Racing thoughts.

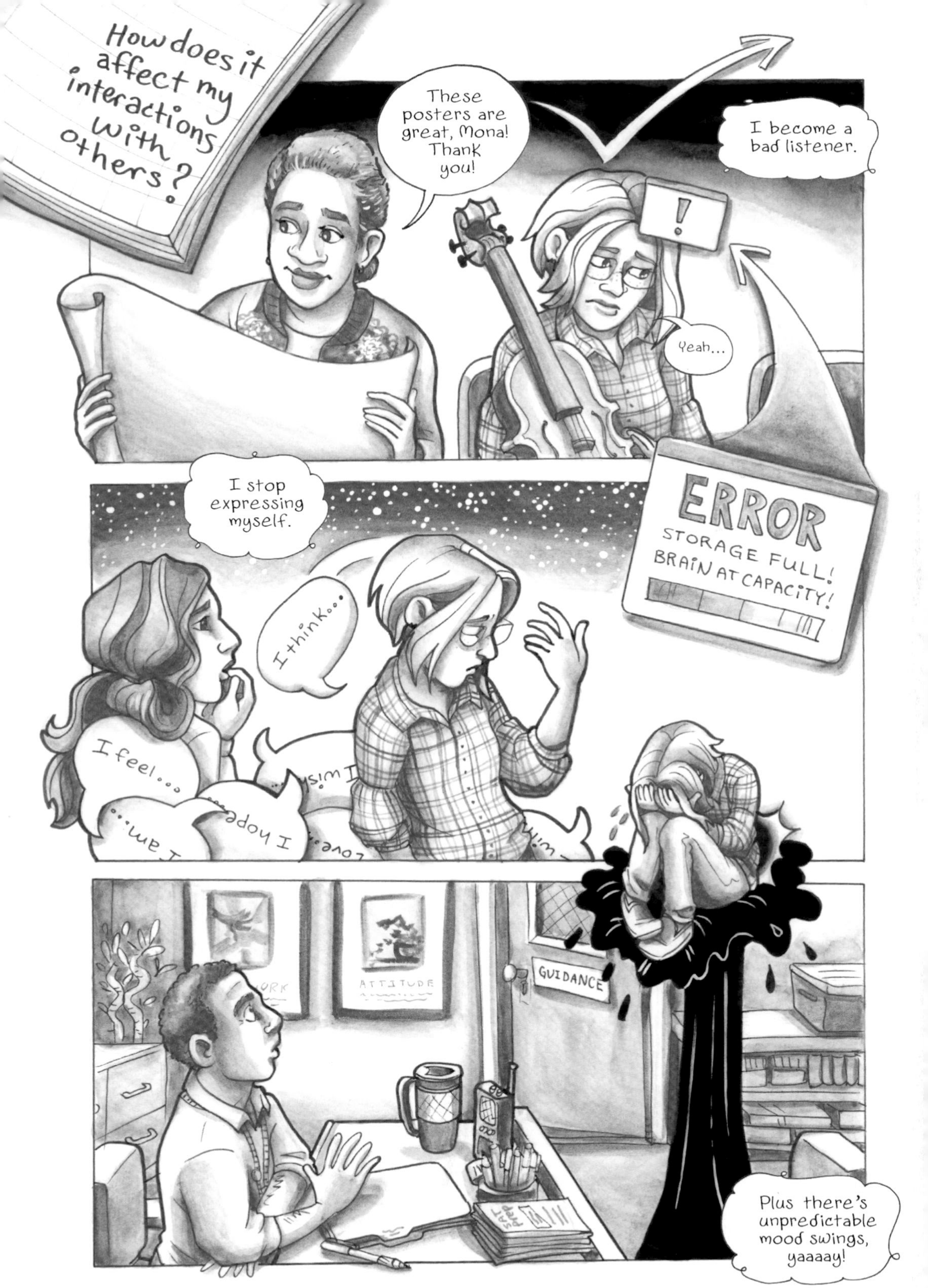
How does it affect my interactions with others?
These posters are great, Mona! Thank you!
I become a bad listener.
!
Yeah...
ERROR
STORAGE FULL!
BRAIN AT CAPACITY!
I stop expressing myself.
I think...
I feel...
I wish...
I hope...
I am...
GUIDANCE
ATTITUDE
Plus there's unpredictable mood swings, yaaaay!

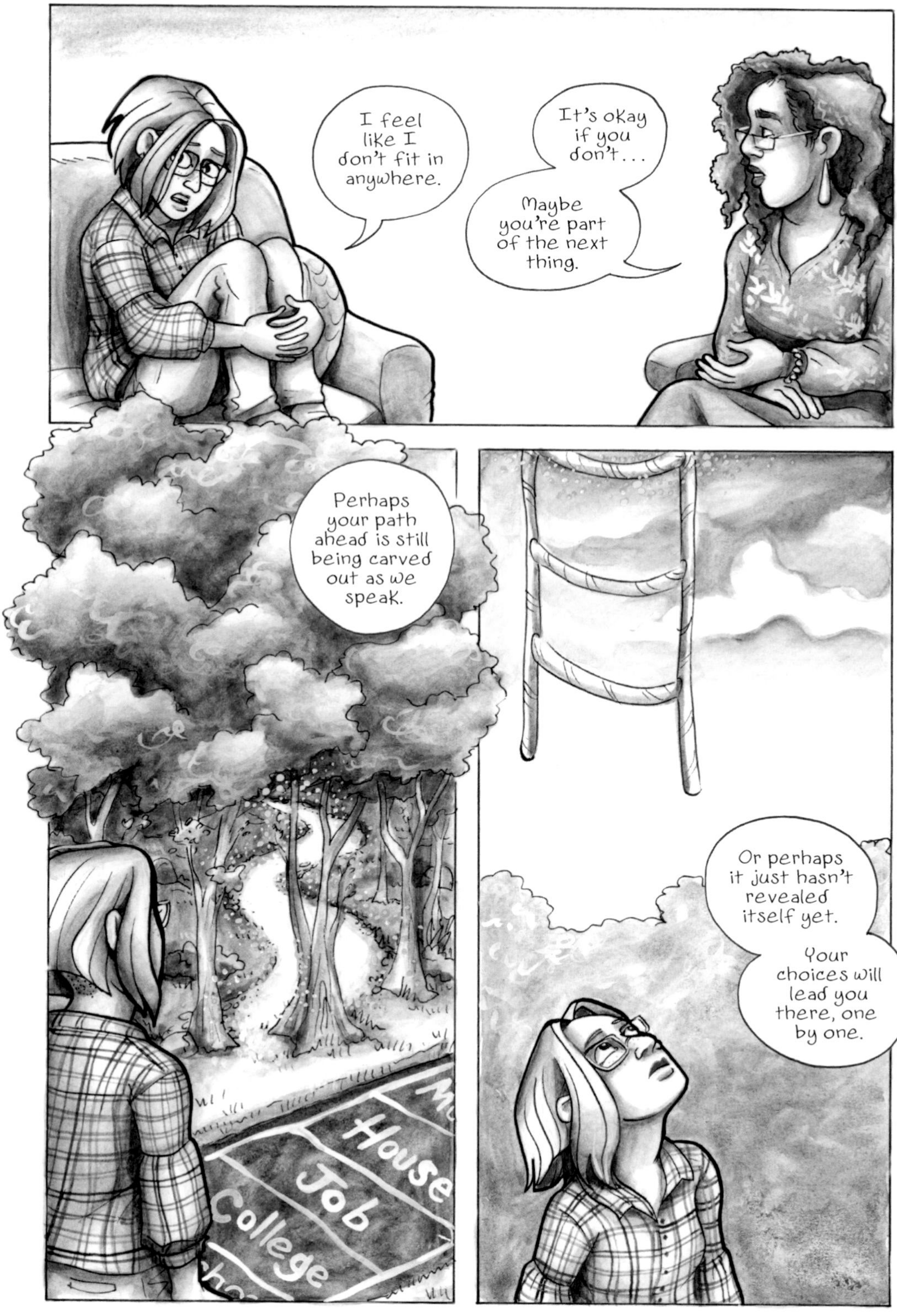
I feel like I don't fit in anywhere.
It's okay if you don't...
Maybe you're part of the next thing.
Perhaps your path ahead is still being carved out as we speak.
House
Job
College
Or perhaps it just hasn't revealed itself yet.
Your choices will lead you there, one by one.

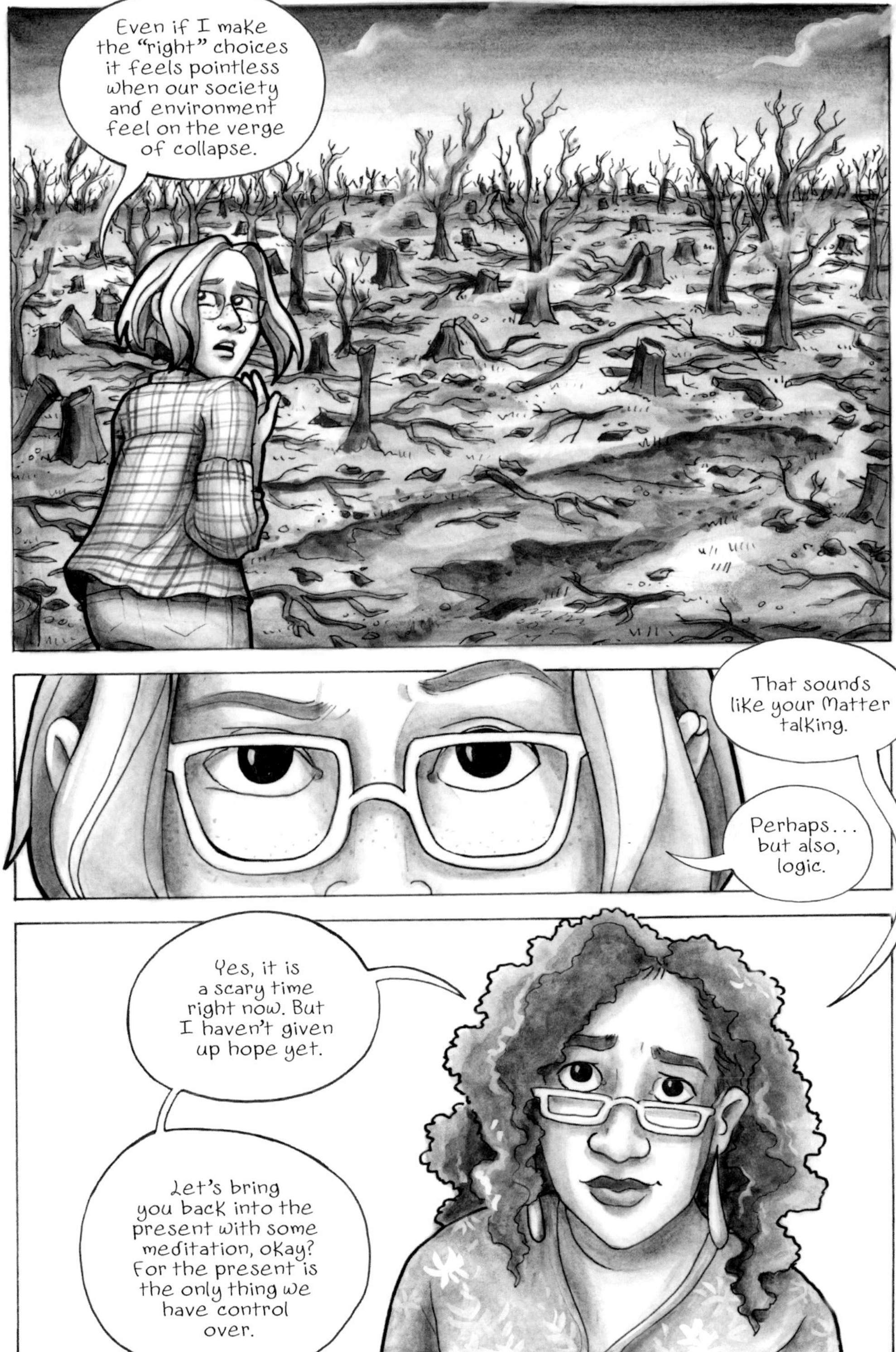
Even if I make the "right" choices it feels pointless when our society and environment feel on the verge of collapse.
That sounds like your Matter talking.
Perhaps... but also, logic.
Yes, it is a scary time right now. But I haven't given up hope yet.
Let's bring you back into the present with some meditation, okay? For the present is the only thing we have control over.

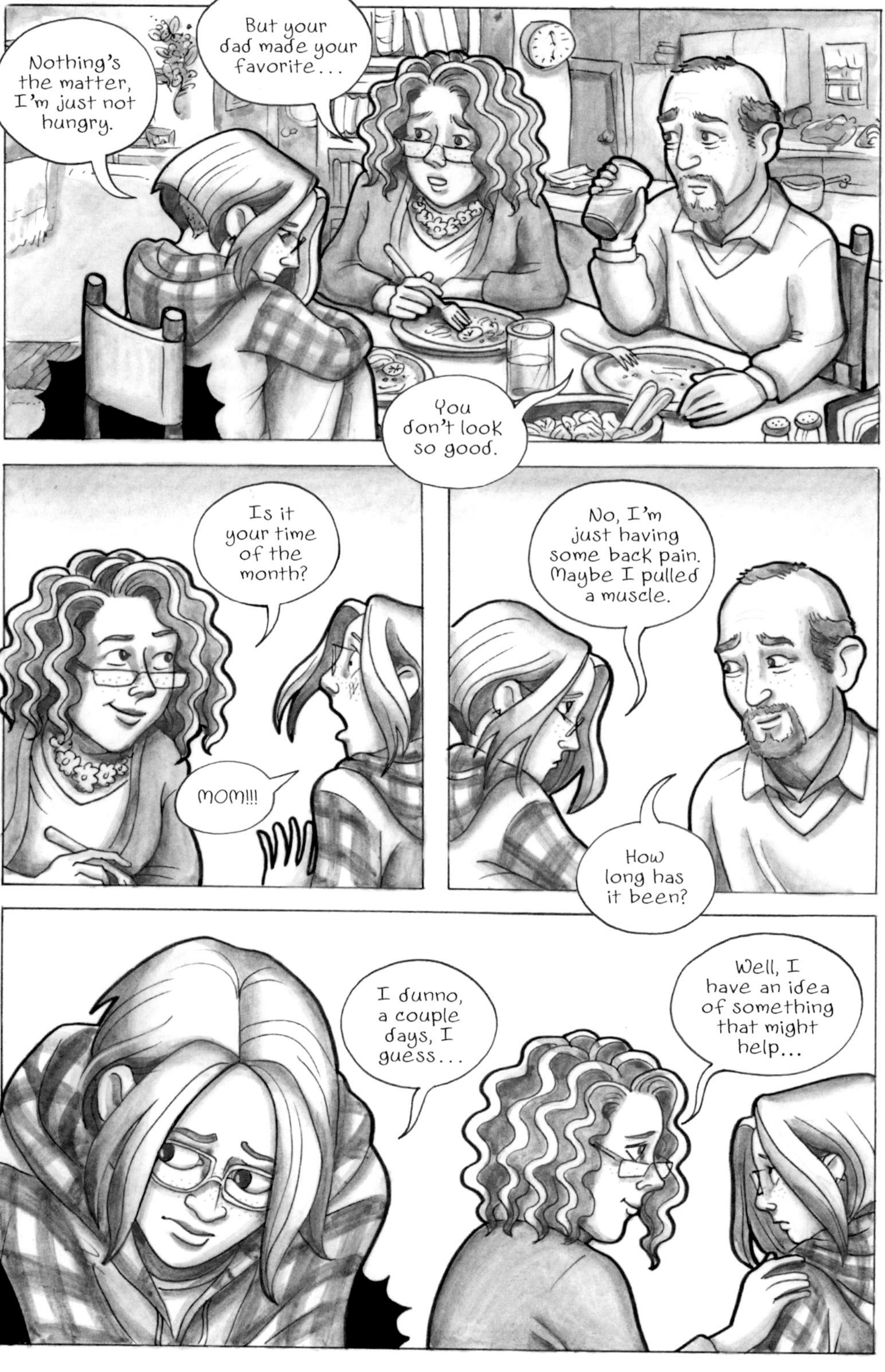
Nothing's the matter, I'm just not hungry.
But your dad made your favorite...
You don't look so good.
Is it your time of the month?
MOM!!!
No, I'm just having some back pain. Maybe I pulled a muscle.
How long has it been?
I dunno, a couple days, I guess...
Well, I have an idea of something that might help...

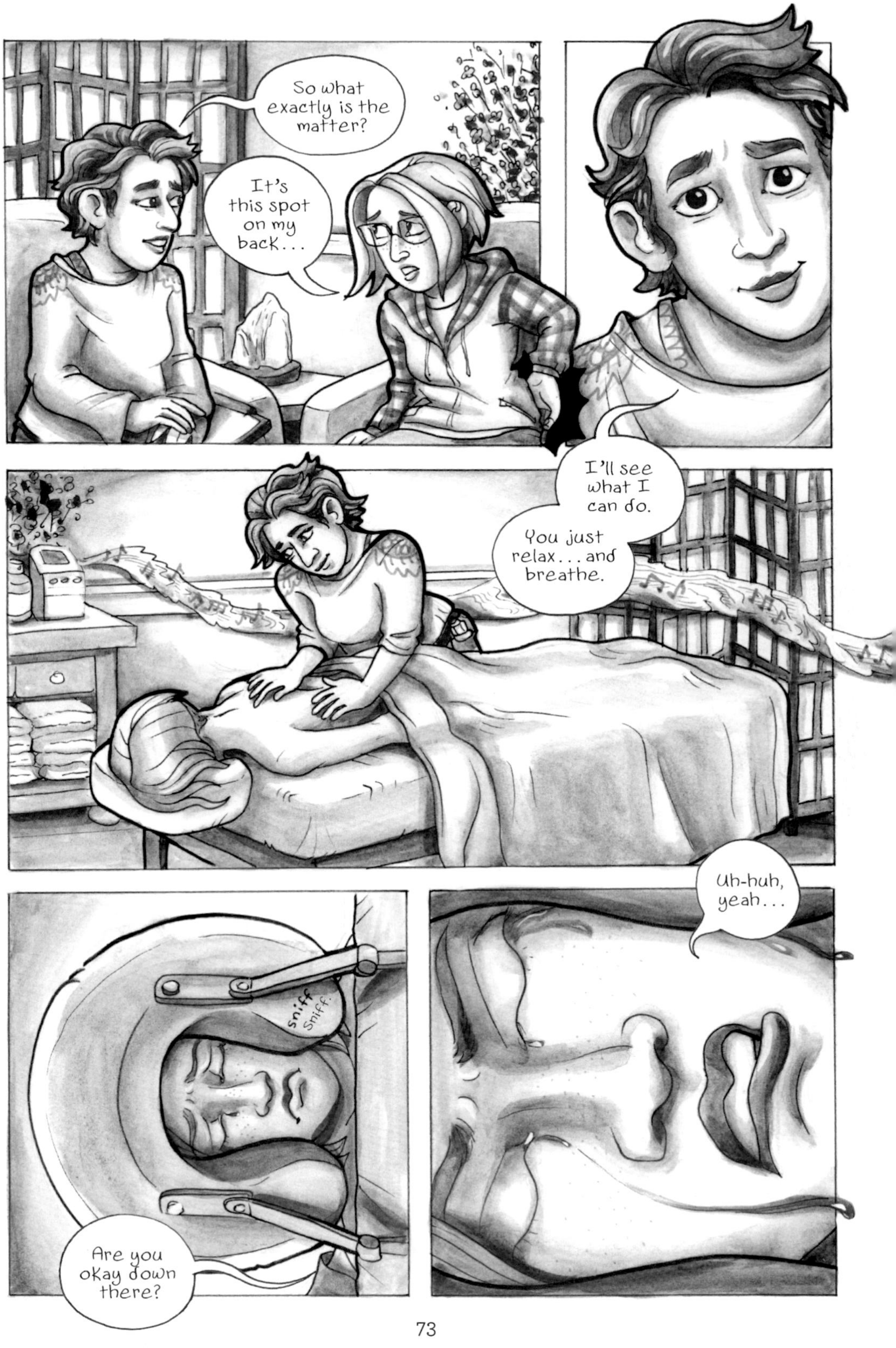
So what exactly is the matter?
It's this spot on my back...
I'll see what I can do.
You just relax... and breathe.
sniff sniff.
Are you okay down there?
Uh-huh, yeah...

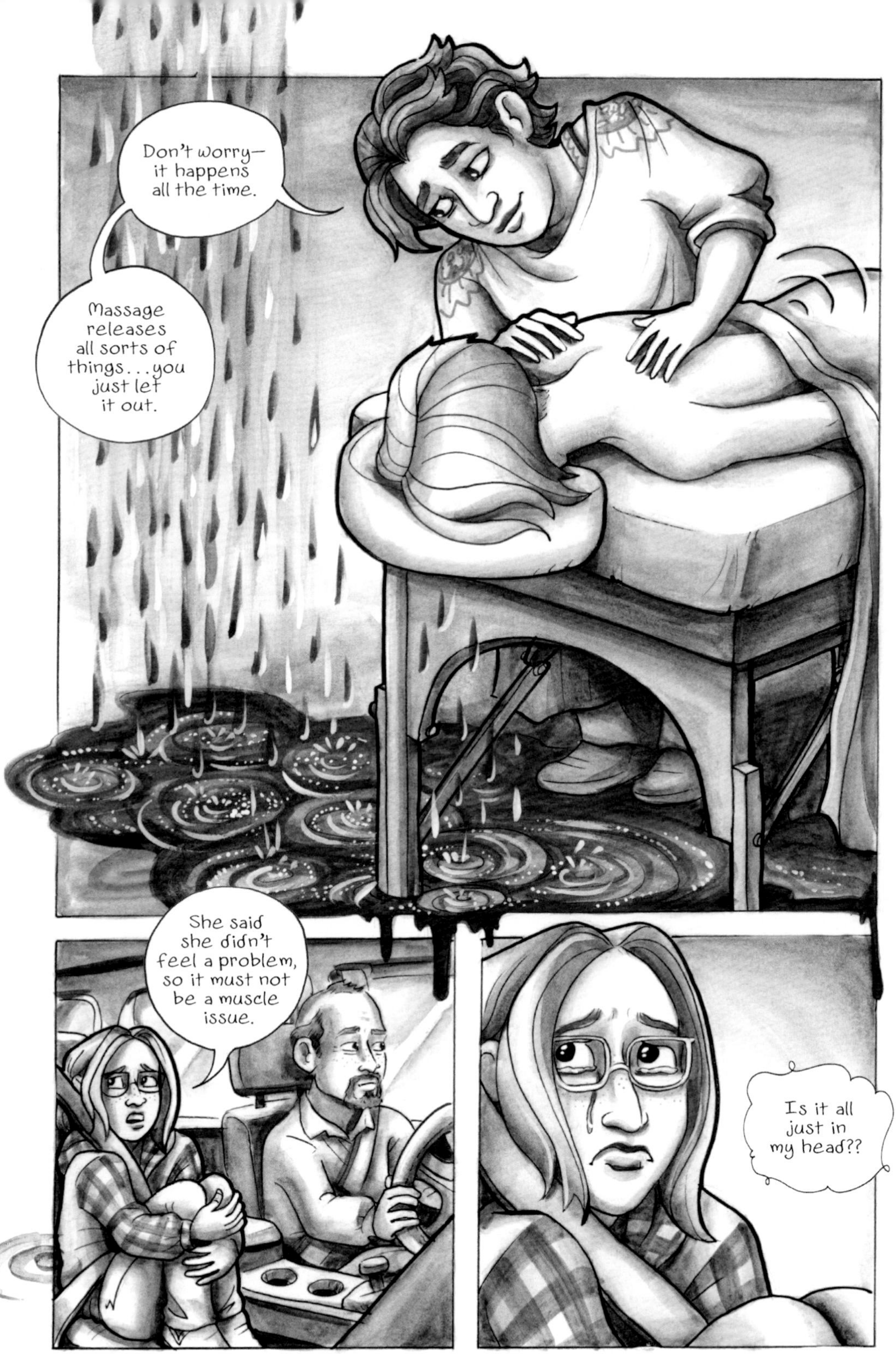
Don't worry—it happens all the time.
Massage releases all sorts of things...you just let it out.
She said she didn't feel a problem, so it must not be a muscle issue.
Is it all just in my head??

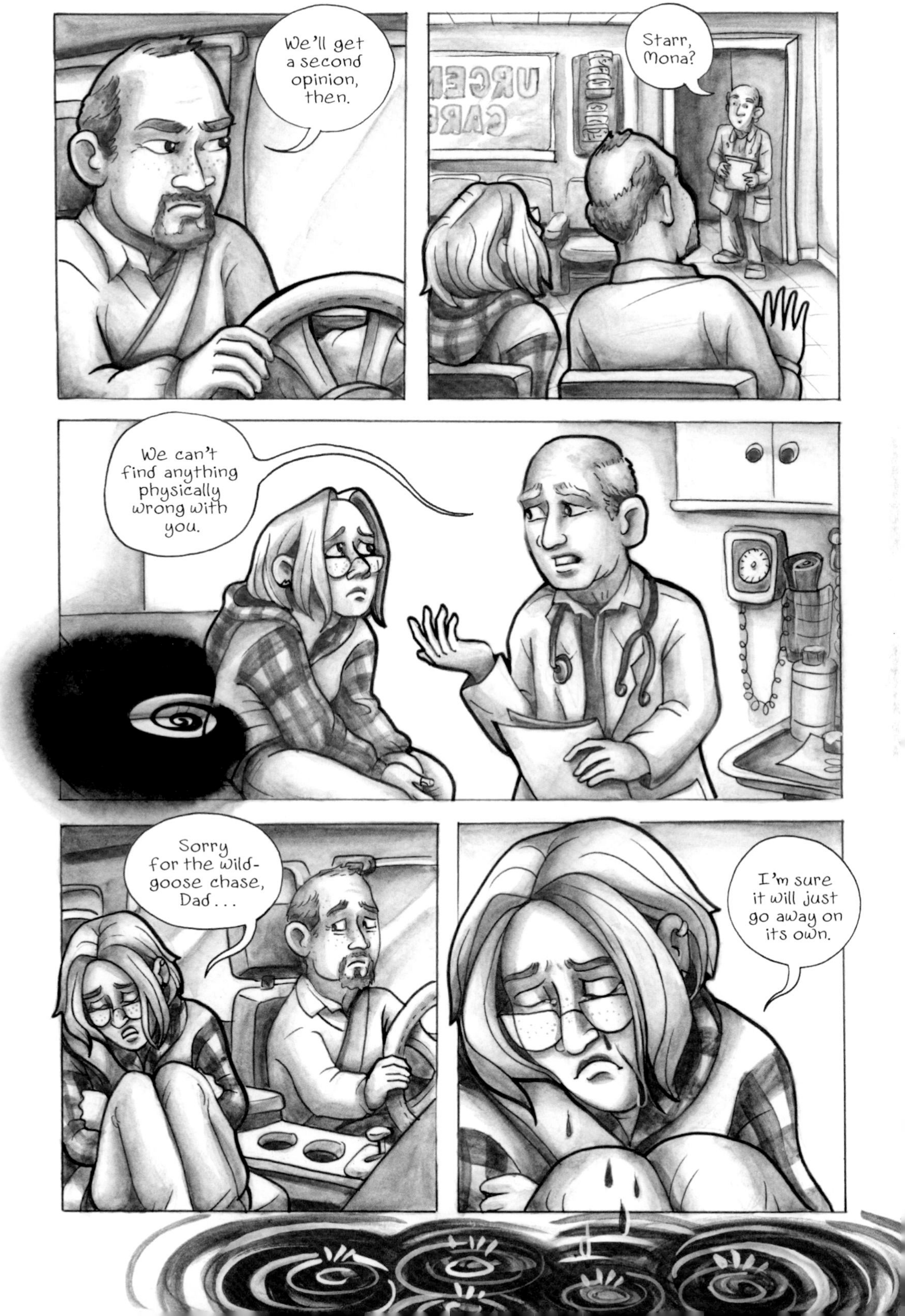
We'll get a second opinion, then.
Starr, Mona?
URGENT CARE
We can't find anything physically wrong with you.
Sorry for the wild-goose chase, Dad . . .
I'm sure it will just go away on its own.

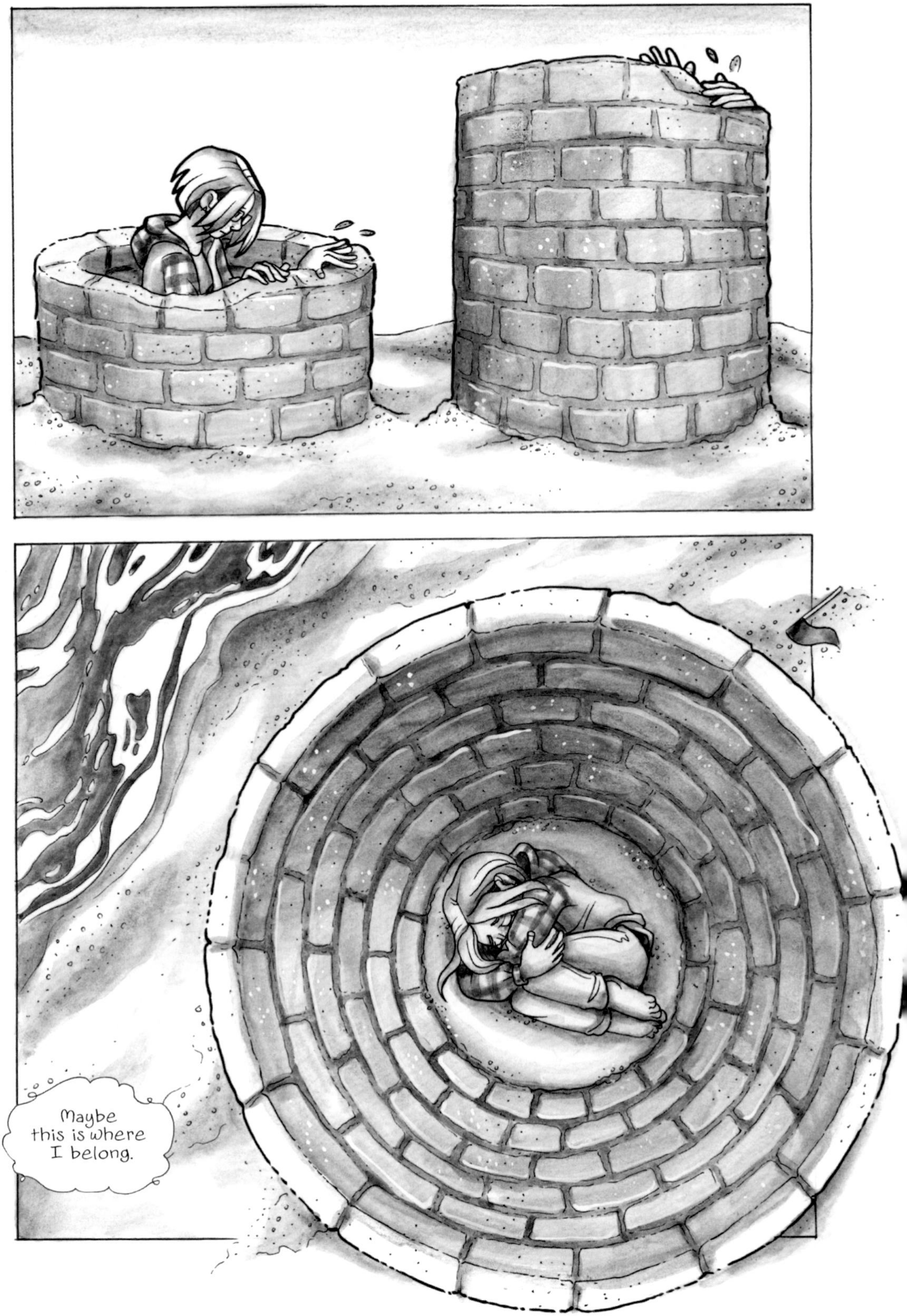
Maybe
this is where
I belong.

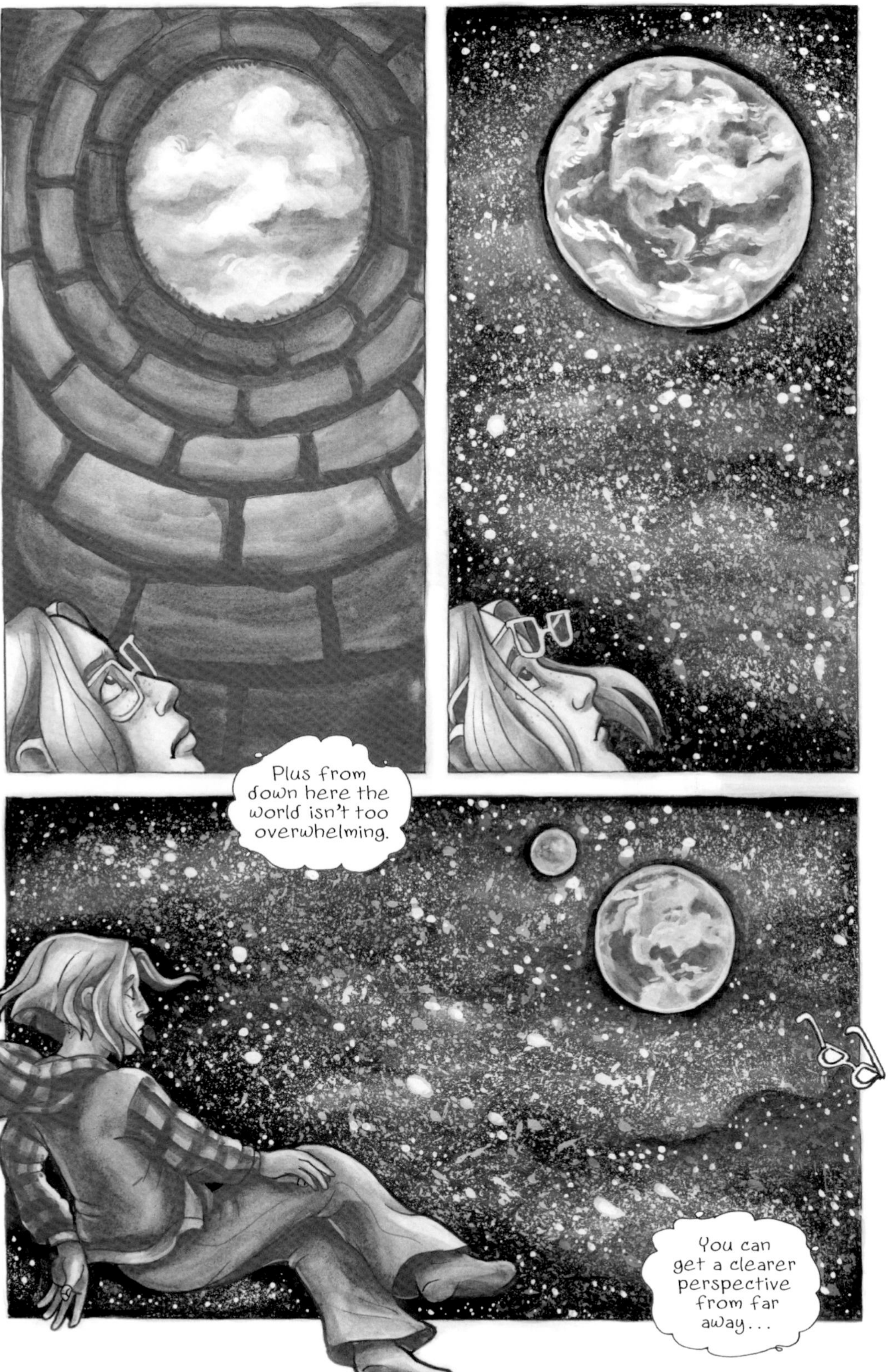
Plus from down here the world isn't too overwhelming.
You can get a clearer perspective from far away...

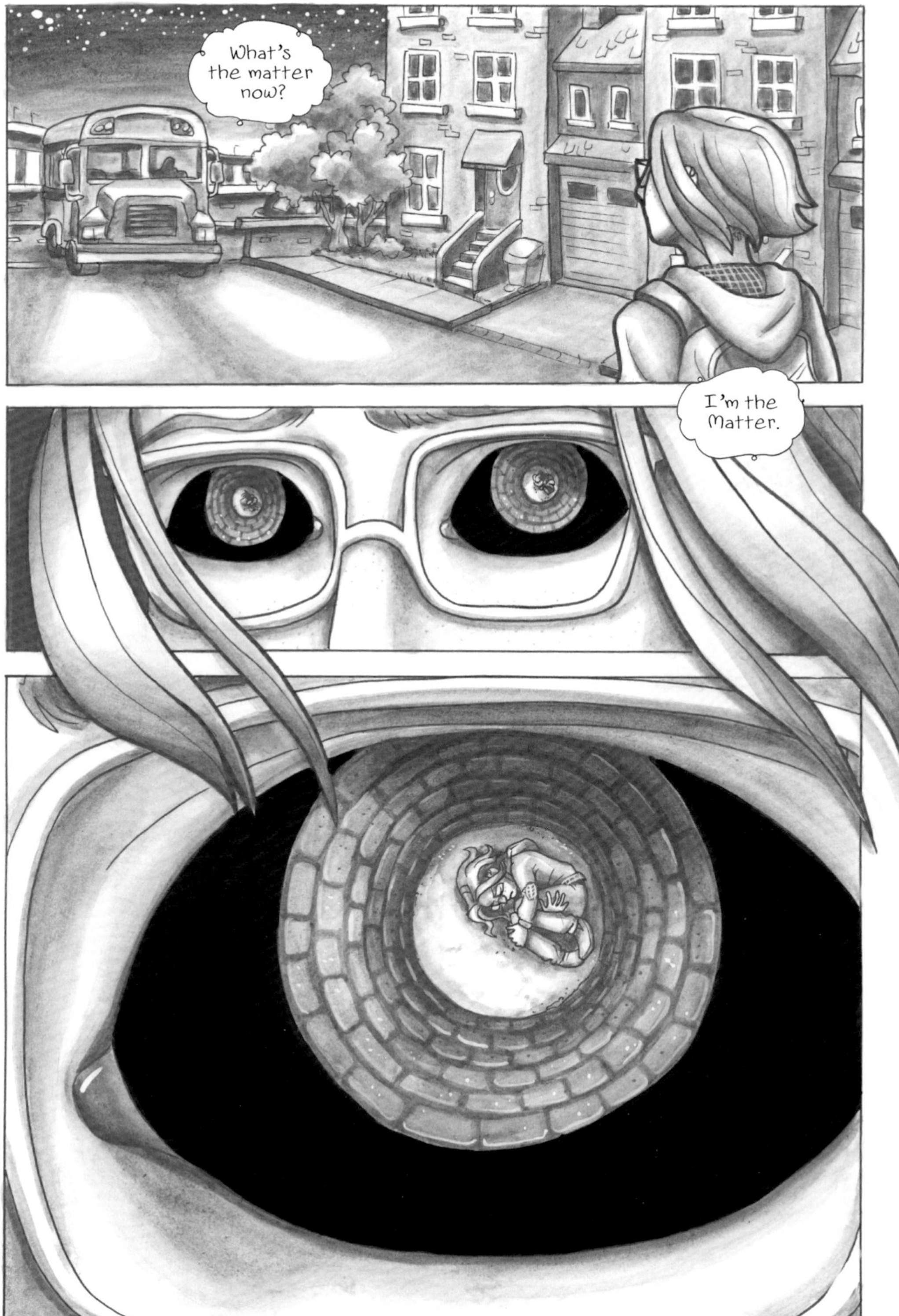
What's the matter now?
I'm the Matter.

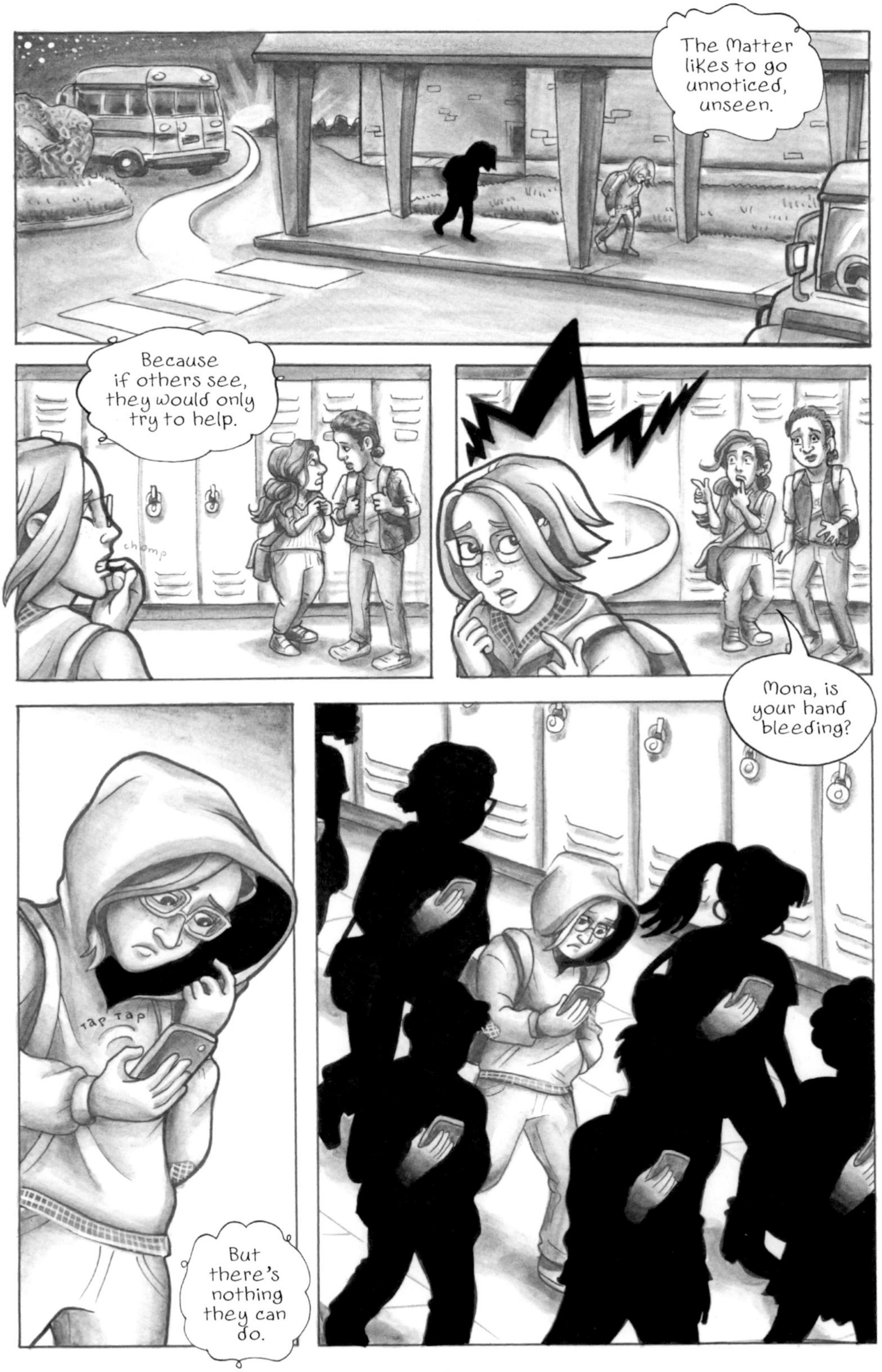
The Matter likes to go unnoticed, unseen.
Because if others see, they would only try to help.
chomp
Mona, is your hand bleeding?
TAP TAP
But there's nothing they can do.

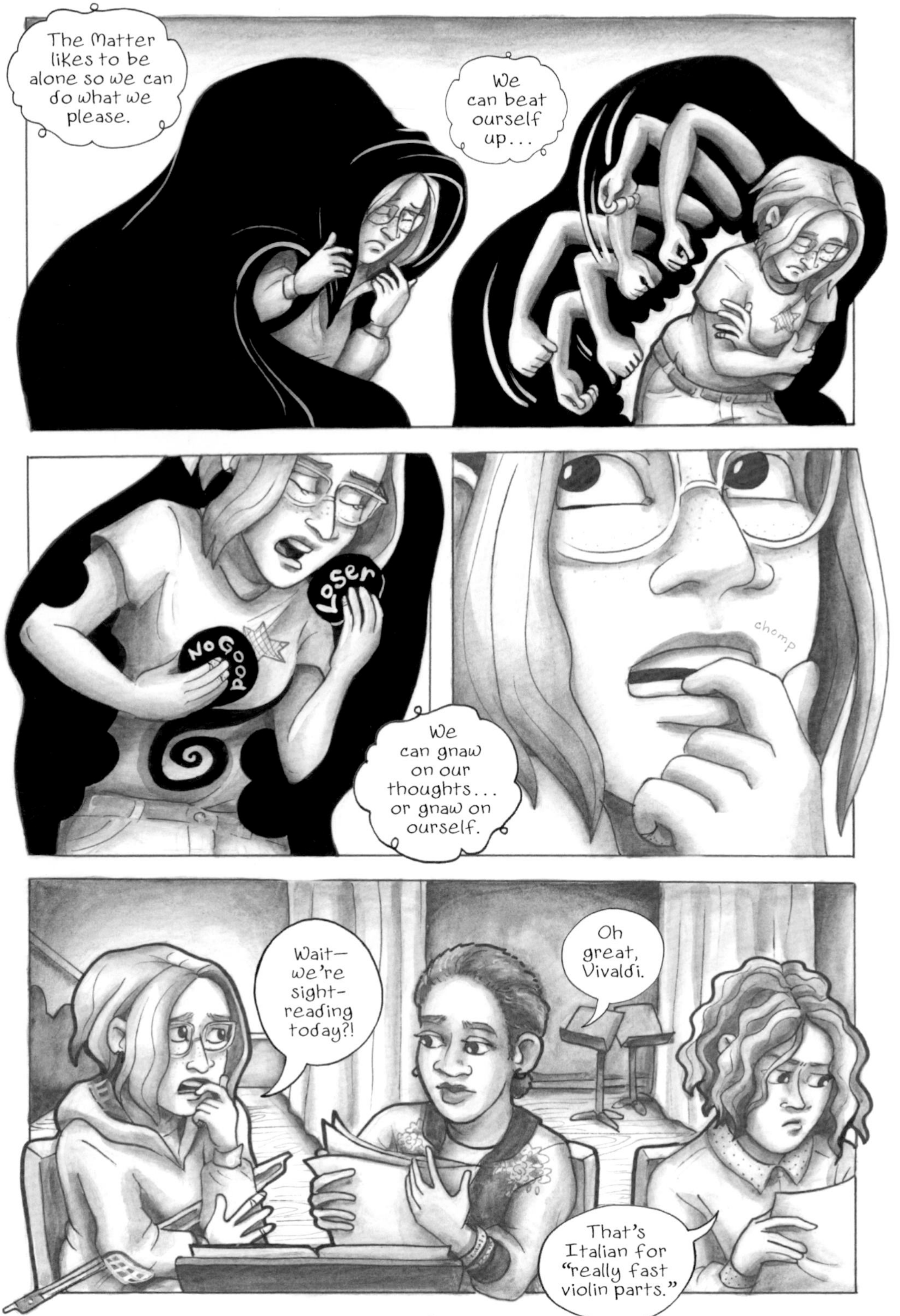
The Matter likes to be alone so we can do what we please.
We can beat ourself up...
Loser
No Good
chomp
We can gnaw on our thoughts... or gnaw on ourself.
Wait—we're sight-reading today?!
Oh great, Vivaldi.
That's Italian for "really fast violin parts."

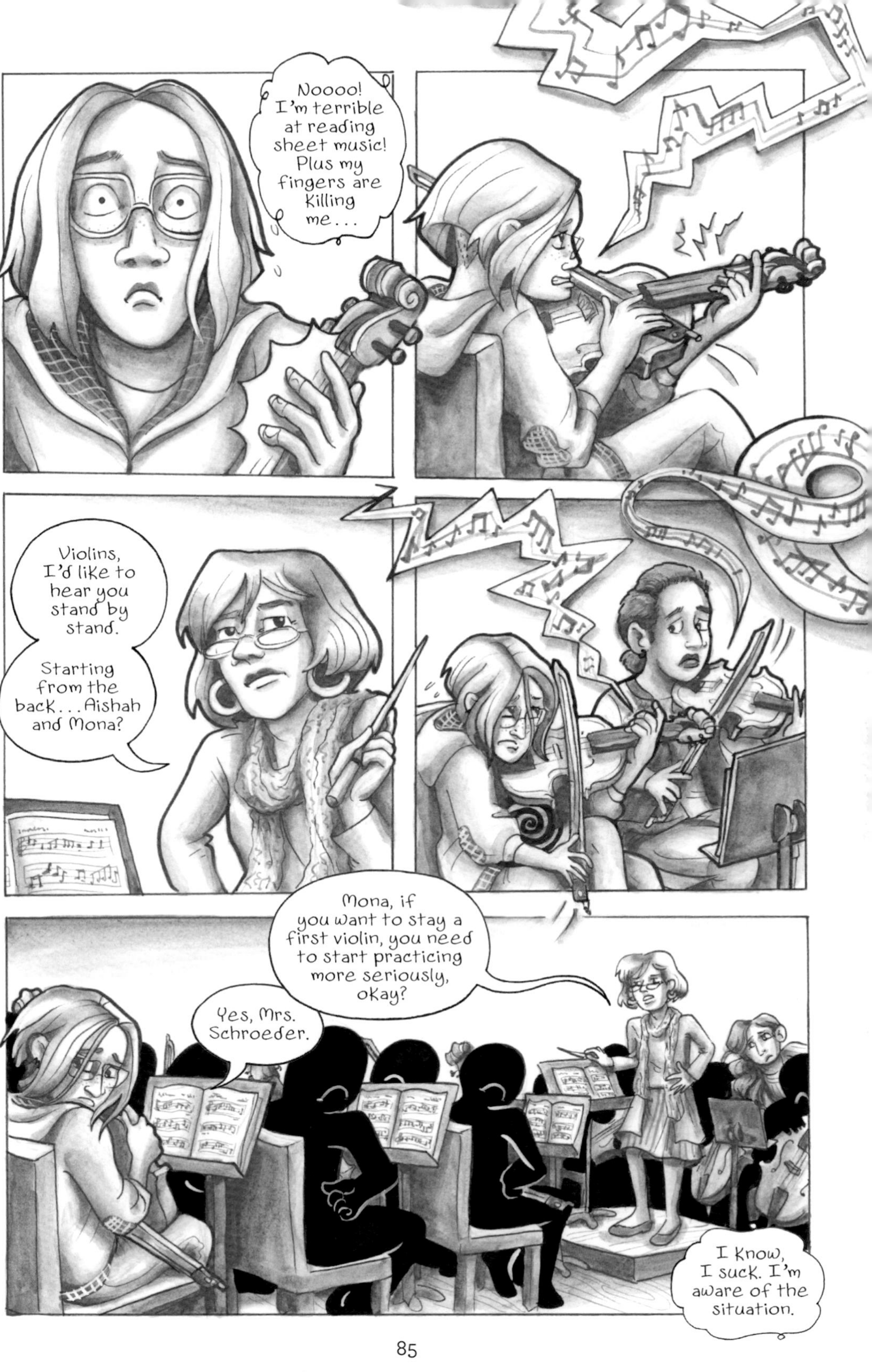
Noooo! I'm terrible at reading sheet music! Plus my fingers are killing me...
Violins, I'd like to hear you stand by stand.
Starting from the back...Aishah and Mona?
Mona, if you want to stay a first violin, you need to start practicing more seriously, okay?
Yes, Mrs. Schroeder.
I know, I suck. I'm aware of the situation.

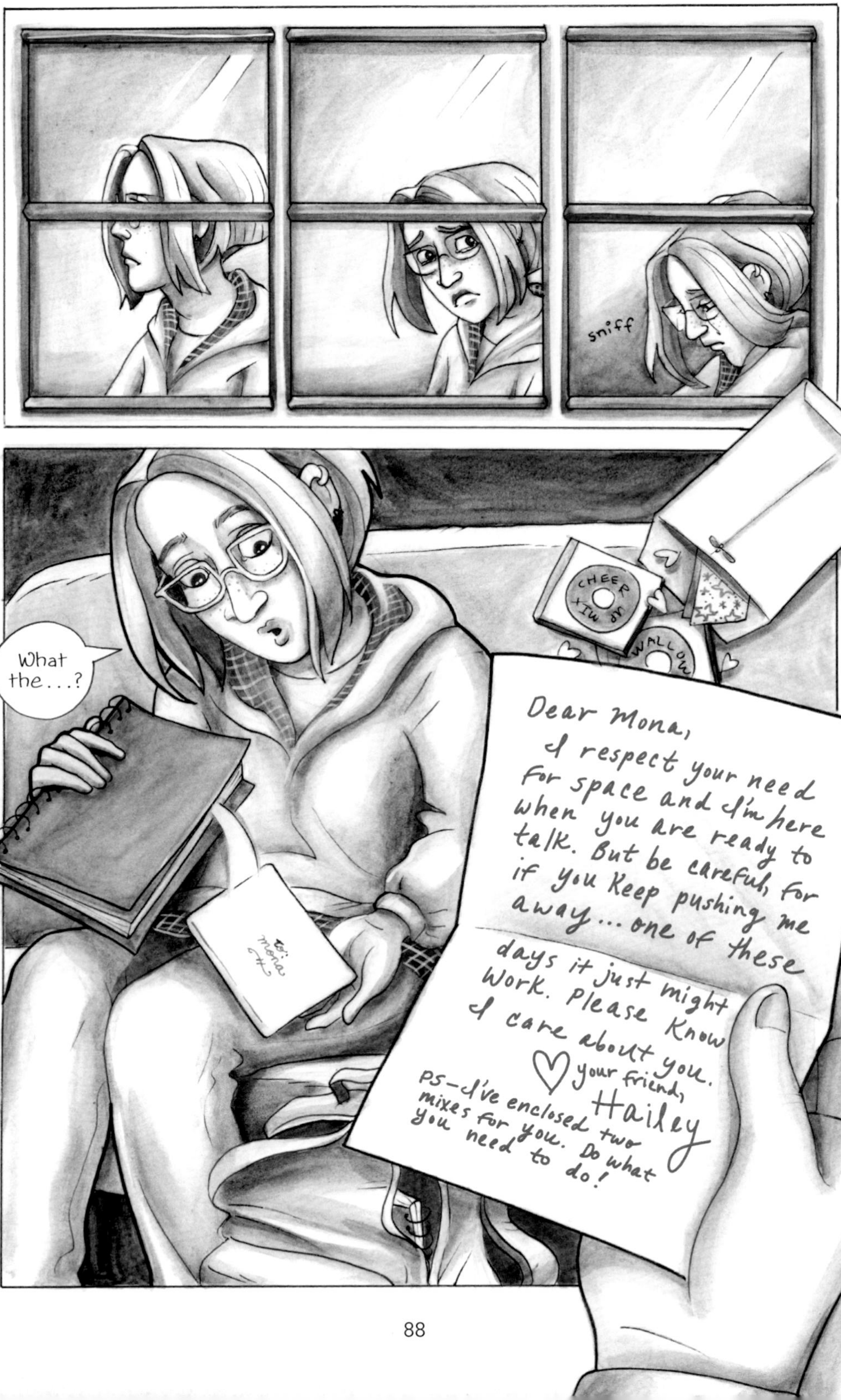
sniff
What the...?
CHEER UP MIX
WALLOW
to: mona
Dear Mona,
I respect your need for space and I'm here when you are ready to talk. But be careful, for if you keep pushing me away... one of these days it just might work. Please know I care about you.
your friend,
Hailey
PS—I've enclosed two mixes for you. Do what you need to do!

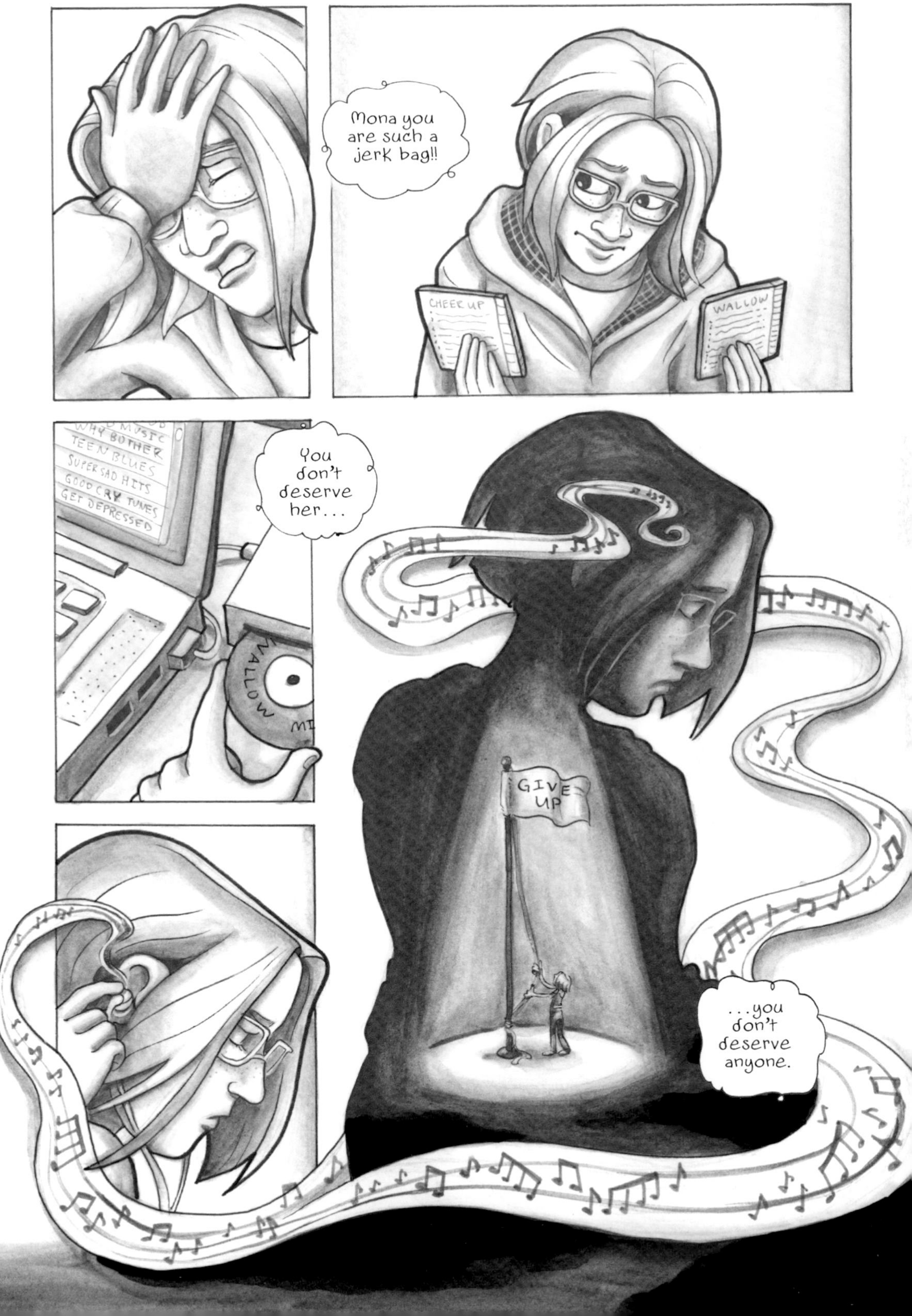
Mona you are such a jerk bag!!
CHEER UP
WALLOW
WHY BOTHER
TEEN BLUES
SUPER SAD HITS
GOOD CRY TUNES
GET DEPRESSED
You don't deserve her...
WALLOW
GIVE UP
...you don't deserve anyone.

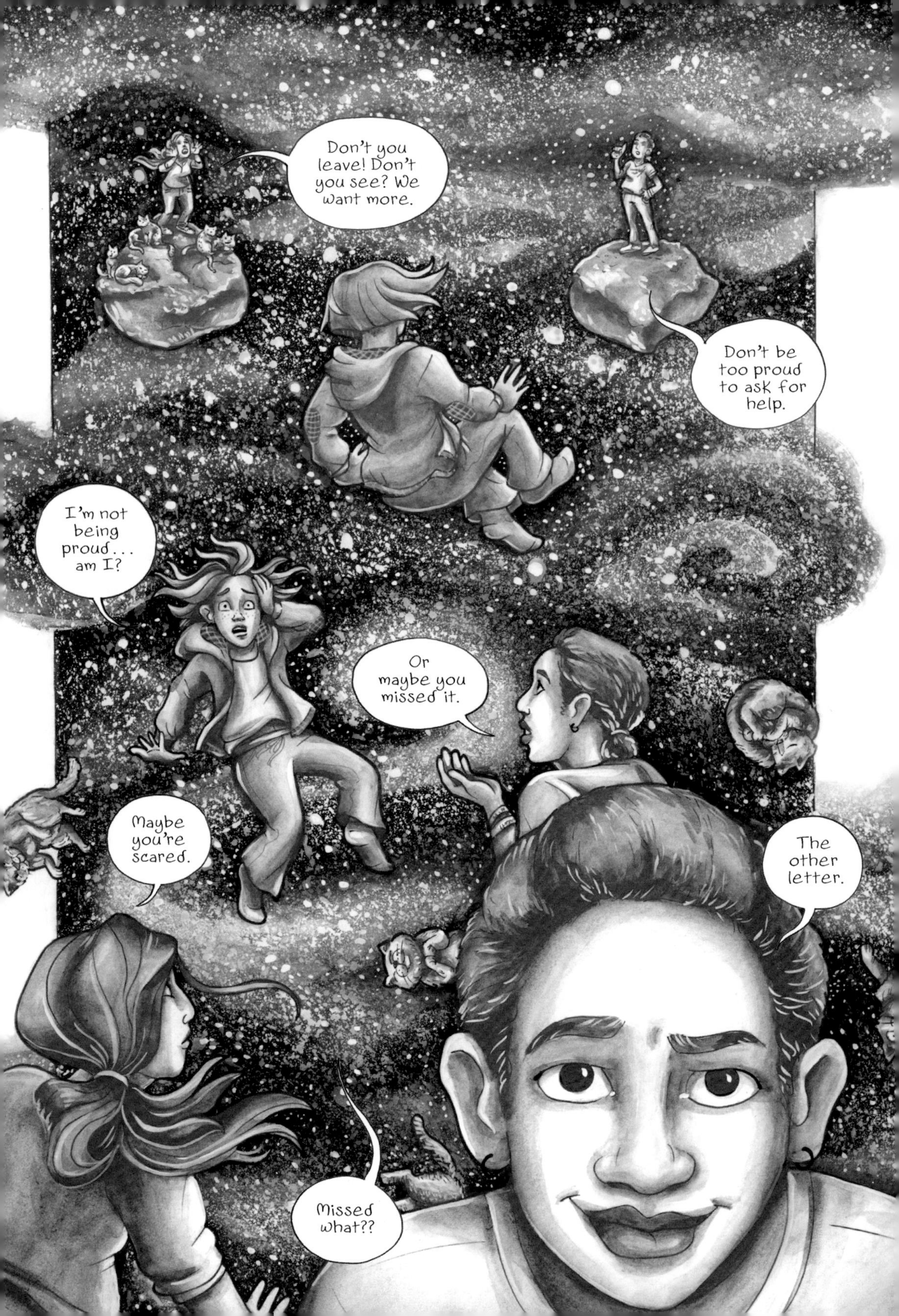
Don't you leave! Don't you see? We want more.
Don't be too proud to ask for help.
I'm not being proud... am I?
Or maybe you missed it.
Maybe you're scared.
The other letter.
Missed what??

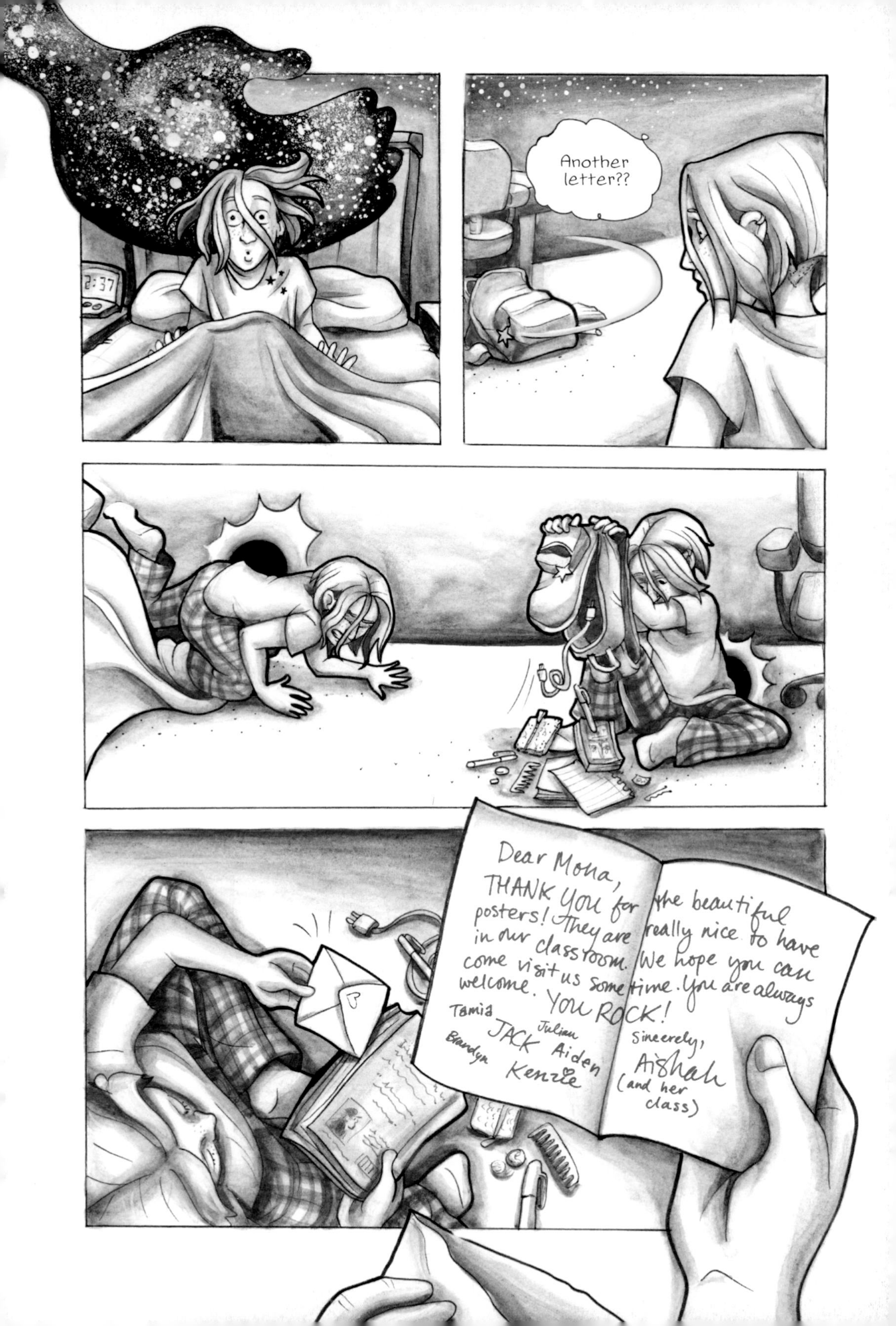
2:37
Another letter??
Dear Mona,
THANK YOU for the beautiful posters! They are really nice to have in our classroom. We hope you can come visit us some time. You are always welcome. YOU ROCK!
Tamia
Julian
JACK
Aiden
Brandyn
Kenzie
Sincerely,
Aishah
(and her class)

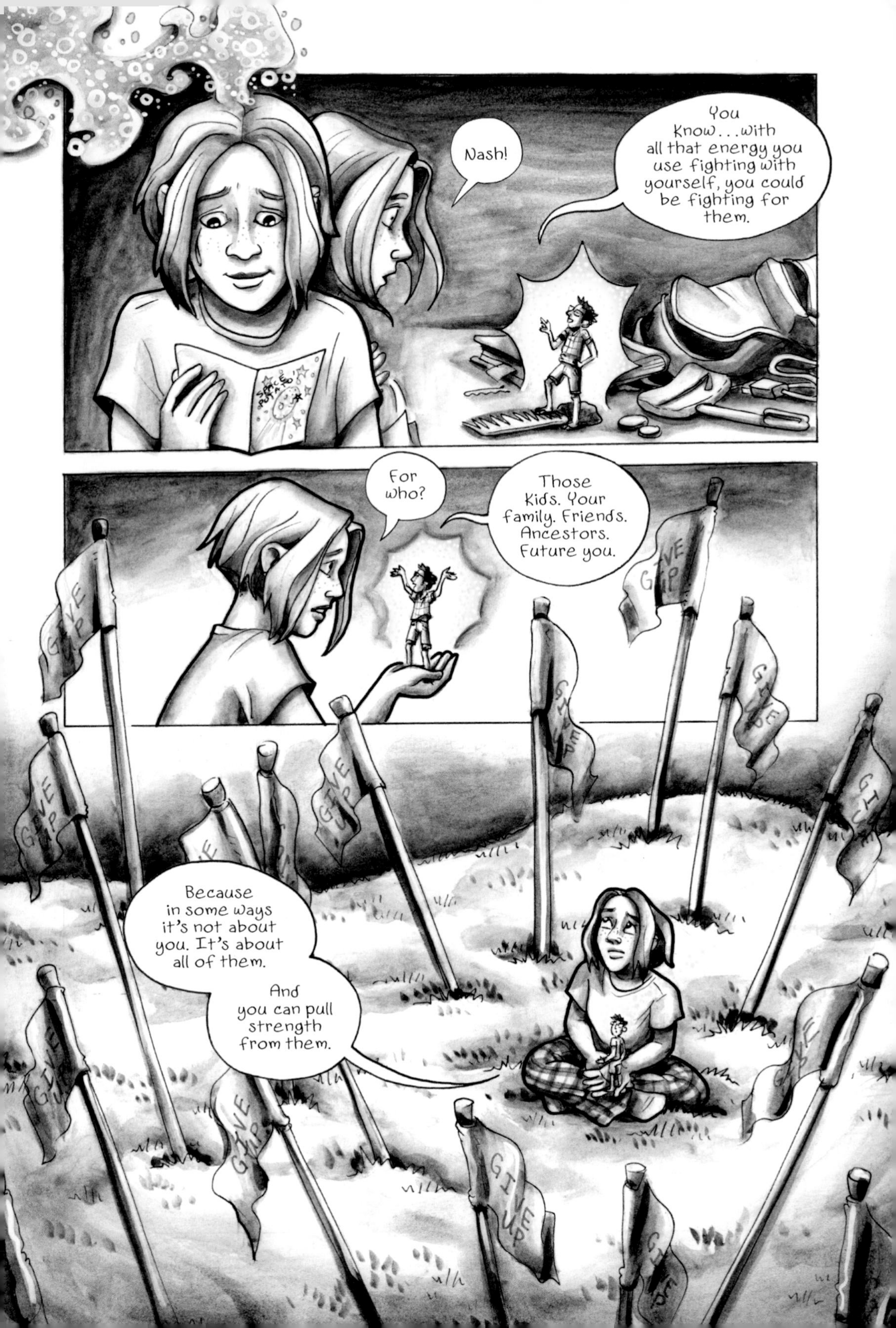
Nash!
You know...with all that energy you use fighting with yourself, you could be fighting for them.
SPACE POTATO
For who?
Those kids. Your family. Friends. Ancestors. Future you.
GIVE UP
Because in some ways it's not about you. It's about all of them.
And you can pull strength from them.

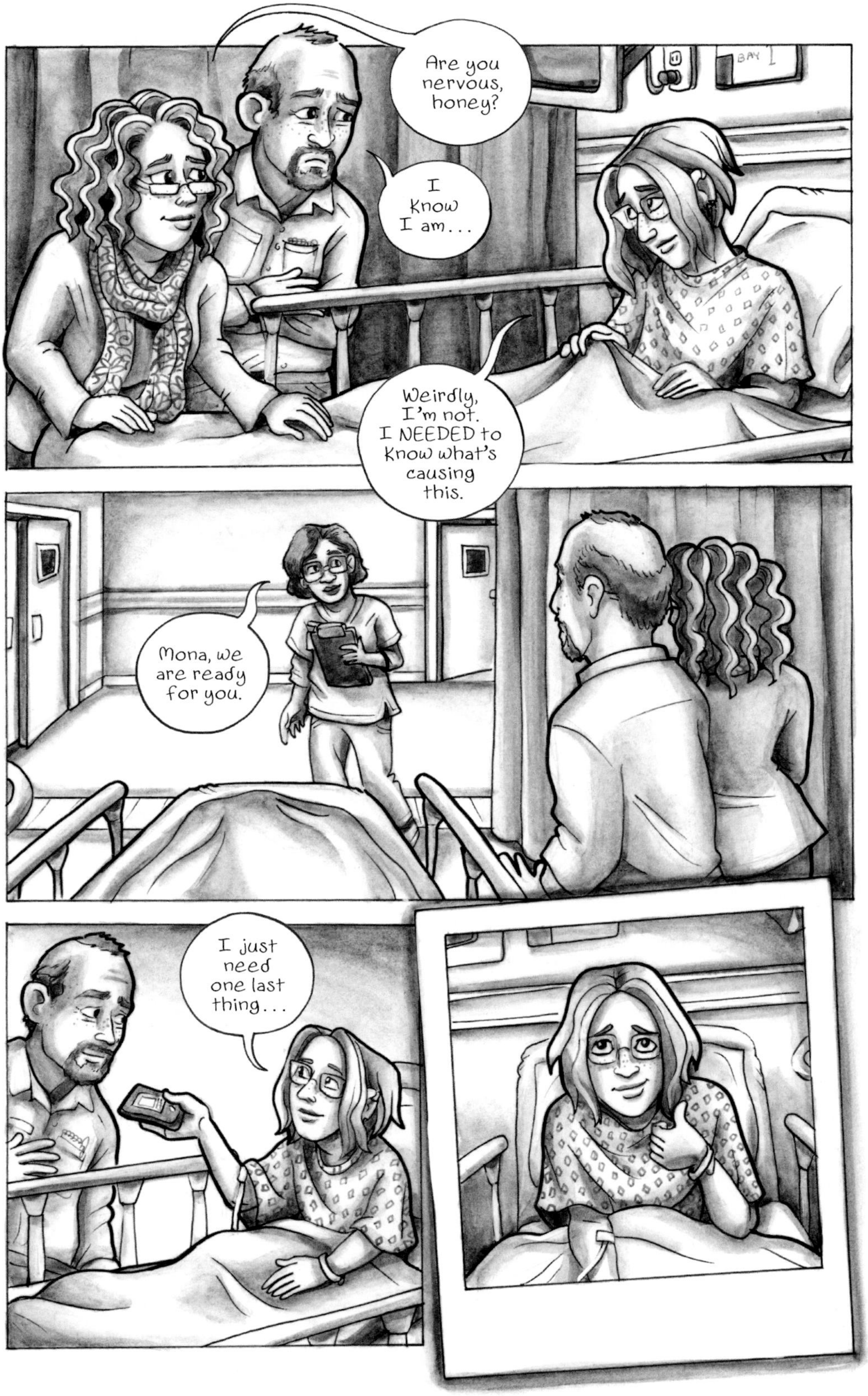
Are you nervous, honey?
I know I am...
Weirdly, I'm not. I NEEDED to know what's causing this.
Mona, we are ready for you.
I just need one last thing...

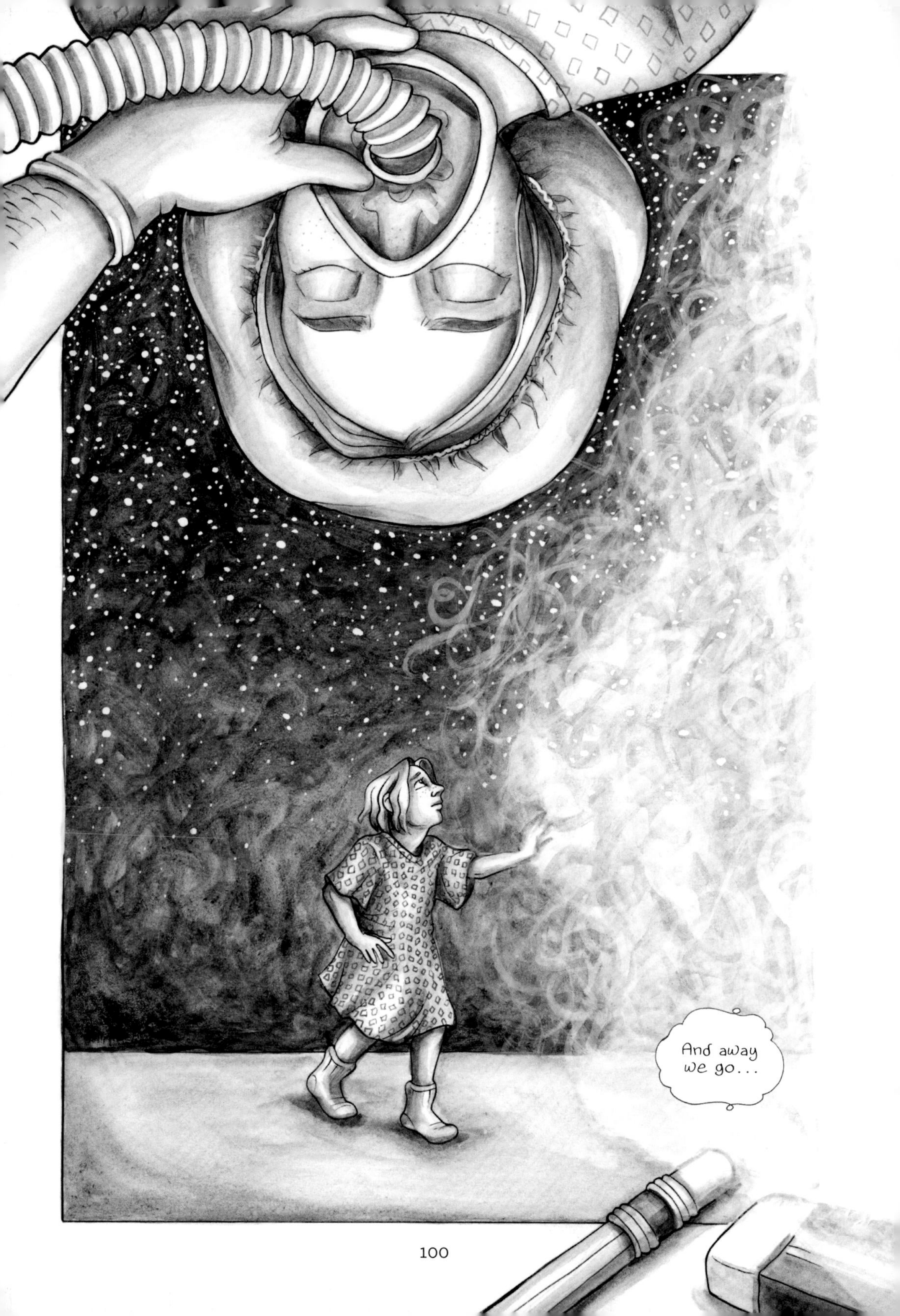
And away we go...

Break Your Cycles

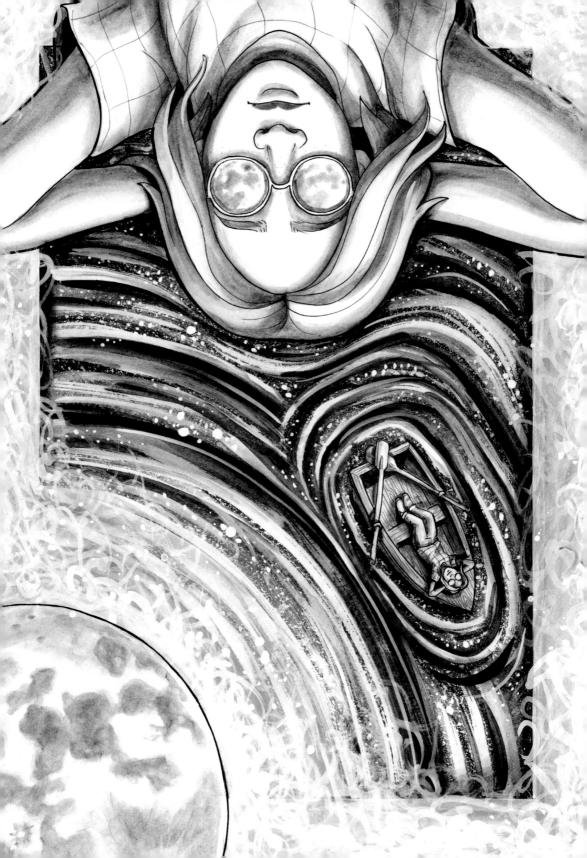

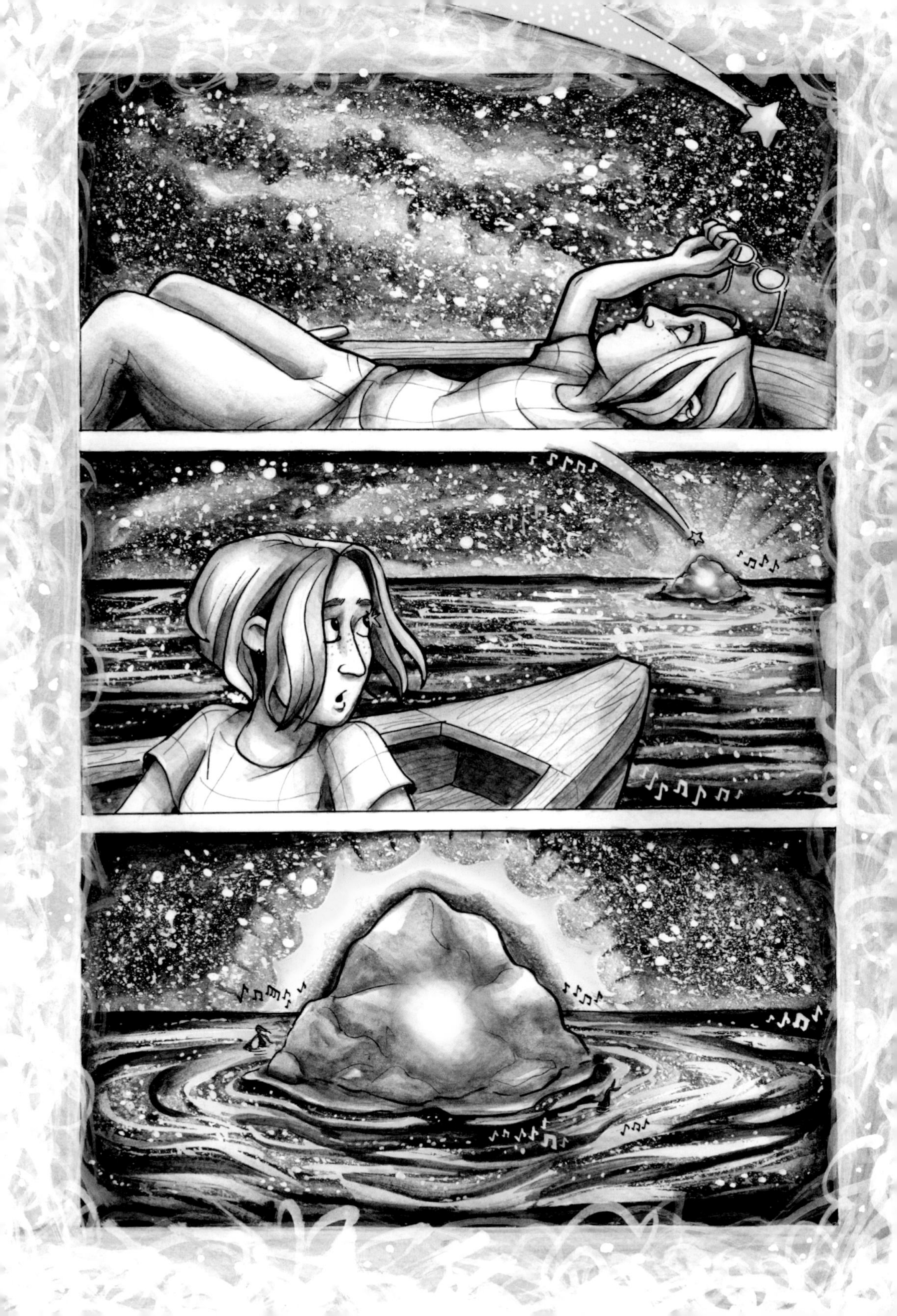

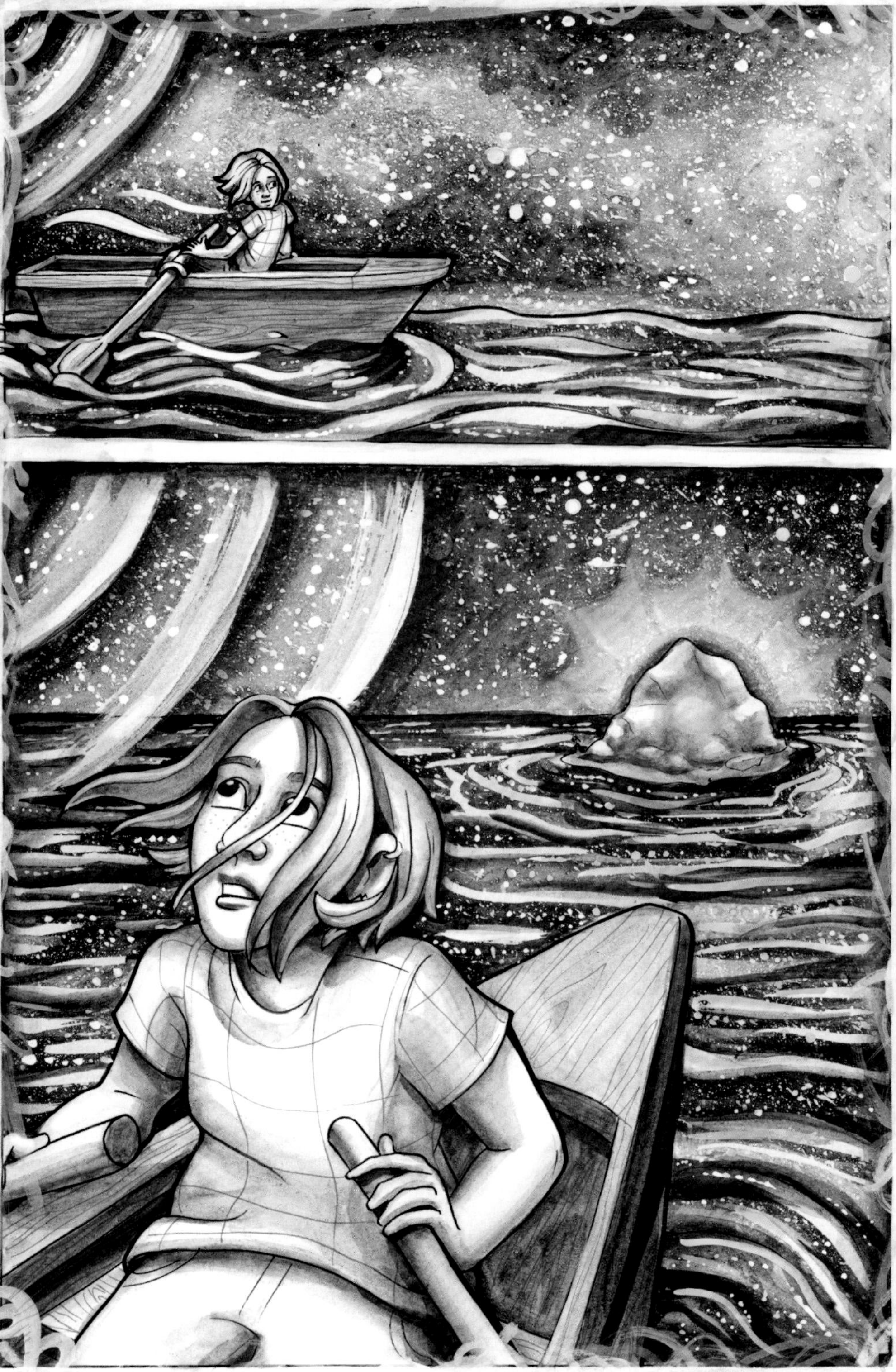

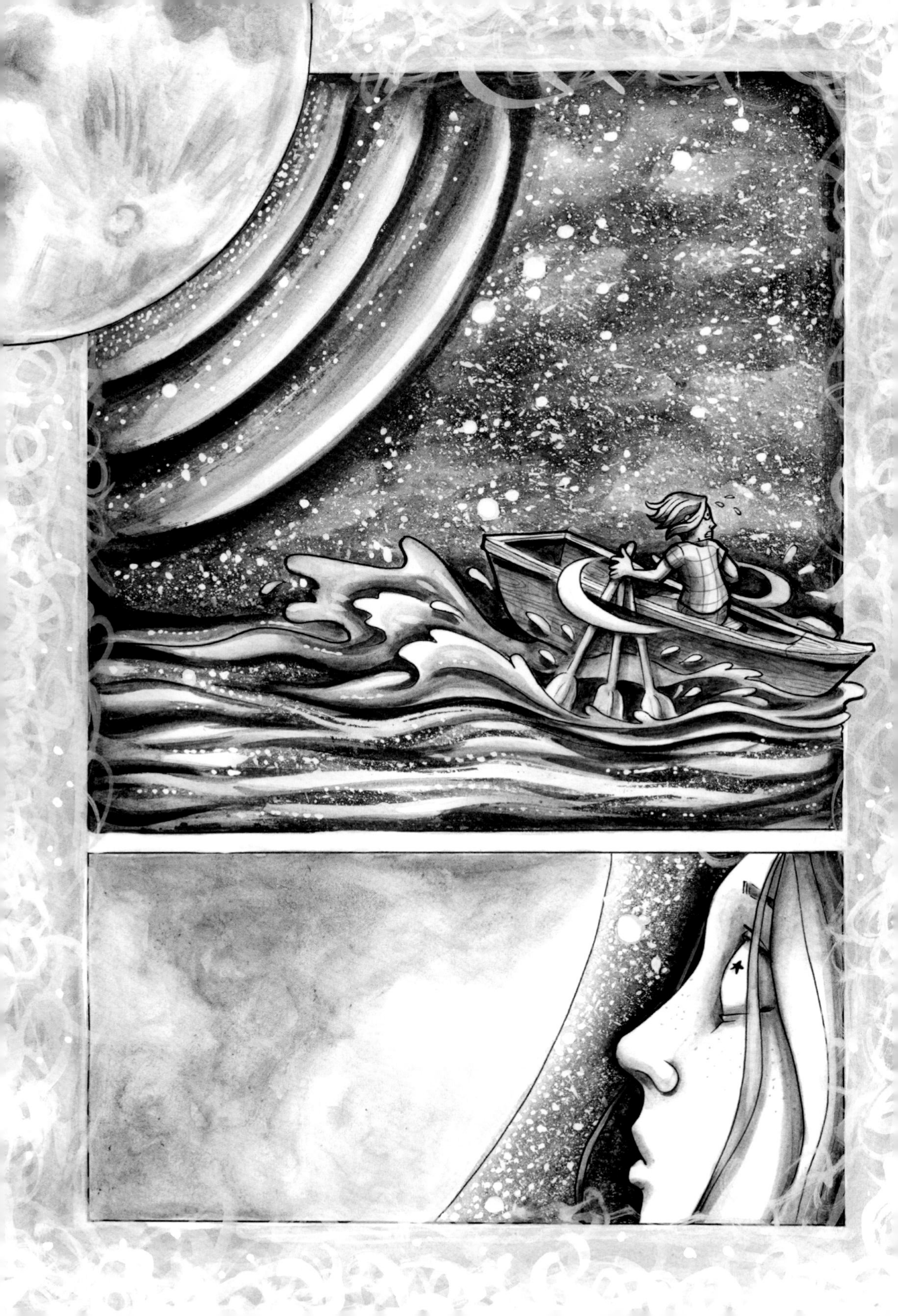

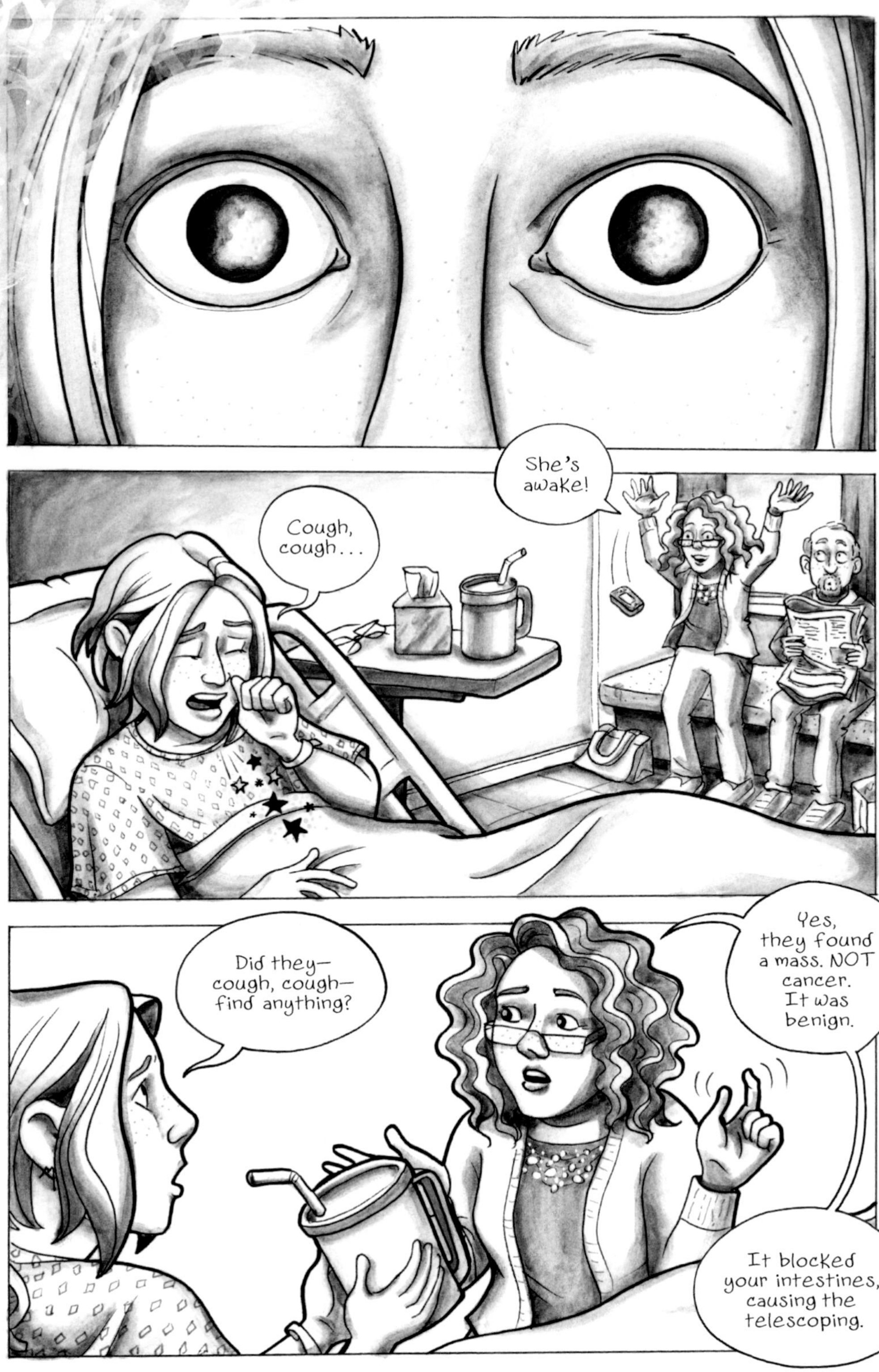

She's awake!
Cough, cough...
Did they—cough, cough—find anything?
Yes, they found a mass. NOT cancer. It was benign.
It blocked your intestines, causing the telescoping.

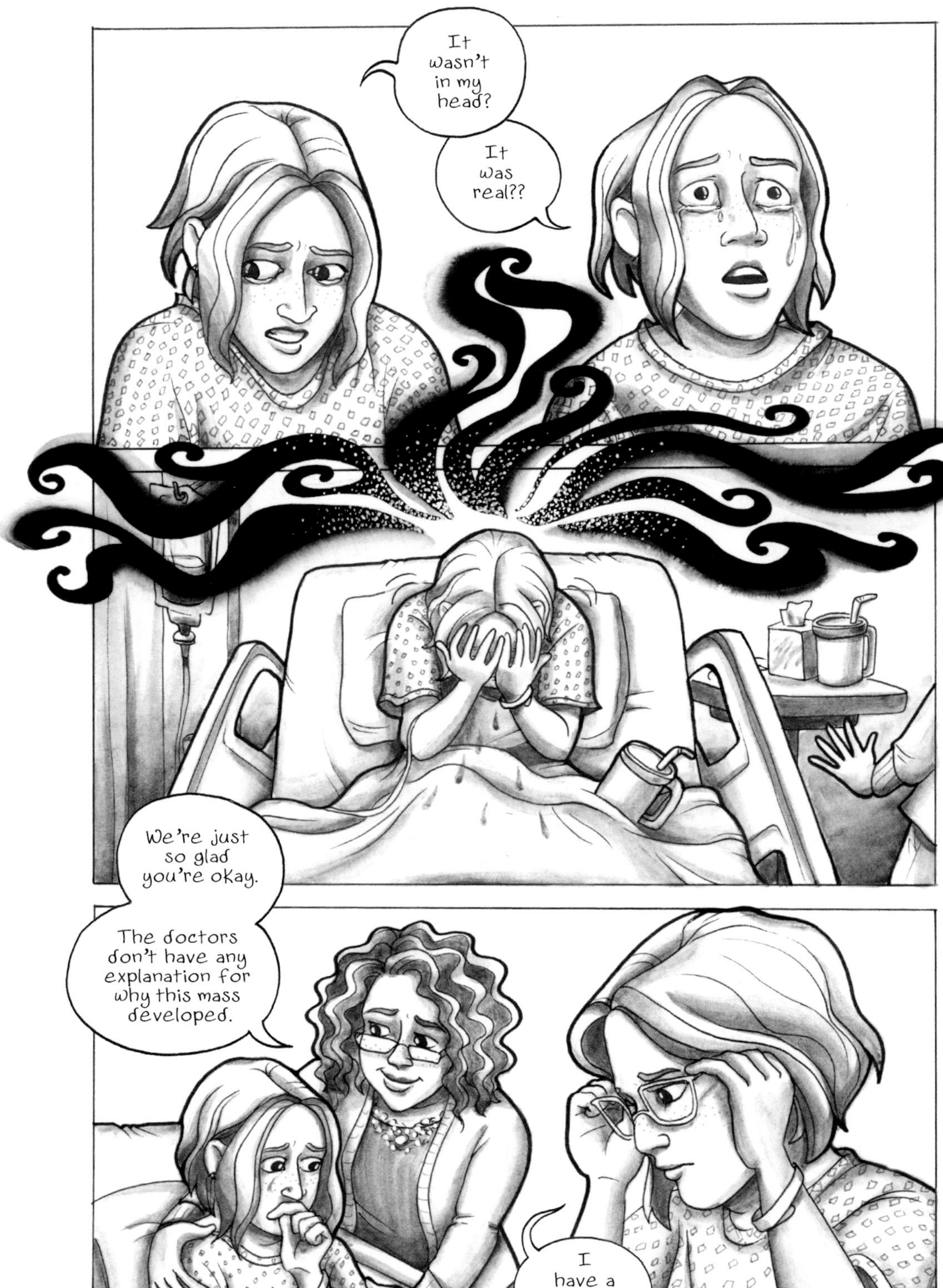
It wasn't in my head?
It was real??
We're just so glad you're okay.
The doctors don't have any explanation for why this mass developed.
I have a theory...

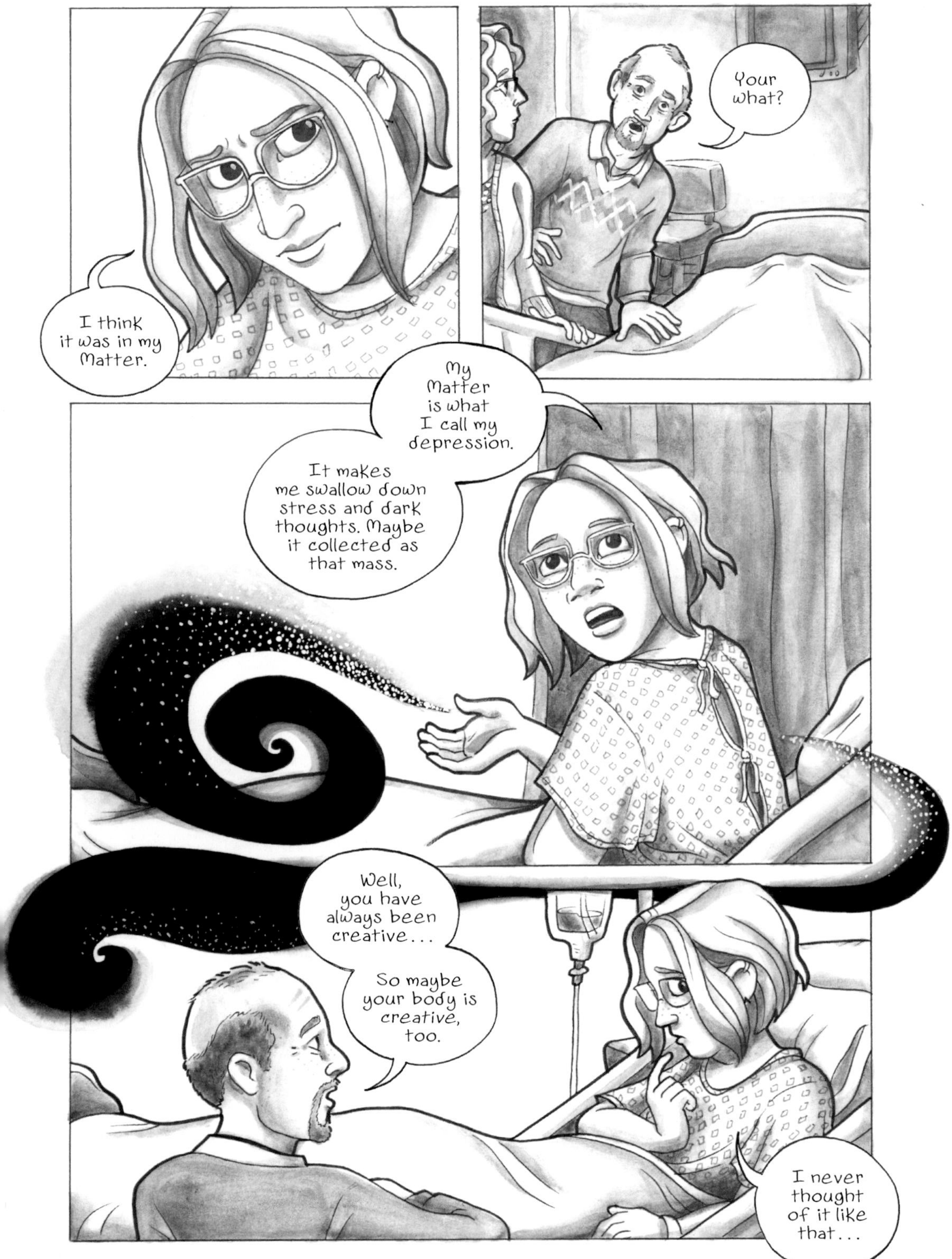
I think it was in my Matter.
Your what?
My Matter is what I call my depression.
It makes me swallow down stress and dark thoughts. Maybe it collected as that mass.
Well, you have always been creative...
So maybe your body is creative, too.
I never thought of it like that...

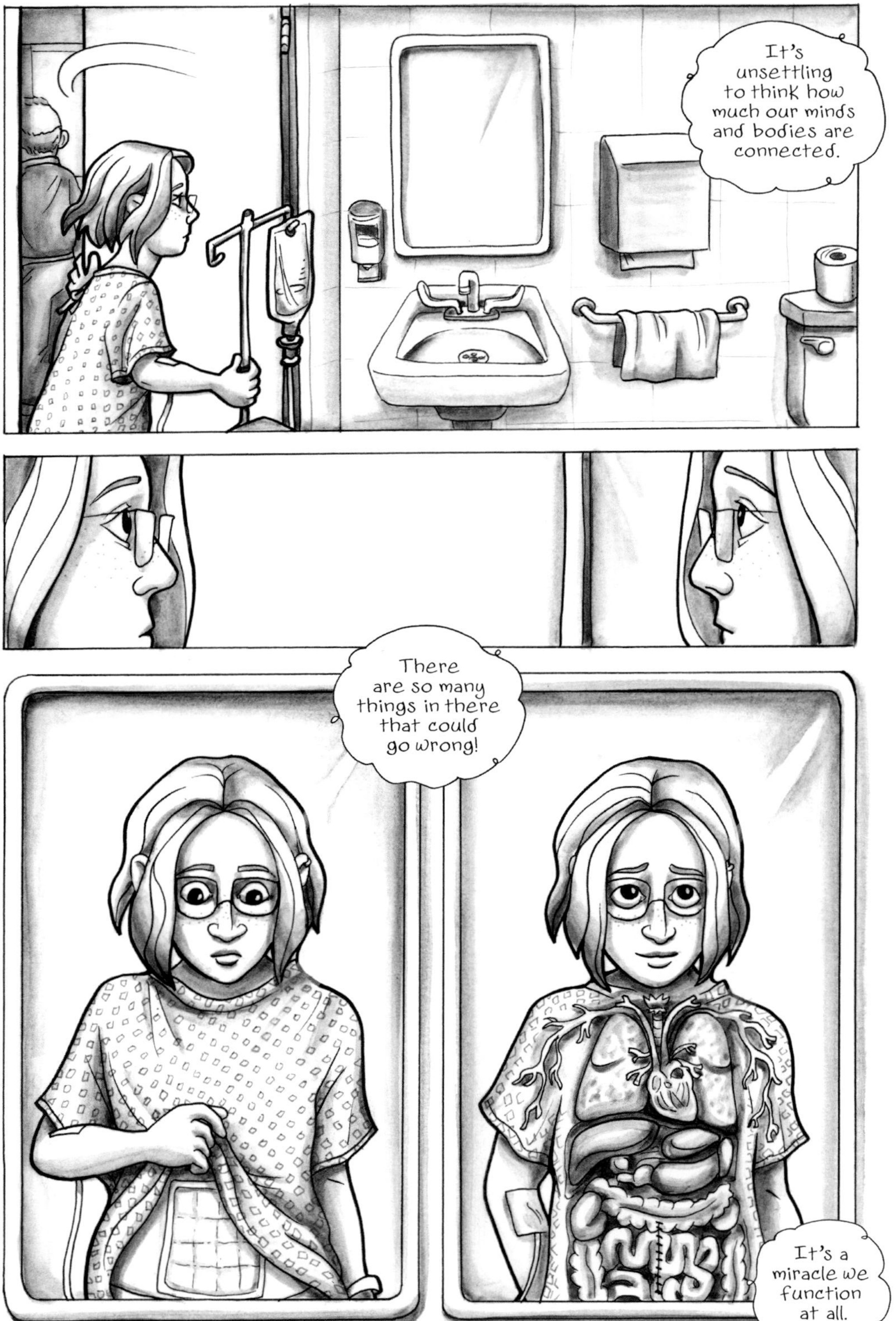
It's unsettling to think how much our minds and bodies are connected.
There are so many things in there that could go wrong!
It's a miracle we function at all.

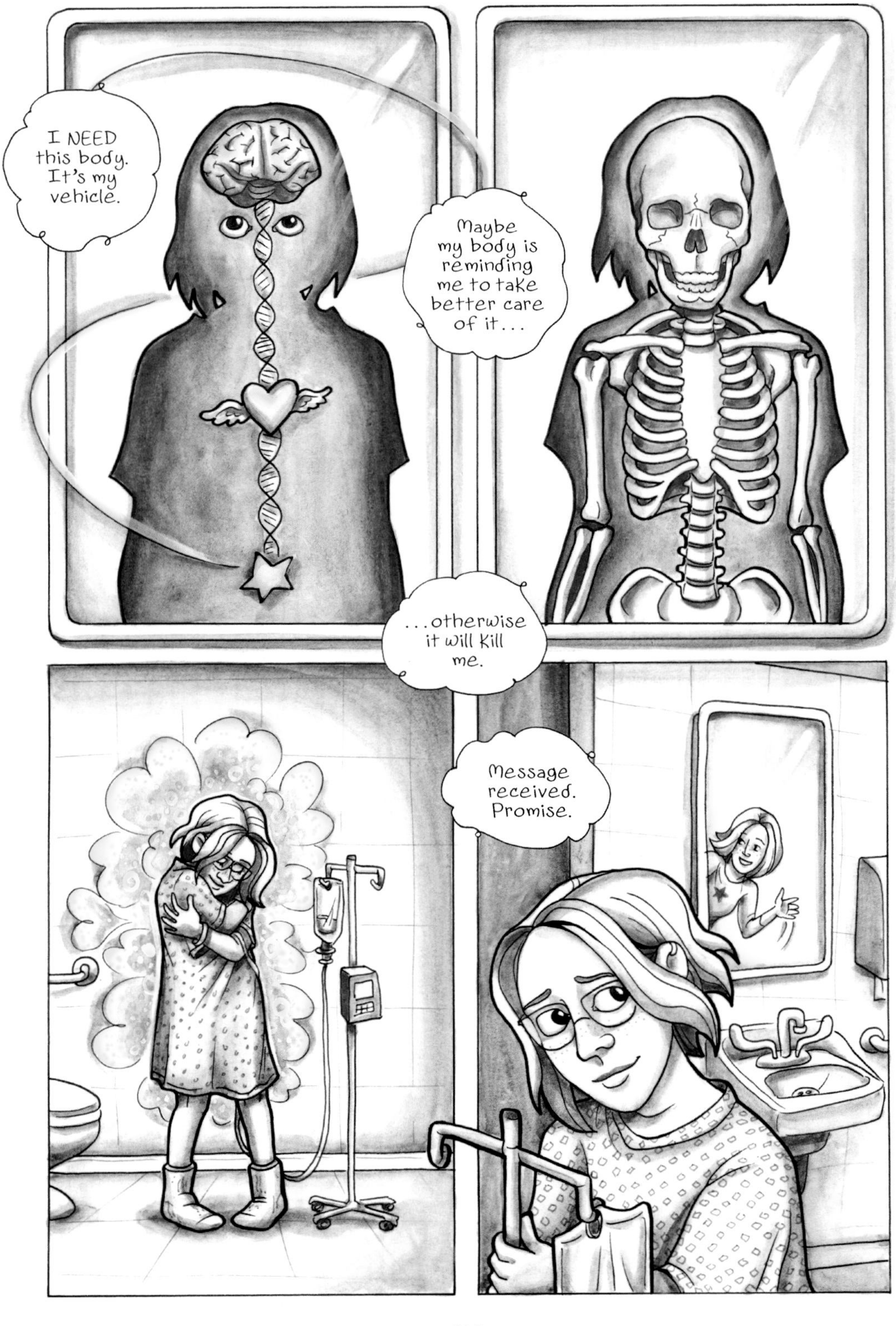
I NEED this body. It's my vehicle.
Maybe my body is reminding me to take better care of it...
...otherwise it will kill me.
Message received. Promise.

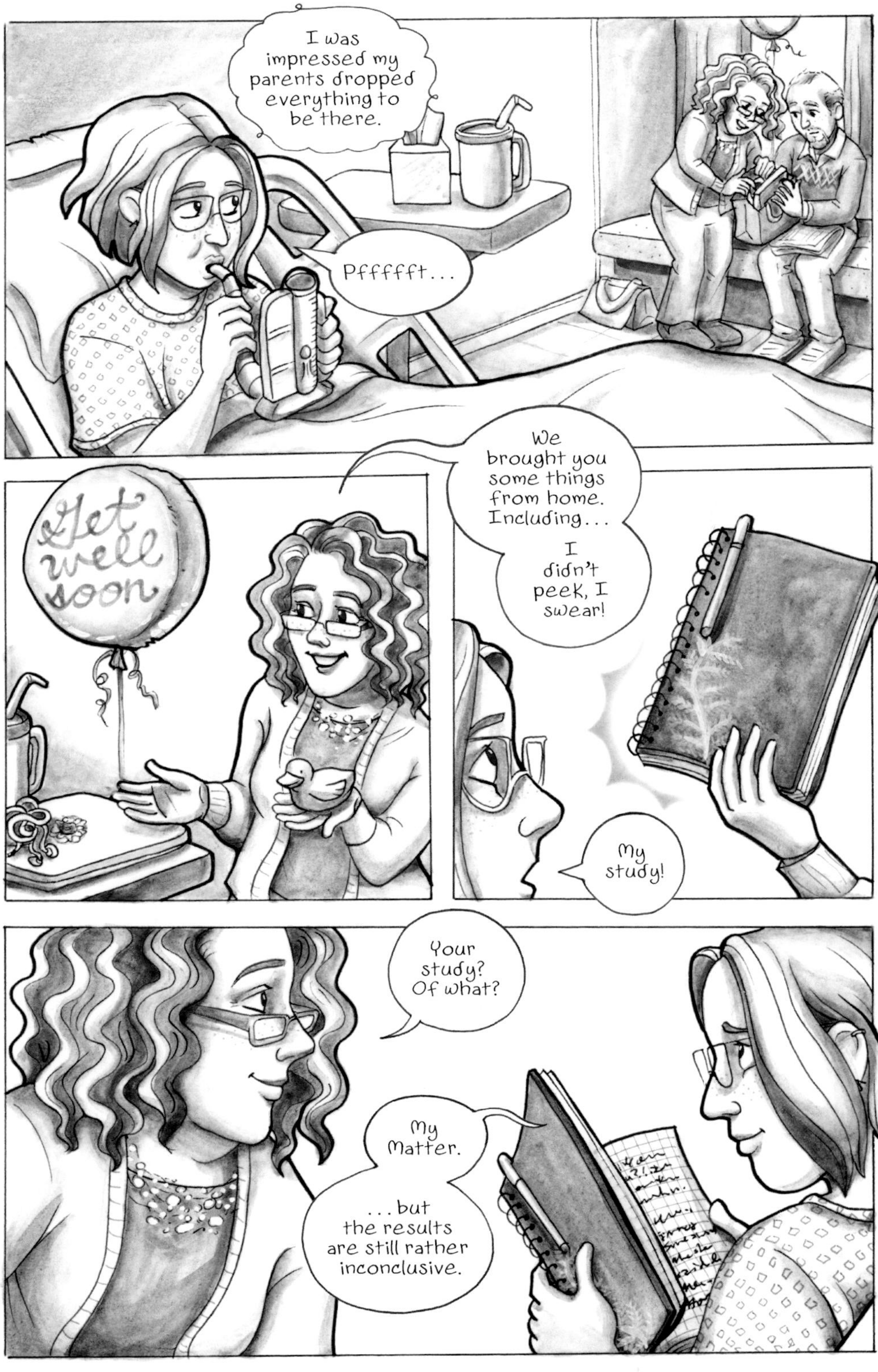
I was impressed my parents dropped everything to be there.
Pffffft...
We brought you some things from home. Including...
I didn't peek, I swear!
My study!
Your study? Of what?
My Matter.
...but the results are still rather inconclusive.
Get well soon

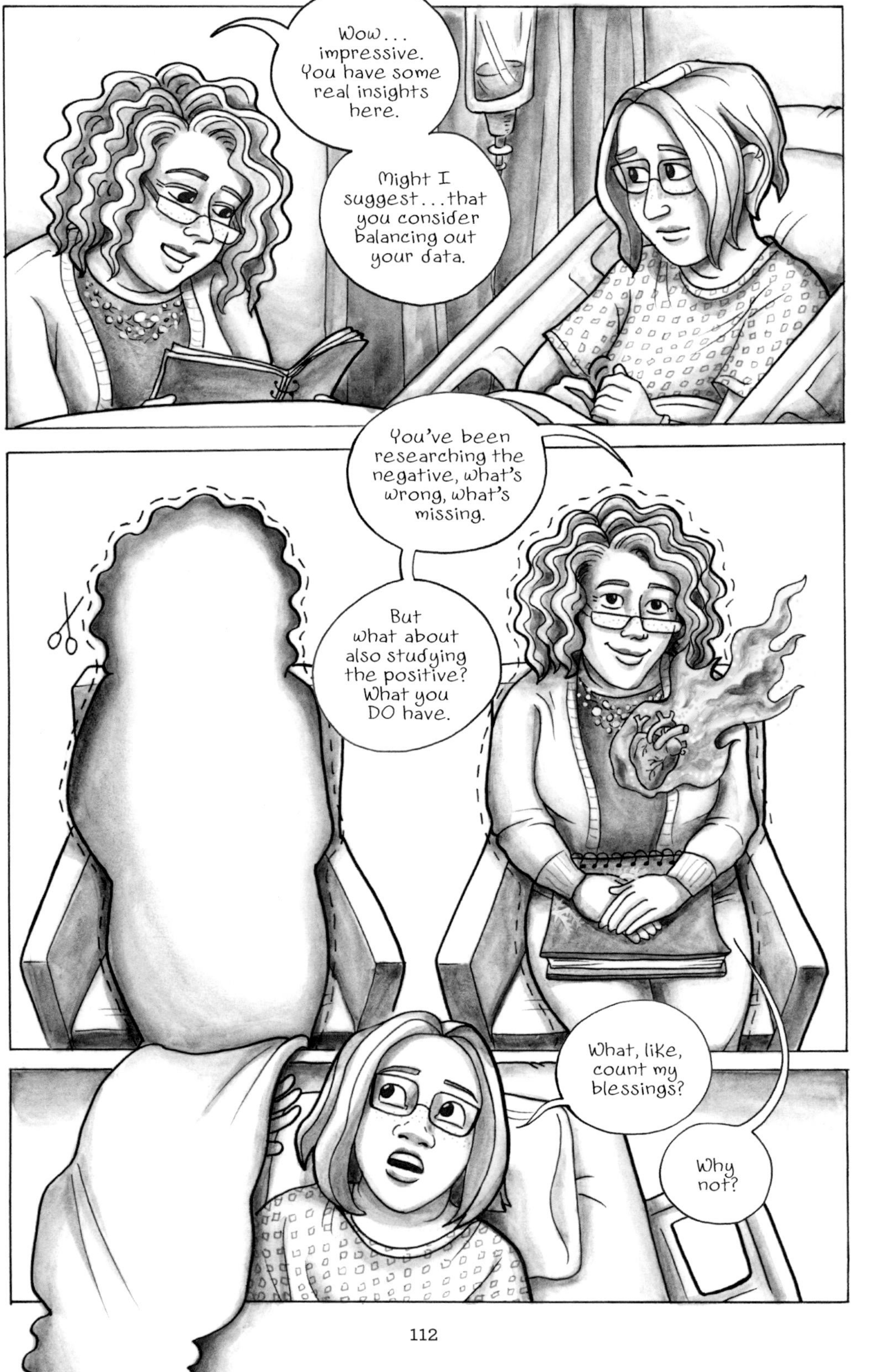
Wow... impressive. You have some real insights here.
Might I suggest...that you consider balancing out your data.
You've been researching the negative, what's wrong, what's missing.
But what about also studying the positive? What you DO have.
What, like, count my blessings?
Why not?

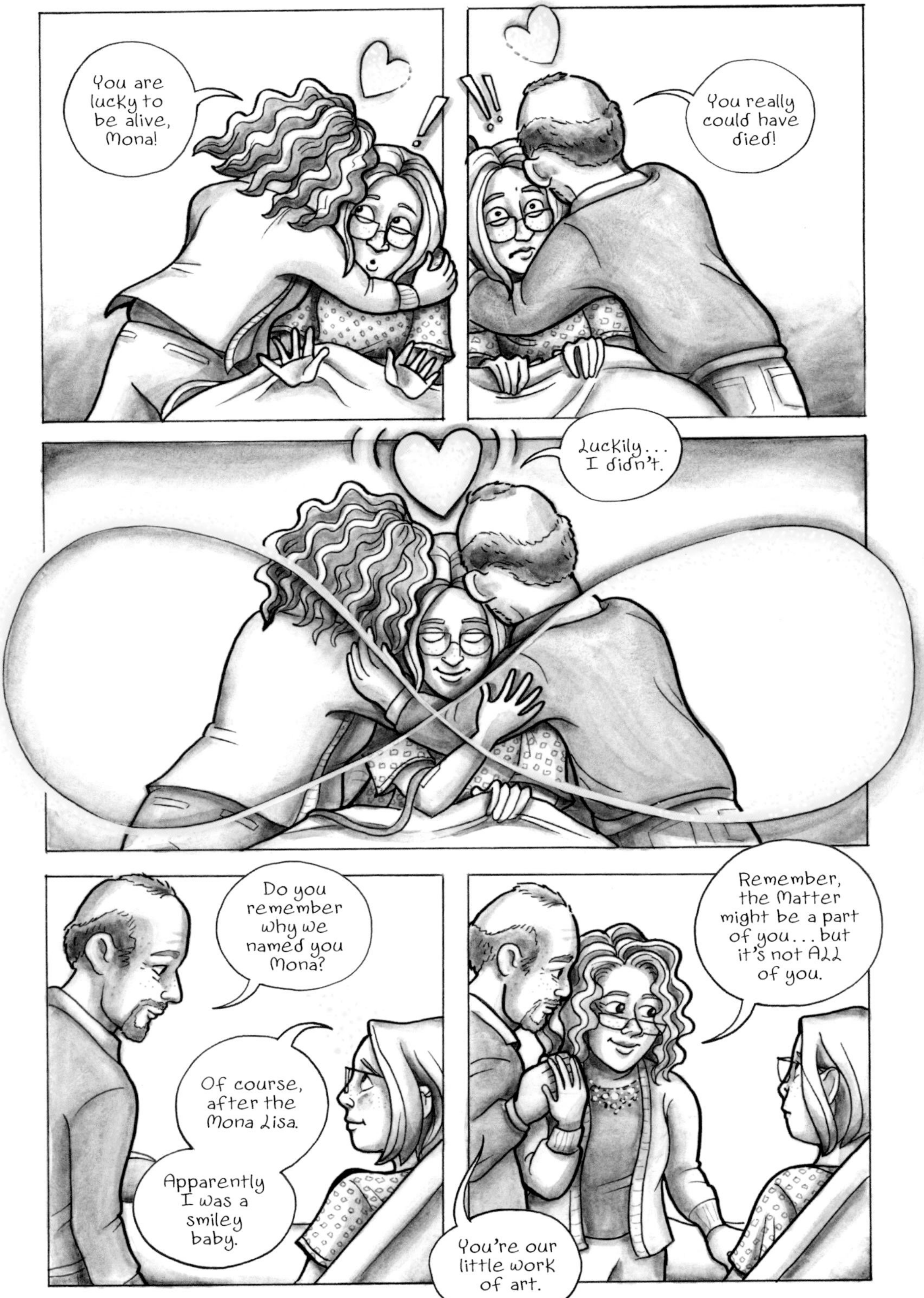
You are lucky to be alive, Mona!
!
!!
You really could have died!
Luckily... I didn't.
Do you remember why we named you Mona?
Of course, after the Mona Lisa.
Apparently I was a smiley baby.
Remember, the Matter might be a part of you... but it's not ALL of you.
You're our little work of art.

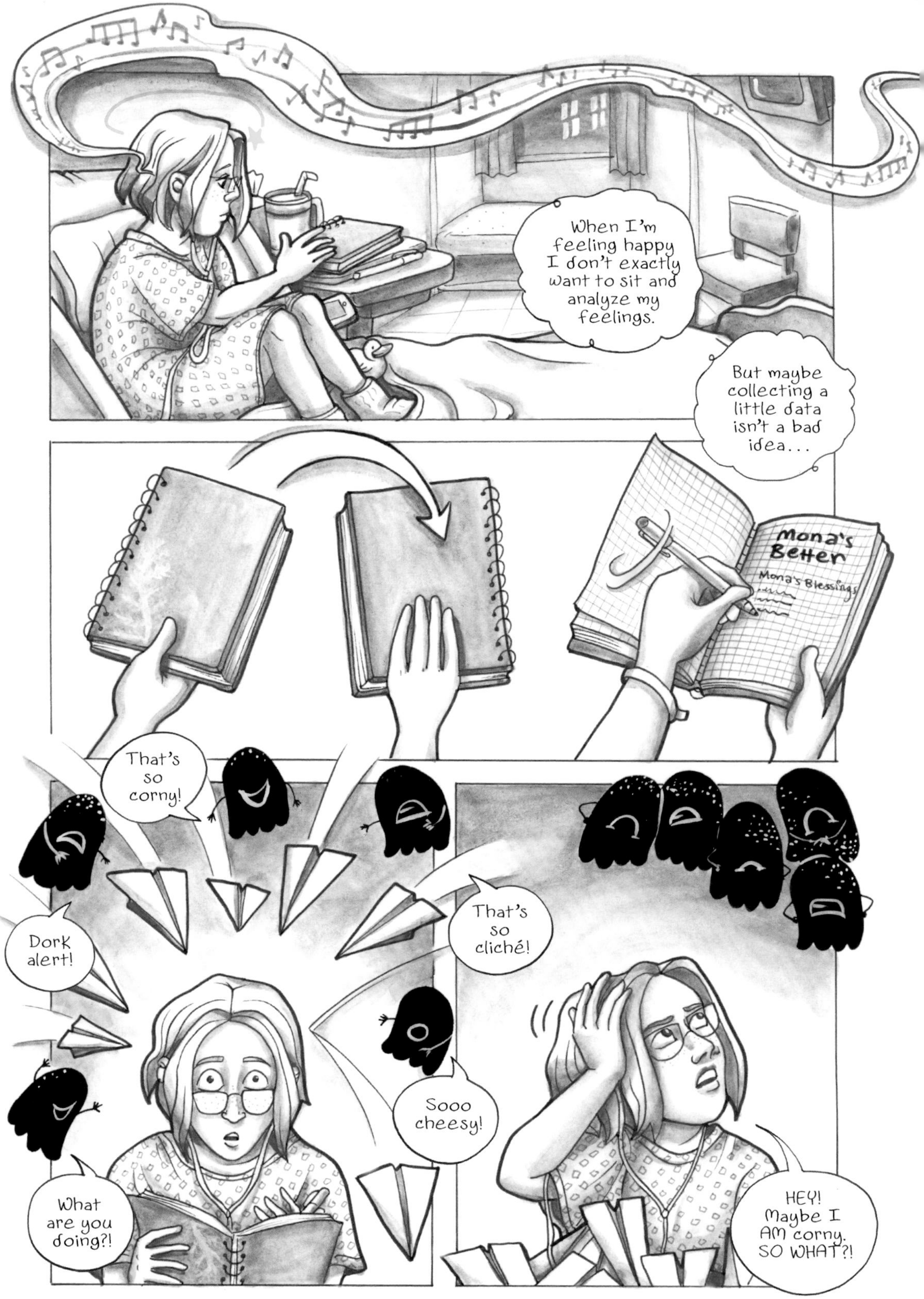
When I'm feeling happy I don't exactly want to sit and analyze my feelings.
But maybe collecting a little data isn't a bad idea...
Mona's Better
Mona's Blessings
That's so corny!
Dork alert!
That's so cliché!
Sooo cheesy!
What are you doing?!
HEY! Maybe I AM corny. SO WHAT?!

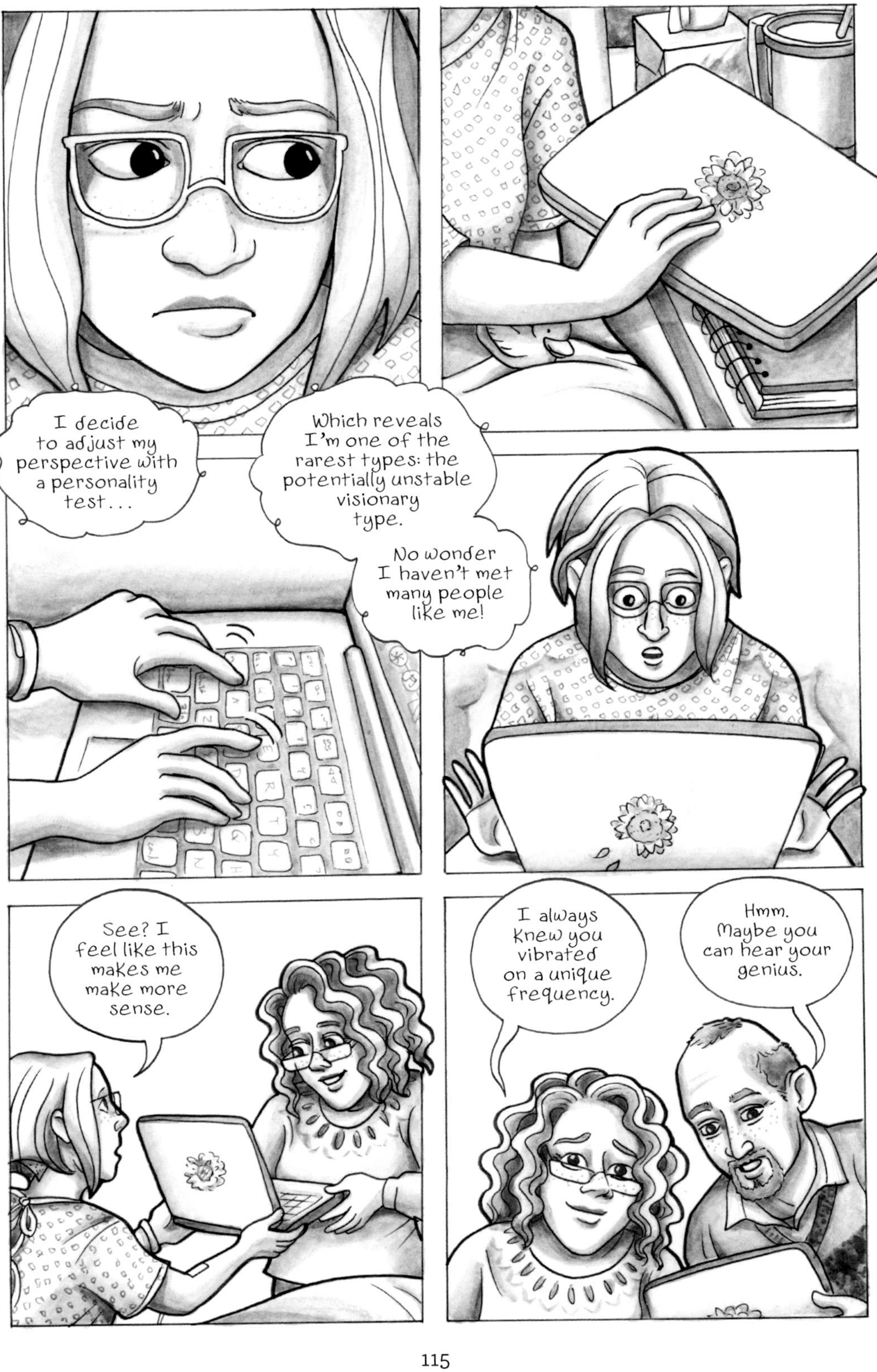
I decide to adjust my perspective with a personality test...
Which reveals I'm one of the rarest types: the potentially unstable visionary type.
No wonder I haven't met many people like me!
See? I feel like this makes me make more sense.
I always knew you vibrated on a unique frequency.
Hmm. Maybe you can hear your genius.

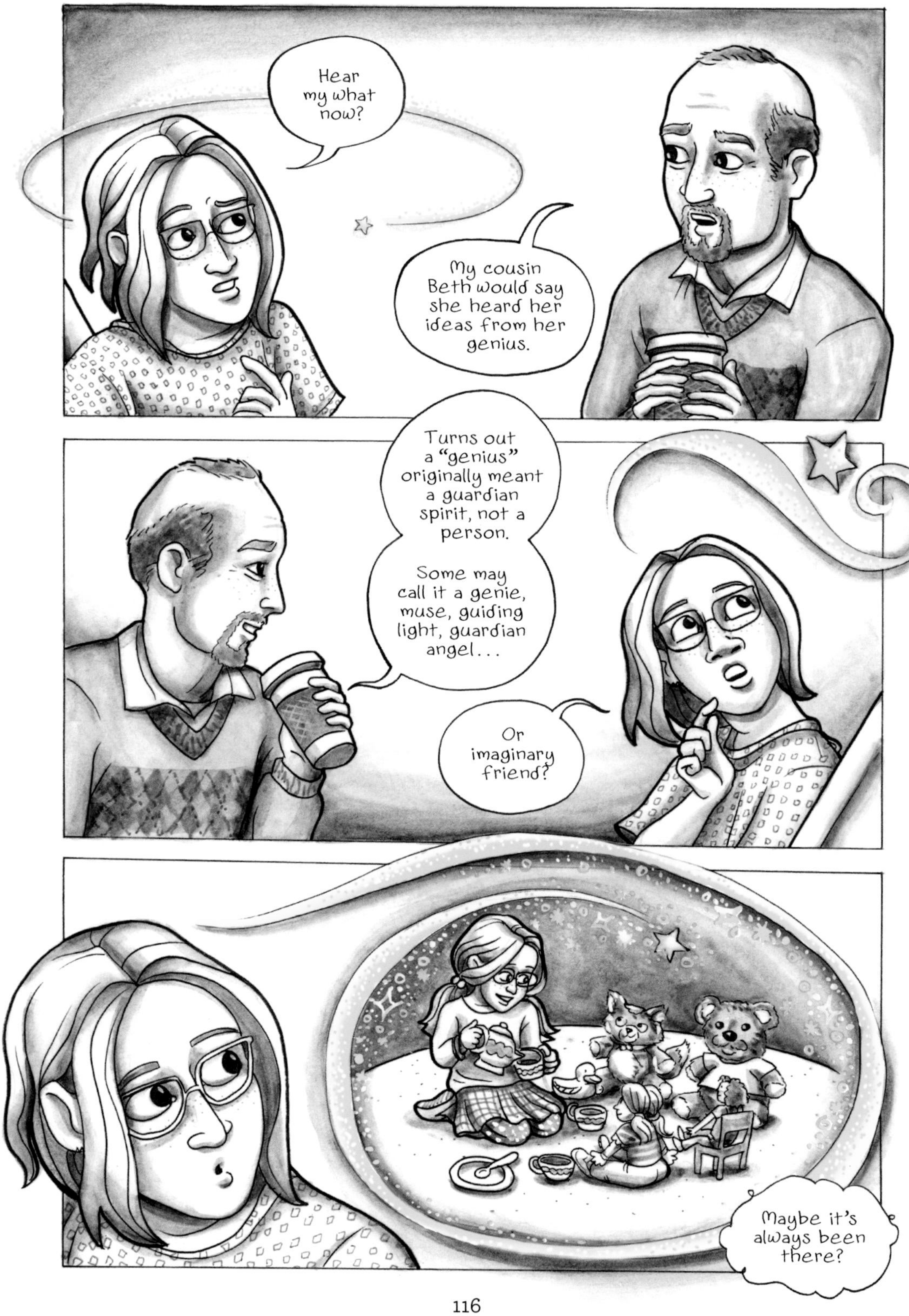
Hear my what now?
My cousin Beth would say she heard her ideas from her genius.
Turns out a "genius" originally meant a guardian spirit, not a person.
Some may call it a genie, muse, guiding light, guardian angel...
Or imaginary friend?
Maybe it's always been there?

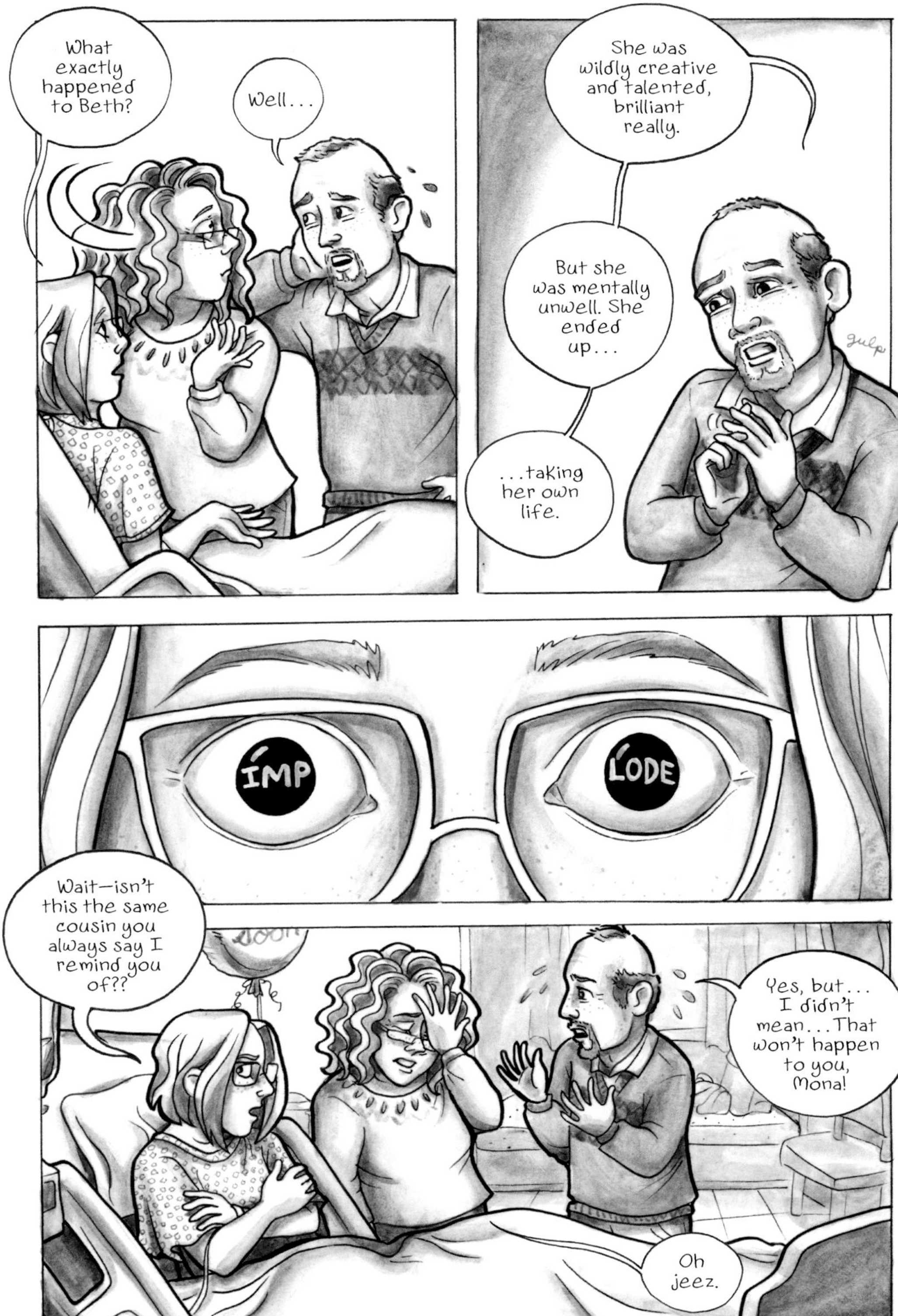
What exactly happened to Beth?
Well...
She was wildly creative and talented, brilliant really.
But she was mentally unwell. She ended up...
...taking her own life.
gulp
IMP
LODE
Wait—isn't this the same cousin you always say I remind you of??
Yes, but... I didn't mean... That won't happen to you, Mona!
Oh jeez.

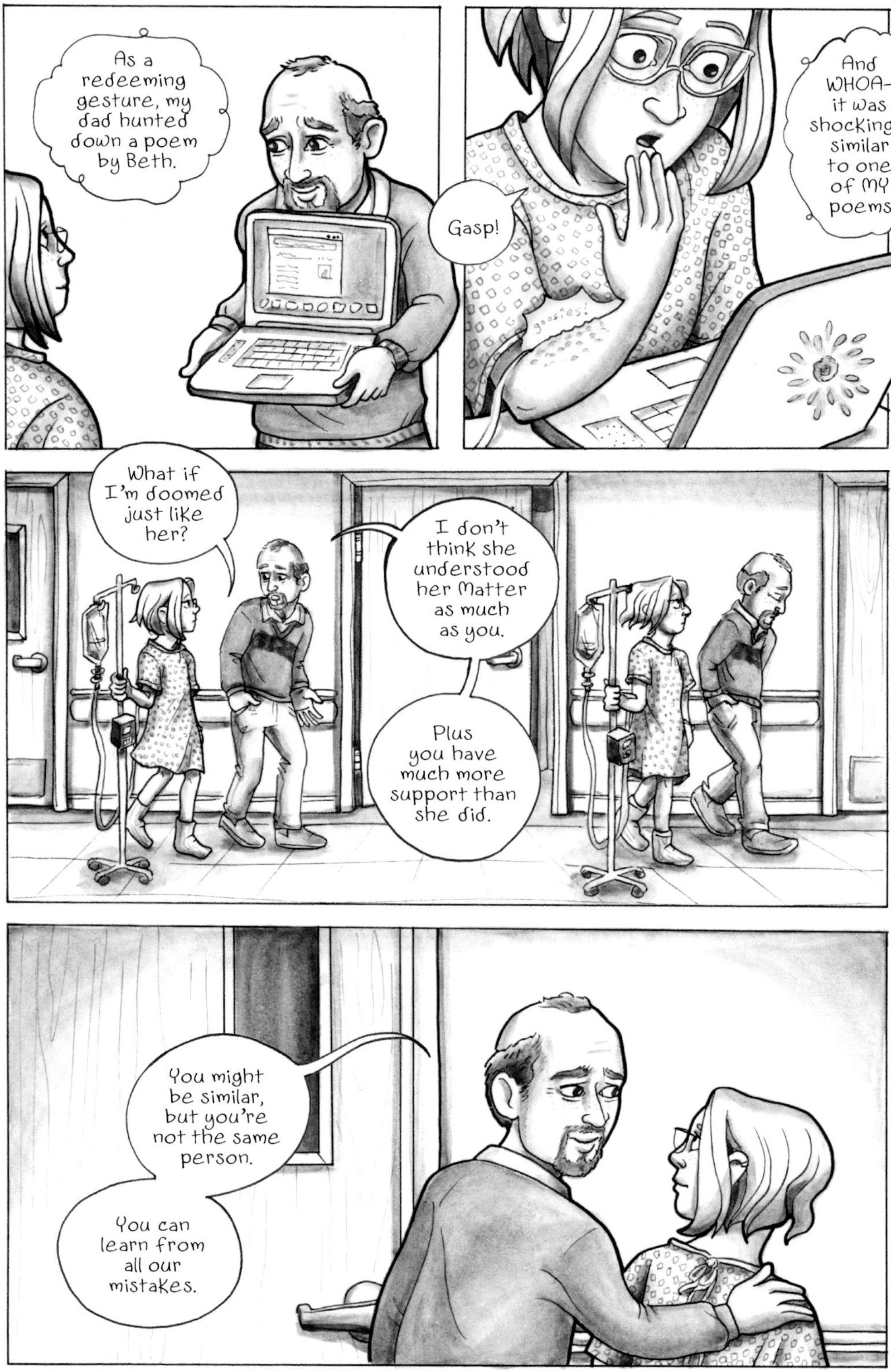
As a redeeming gesture, my dad hunted down a poem by Beth.
Gasp!
And WHOA— it was shockingly similar to one of MY poems.
goosies!
What if I'm doomed just like her?
I don't think she understood her Matter as much as you.
Plus you have much more support than she did.
You might be similar, but you're not the same person.
You can learn from all our mistakes.

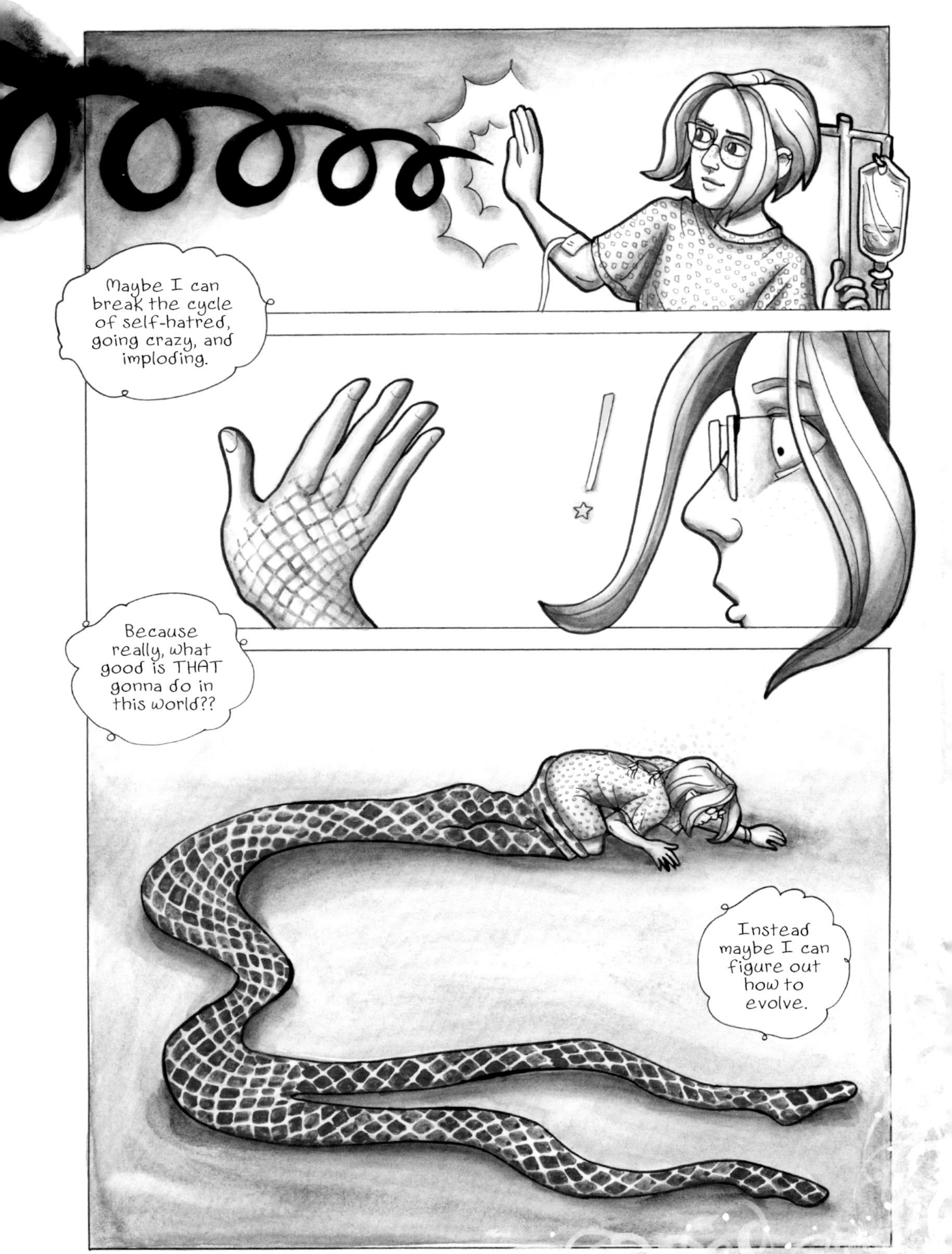
Maybe I can break the cycle of self-hatred, going crazy, and imploding.
Because really, what good is THAT gonna do in this world??
Instead maybe I can figure out how to evolve.

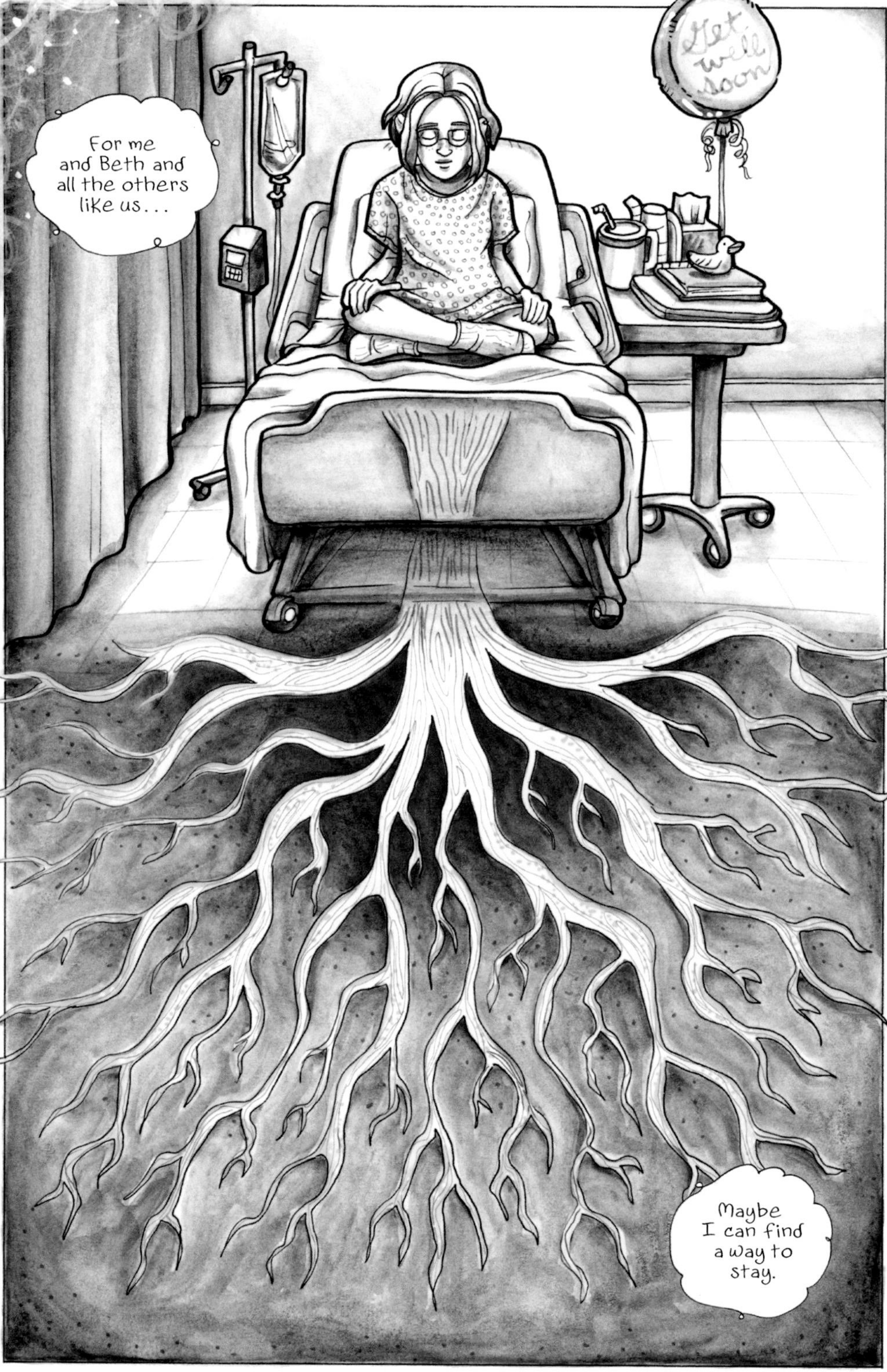
For me and Beth and all the others like us...
Get well soon
Maybe I can find a way to stay.

Turn emotion into action

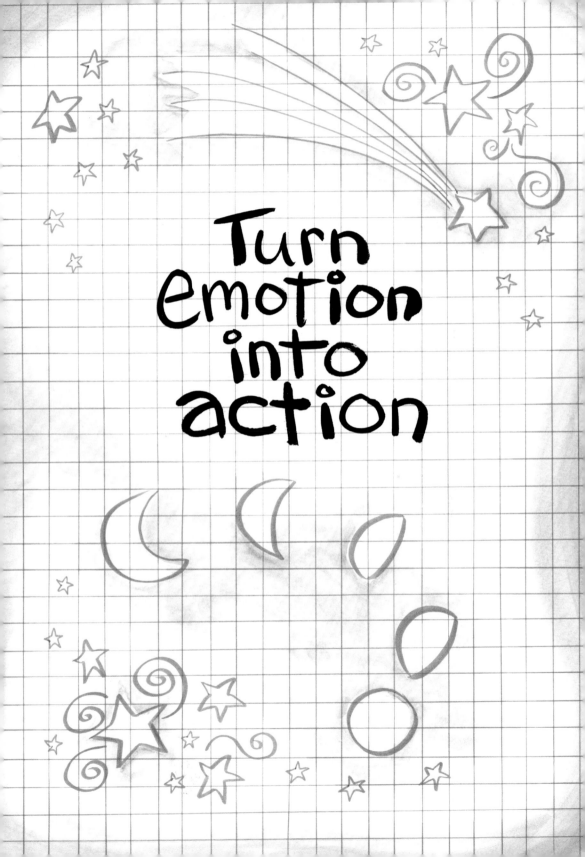

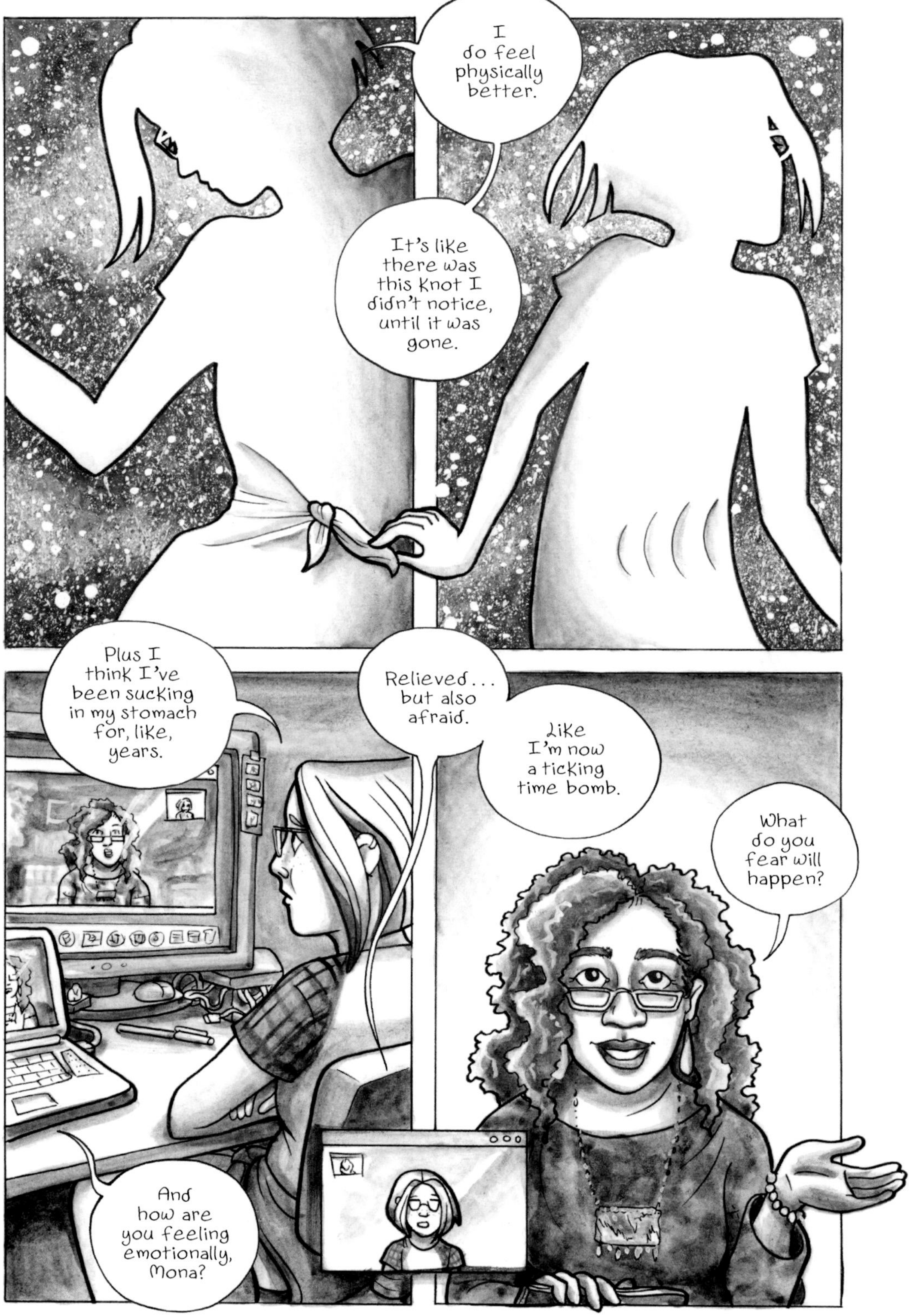
I do feel physically better.
It's like there was this knot I didn't notice, until it was gone.
Plus I think I've been sucking in my stomach for, like, years.
And how are you feeling emotionally, Mona?
Relieved . . . but also afraid.
Like I'm now a ticking time bomb.
What do you fear will happen?

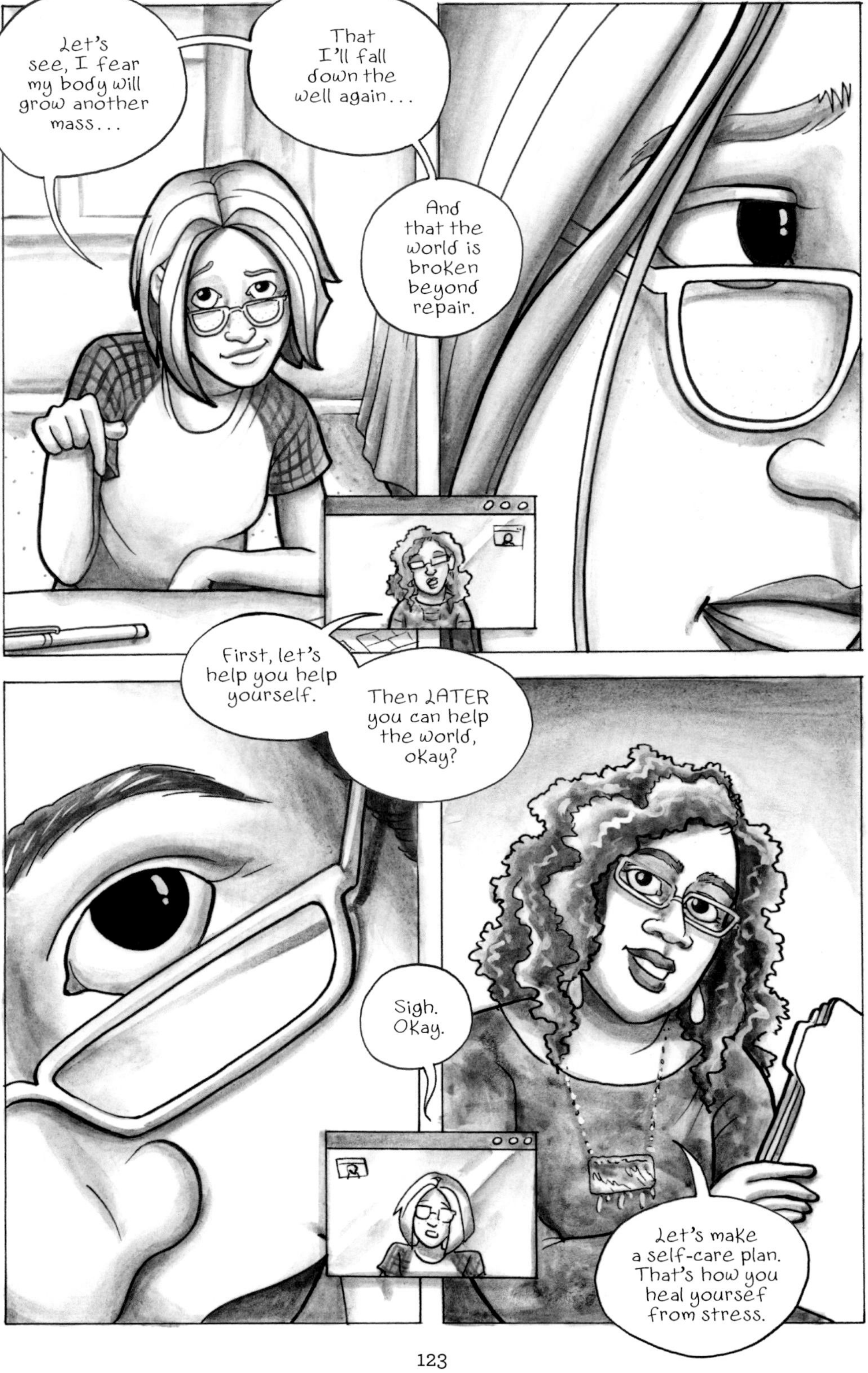
Let's see, I fear my body will grow another mass...
That I'll fall down the well again...
And that the world is broken beyond repair.
First, let's help you help yourself.
Then LATER you can help the world, okay?
Sigh. Okay.
Let's make a self-care plan. That's how you heal yoursef from stress.

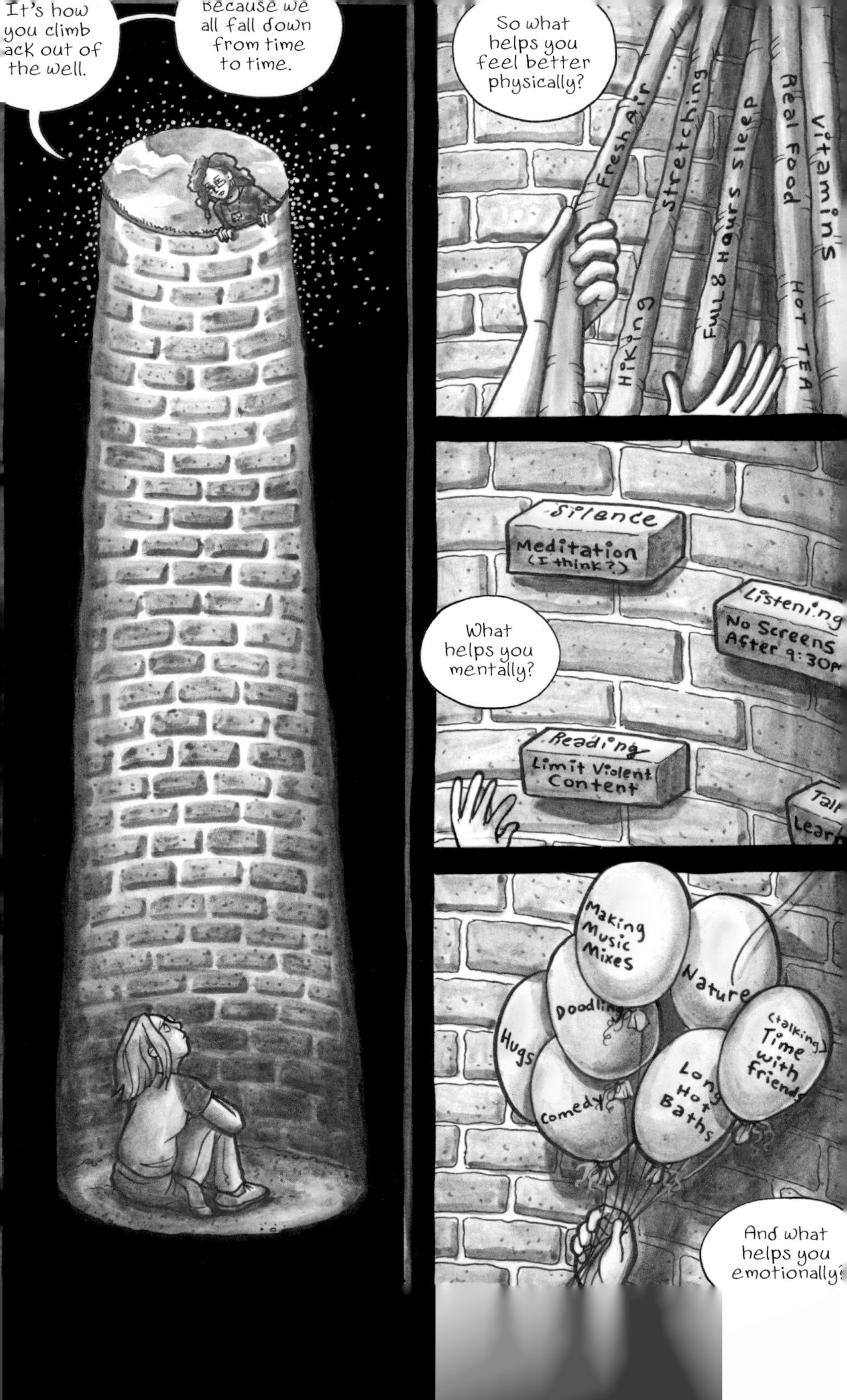

It's how you climb ack out of the well.
Because we all fall down from time to time.
So what helps you feel better physically?
Fresh Air
Stretching
Real Food
Vitamins
Full 8 Hours Sleep
Hiking
Hot Tea
Silence
Meditation (I think?)
Listening
No Screens After 9:30
What helps you mentally?
Reading
Limit Violent Content
Making Music Mixes
Nature
Doodling
Hugs
(talking) Time with friends
Long Hot Baths
Comedy
And what helps you emotionally?

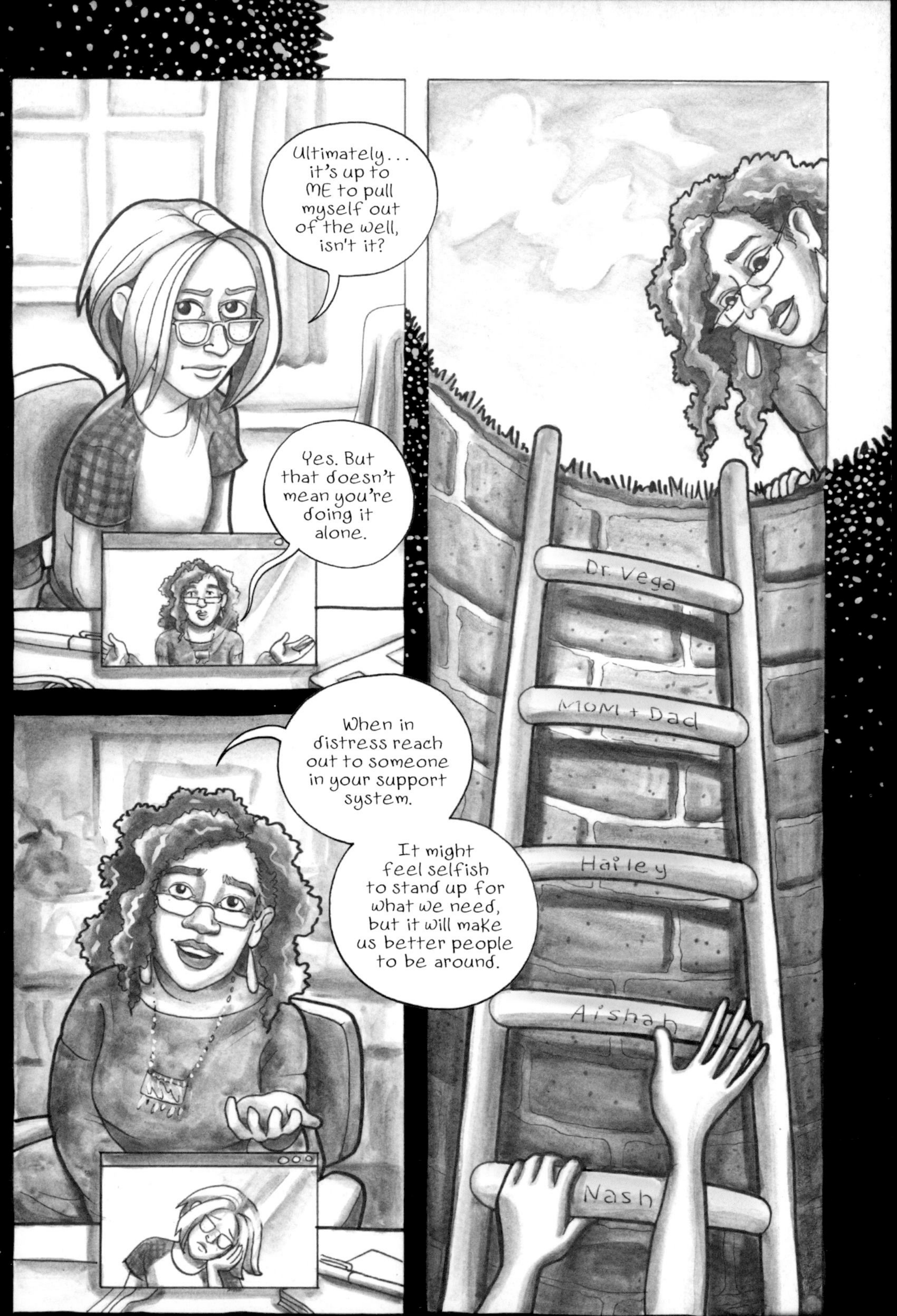

Ultimately... it's up to ME to pull myself out of the well, isn't it?
Yes. But that doesn't mean you're doing it alone.
When in distress reach out to someone in your support system.
It might feel selfish to stand up for what we need, but it will make us better people to be around.
Dr. Vega
MOM + Dad
Hailey
Aishah
Nash

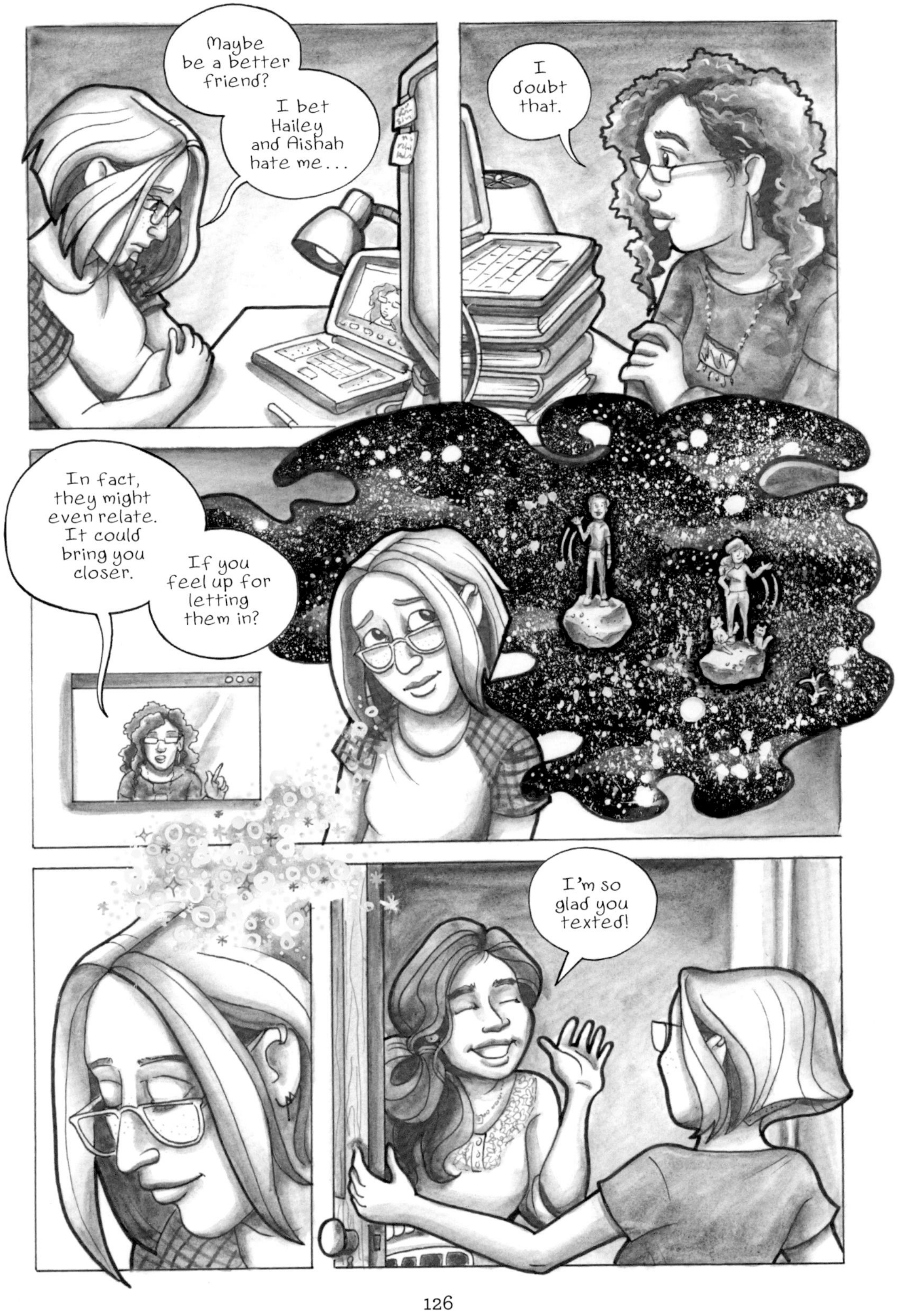
Maybe be a better friend?
I bet Hailey and Aishah hate me...
I doubt that.
In fact, they might even relate. It could bring you closer.
If you feel up for letting them in?
I'm so glad you texted!

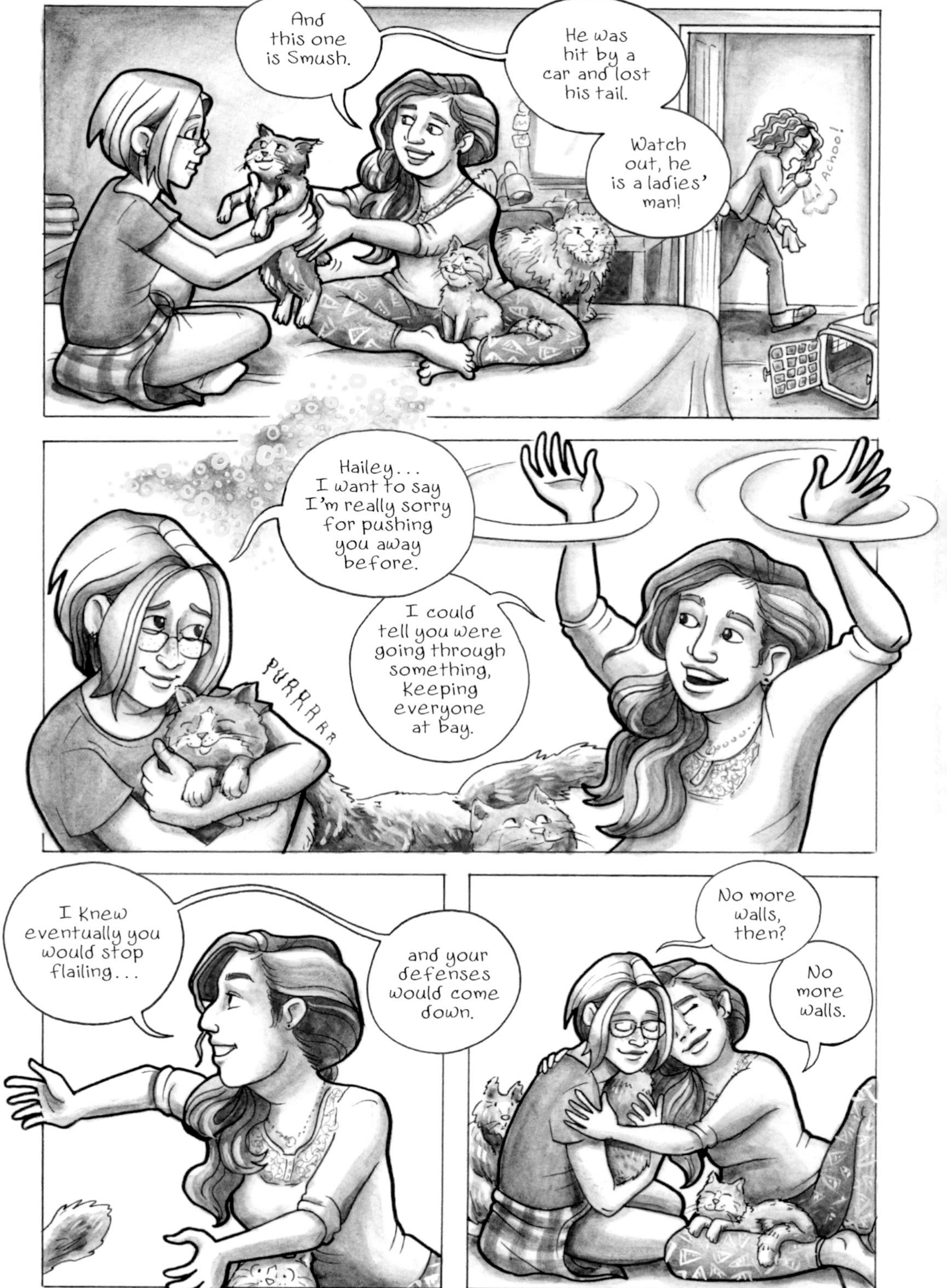
And this one is Smush.
He was hit by a car and lost his tail.
Watch out, he is a ladies' man!
Achoo!
Hailey... I want to say I'm really sorry for pushing you away before.
PURRRRRR
I could tell you were going through something, keeping everyone at bay.
I knew eventually you would stop flailing...
and your defenses would come down.
No more walls, then?
No more walls.

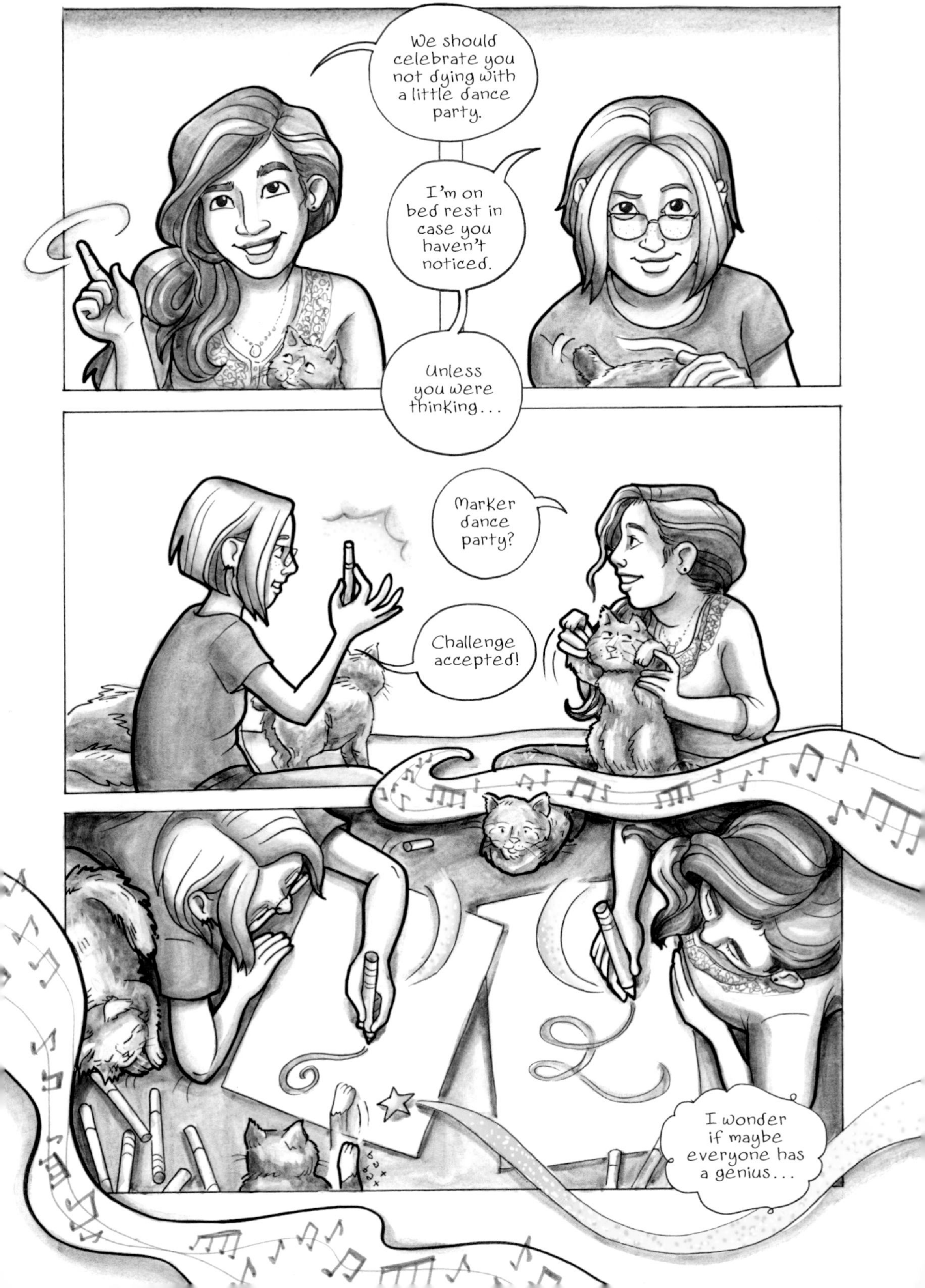
We should celebrate you not dying with a little dance party.
I'm on bed rest in case you haven't noticed.
Unless you were thinking...
Marker dance party?
Challenge accepted!
I wonder if maybe everyone has a genius...

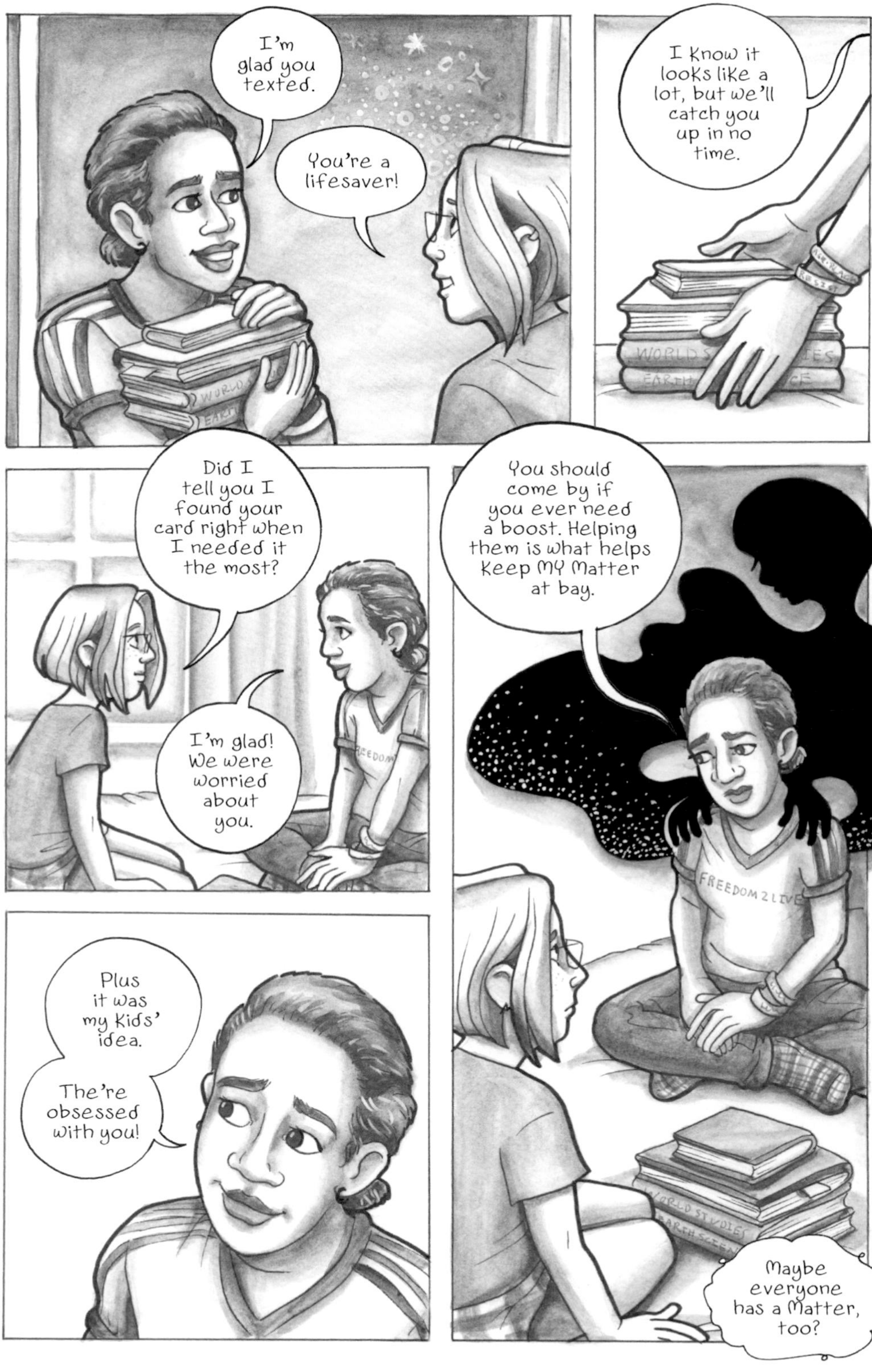
I'm glad you texted.
You're a lifesaver!
I know it looks like a lot, but we'll catch you up in no time.
Did I tell you I found your card right when I needed it the most?
I'm glad! We were worried about you.
You should come by if you ever need a boost. Helping them is what helps keep MY Matter at bay.
FREEDOM 2 LIVE
Plus it was my kids' idea.
The're obsessed with you!
Maybe everyone has a Matter, too?

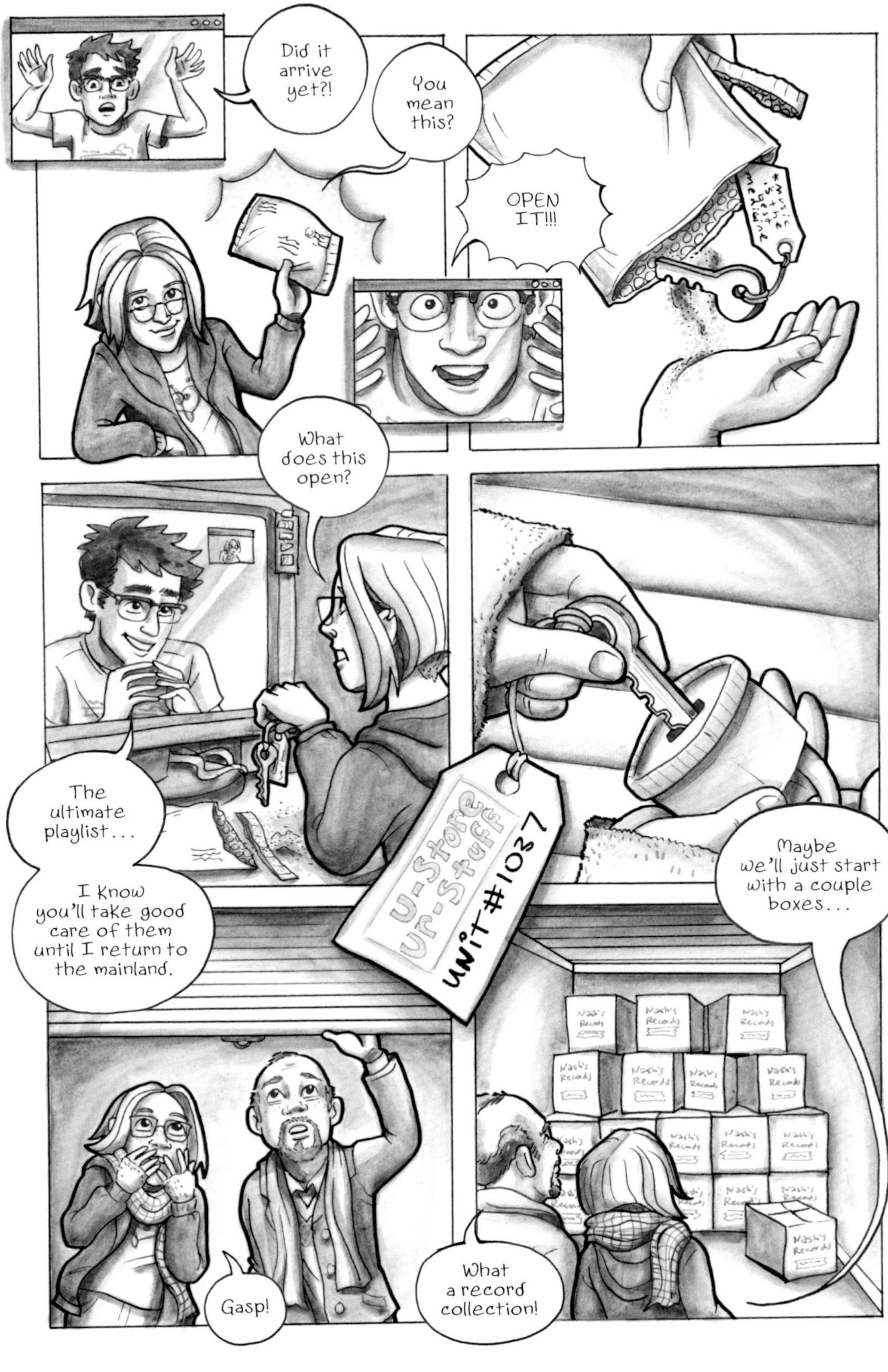

Did it arrive yet?!
You mean this?
OPEN IT!!!
Music is the best medicine
What does this open?
The ultimate playlist...
I know you'll take good care of them until I return to the mainland.
U-Store Ur-Stuff
UNIT #1037
Maybe we'll just start with a couple boxes...
Gasp!
What a record collection!

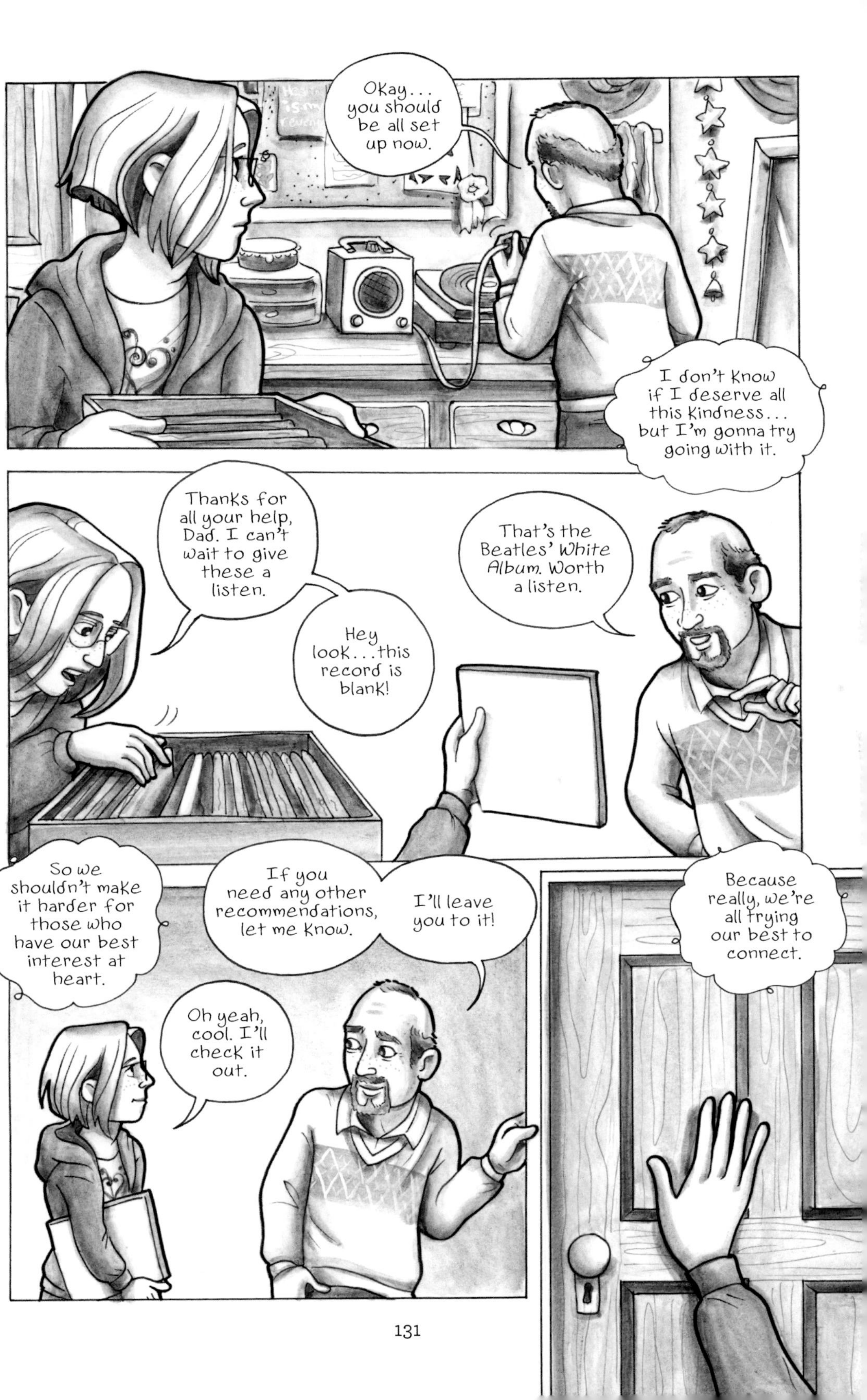
Okay... you should be all set up now.
I don't know if I deserve all this kindness... but I'm gonna try going with it.
Thanks for all your help, Dad. I can't wait to give these a listen.
Hey look...this record is blank!
That's the Beatles' White Album. Worth a listen.
So we shouldn't make it harder for those who have our best interest at heart.
If you need any other recommendations, let me know.
I'll leave you to it!
Oh yeah, cool. I'll check it out.
Because really, we're all trying our best to connect.

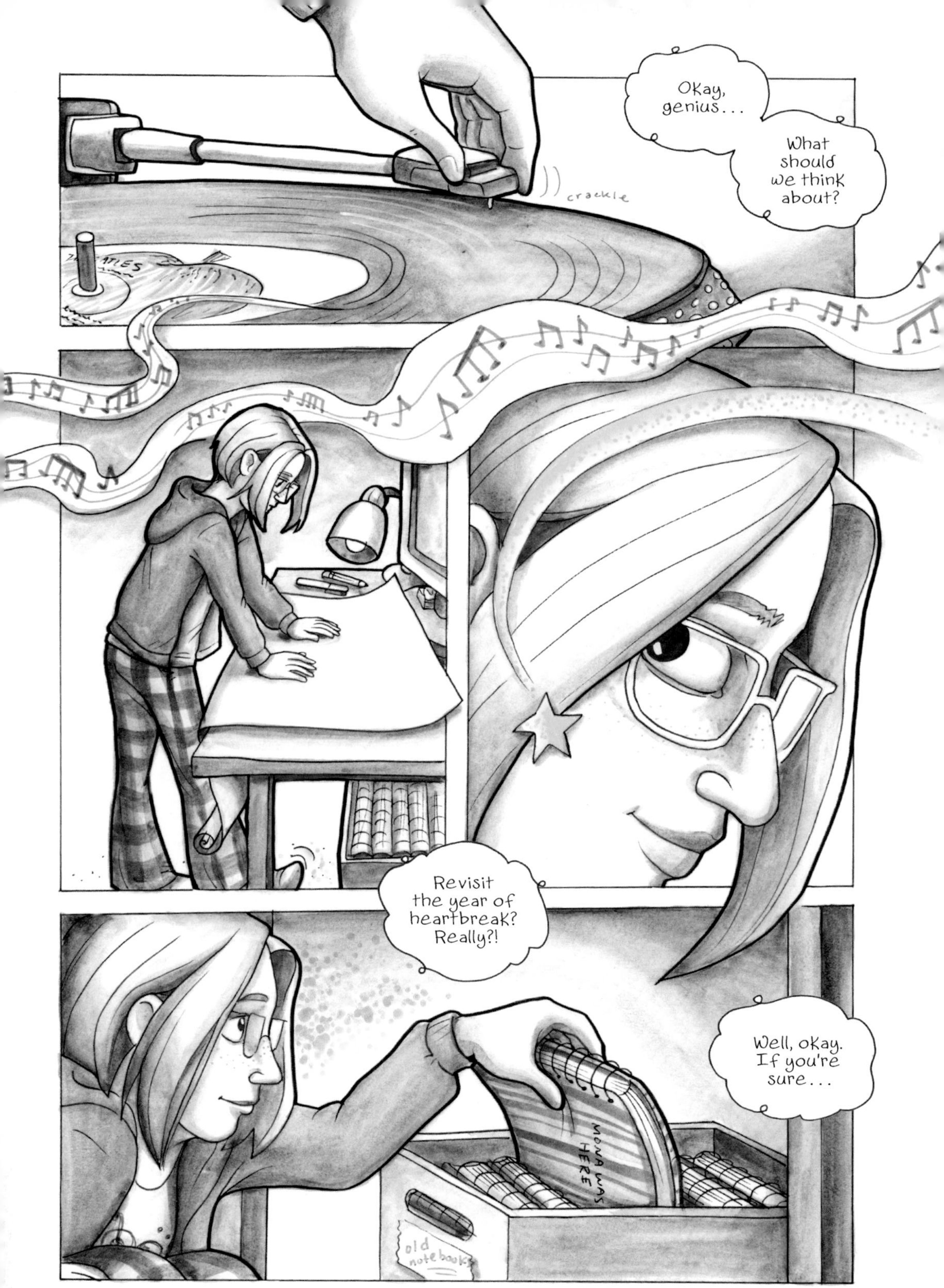
Okay, genius...
What should we think about?
crackle
Revisit the year of heartbreak? Really?!
Well, okay. If you're sure...
MONA WAS HERE
old notebooks

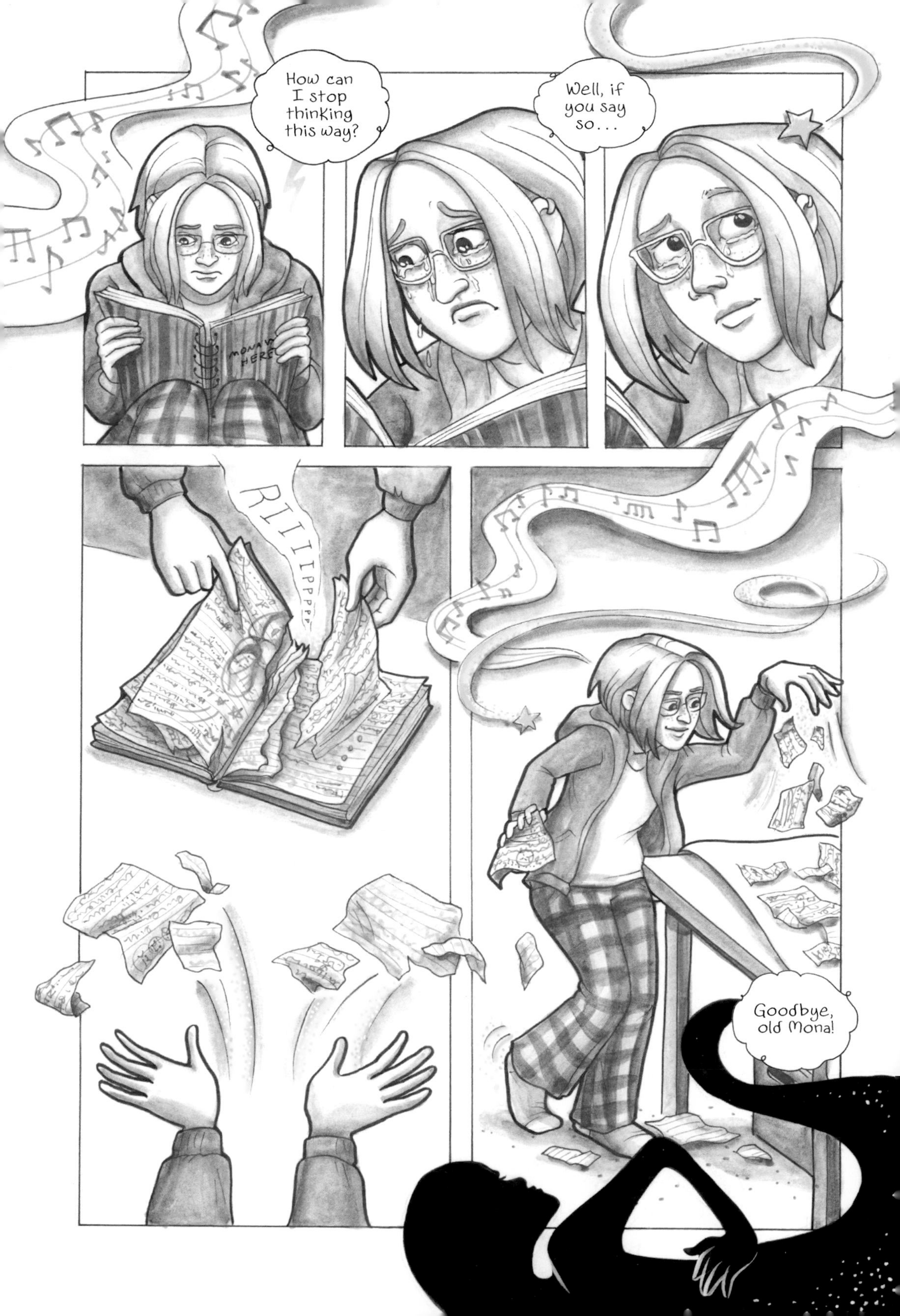
How can I stop thinking this way?
MONA WAS HERE
Well, if you say so...
RIIIIIPPPPP
Goodbye, old Mona!

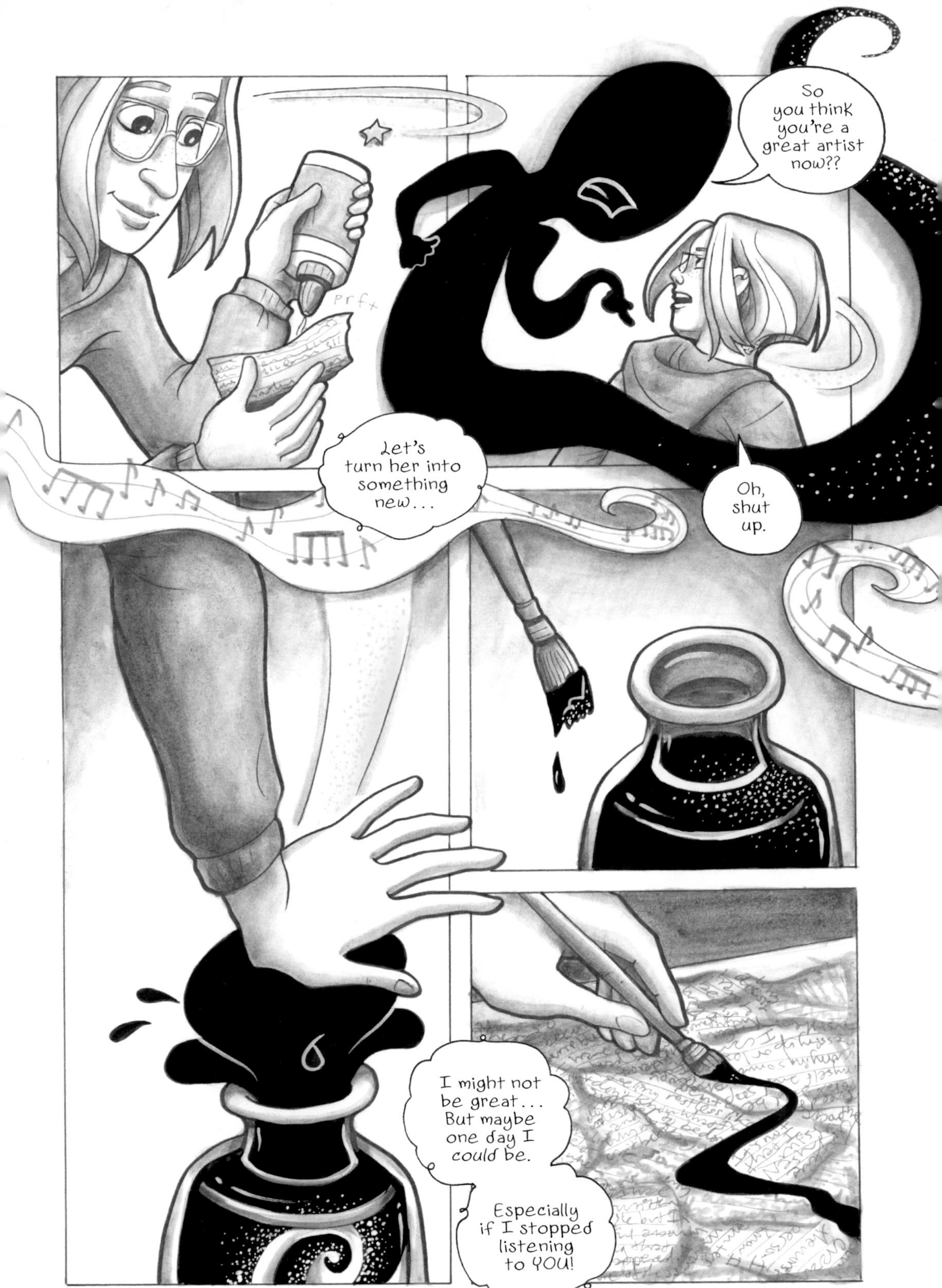
prfx
So you think you're a great artist now??
Oh, shut up.
Let's turn her into something new...
I might not be great... But maybe one day I could be.
Especially if I stopped listening to YOU!

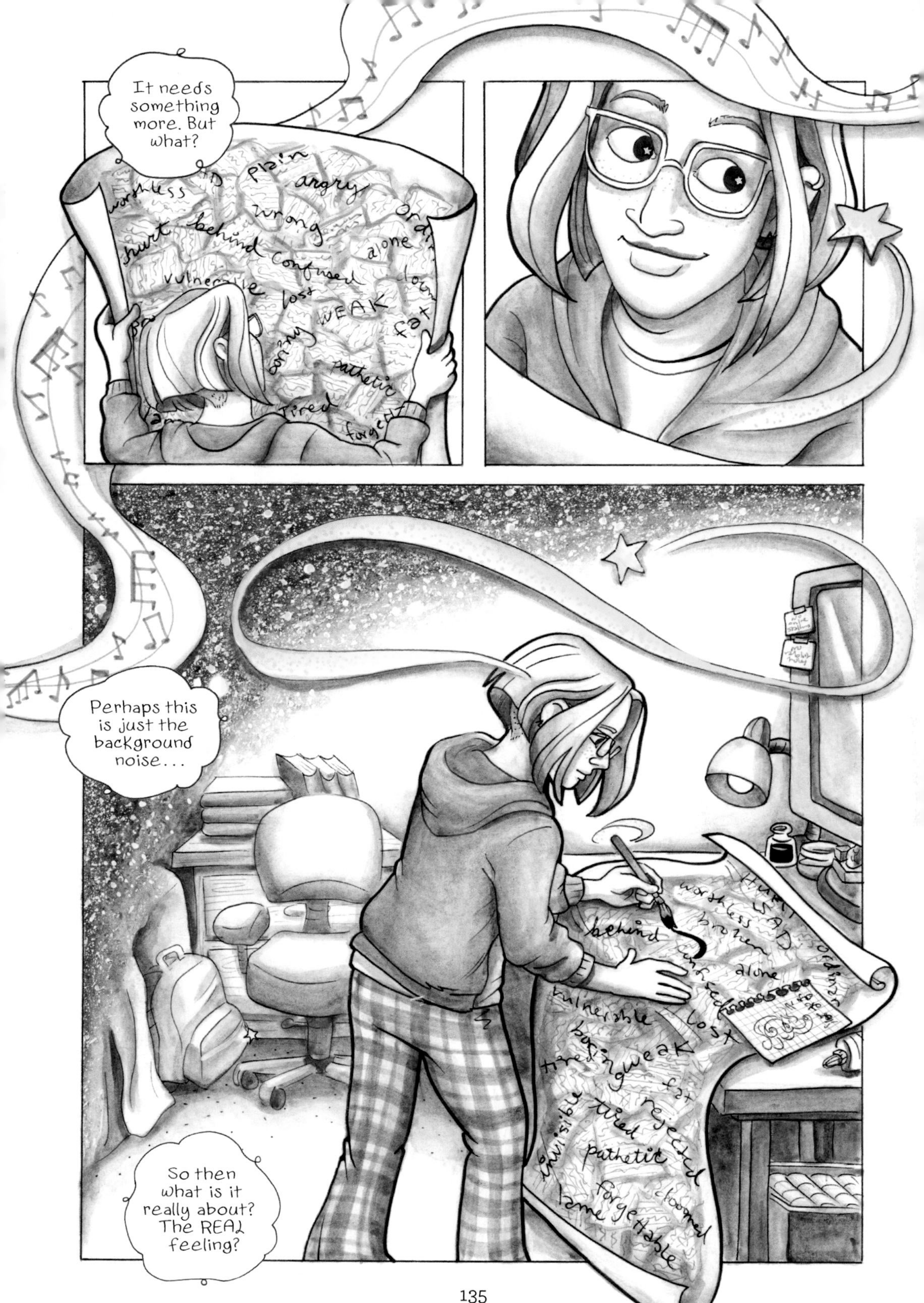
It needs something more. But what?
Perhaps this is just the background noise...
So then what is it really about? The REAL feeling?

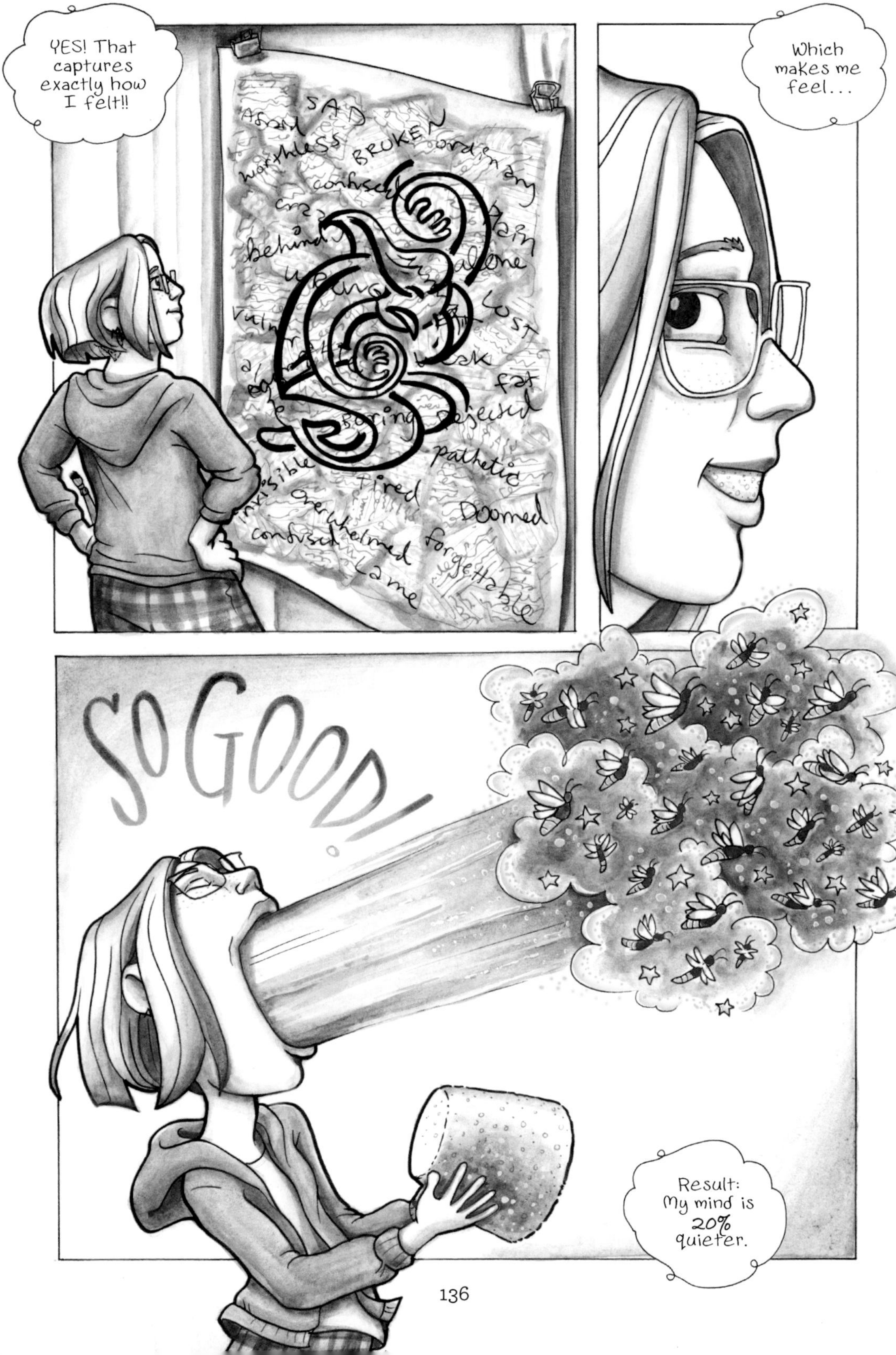
YES! That captures exactly how I felt!!
SAD
worthless
BROKEN
ordinary
confused
behind
alone
LOST
Boring
Rejected
pathetic
invisible
Tired
Doomed
overwhelmed
confused
forgettable
Lame
Which makes me feel...
SO GOOD!
Result: My mind is 20% quieter.

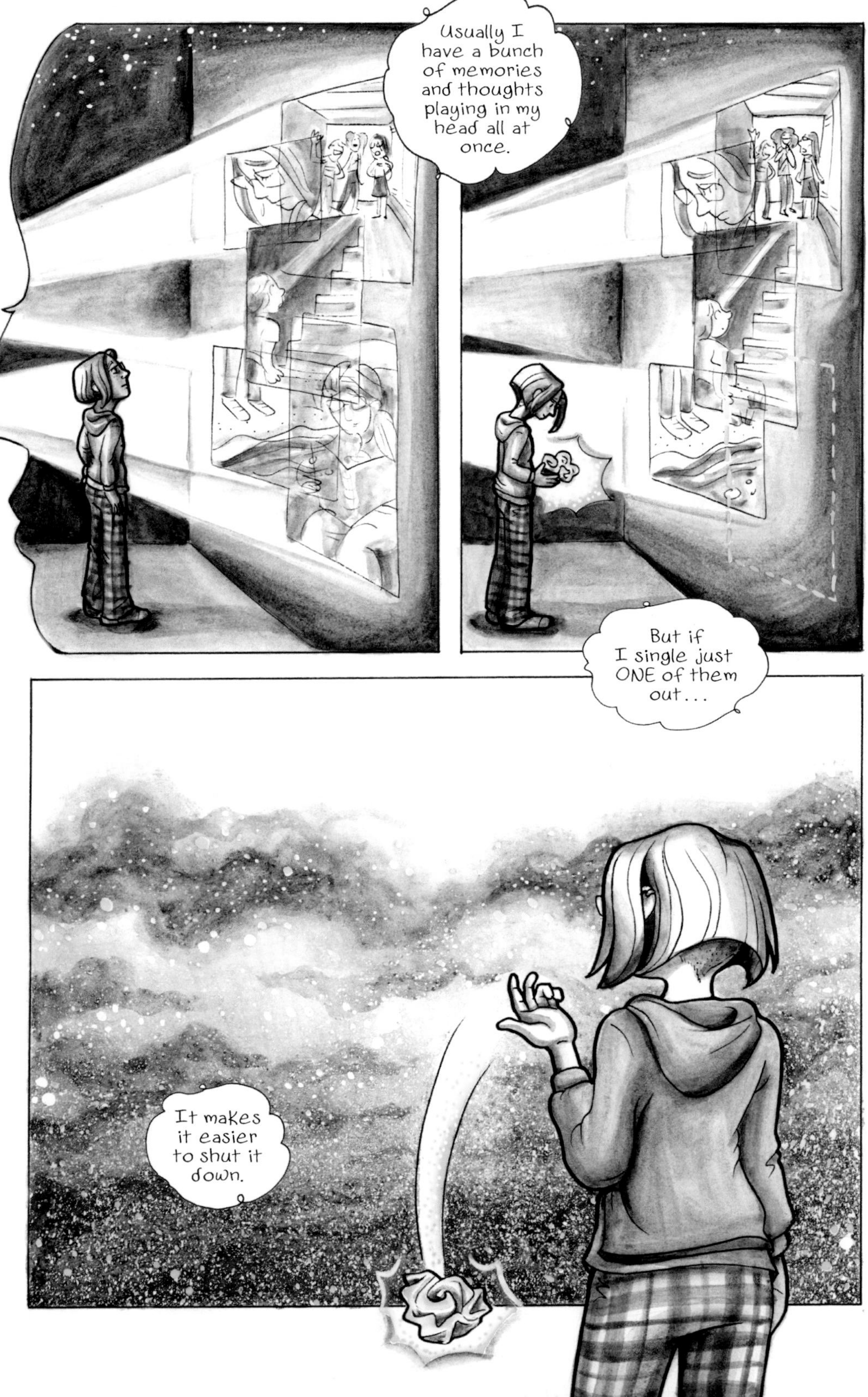
Usually I have a bunch of memories and thoughts playing in my head all at once.
But if I single just ONE of them out...
It makes it easier to shut it down.

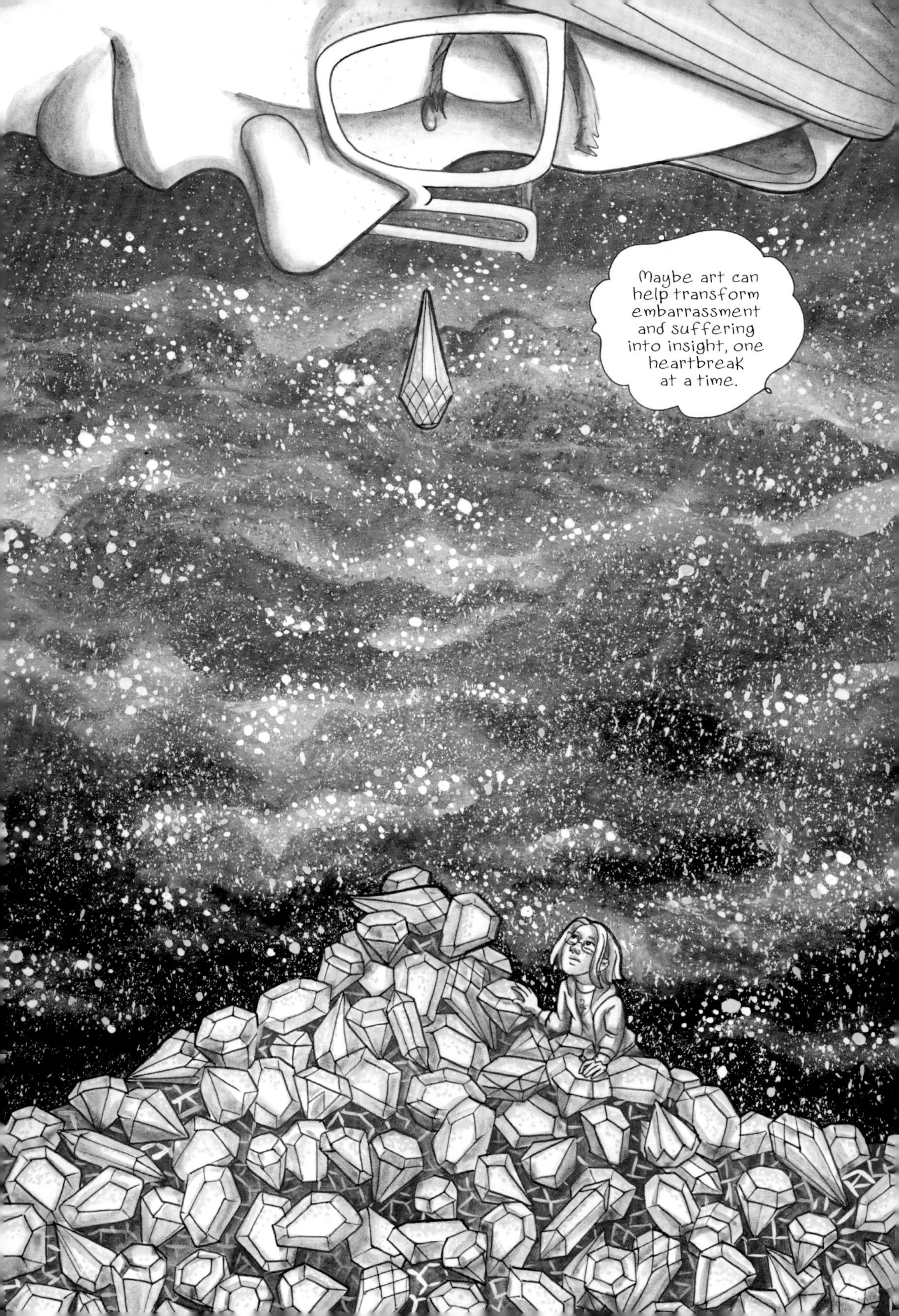
Maybe art can help transform embarrassment and suffering into insight, one heartbreak at a time.

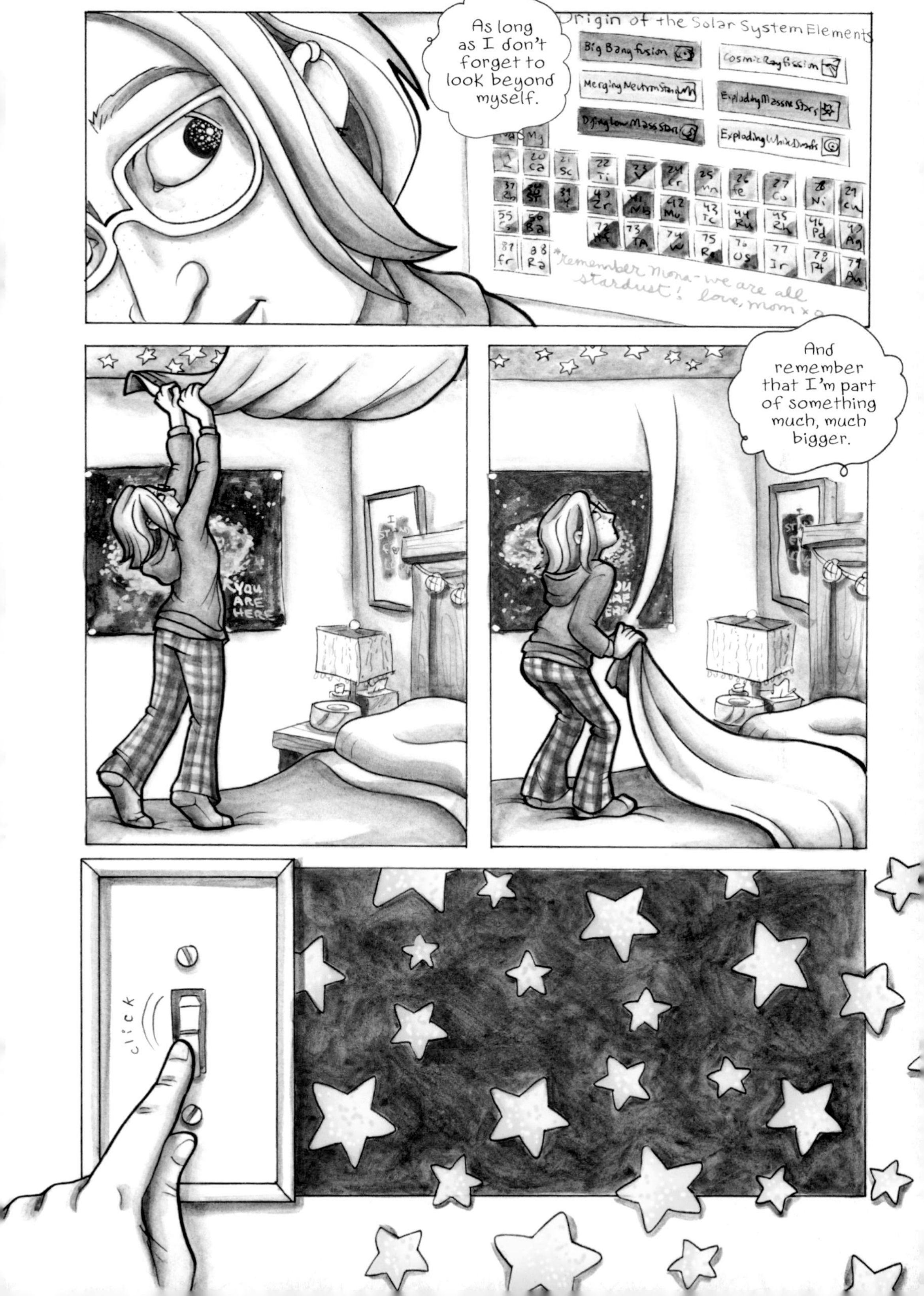
As long as I don't forget to look beyond myself.
Origin of the Solar System Elements
Big Bang fusion
Cosmic Ray fission
Merging Neutron Stars
Exploding Massive Stars
Dying Low Mass Stars
Exploding White Dwarfs
*remember Mona- we are all stardust! love, mom x
YOU ARE HERE
And remember that I'm part of something much, much bigger.
click

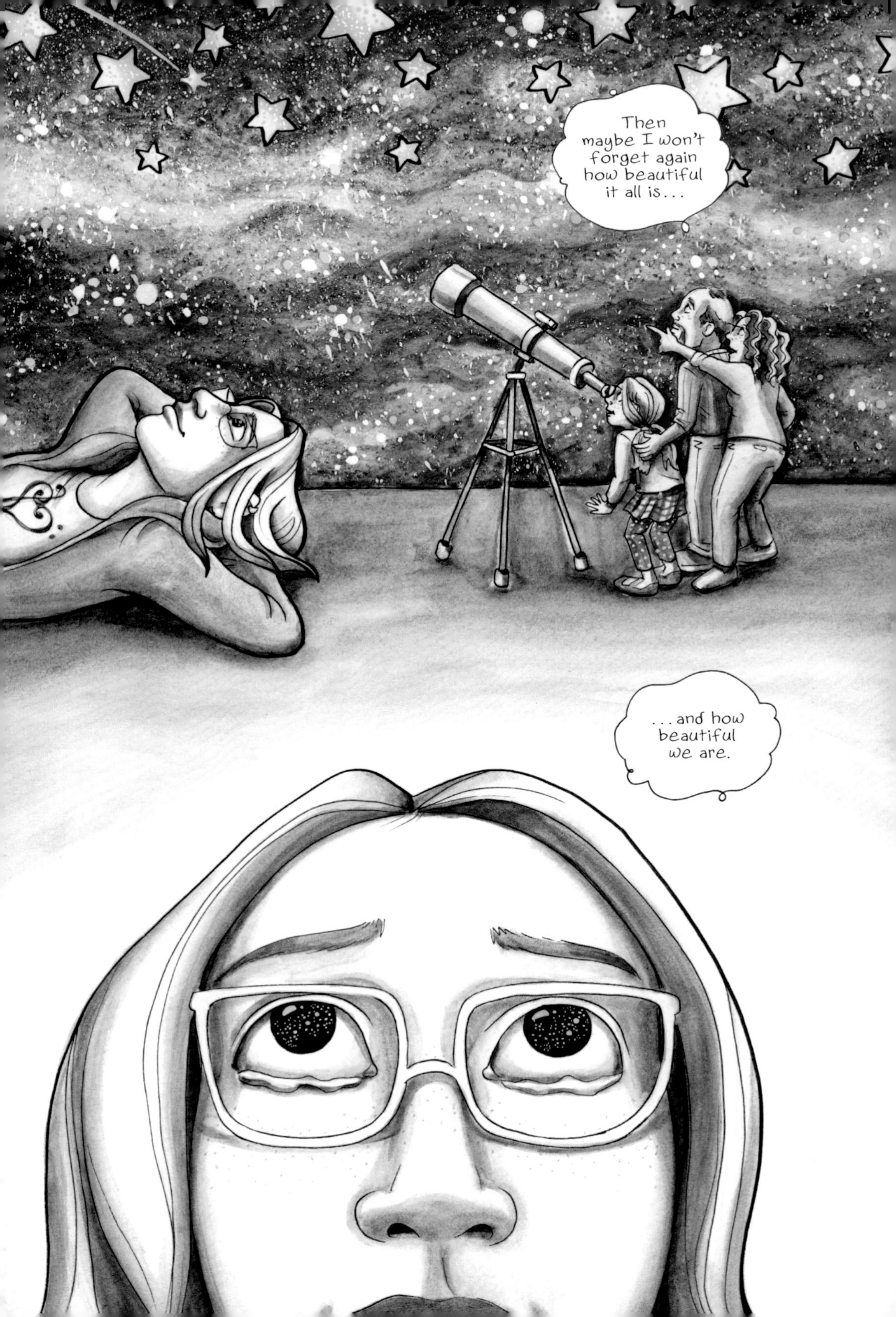
Then maybe I won't forget again how beautiful it all is . . .
. . . and how beautiful we are.

Replace what You can't erase

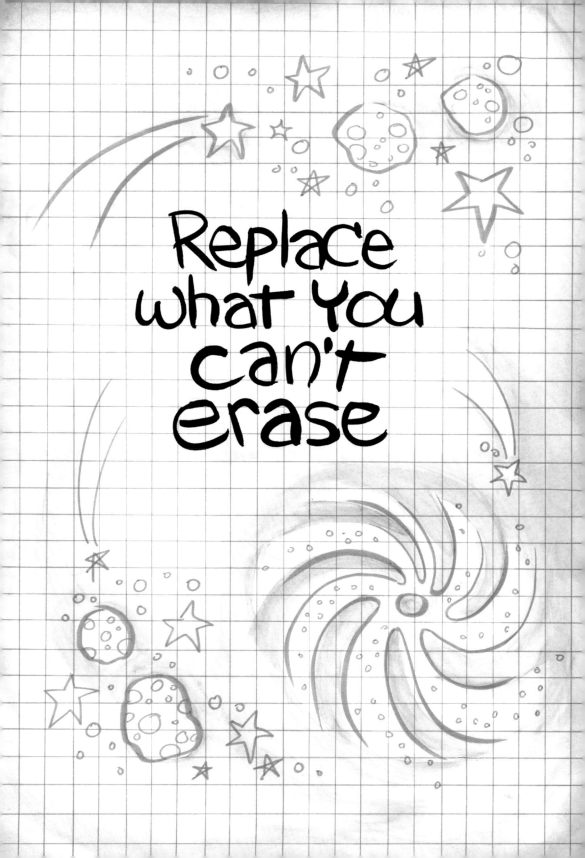

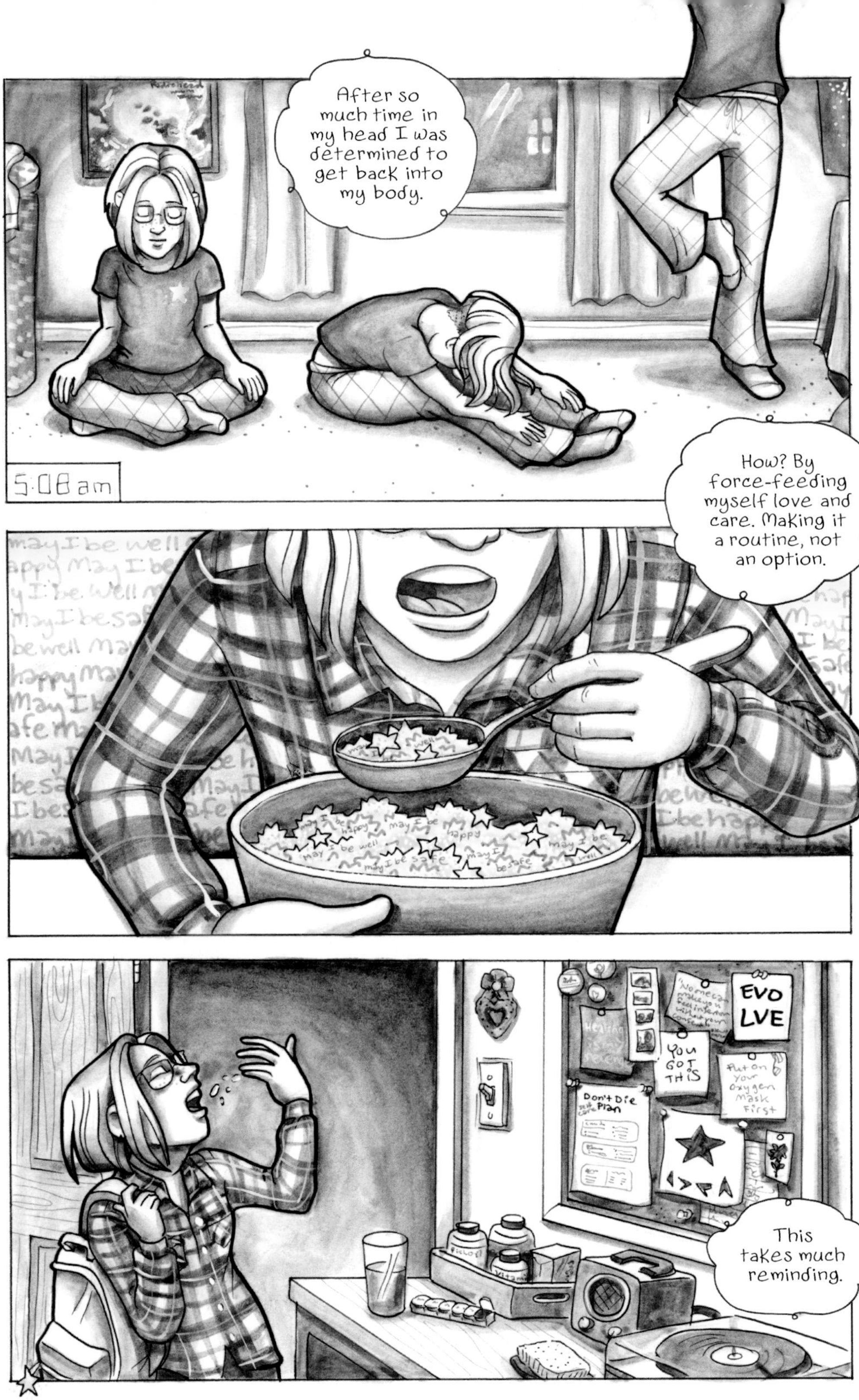
After so much time in my head I was determined to get back into my body.
5:08 am
How? By force-feeding myself love and care. Making it a routine, not an option.
EVO LVE
YOU GOT THIS
Put on your oxygen mask first
Don't Die Plan
This takes much reminding.

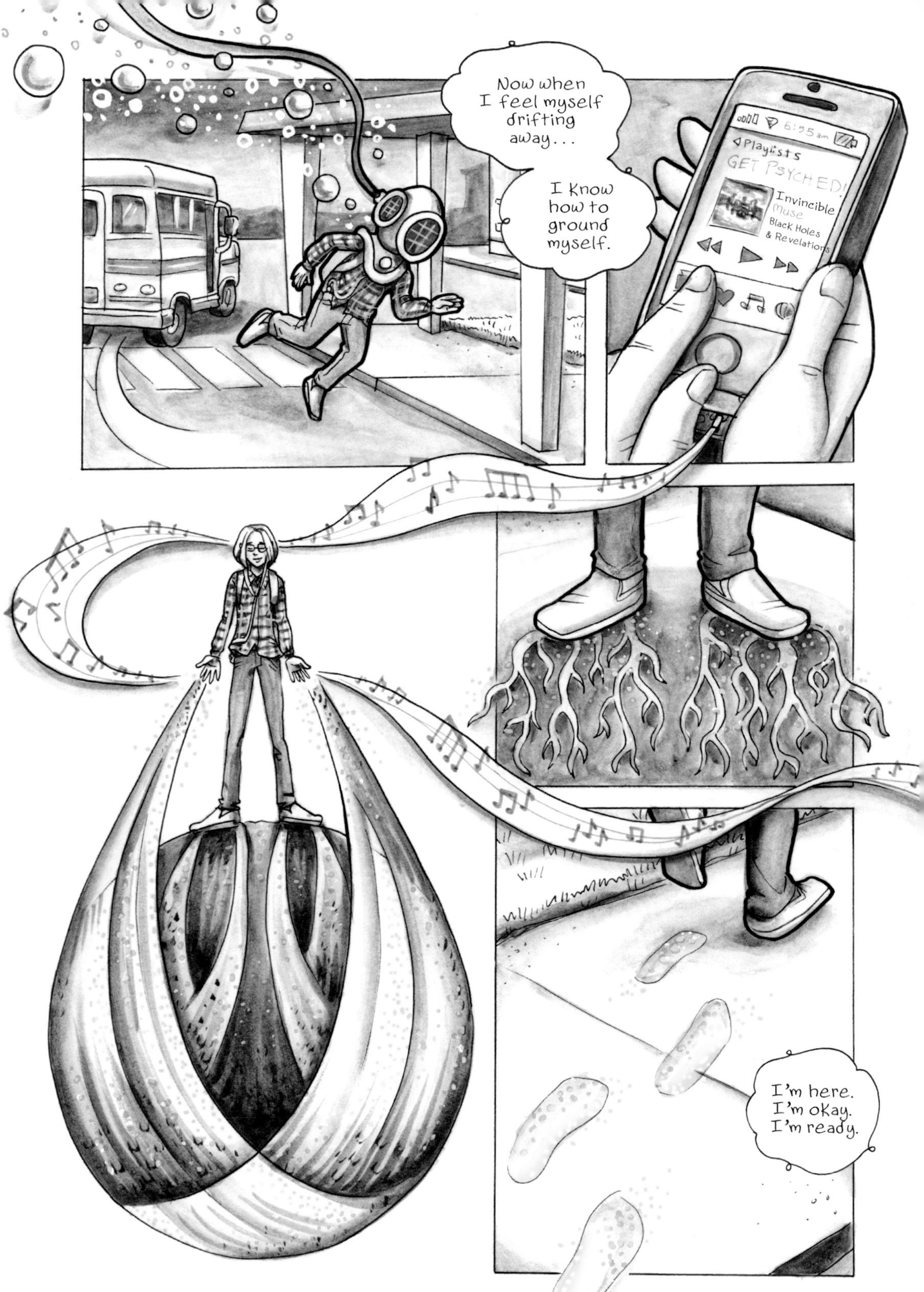
Now when I feel myself drifting away...
I know how to ground myself.
6:55 am
Playlists
GET PSYCHED!
Invincible
Muse
Black Holes & Revelations
I'm here. I'm okay. I'm ready.

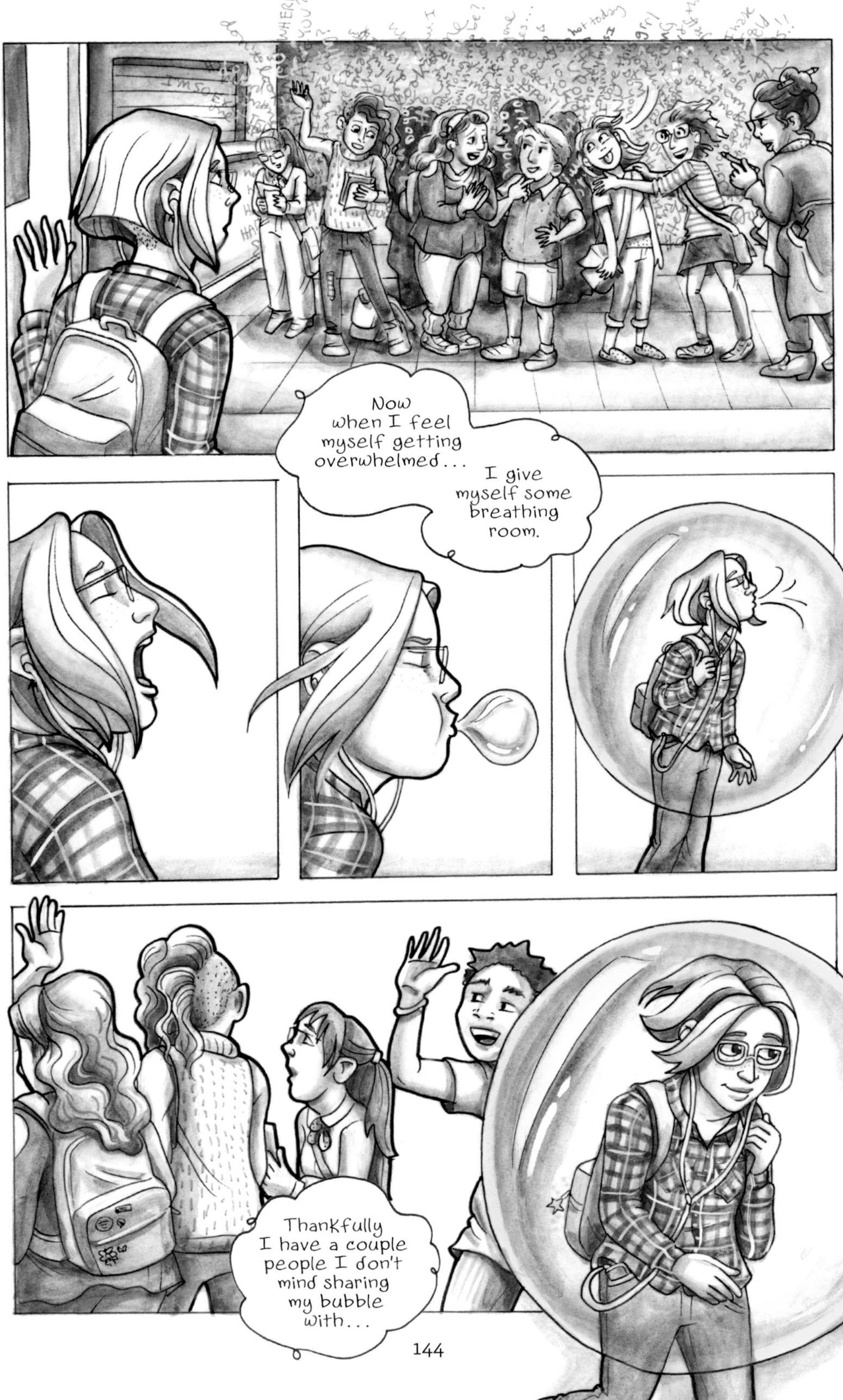
Now when I feel myself getting overwhelmed...
I give myself some breathing room.
Thankfully I have a couple people I don't mind sharing my bubble with...

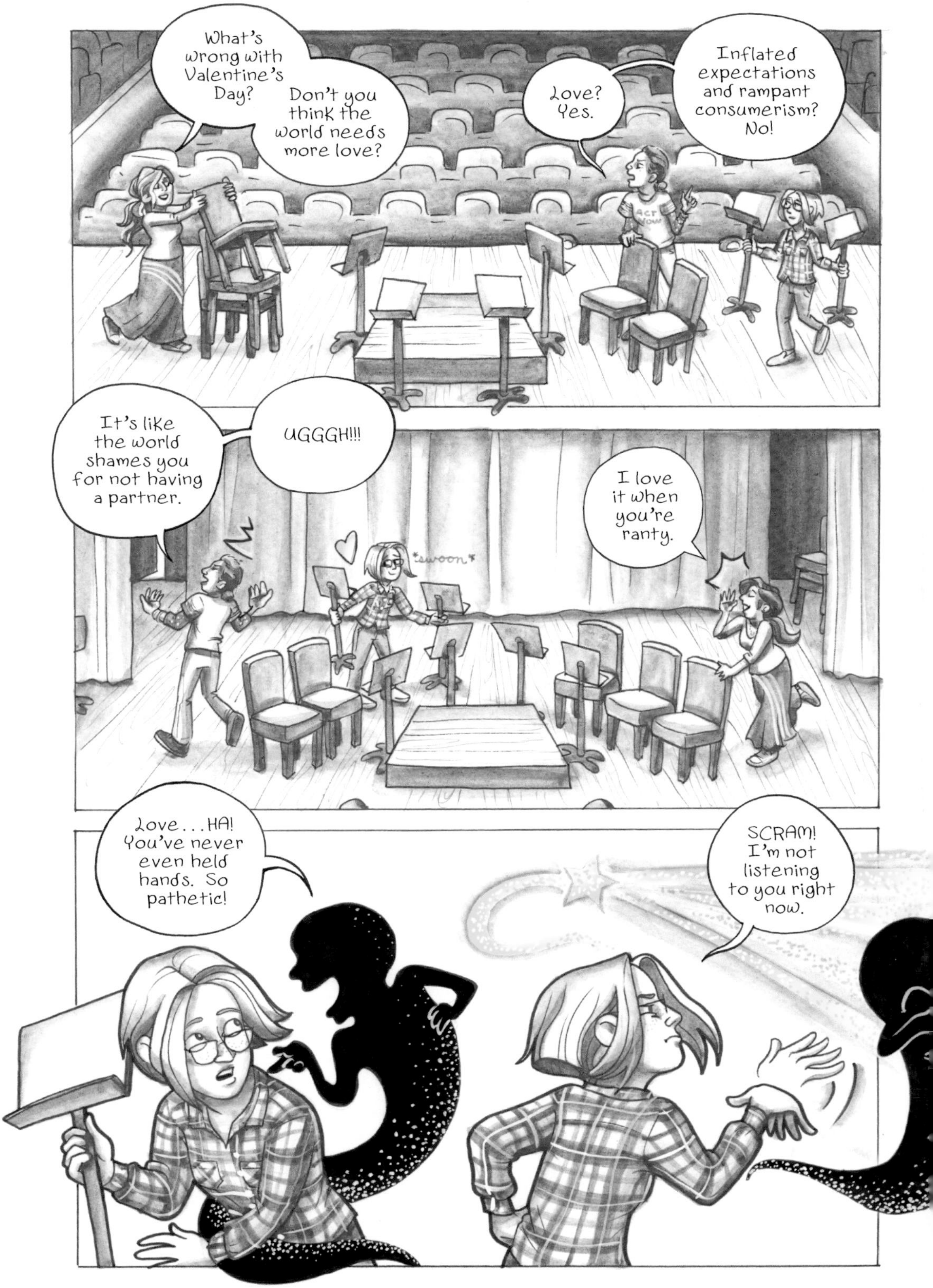
What's wrong with Valentine's Day?
Don't you think the world needs more love?
Love? Yes.
Inflated expectations and rampant consumerism? No!
It's like the world shames you for not having a partner.
UGGGH!!!
swoon
I love it when you're ranty.
Love...HA! You've never even held hands. So pathetic!
SCRAM! I'm not listening to you right now.

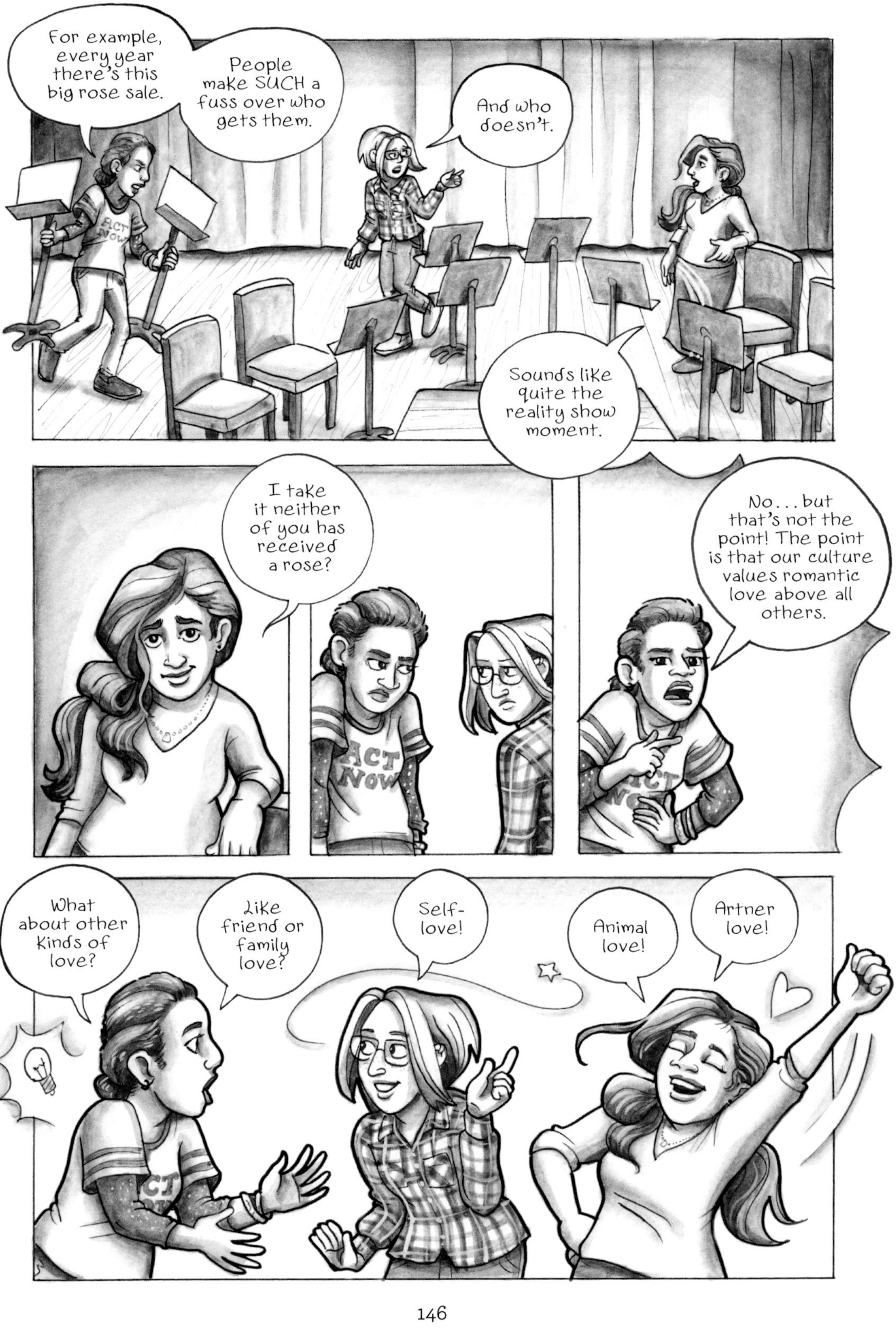

For example, every year there's this big rose sale.
People make SUCH a fuss over who gets them.
And who doesn't.
ACT NOW
Sounds like quite the reality show moment.
I take it neither of you has received a rose?
ACT NOW
No... but that's not the point! The point is that our culture values romantic love above all others.
What about other kinds of love?
Like friend or family love?
Self-love!
Animal love!
Artner love!

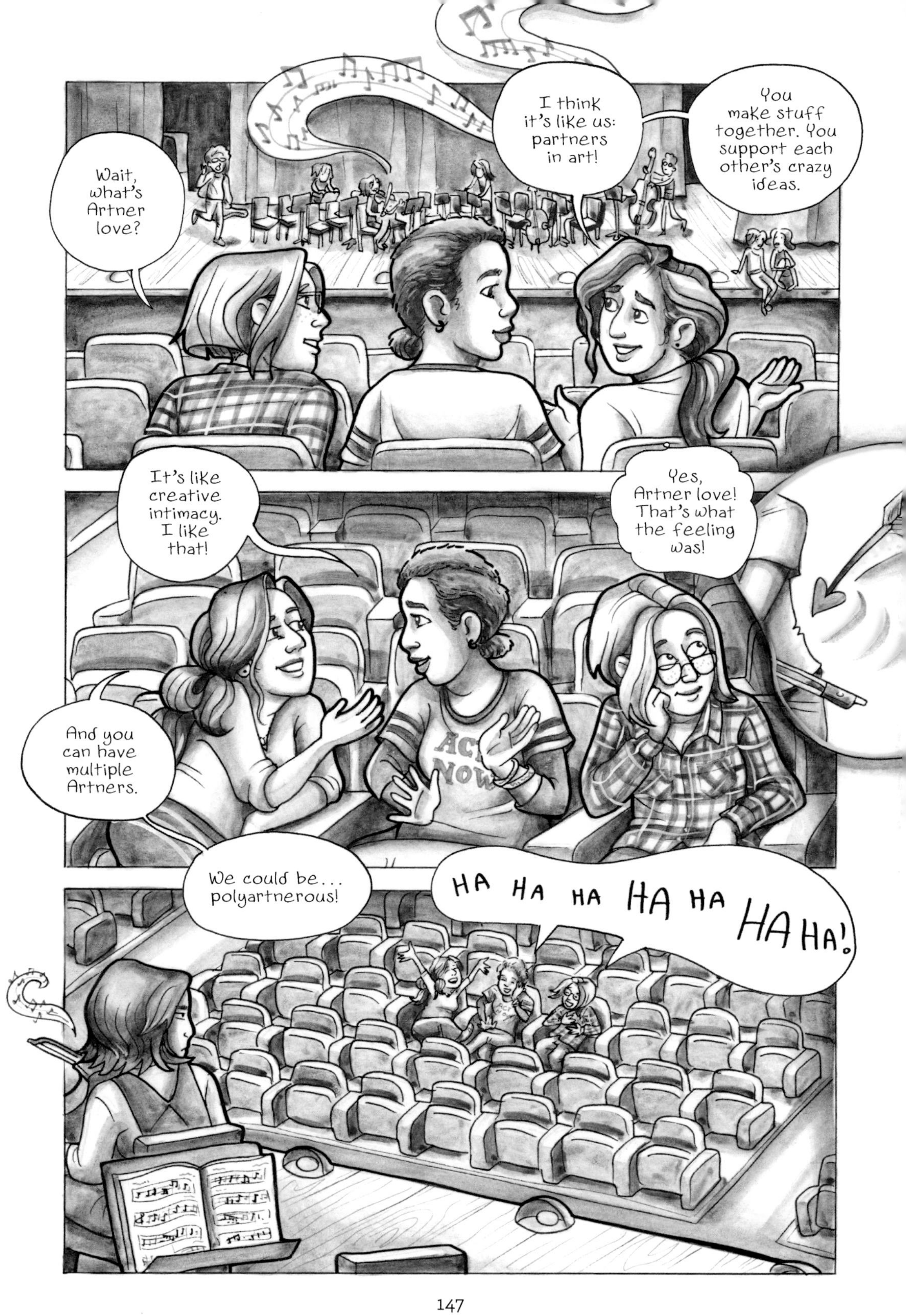
Wait, what's Artner love?
I think it's like us: partners in art!
You make stuff together. You support each other's crazy ideas.
It's like creative intimacy. I like that!
Yes, Artner love! That's what the feeling was!
And you can have multiple Artners.
We could be... polyartnerous!
HA HA HA HA HA HA HA!

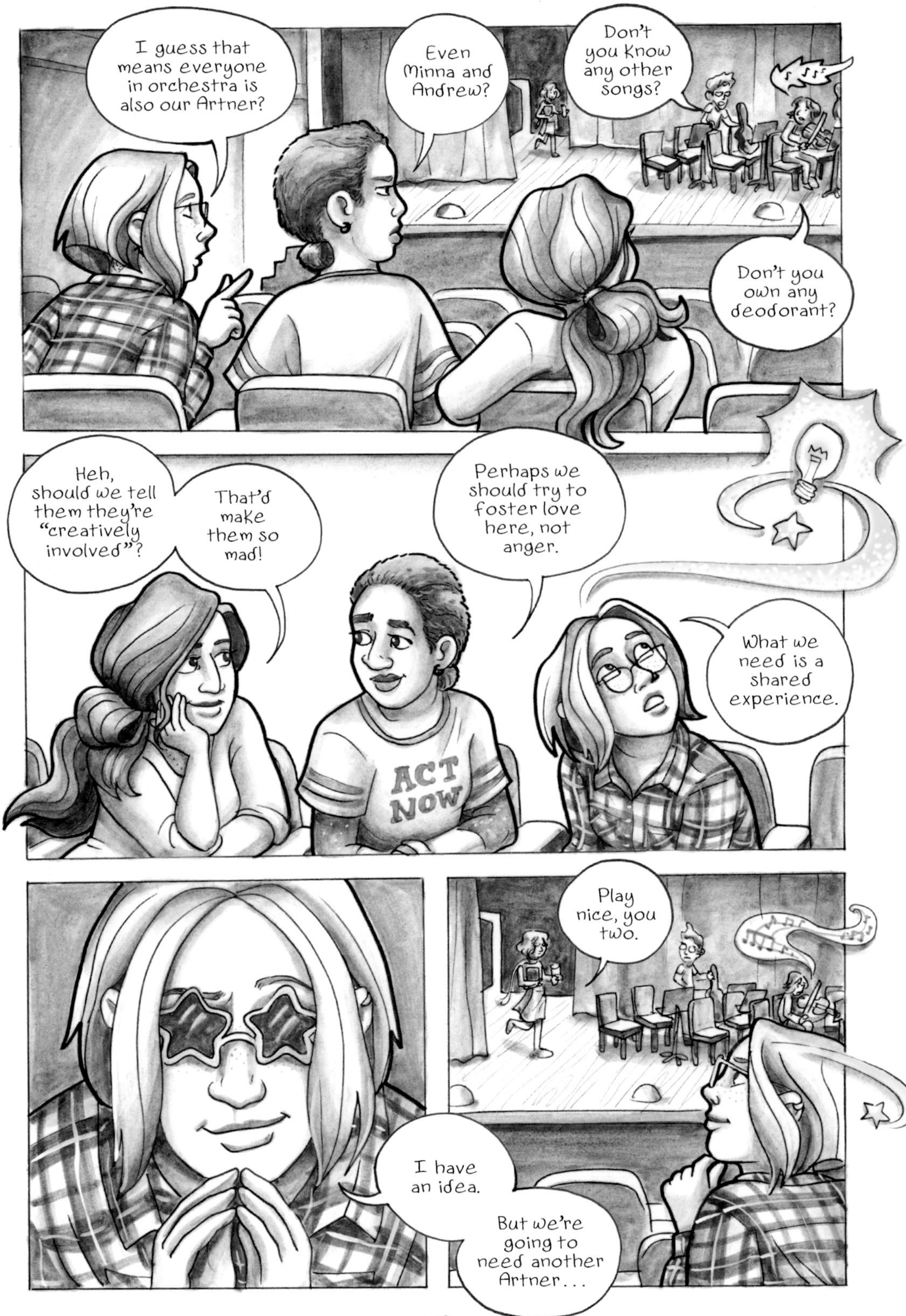
I guess that means everyone in orchestra is also our Artner?
Even Minna and Andrew?
Don't you know any other songs?
Don't you own any deodorant?
Heh, should we tell them they're "creatively involved"?
That'd make them so mad!
Perhaps we should try to foster love here, not anger.
What we need is a shared experience.
ACT NOW
Play nice, you two.
I have an idea.
But we're going to need another Artner . . .

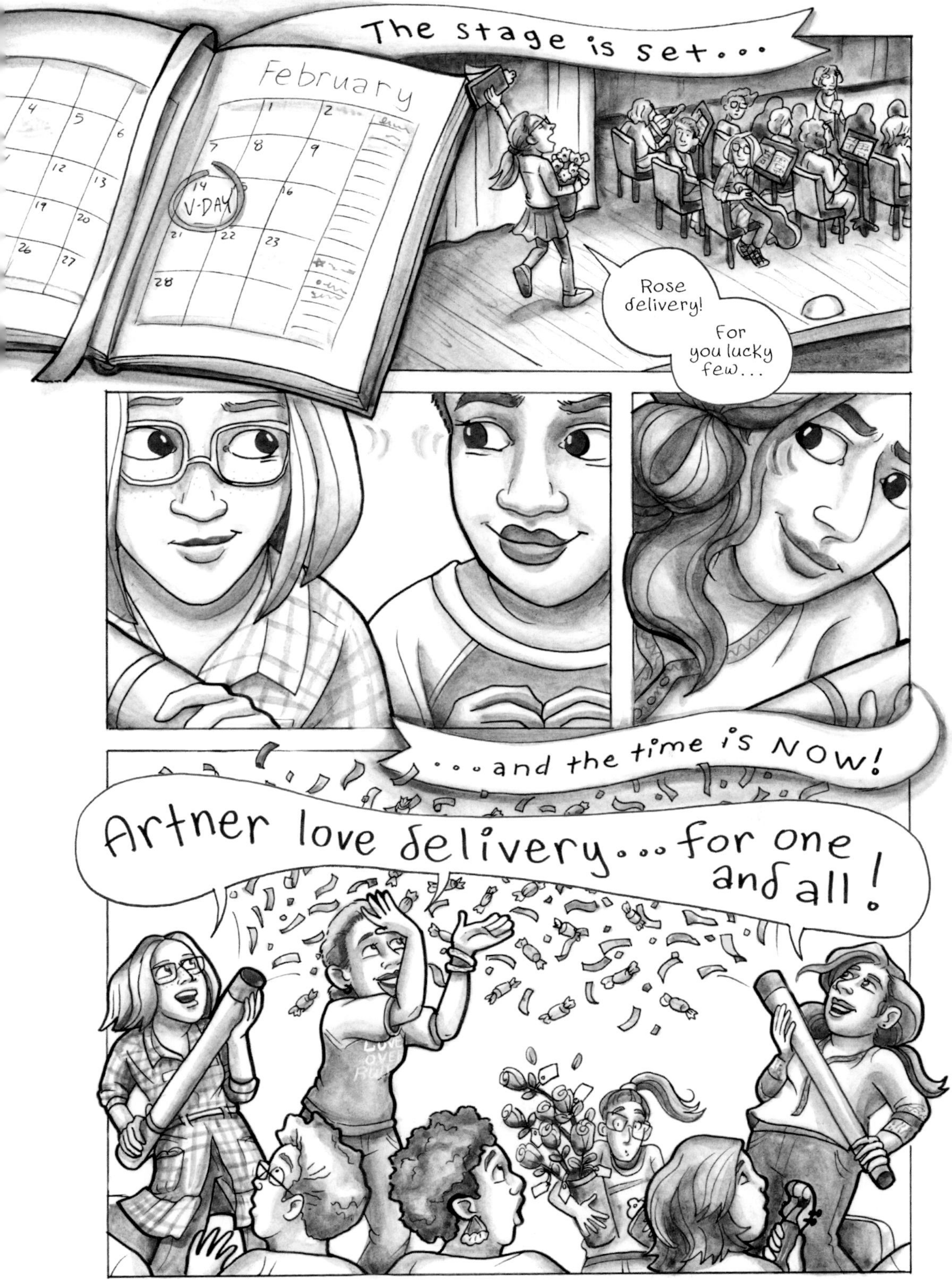

The stage is set...
February
V-DAY
Rose delivery!
For you lucky few...
...and the time is NOW!
Artner love delivery... for one and all!

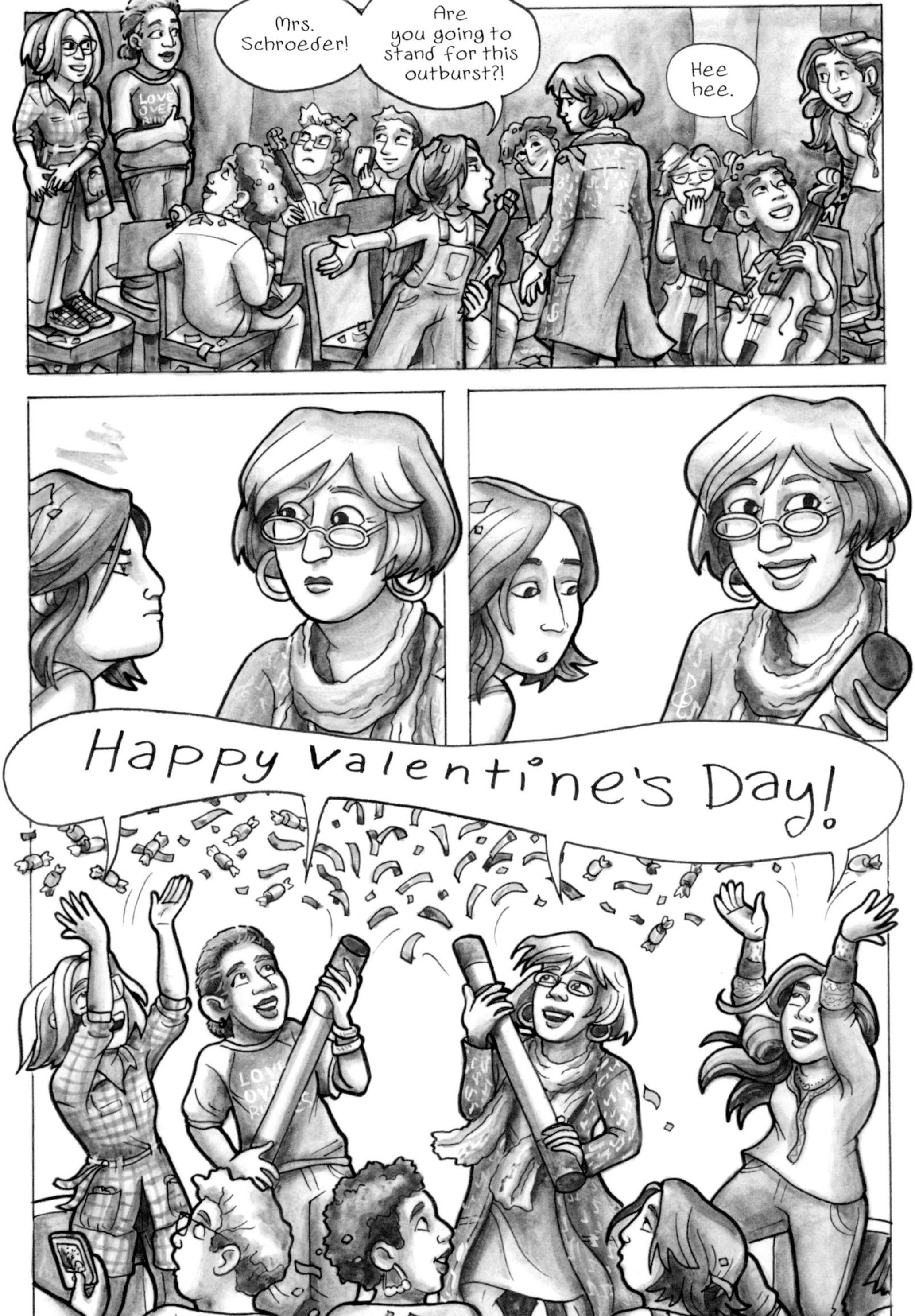
Mrs. Schroeder!
Are you going to stand for this outburst?!
Hee hee.
Happy Valentine's Day!

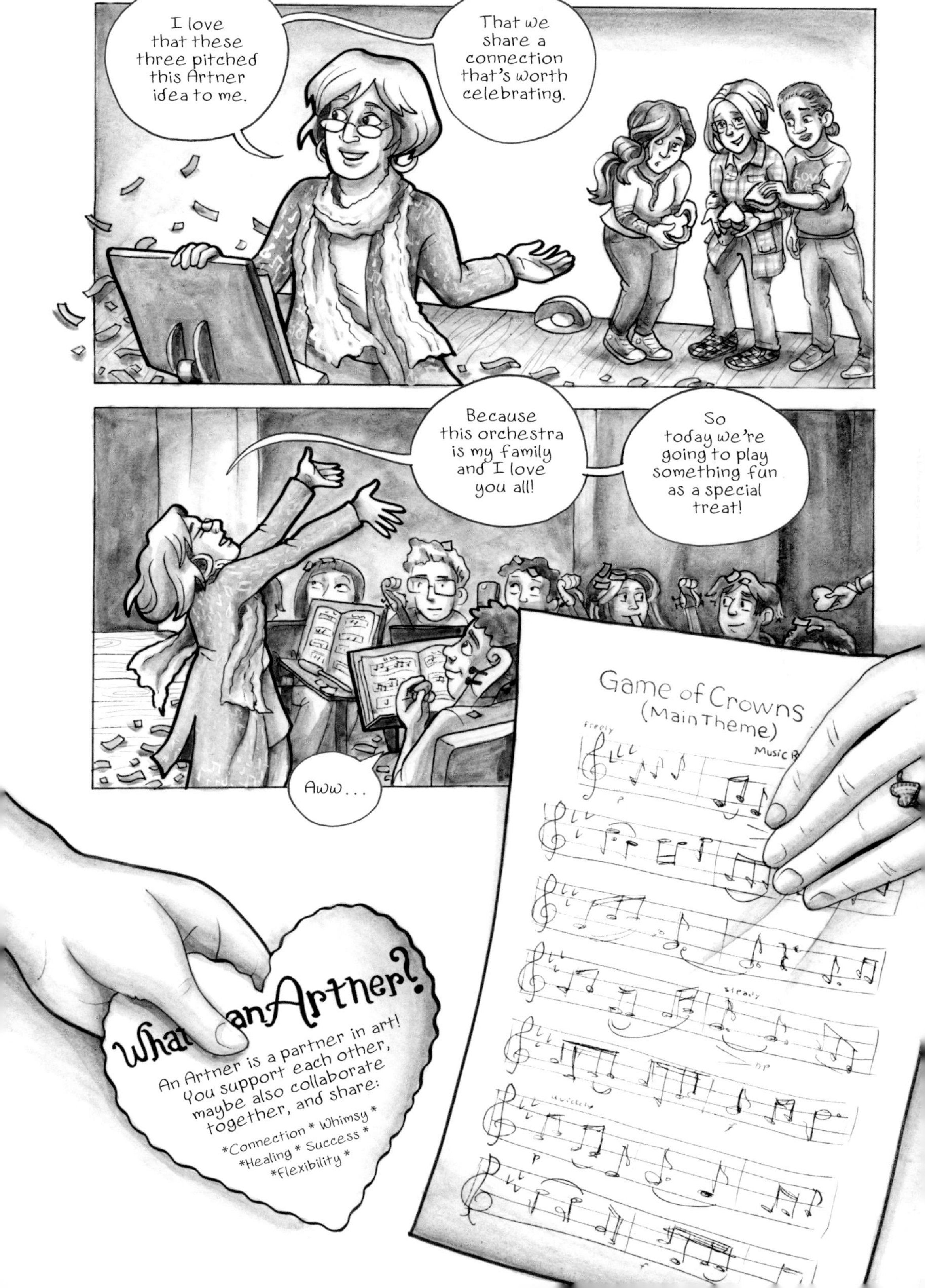
I love that these three pitched this Artner idea to me.
That we share a connection that's worth celebrating.
LOVE
Because this orchestra is my family and I love you all!
So today we're going to play something fun as a special treat!
Aww...
Game of Crowns
(Main Theme)
Freely
steady
Wha
an Artner?
An Artner is a partner in art! You support each other, maybe also collaborate together, and share:
*Connection * Whimsy *
*Healing * Success *
*Flexibility *

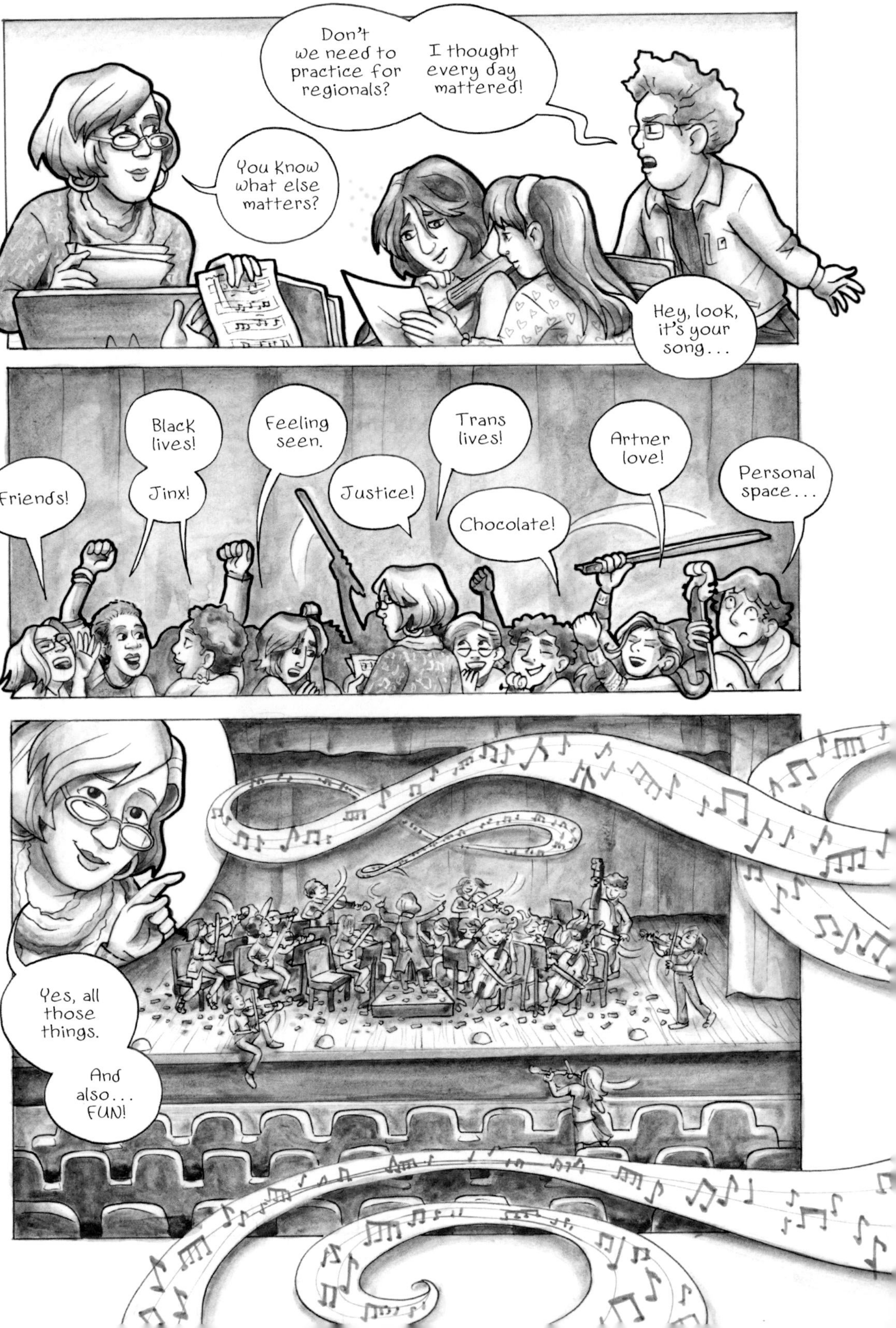
Don't we need to practice for regionals?
I thought every day mattered!
You know what else matters?
Hey, look, it's your song...
Friends!
Black lives!
Jinx!
Feeling seen.
Justice!
Trans lives!
Chocolate!
Artner love!
Personal space...
Yes, all those things.
And also... FUN!

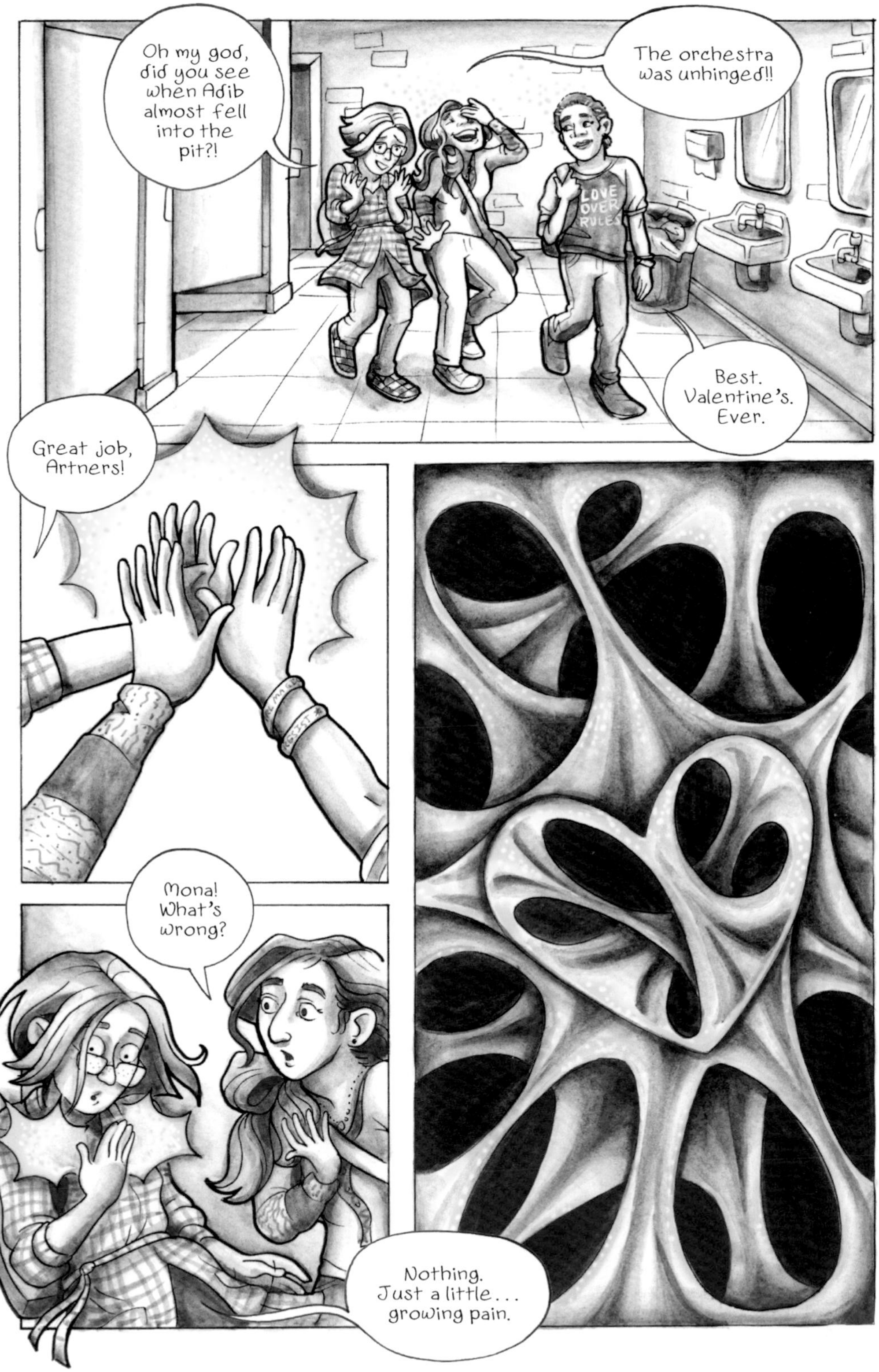
Oh my god, did you see when Adib almost fell into the pit?!
The orchestra was unhinged!!
LOVE OVER RULES
Best. Valentine's. Ever.
Great job, Artners!
Mona! What's wrong?
Nothing. Just a little . . . growing pain.

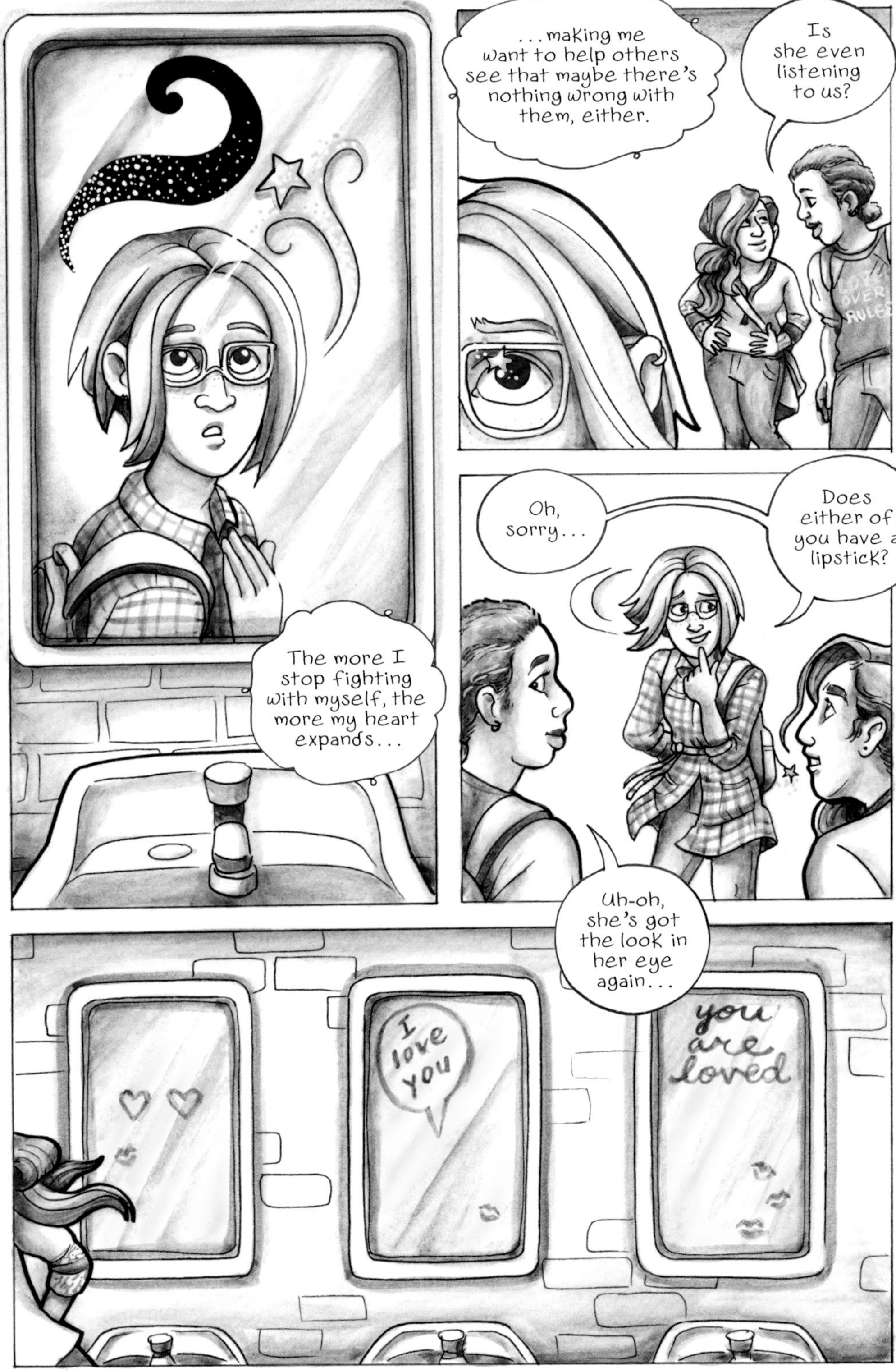

The more I stop fighting with myself, the more my heart expands...
...making me want to help others see that maybe there's nothing wrong with them, either.
Is she even listening to us?
LOVE OVER RULES
Oh, sorry...
Does either of you have a lipstick?
Uh-oh, she's got the look in her eye again...
I love you
you are loved

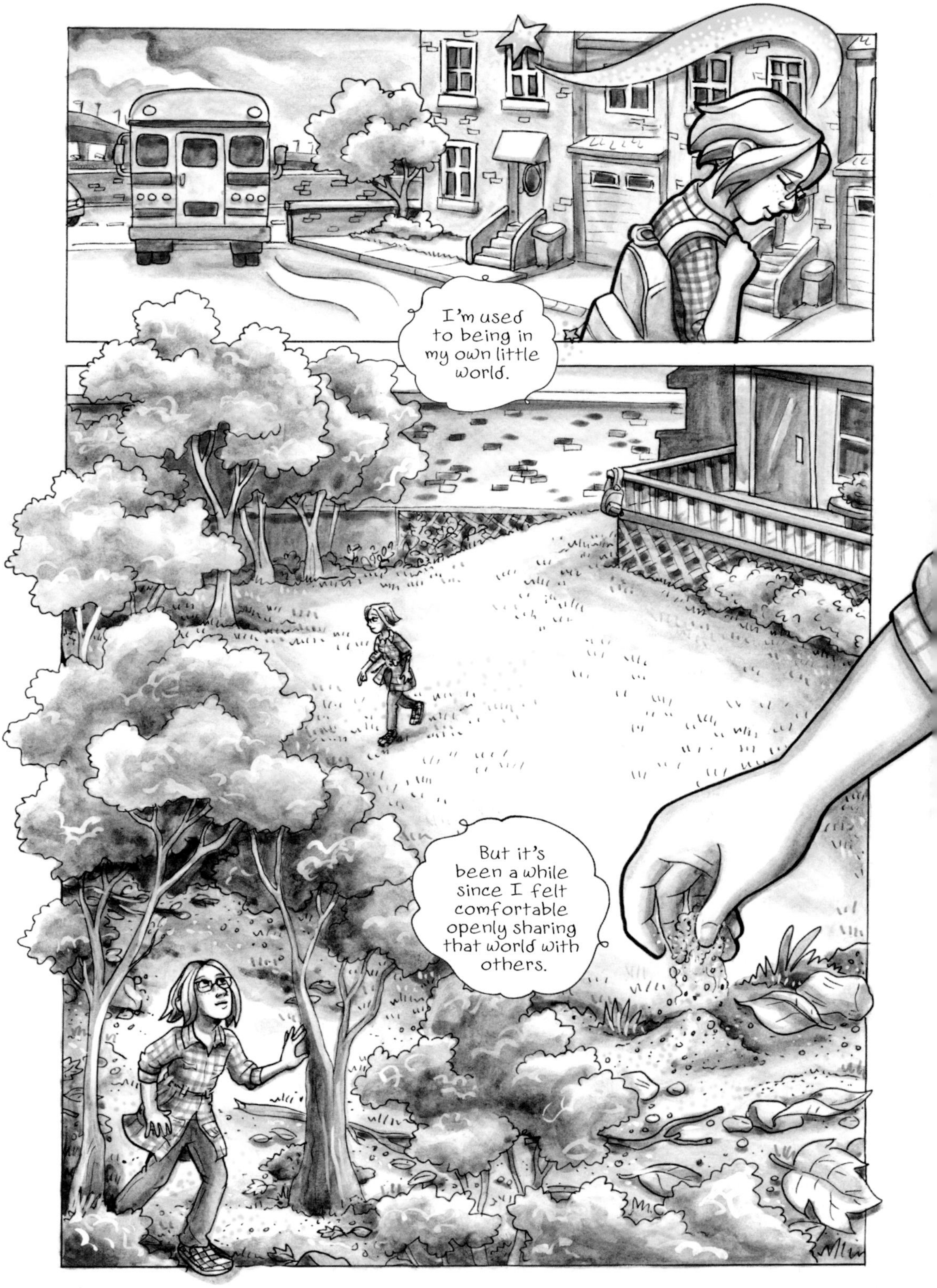
I'm used to being in my own little world.
But it's been a while since I felt comfortable openly sharing that world with others.

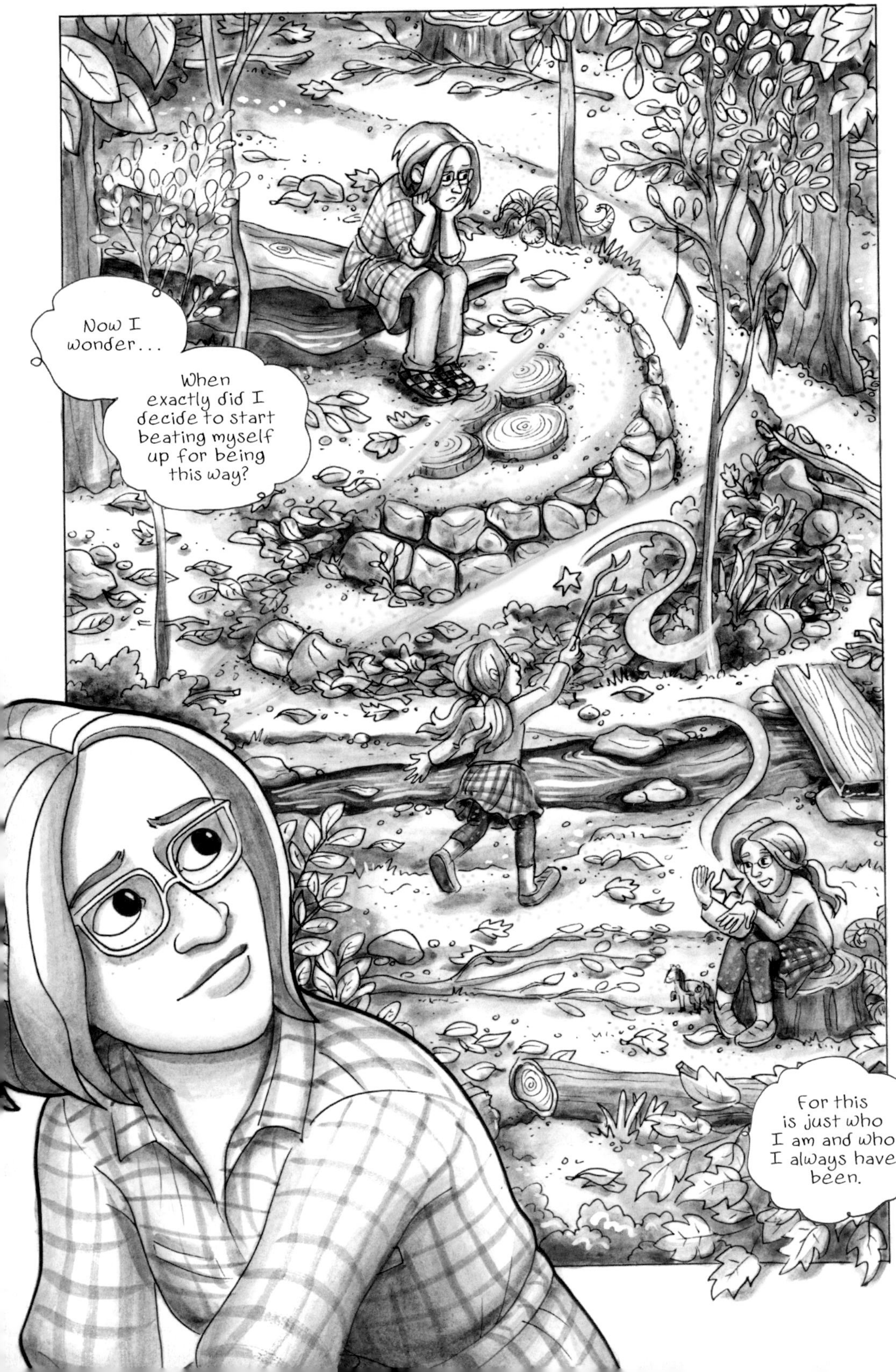
Now I wonder...
When exactly did I decide to start beating myself up for being this way?
For this is just who I am and who I always have been.

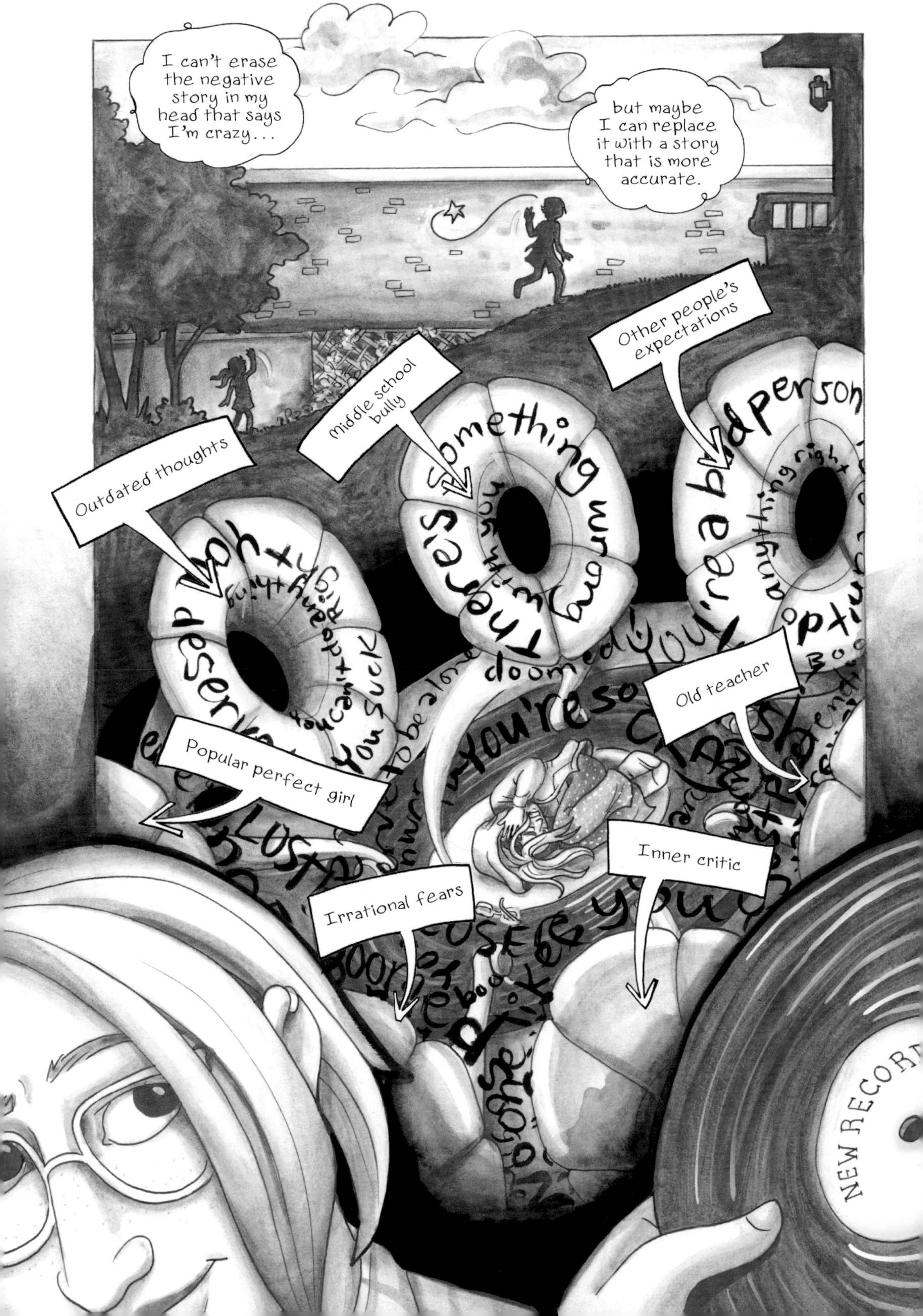

I can't erase the negative story in my head that says I'm crazy . . .
but maybe I can replace it with a story that is more accurate.
Other people's expectations
Middle school bully
Outdated thoughts
Old teacher
Popular perfect girl
Inner critic
Irrational fears
NEW RECORD

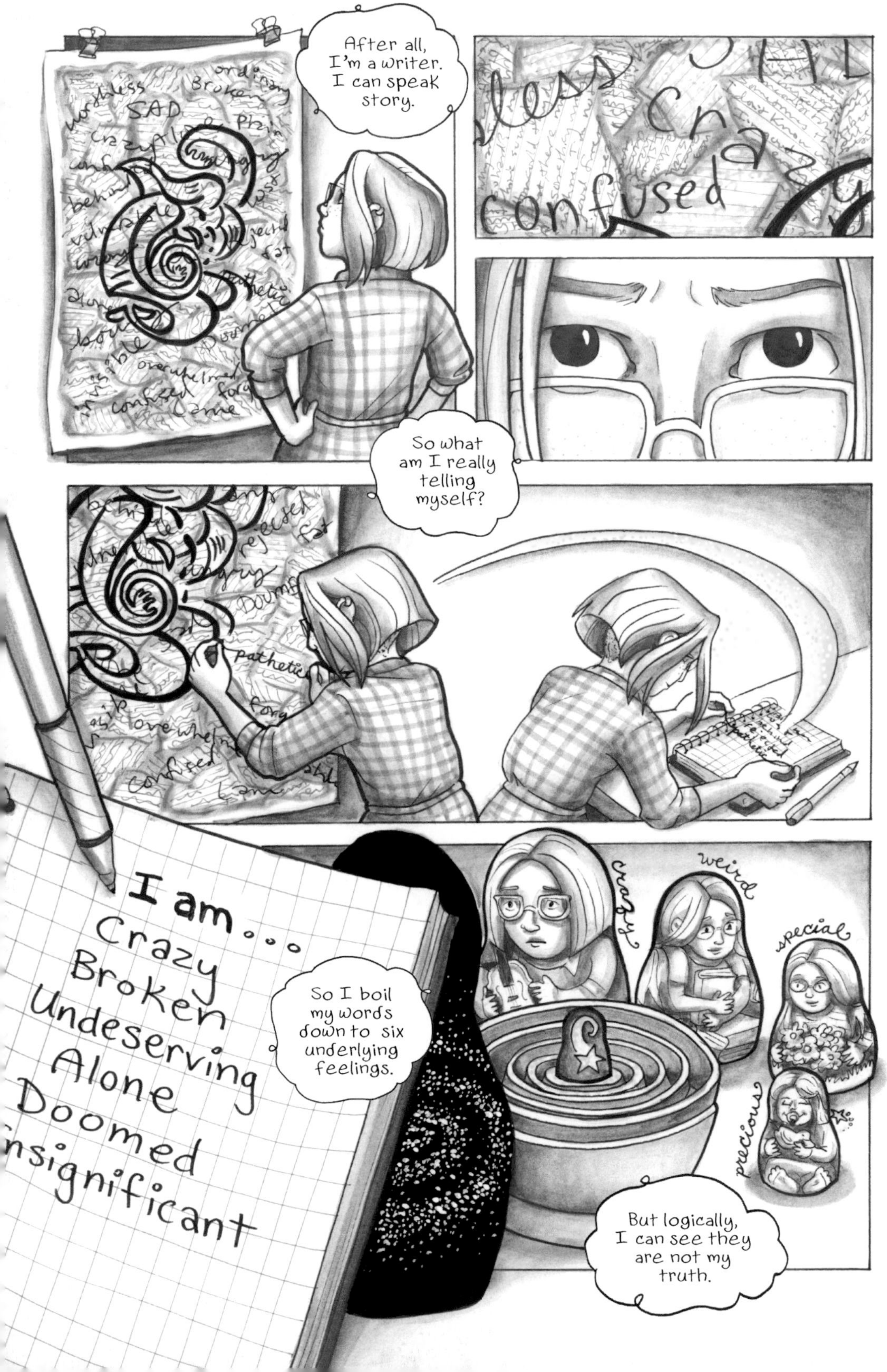

After all, I'm a writer. I can speak story.
confused
So what am I really telling myself?
I am...
Crazy
Broken
Undeserving
Alone
Doomed
Insignificant
So I boil my words down to six underlying feelings.
crazy
weird
special
precious
But logically, I can see they are not my truth.

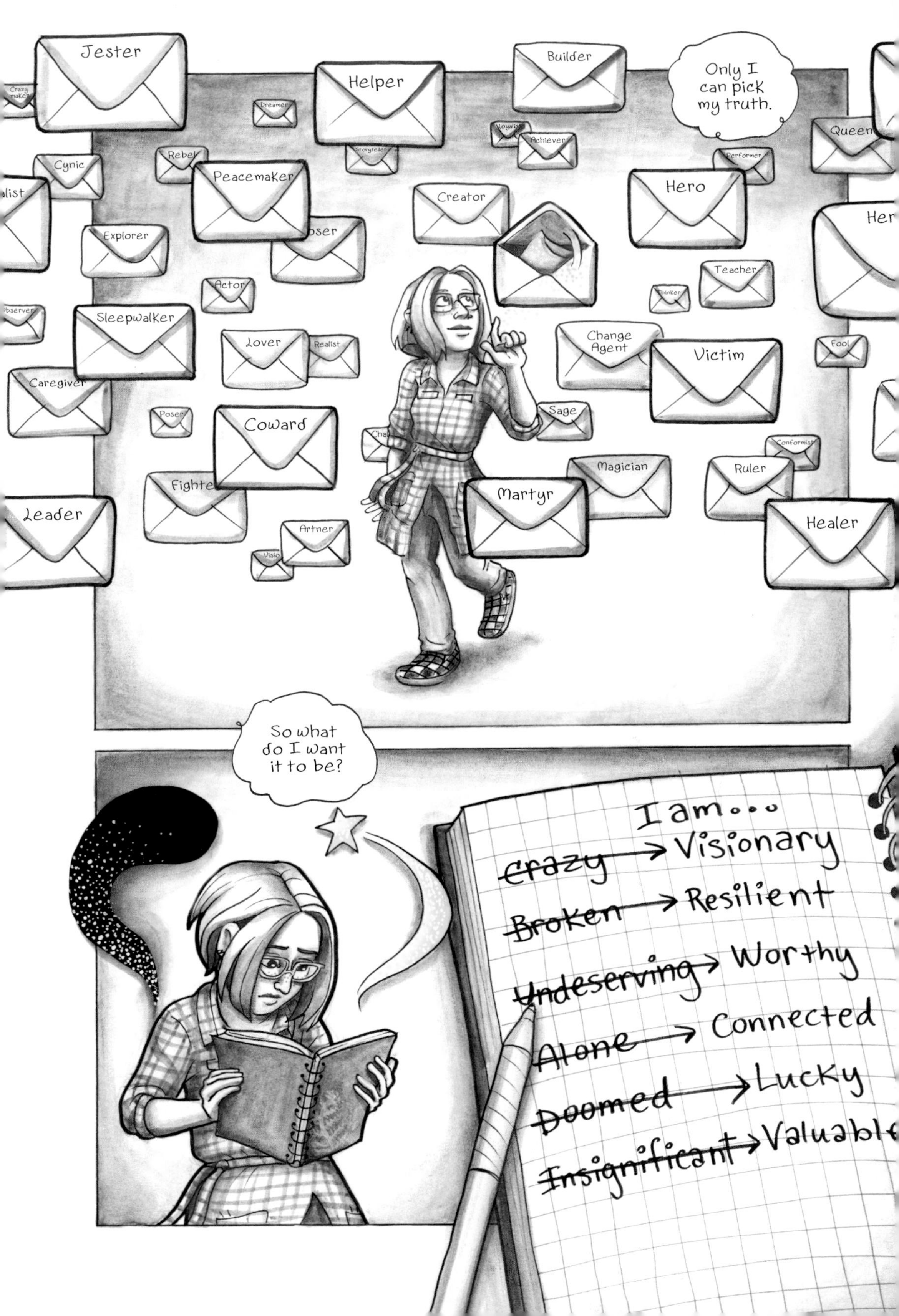
Jester
Crazy maker
Dreamer
Helper
Storyteller
Builder
Loyalist
Achiever
Only I can pick my truth.
Queen
Cynic
Rebel
Peacemaker
Creator
Performer
Hero
Explorer
Teacher
Actor
Thinker
Sleepwalker
Lover
Realist
Change Agent
Victim
Fool
Caregiver
Poser
Coward
Sage
Conformist
Magician
Ruler
Leader
Martyr
Healer
Artner
So what do I want it to be?
I am...
~~Crazy~~ → Visionary
~~Broken~~ → Resilient
~~Undeserving~~ → Worthy
~~Alone~~ → Connected
~~Doomed~~ → Lucky
~~Insignificant~~ → Valuable

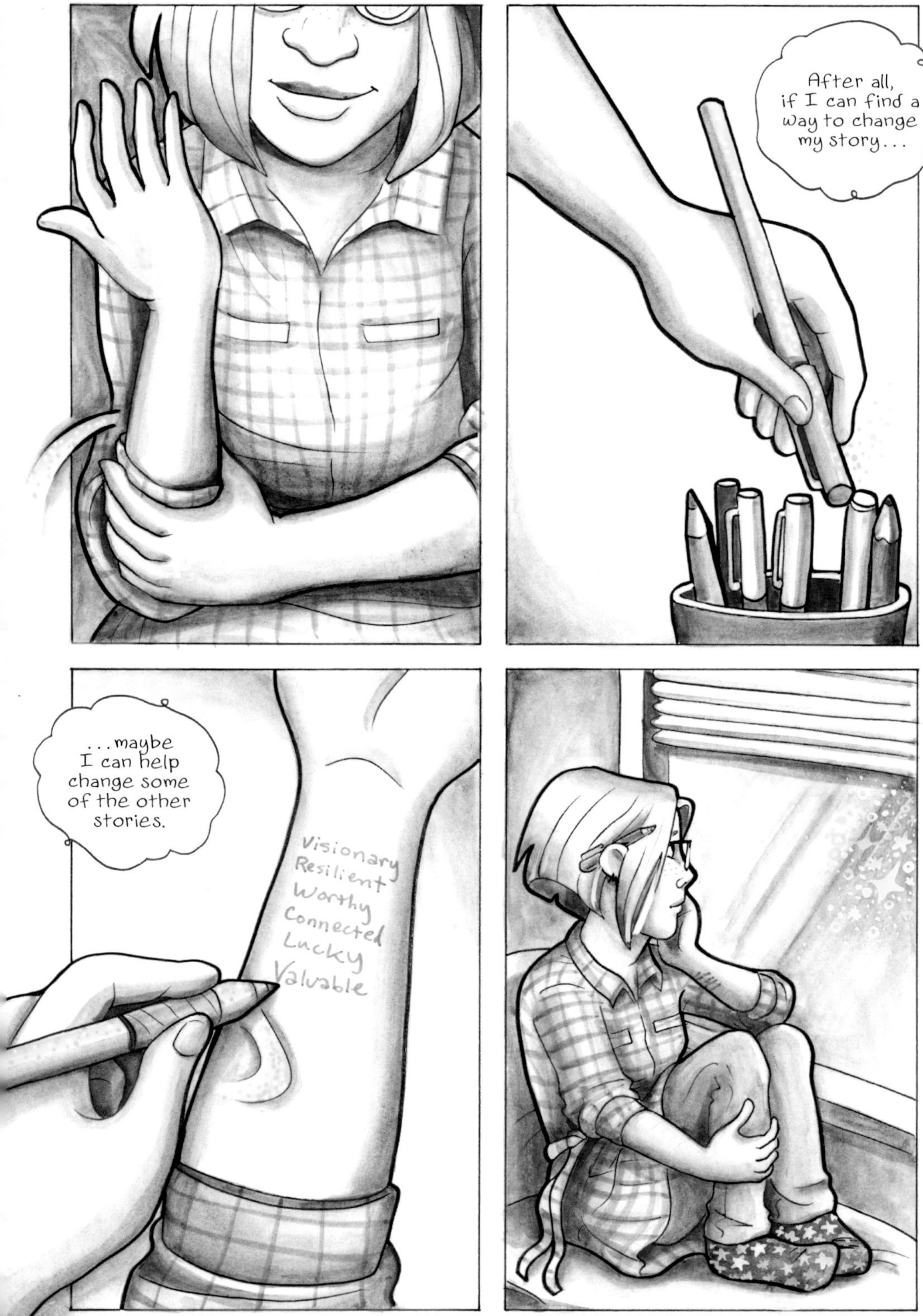
After all, if I can find a way to change my story...
...maybe I can help change some of the other stories.
Visionary
Resilient
Worthy
Connected
Lucky
Valuable

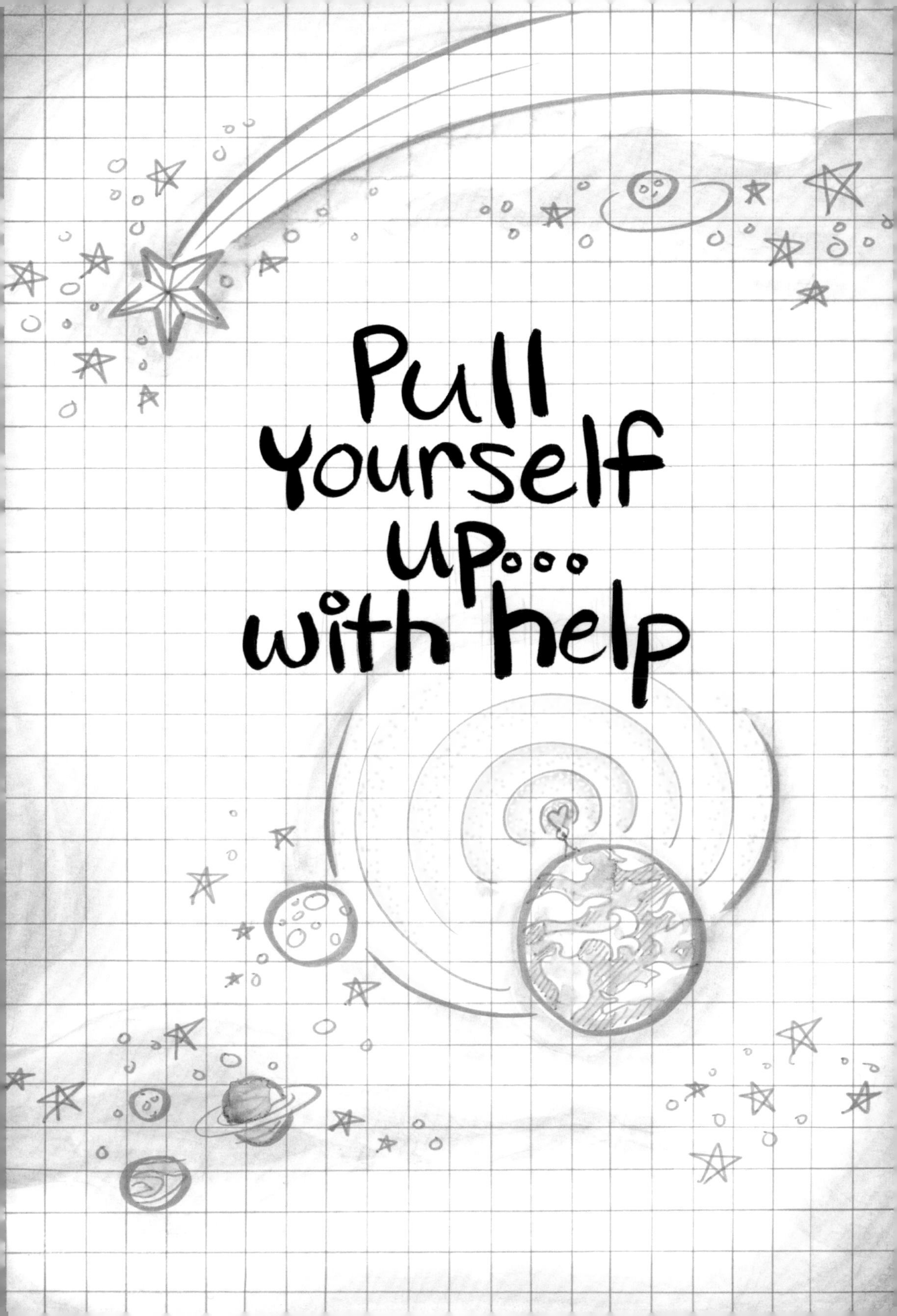
Pull
Yourself
up...
with help

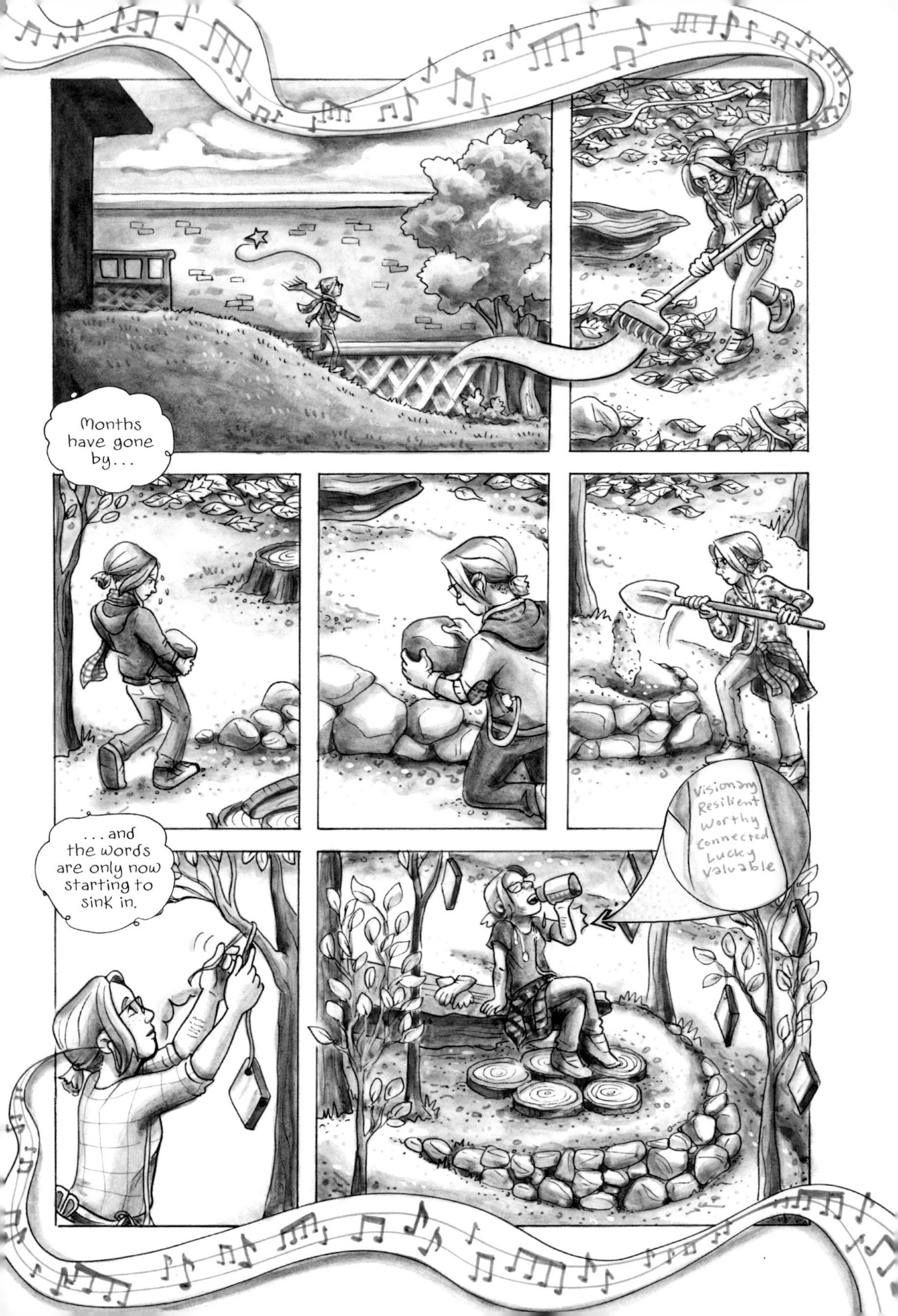

Months have gone by...
...and the words are only now starting to sink in.
Visionary
Resilient
Worthy
Connected
Lucky
Valuable

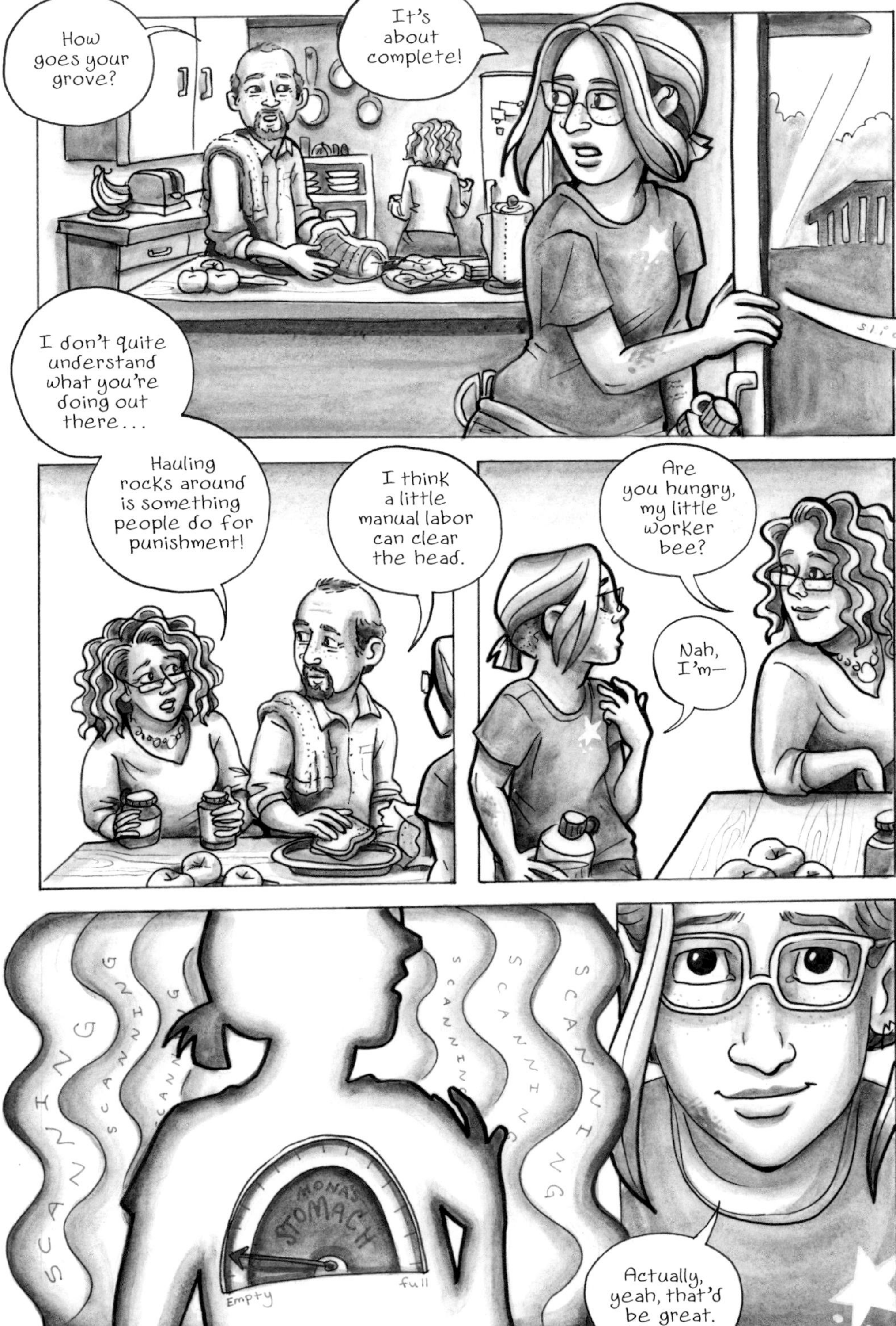
How goes your grove?
It's about complete!
slide
I don't quite understand what you're doing out there...
Hauling rocks around is something people do for punishment!
I think a little manual labor can clear the head.
Are you hungry, my little worker bee?
Nah, I'm—
SCANNING
SCANNING
SCANNING
SCANNING
SCANNING
SCANNING
MONA'S STOMACH
Empty
full
Actually, yeah, that'd be great.

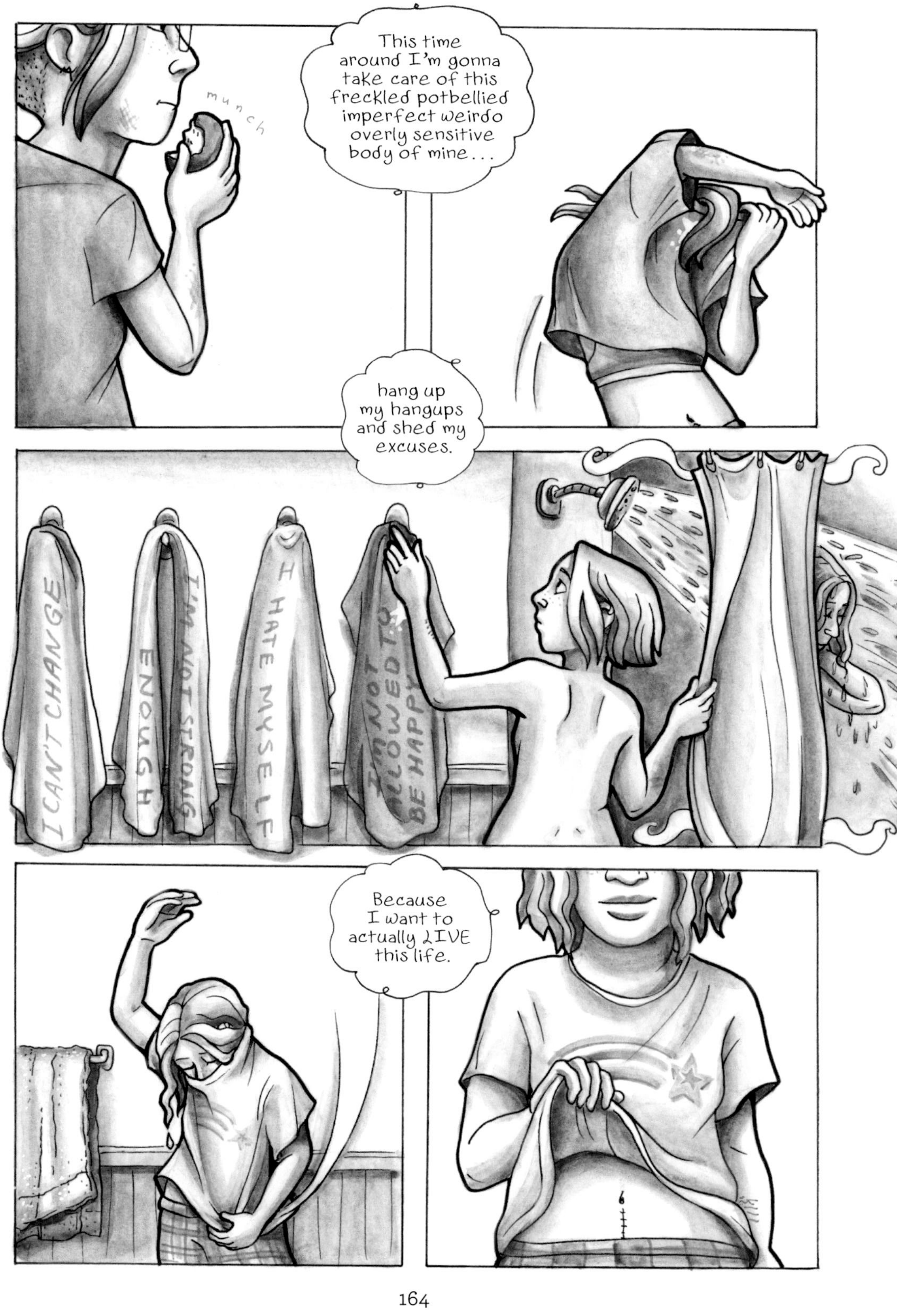
munch
This time around I'm gonna take care of this freckled potbellied imperfect weirdo overly sensitive body of mine . . .
hang up my hangups and shed my excuses.
I CAN'T CHANGE
I'M NOT STRONG ENOUGH
I HATE MYSELF
I'M NOT ALLOWED TO BE HAPPY
Because I want to actually LIVE this life.

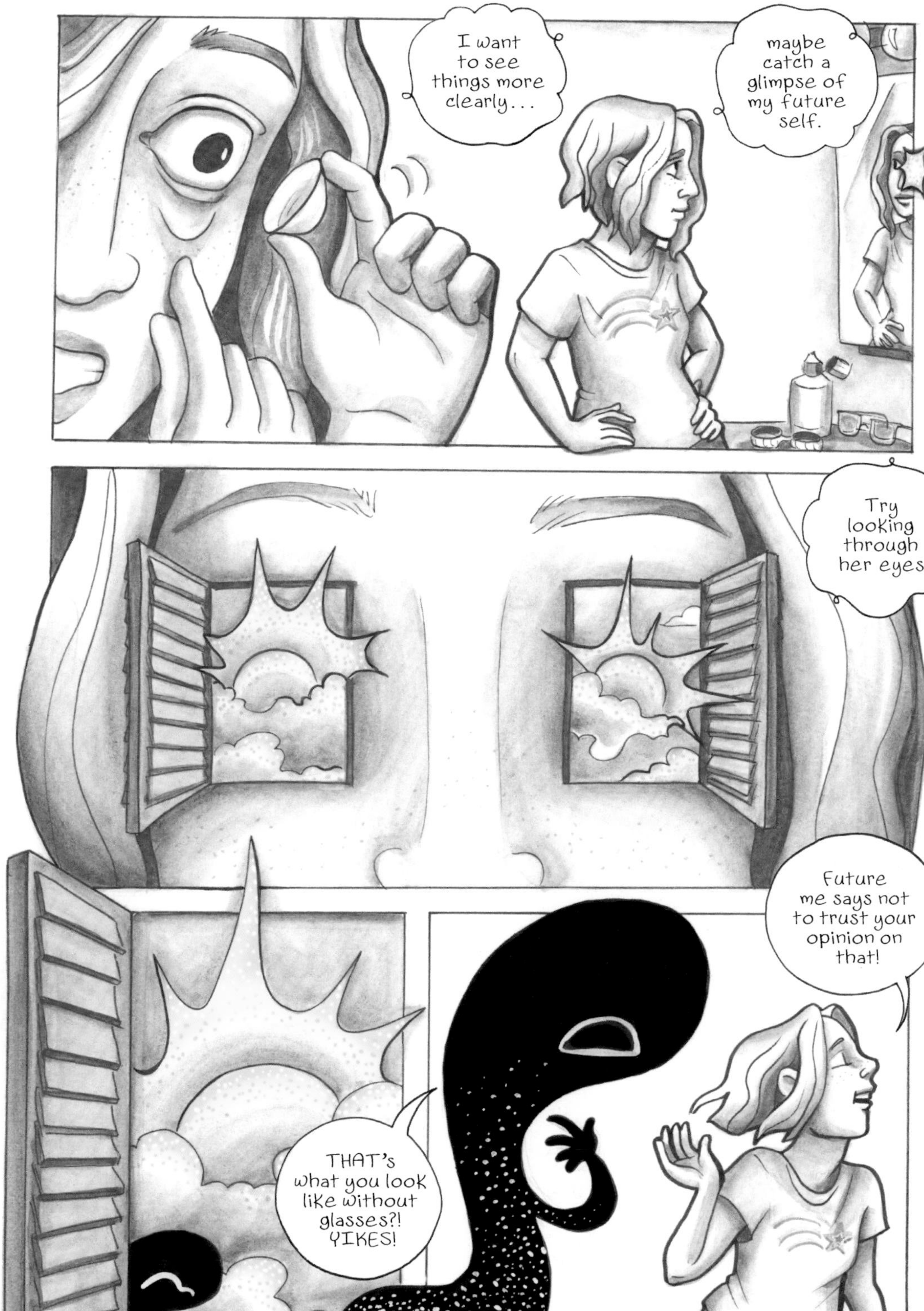
I want to see things more clearly...
maybe catch a glimpse of my future self.
Try looking through her eyes.
Future me says not to trust your opinion on that!
THAT's what you look like without glasses?! YIKES!

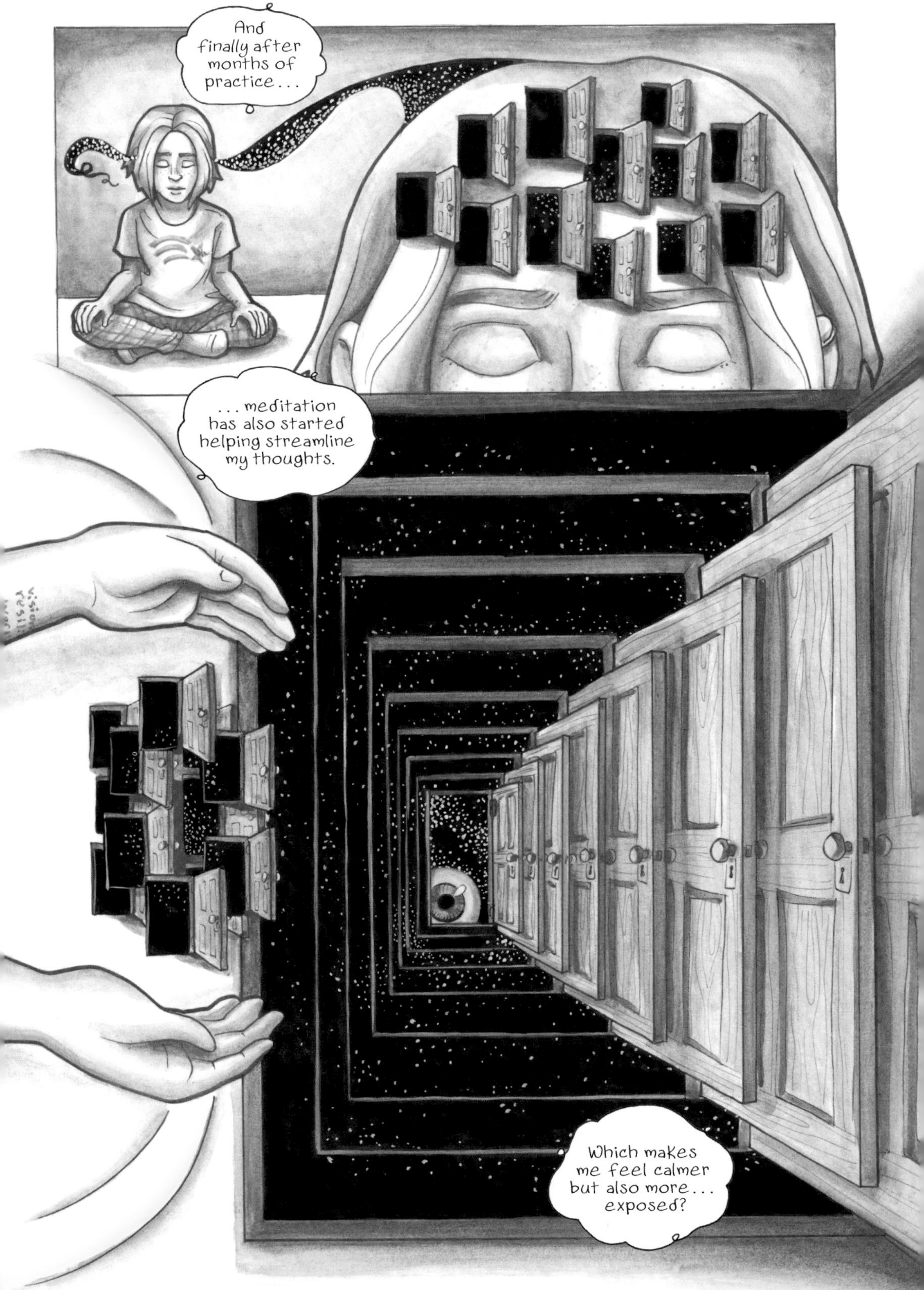
And finally after months of practice . . .
. . . meditation has also started helping streamline my thoughts.
Which makes me feel calmer but also more . . . exposed?

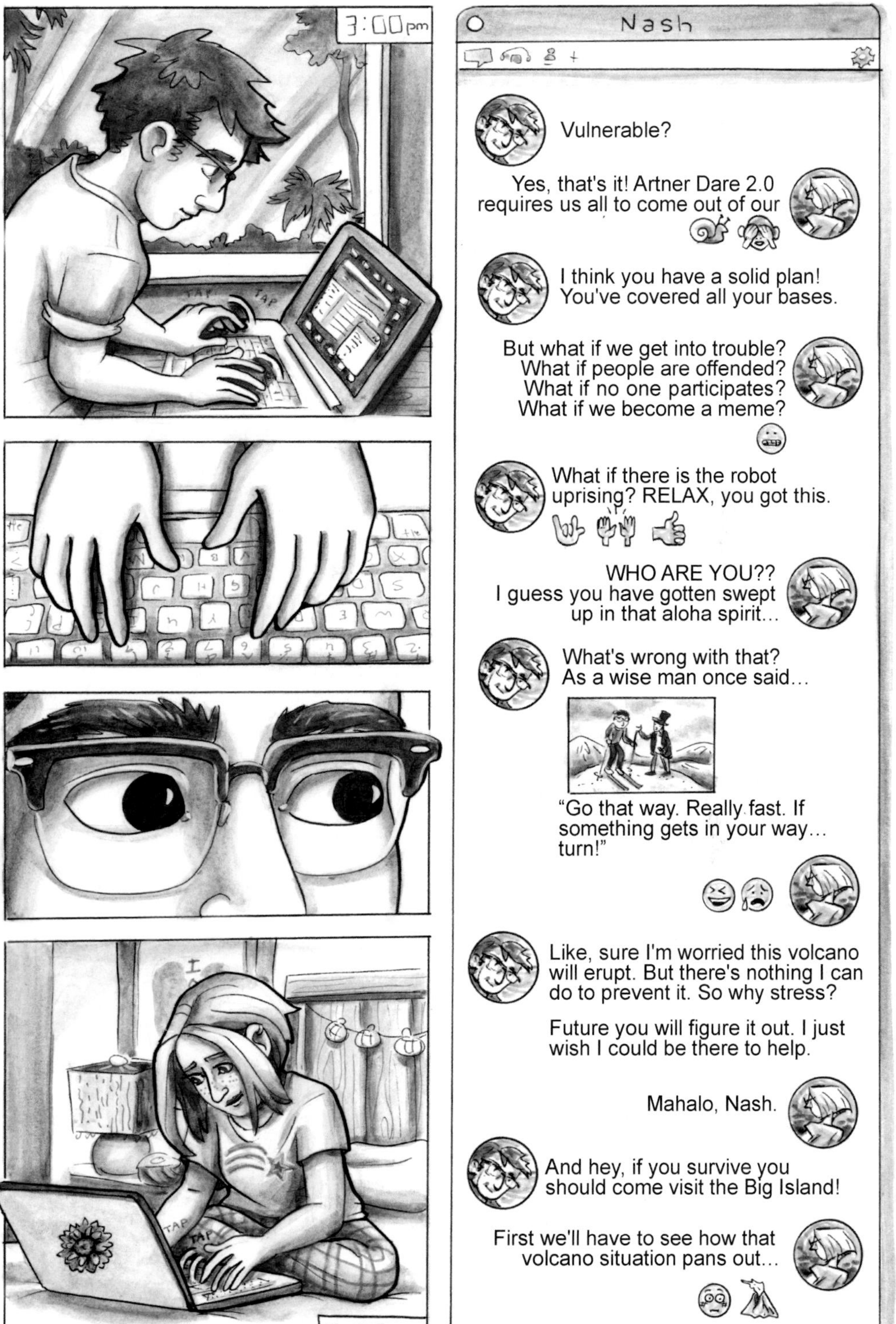
3:00pm
TAP
TAP
Nash
Vulnerable?
Yes, that's it! Artner Dare 2.0 requires us all to come out of our
I think you have a solid plan! You've covered all your bases.
But what if we get into trouble? What if people are offended? What if no one participates? What if we become a meme?
What if there is the robot uprising? RELAX, you got this.
WHO ARE YOU?? I guess you have gotten swept up in that aloha spirit…
What's wrong with that? As a wise man once said…
"Go that way. Really fast. If something gets in your way… turn!"
Like, sure I'm worried this volcano will erupt. But there's nothing I can do to prevent it. So why stress?
Future you will figure it out. I just wish I could be there to help.
Mahalo, Nash.
And hey, if you survive you should come visit the Big Island!
First we'll have to see how that volcano situation pans out…
TAP
TAP
9:00pm

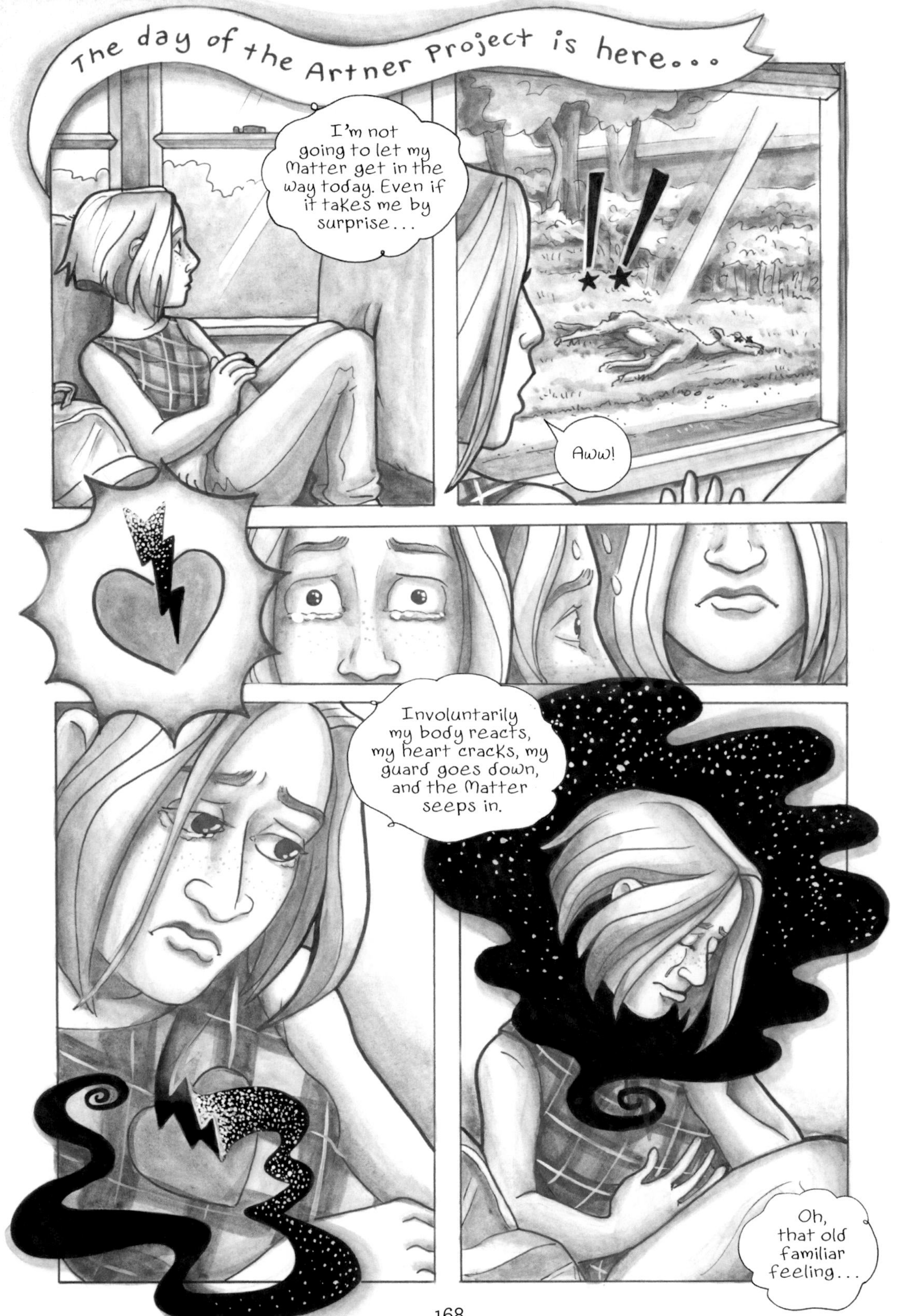
The day of the Artner Project is here...
I'm not going to let my Matter get in the way today. Even if it takes me by surprise...
Aww!
Involuntarily my body reacts, my heart cracks, my guard goes down, and the Matter seeps in.
Oh, that old familiar feeling...

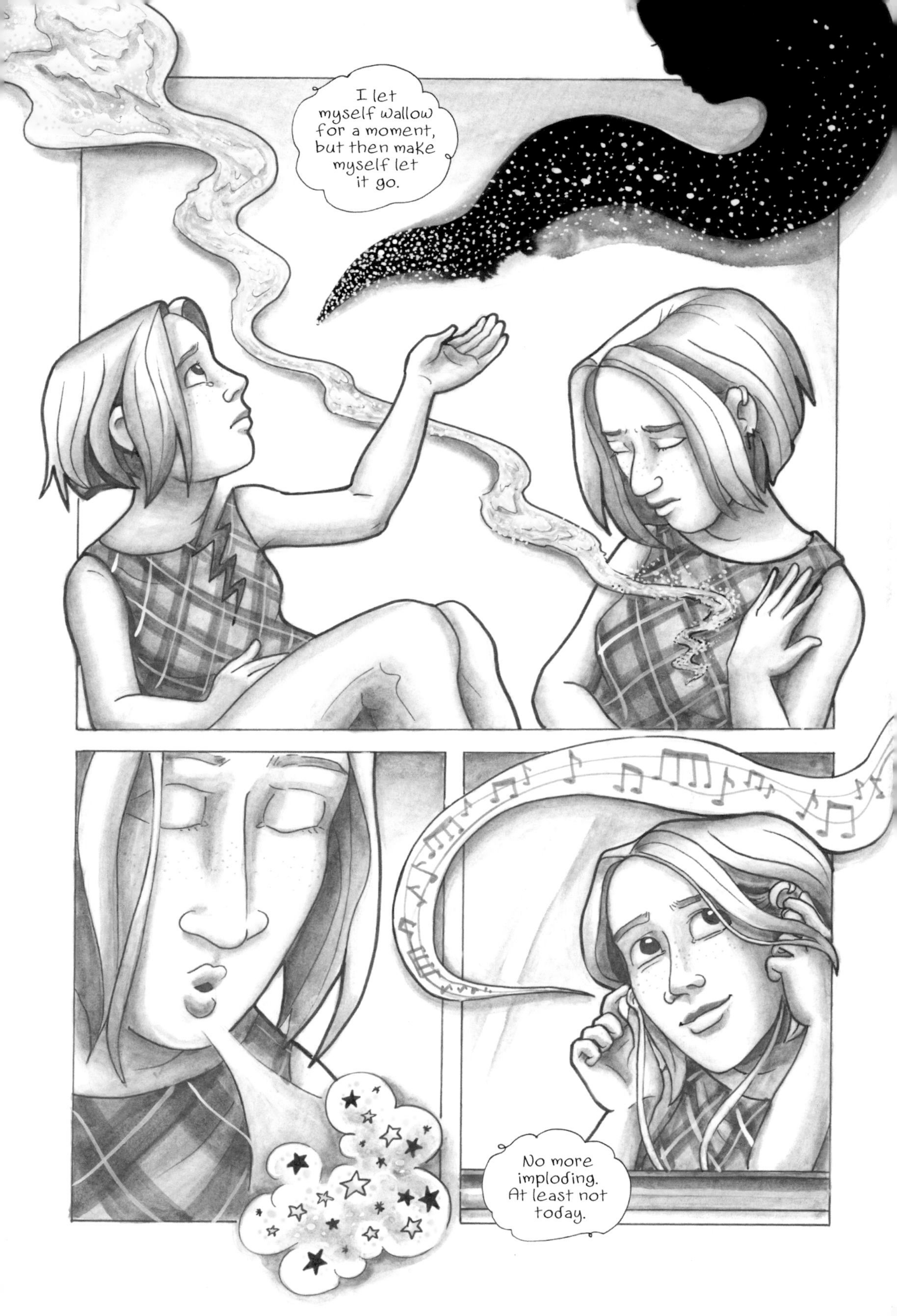
I let myself wallow for a moment, but then make myself let it go.
No more imploding. At least not today.

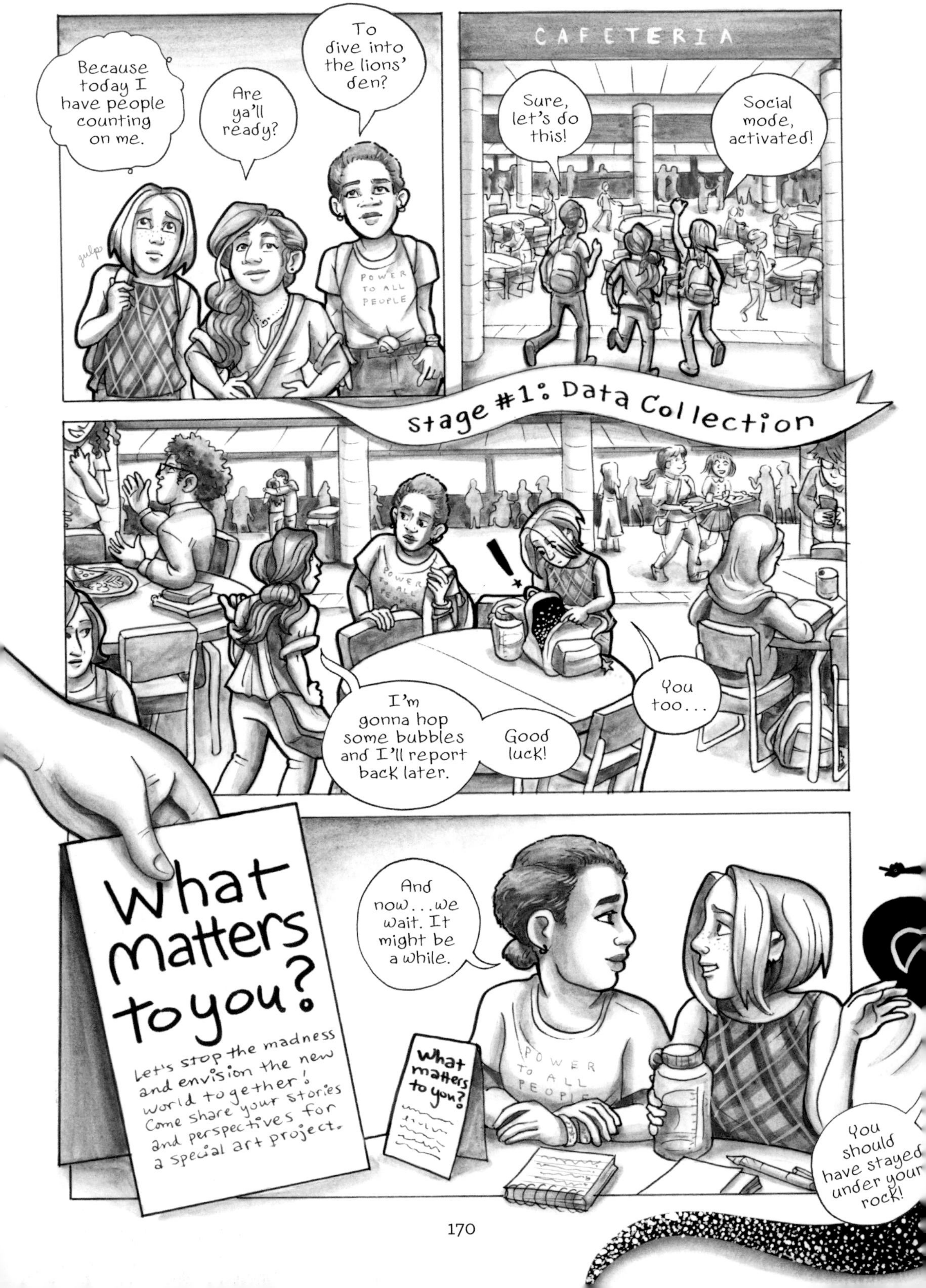
Because today I have people counting on me.
gulps
Are ya'll ready?
To dive into the lions' den?
POWER TO ALL PEOPLE
CAFETERIA
Sure, let's do this!
Social mode, activated!
Stage #1: Data Collection
POWER TO ALL PEOPLE
I'm gonna hop some bubbles and I'll report back later.
Good luck!
You too...
What matters to you?
Let's stop the madness and envision the new world together! Come share your stories and perspectives for a special art project.
And now...we wait. It might be a while.
What matters to you?
POWER TO ALL PEOPLE
You should have stayed under your rock!

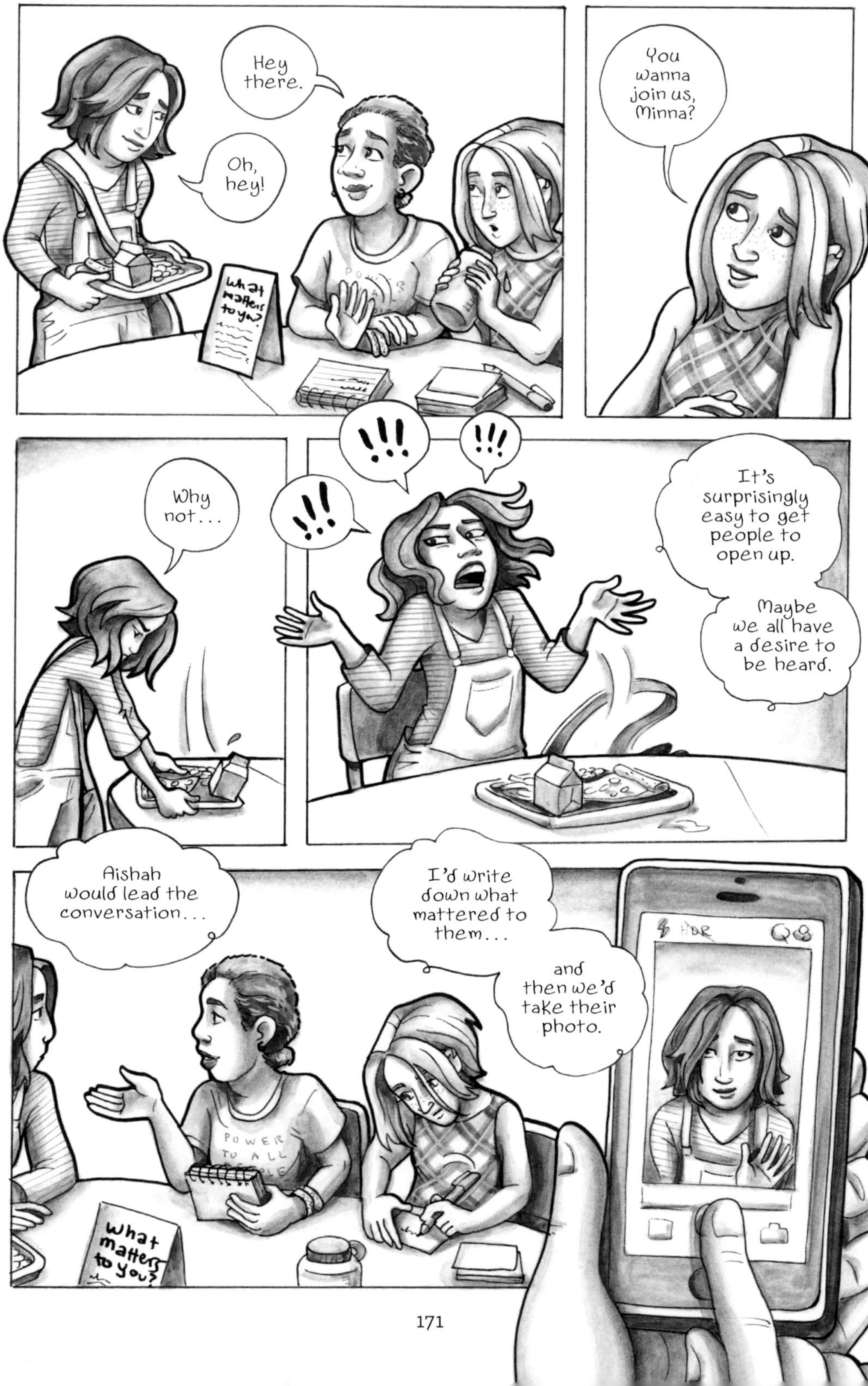
Hey there.
Oh, hey!
what matters to you?
You wanna join us, Minna?
Why not...
!!!
!!!
!!!
It's surprisingly easy to get people to open up.
Maybe we all have a desire to be heard.
Aishah would lead the conversation...
I'd write down what mattered to them...
and then we'd take their photo.
POWER TO ALL
what matters to you?

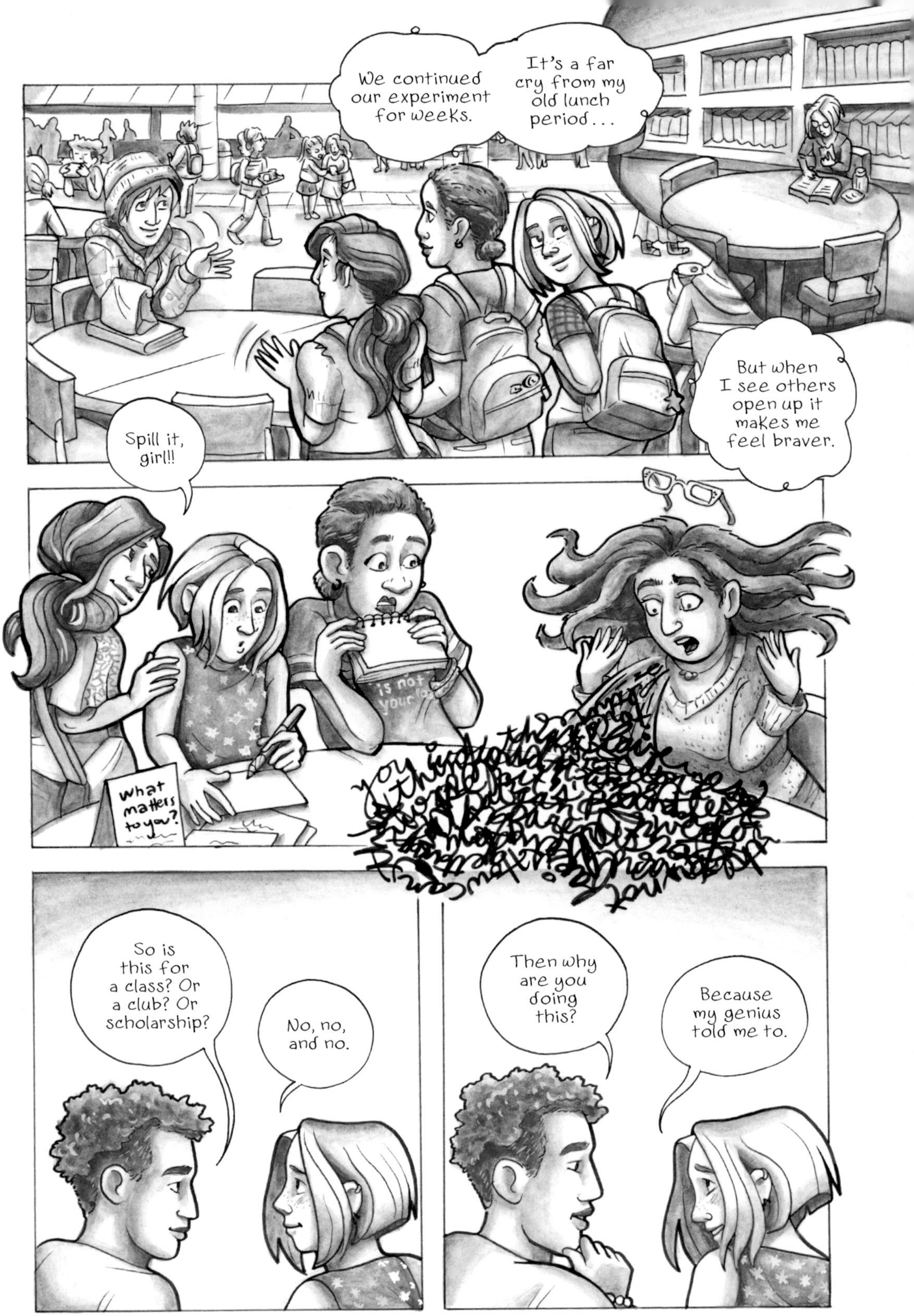
We continued our experiment for weeks.
It's a far cry from my old lunch period . . .
But when I see others open up it makes me feel braver.
Spill it, girl!!
what matters to you?
is not your
So is this for a class? Or a club? Or scholarship?
No, no, and no.
Then why are you doing this?
Because my genius told me to.

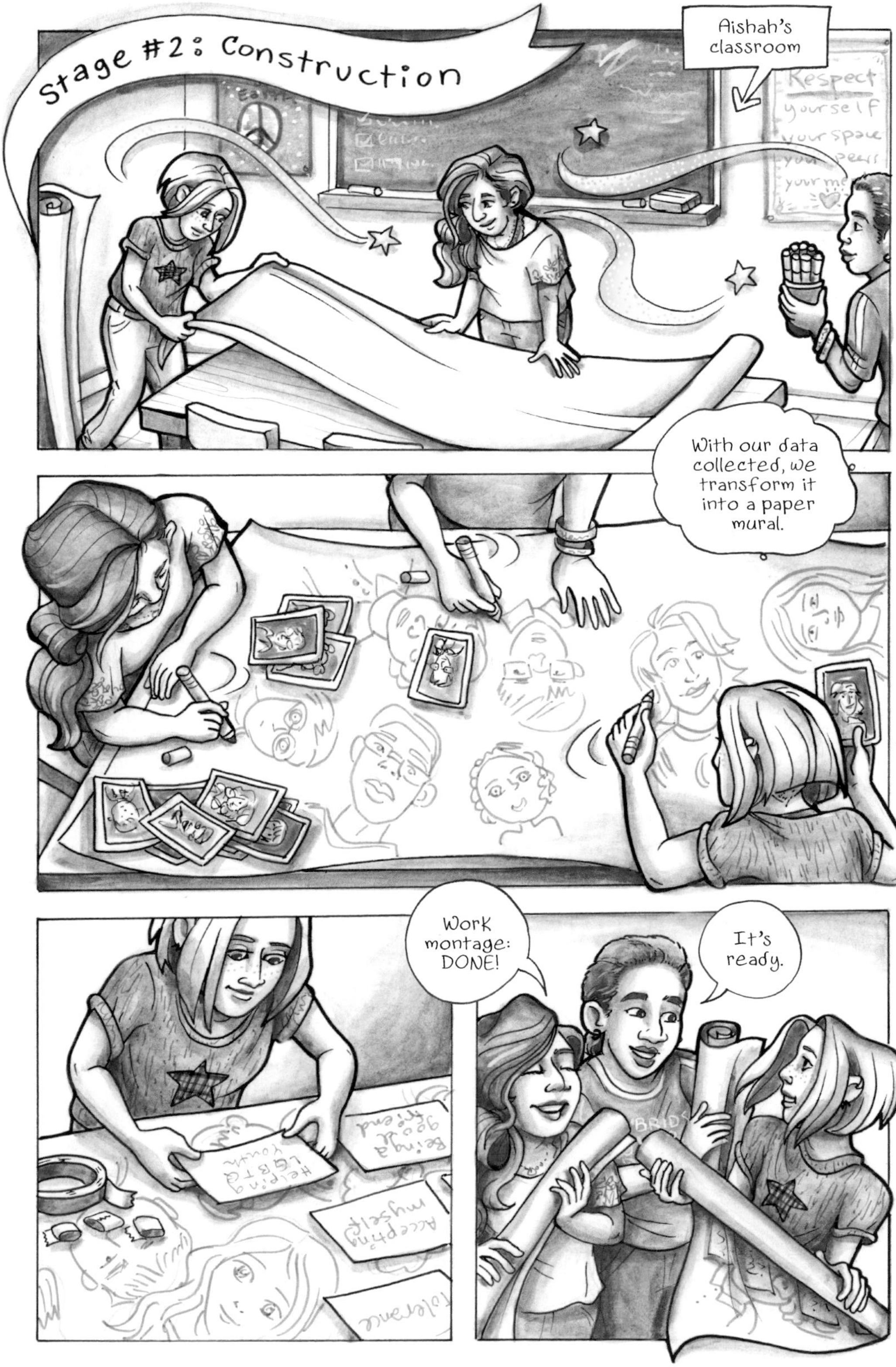
Stage #2: Construction
Aishah's classroom
Respect yourself your space your peers your me
With our data collected, we transform it into a paper mural.
Helping LGBTQ Youth
Being a good friend
Accepting myself
Tolerance
Work montage: DONE!
It's ready.

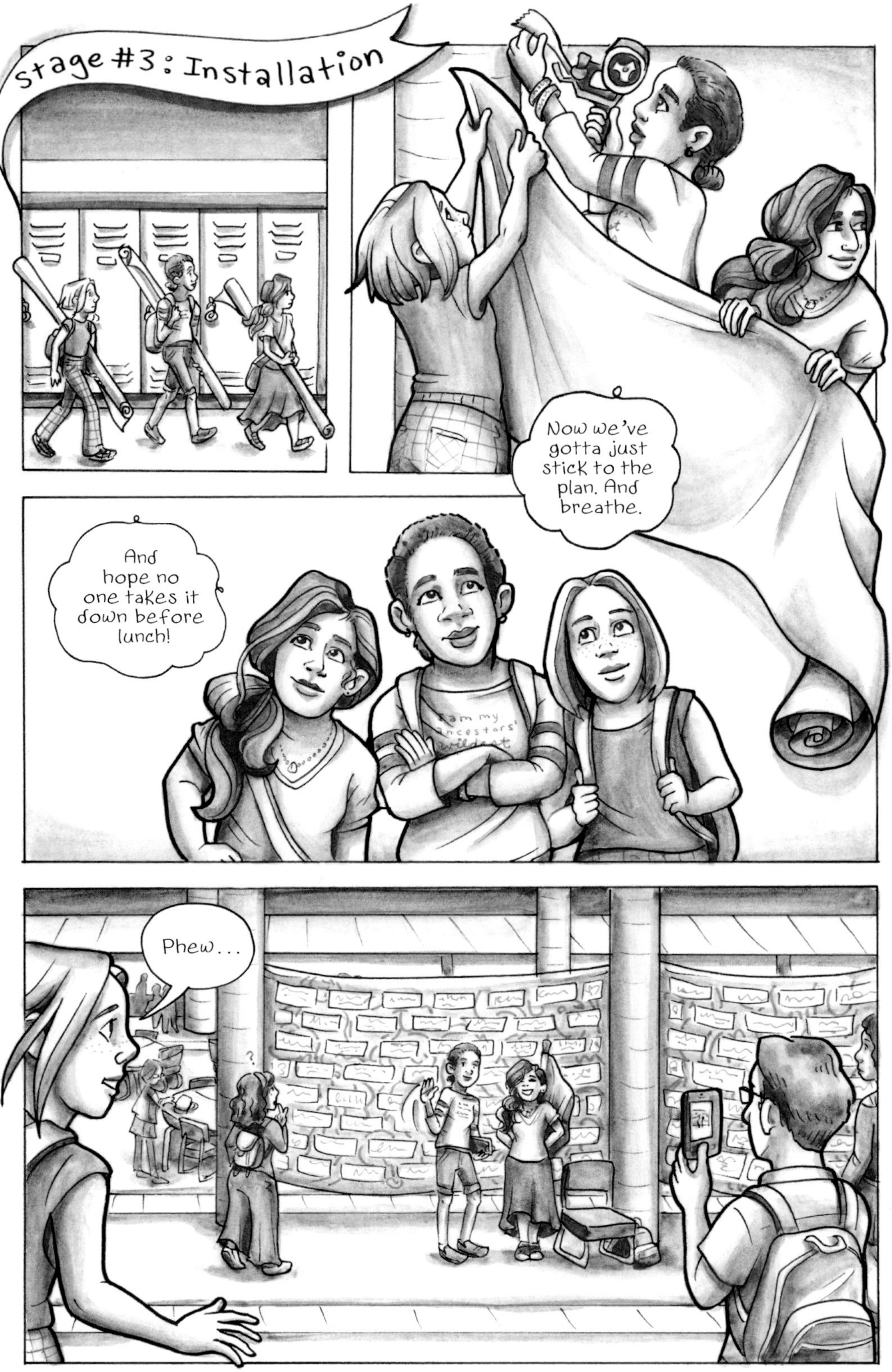
Stage #3: Installation
Now we've gotta just stick to the plan. And breathe.
And hope no one takes it down before lunch!
Phew...

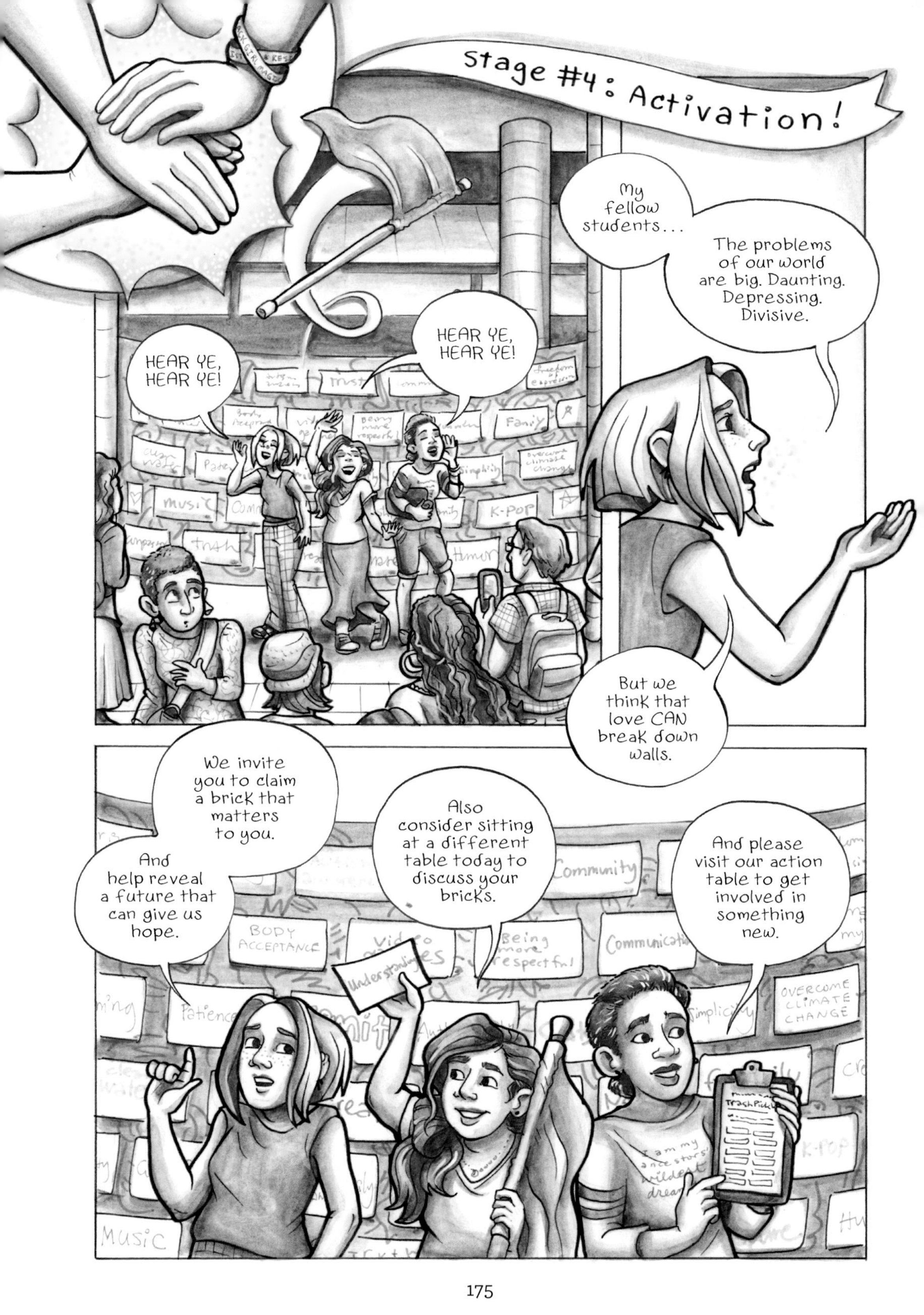

Stage #4: Activation!
HEAR YE, HEAR YE!
HEAR YE, HEAR YE!
My fellow students...
The problems of our world are big. Daunting. Depressing. Divisive.
But we think that love CAN break down walls.
We invite you to claim a brick that matters to you.
And help reveal a future that can give us hope.
Also consider sitting at a different table today to discuss your bricks.
And please visit our action table to get involved in something new.

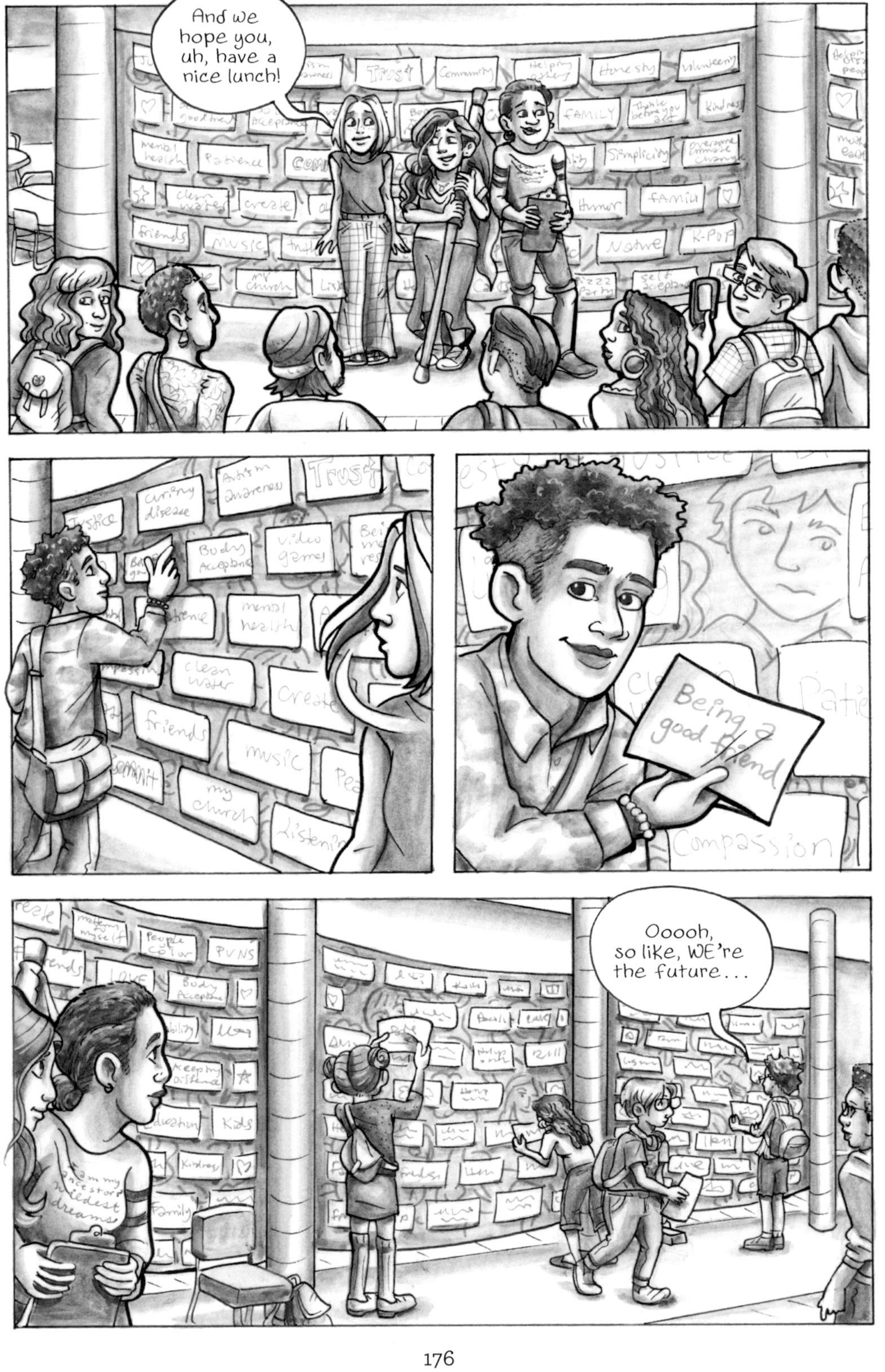
And we hope you, uh, have a nice lunch!
Being a good friend
Ooooh, so like, WE're the future...

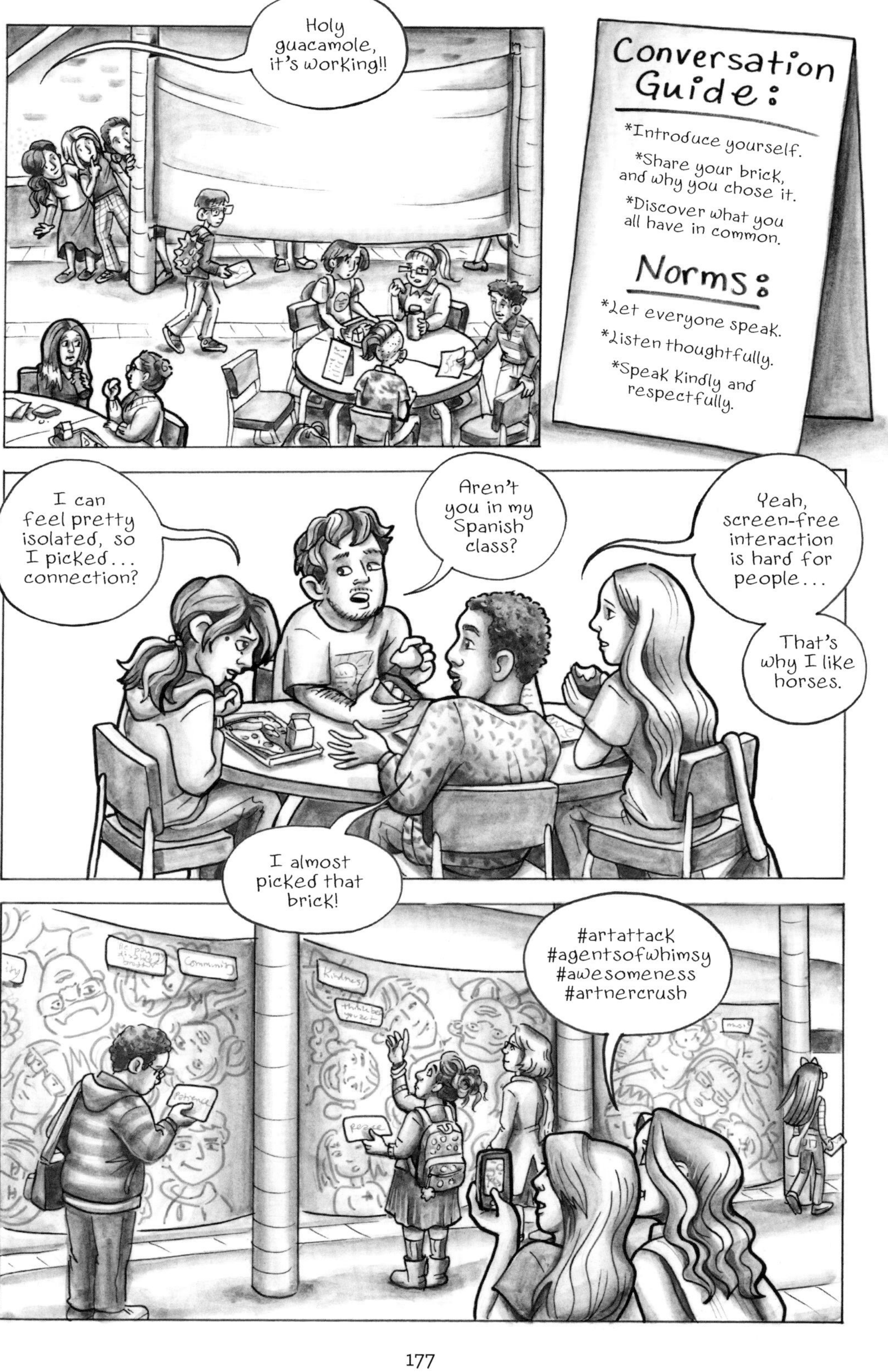
Holy guacamole, it's working!!
Conversation Guide:
*Introduce yourself.
*Share your brick, and why you chose it.
*Discover what you all have in common.
Norms:
*Let everyone speak.
*Listen thoughtfully.
*Speak kindly and respectfully.
I can feel pretty isolated, so I picked... connection?
Aren't you in my Spanish class?
Yeah, screen-free interaction is hard for people...
That's why I like horses.
I almost picked that brick!
#artattack
#agentsofwhimsy
#awesomeness
#artnercrush

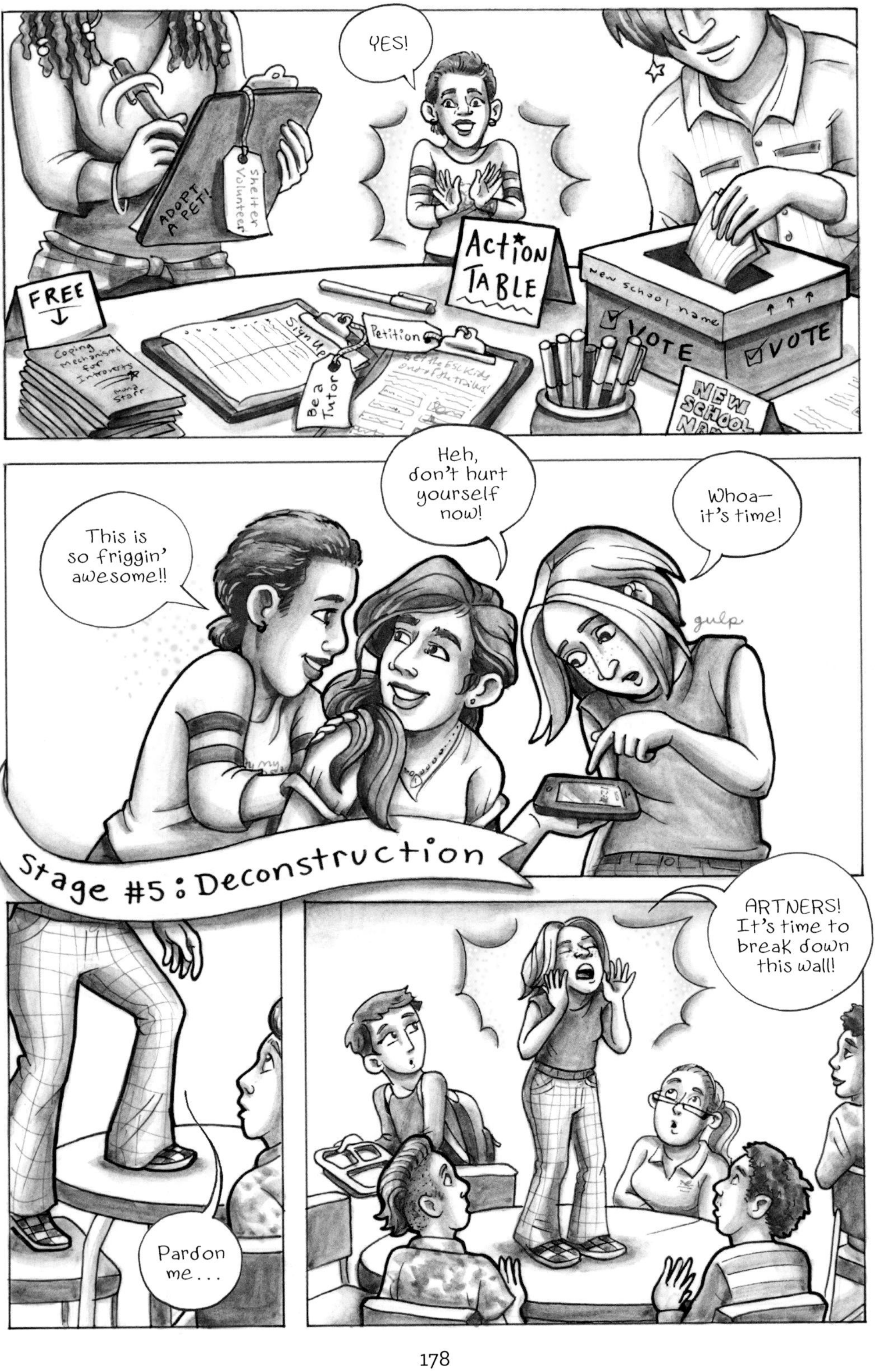
YES!
Shelter Volunteer
ADOPT A PET!
Action TABLE
FREE
Coping Mechanisms for Introverts
Sign Up
Petition
Be a Tutor
New school name
VOTE
VOTE
NEW SCHOOL
This is so friggin' awesome!!
Heh, don't hurt yourself now!
Whoa— it's time!
gulp
Stage #5: Deconstruction
Pardon me...
ARTNERS! It's time to break down this wall!

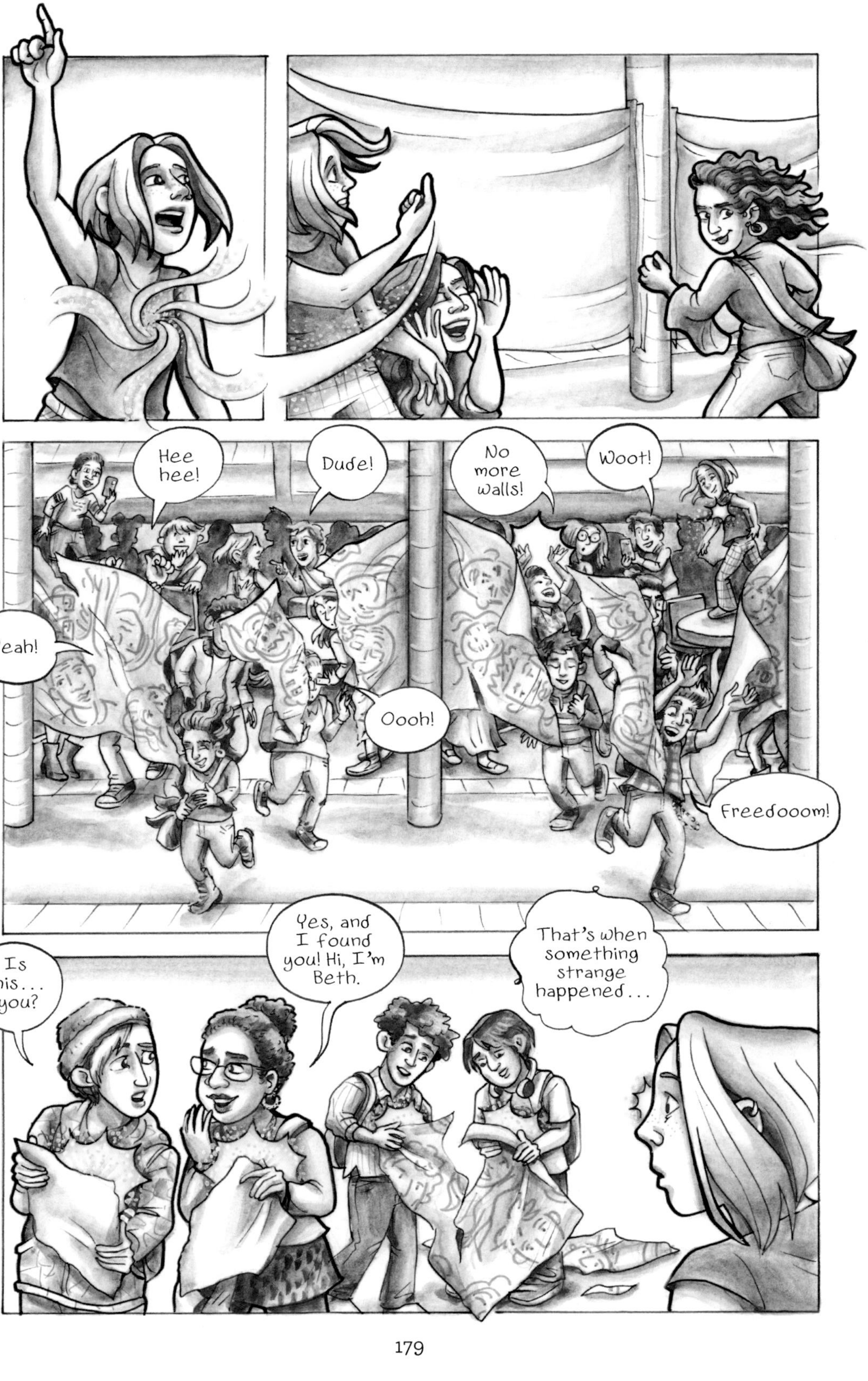

Hee hee!
Dude!
No more walls!
Woot!
Yeah!
Oooh!
Freedooom!
Is this... you?
Yes, and I found you! Hi, I'm Beth.
That's when something strange happened...

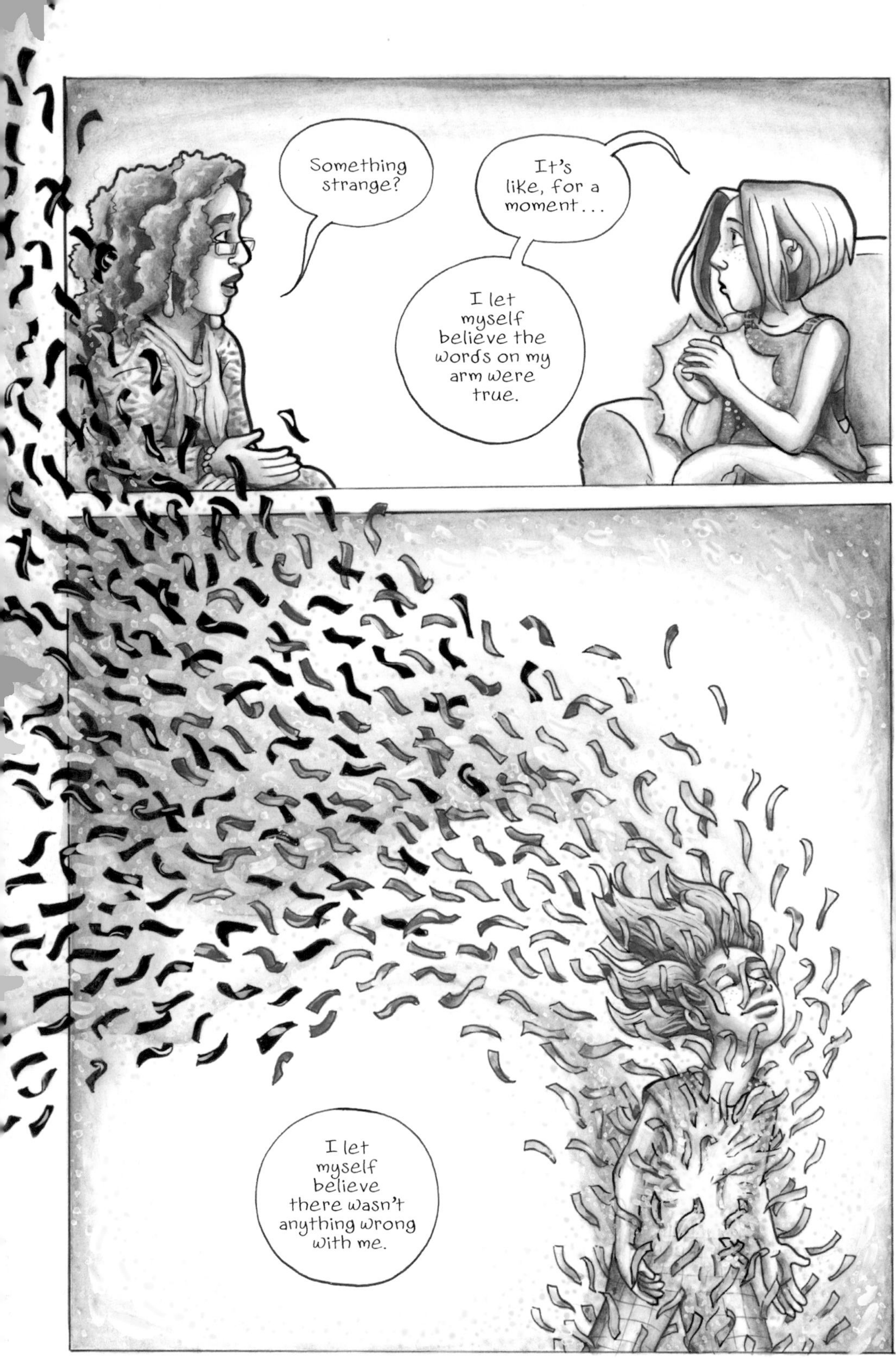
Something strange?
It's like, for a moment...
I let myself believe the words on my arm were true.
I let myself believe there wasn't anything wrong with me.

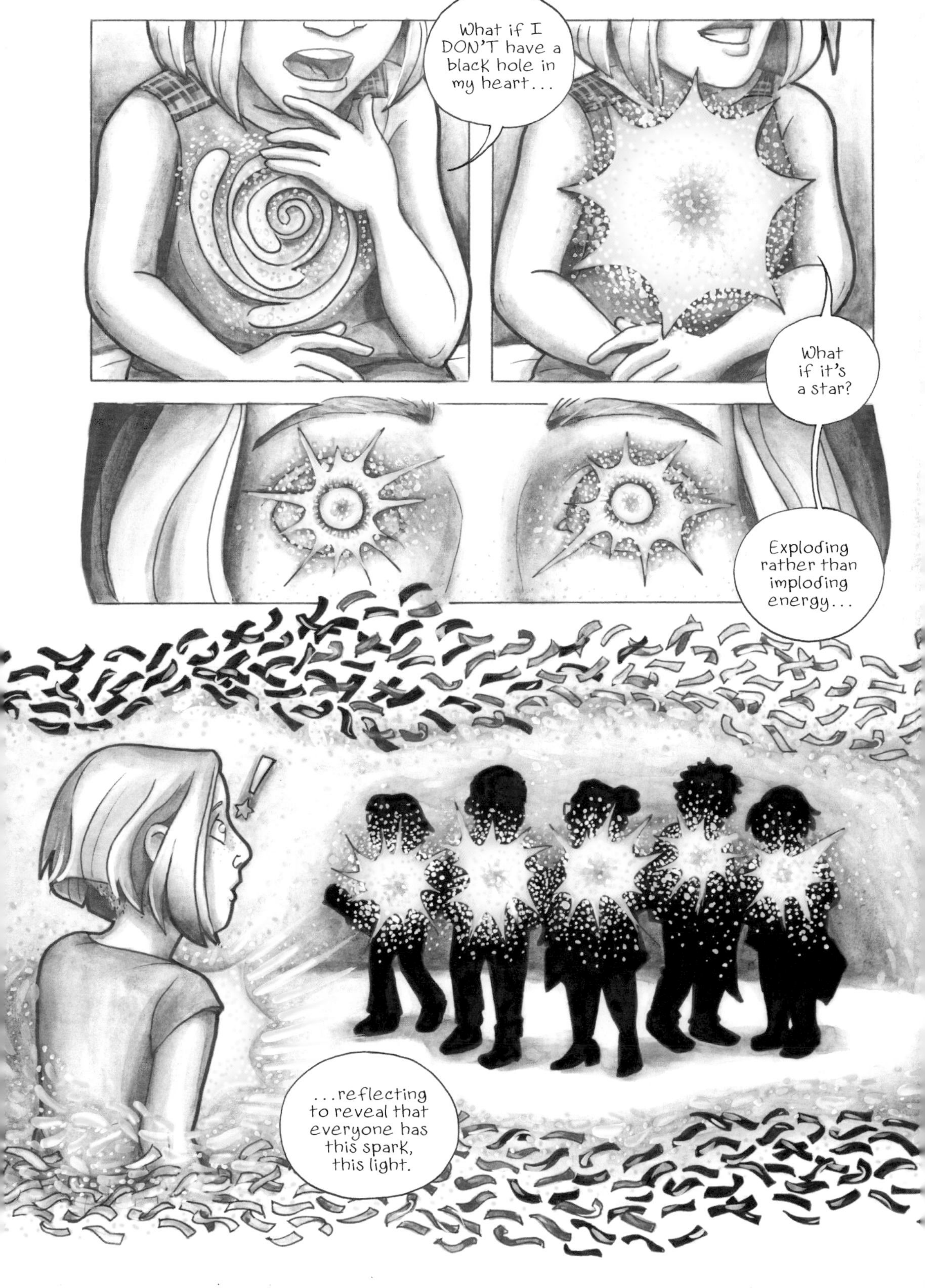
What if I DON'T have a black hole in my heart...
What if it's a star?
Exploding rather than imploding energy...
...reflecting to reveal that everyone has this spark, this light.

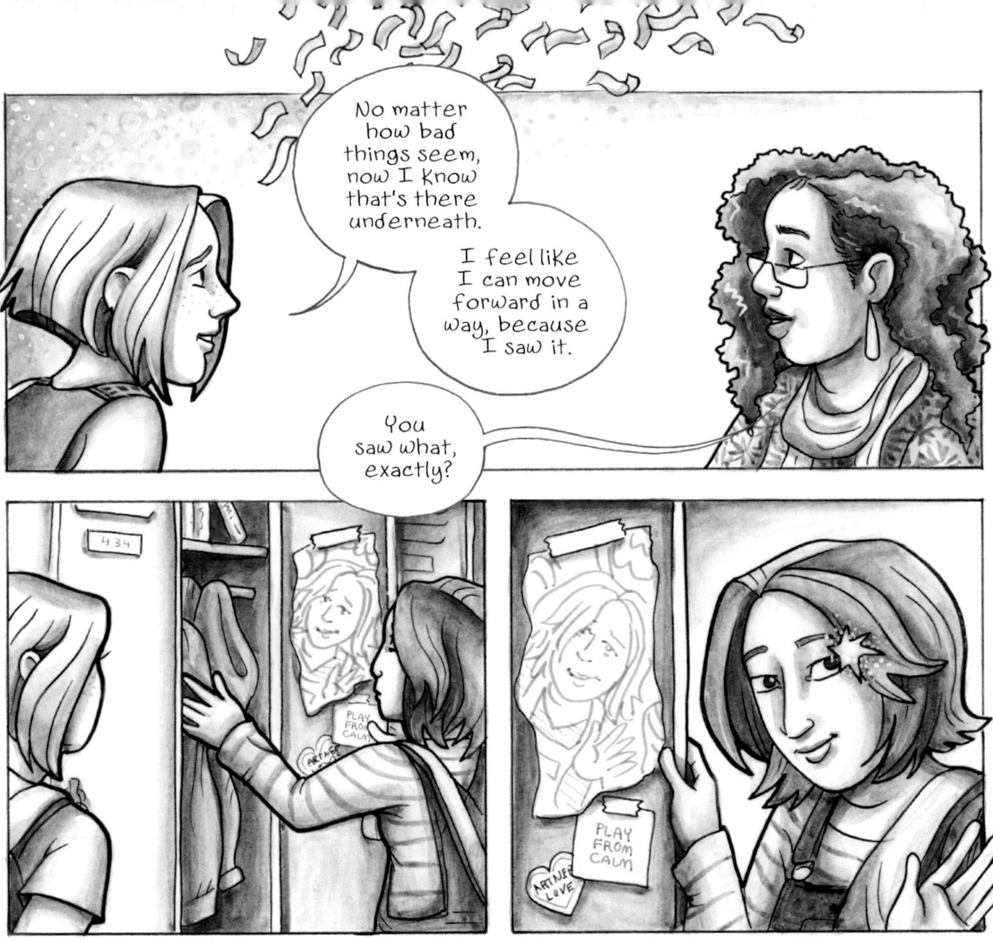
No matter how bad things seem, now I know that's there underneath.
I feel like I can move forward in a way, because I saw it.
You saw what, exactly?
434
PLAY FROM CALM
PLAY FROM CALM

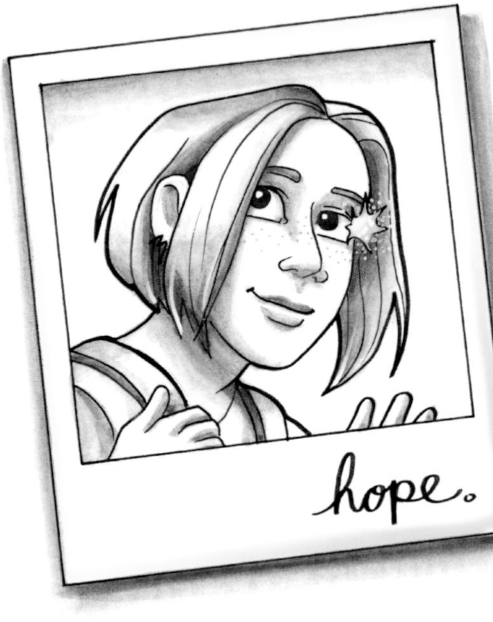
hope.

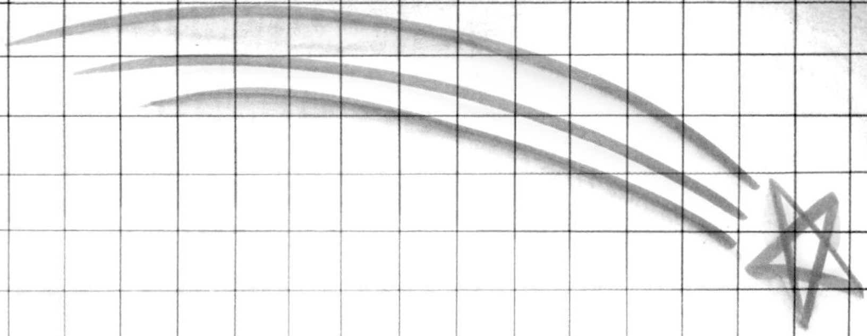

Acknowledgments

The support I've received to help bring this book
into the world has changed my heart forever.

First I need to thank my LITERARY ARTNERS: editors Emily Daluga
and Maggie Lehrman along with designers Siobhan Gallagher and Max
Temescu at Abrams Books, plus my literary agent Daniel Lazar at
Writers House. You wanted a story I was reluctant to tell but your
faith in Mona made be brave enough to trust where she was taking us.

Another big thanks goes to my CONTRIBUTING ARTNERS Andrea
Spracaio, Bonnie Rubrecht, Lauren Larken, Earl Vallery, and John K.
Snyder III for your incredibly helpful feedback during the editing
process. Plus extra thanks to Andrea, Bonnie, and Earl for contibuting
handwriting. And I'm extra excited to acknowledge the 37 real life
students* who gave voice to Mona's classmates in the wall installation
at the end of the book! Thanks for accepting my Artner Dare.
(*See copyright page for the full list.)

I'm especially grateful to thank all the GENEROUS PATRONS who
provided financial support which covered my housing costs during the
11 months of drawing production. This includes everyone who voted
for me to receive the local SOUP GRANT through New City Arts
Initiative in Charlottesville. Plus all the contributors to my online
PATREON CAMPAIGN: Artistic Evolution, Hina Ansari, Diana Arge
Bendixen, Bernie Beitman, Maurice and Patty Gulledge, Brian Gulledge,
Chris Grandjean, Earl Vallery, Jamie Bernstein, Jamie Linck, Jennifer
Hayden, Juliet Trail, Kenneth Hill, Lindsay Heider Diamond, Matt Mikas,
Melissa Charles, Natalie Anderson, The Moxley Family, Vivek Tiwary,
Chris Calloway, Francis Mitchell, Caitlin Adams, Ray Keilman, Alan
Reynolds, John Steimke, and Wendy Addison. It was such a
pleasure to share this journey with you all!

Special thanks go out to ARTNER ANGELS Eileen French for
welcoming me into her studio at McGuffey Arts Center while I
finished inking, my Dad for all his sanity-saving help with Photoshop,
and especially Earl for being so supportive through this emotionally
challenging process. I don't know if I could have done it without
you . . . and I will never forget all you did for Mona and I.

Finally I'd like to thank all my friends, family, Artners, students,
readers, ancestors, and animal friends who have kindly encouraged
and supported me on this long journey. This story belongs to all of us.

Thank You!

artnerlove,
Laura Lee

Nash's
READING LIST

1. American Nations by Colin Woodard
2. Ishmael by Daniel Quinn
3. The Fire Next Time by James Baldwin
4. The Miracle of Mindfulness
   by Thich Nhat Hanh
5. Women Who Run with the Wolves
   by Clarissa Pinkola Estés
6. Quiet: The Power of Introverts in a World
   that Can't Stop Talking by Susan Cain
7. Party of One: The Loner's Manifesto
   by Anneli Rufus
8. The Highly Sensitive Person
   by Elaine N. Aron
9. Lighter Than My Shadow by Katie Green
10. Marbles: Mania, Depression, Michelangelo
    and Me by Ellen Forney

Mona's
SOUNDTRACK

1. "Ode to My Family" - The Cranberries
2. "Tomorrow, Tomorrow" - Elliott Smith
3. "Saying Goodbye" - J.S. Ondara
4. "Everybody Here Hates You" - Courtney Barnett
5. "Phenomenal Woman" - Laura Mvula
6. "Breaking Down" - Florence + the Machine
7. "Comptine D'Un Autre Été L'Après Midi" - Yann Tiersen
8. "Hospital Beds" - Cold War Kids
9. "Cosmic Girl" - Jamiroquai
10. "While My Guitar Gently Weeps" - The Beatles
11. "Without You" - Harry Nilsson
12. "Invisible Sun" - The Police
13. "Remind Me" - Emily King
14. "Turn the Light" - Karen O & Danger Mouse
15. "Invincible" - Muse
16. "Dark Matter" - Andrew Bird
17. "Bad Day" - R.E.M.
18. "Lightning Bolt" - Jake Bugg
(and the entire album A Moon Shaped Pool by Radiohead)

NOTE: I don't always do everything listed here! It's an ideal list since real life demands flexibility. But I manage to do most of it, which has vastly improved my life and helped me make smarter decisions . . .

Laura Lee's Self-Care Plan

(Hero's Training Regimen)

Physical Needs

DAILY
- 8 hours of sleep
- Supplements & Food Medicine
- No caffeine after 2 pm
- Affection XO (8 hugs a day!)
- Stretching breaks from desk work

WEEKLY
- Walking in nature 2 hours
- Yoga 1 hour
- Physical Therapy 1 hour
- (Adult beverages: limit 3x)
- Flossing & face scrub

REGULARLY
- Wear wrist brace while cleaning
- Hot baths & steaming
- Seasonal healing (like massage)

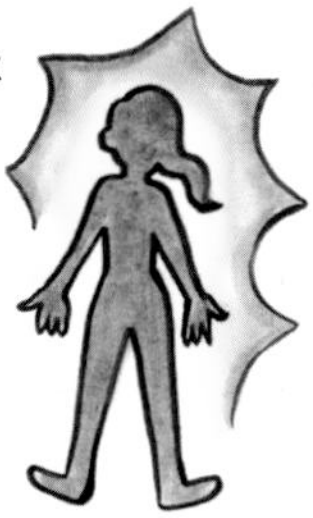

Daily Supplements

- Wheat germ
- Prunes
- Kombucha
- Tulsi tea
- Local, fresh real food
- Ginger turmeric shots
- Multivitamin
- Fish oil
- Probiotic
- Vitamin D
- Calcium

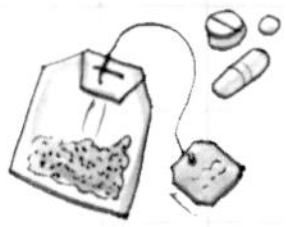

Support System

WORLD FAMILY:
- Earl
- Juliet
- LarKen
- Bonnie
- Sam

BIOLOGICAL FAMILY:
- Mom
- Dad
- Brian
- Anna
- Elaine

+ Artners, Readers, Historical Mentors, Ancestors, & Magical Helpers

Emotional Needs

- Time in nature
- Time with animals
- Time with Kids
- Time in water
- Growing plants
- Singing in studio & car
- Making playlists & listening to radio
- Ecstatic Dance
- Prayer/devotion rituals
- Exploring new places
- Introvert Social recovery time
- Aromatherapy/scent scene changes
- Phone dates with support system
- Friend dates in person
- Sending snail mail
- Volunteering

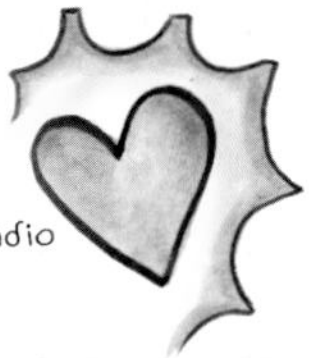

When stress symptoms flare up. . . do some things from your self-care plan! And reach out to someone in your support system.

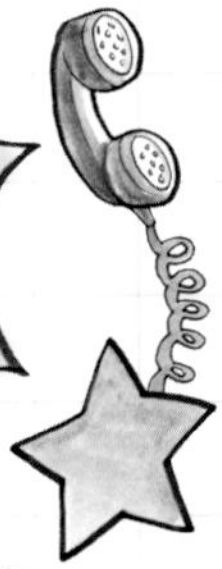

Mental Needs

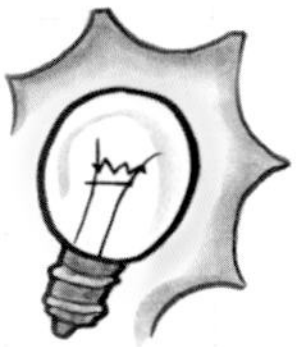

WEEKLY
- 1–2 days off & flex time
- Fictional assistant time
- Contemplative chores (like washing dishes)

REGULARLY
- Personal art time
- Journaling
- Alone time
- Artnering with others
- Learning new things

DAILY
- Know my WARNING SIGNS
- Meditate 10 min
- Avoid violent content
- No screens after 9:30 pm
- Limited social media
- Controlled news intake
- Periods of silence
- Reading for fun

Stress Warning Signs

- Insomnia
- Melancholia
- Appetite loss
- Overindulgence $
- Working late
- Racing thoughts
- Racing heart
- Excessive nail/cuticle biting
- Feeling overwhelmed
- Increased insecurity/doubt
- Pain in neck, back, wrist, or belly
- Hunched over posture
- Excessive future tripping or nostalgia
- Eye styes/twitching, avoiding eye contact
- Trouble communicating or listening

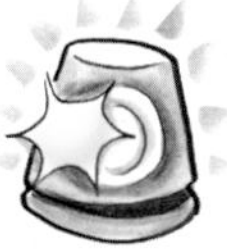

☆ When in doubt, take a shower or make tea!

What helps YOU feel better? Fill out your own self-care plan and post it somewhere in your home or studio. Share it with the people in your life who care about you so they know your needs and help remind you to do the things that keep you healthy when you are struggling.

Self-Care Plan

Physical Needs

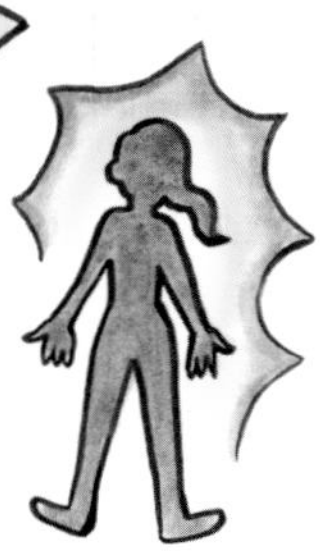

Emotional Needs

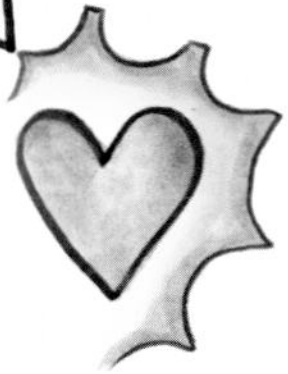

Mental Needs

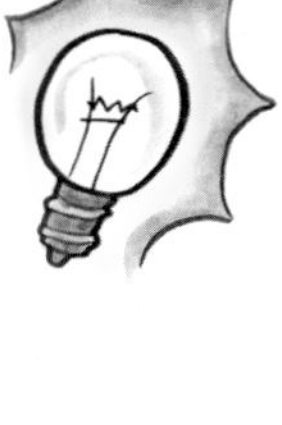

Daily Supplements

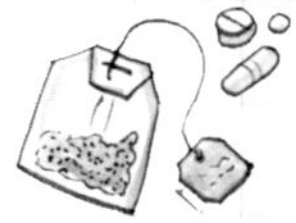

Support System

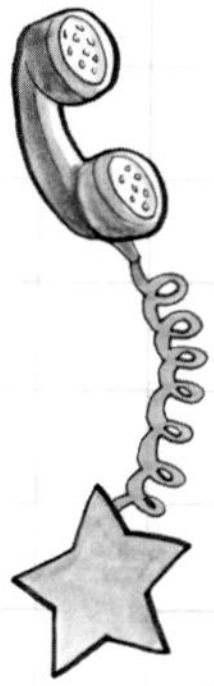

Stress Warning Signs

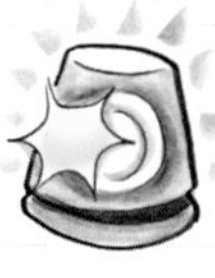

Need more time? Make a TIME CHART of how you honestly spend your time during an average week. What can you take time away from to devote to self-care?

When in doubt,

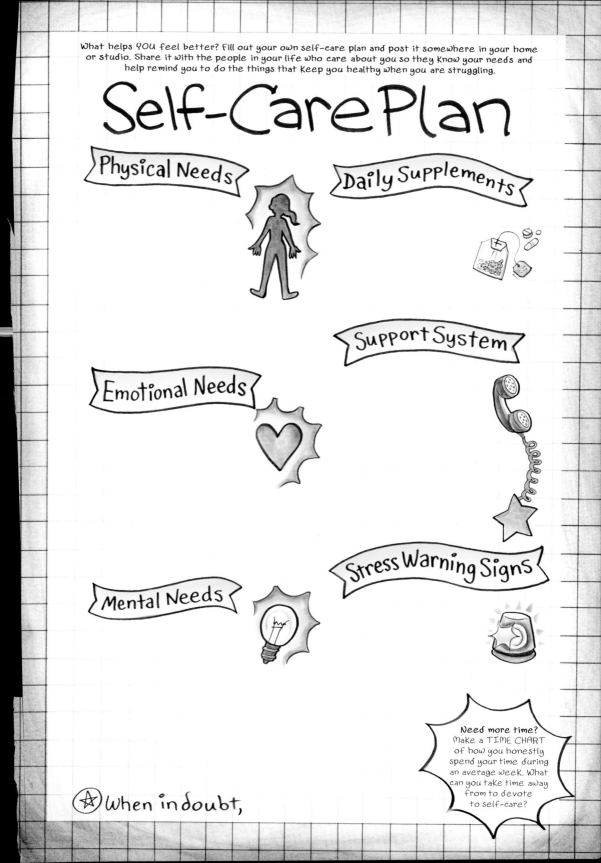

About the Author

LAURA LEE GULLEDGE is an author, illustrator, teaching artist, and proponent of Artner love.

Her debut YA graphic novel Page by Paige was nominated for the prestigious Eisner and Harvey Awards. Her second graphic novel Will & Whit was selected as a YALSA Top Ten Book for Teens and has been adapted into an innovative multidisciplinary musical. Then her interactive book Sketchbook Dares: 24 Ways to Draw Out Your Inner Artist invites you to try out her favorite drawing activities.

Laura Lee also enjoys exploring comics journalism, interactive event production, ecstatic dance, live art performance, and sustainable creativity. She currently lives in Charlottesville, Virginia, where she posts new art and adventures weekly in her blog at WHOISLAURALEE.COM.

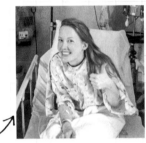

*A couple examples of art imitating life: Laura Lee playing violin in high school orchestra and about to go into emergency surgery, just like Mona.

Author's Note

I used to fear that embracing my artistic side would make me more "crazy," or it would reveal there was something deeply wrong with me. But it turns out it's not the art that makes you mentally unhealthy . . . it's NOT making art. Because no matter how "normal" I acted, my overwhelming thoughts were still there eating away at me.

Thankfully, I surrendered to my creative impulses and learned to use them as a resource to help me express, understand, and heal myself. I got to know the voices in my head and how to manage them, which has saved my life in so many ways.

And miraculously, this resource is available to everyone.

If YOU have a creative outlet, no matter what medium or level of quality it may be, I encourage you to please use it. Use your gifts and resources. Pay attention to your thoughts and emotions. Find a way to get them out. Share the journey. Find your Artners. And ask for help if you need it.

. . . I ARTNER DARE YOU.

*Laura Lee's artwork from high school.